Praise for

The Library of the Unwritten

"This book is so much fun, and you should be reading it. Trust me. Stories about story are some of my favorite kinds. This book definitely makes the list. I am so glad I read this."

—Seanan McGuire, author of *In an Absent Dream*

"A muse, an undead librarian, a demon, and a ghost walk into Valhalla. . . . What follows is a delightful and poignant fantasy adventure that delivers a metric ton of found-family feels and reminds us that the hardest stories to face can be the ones we tell about ourselves."

—*New York Times* bestselling author Kit Rocha

"*The Library of the Unwritten* is a tiered dark chocolate cake of a book. The read is rich and robust, the prose has layers upon layers, and the characters melt like ganache upon the tongue. A saturated, decadent treat. An unforgettable, crave-worthy experience. A book lovers' book; a supreme and masterful concoction that makes fresh fiction out of dusty Dante and boring Bible bits. An erudite and engaging pleasure cruise through Hell. A new voice rises in the jewel-toned arena of Valente, Gaiman, and Funke. A baroquely imagined and totally unexpected original take on such well-worn topics as Hell, libraries, and the difference between what never was and what never will be. Put coins over your eyes and climb aboard with your library card in hand; this book will take you where you need to go. With a masterful sense of the canon that is and the canon that never was, Hackwith has presented the world with a flashing, flaming jewel of a book. It's as unforgettable as your first taste of chocolate or your first glimpse of Hell. Unmissable and unforgettable; prepare to read the Unwritten."

—Philip K. Dick Award–winning author Meg Elison

"*The Library of the Unwritten* is a story about stories: ones we tell ourselves, the ones we tell others, and the ones buried so deep we hope no one ever finds them. Hackwith has artfully penned a love letter to books and readers alike and filled it with lush, gorgeous prose; delightfully real characters; a nonstop, twisty, and heart-wrenching plot; and an explosive ending that gave me chills."

—K. A. Doore, author of *The Perfect Assassin*

"A delightful romp through Heaven, Hell, and everything in between, which reveals itself in layers: an exploration of the nuances of belief, a demonstration of the power of the bonds that connect us, and a love letter to everybody who has ever heard the call of their own story."

—Caitlin Starling, author of *The Luminous Dead*

"*The Library of the Unwritten* is like *Good Omens* meets Jim Hines's Ex Libris series, a must-read for any book lover. If you love the smell of freshly printed books, the comfort of walking along tall shelves filled with new adventures, or the feeling of returning to an old favorite read, then grab *The Library of the Unwritten* and join Claire's dimension-hopping team for a Hellishly good time. Hackwith has penned a tale filled with unforgettable characters fighting with the power of creativity against a stunning array of foes from across the multiverse. *The Library of the Unwritten* rocks!"

—Michael R. Underwood,
author of the Stabby Award finalist Genrenauts series

"The only book I've ever read that made the writing process look like fun. A delight for readers and writers alike!"

—Hugo Award finalist Elsa Sjunneson-Henry

"A wry, high-flying, heartfelt fantasy, told with sublime prose and sheer joy even at its darkest moments (and there are many). I want this entire series on my shelf yesterday."

—Tyler Hayes, author of *The Imaginary Corpse*

THE
LIBRARY
OF THE
UNWRITTEN

A. J. Hackwith

ACE

NEW YORK

ACE
Published by Berkley
An imprint of Penguin Random House LLC
penguinrandomhouse.com

Copyright © 2019 by A. J. Hackwith

Library of Congress Cataloging-in-Publication Data

Names: Hackwith, A. J., author.
Title: The library of the unwritten / A. J. Hackwith.
Description: First edition. | New York : Ace, 2019. | Series: Hell's library ; 1
Identifiers: LCCN 2019012345| ISBN 9781984806376 (paperback) |
ISBN 9781984806383 (ebook)
Subjects: | BISAC: FICTION / Fantasy / Contemporary. | FICTION / Fantasy /
General. | GSAFD: Fantasy fiction.
Classification: LCC PS3608.A254 L53 2019 | DDC 813/.6--dc23
LC record available at https://lccn.loc.gov/2019012345

First Edition: October 2019

Printed in the United States of America
1 3 5 7 9 10 8 6 4 2

Cover art: image of book page by Ryan Jorgensen/Arcangel; image of arm by Samantha Pugsley/Arcangel
Cover design by Faceout Studio/Jeff Miller
Book design by Alison Cnockaert

To Levi

THE
LIBRARY
OF THE
UNWRITTEN

1

CLAIRE

Stories want to change, and it is a librarian's job to preserve them; that's the natural order of things. The Unwritten Wing of the Library, for all its infinite magic and mystery, is in some ways a futile project. No story, written or unwritten, is static. Left abandoned too long and given the right stimulation, a book goes wrong in the head. It is a story's natural ambition to wake up and start telling itself to the world.

This, of course, is a buggered pain in the arse.

Librarian Fleur Michel, 1782 CE, Unwritten Wing,
Librarian's Log entry, Personal Ephemera and Errata

BOOKS RAN WHEN THEY grew restless, when they grew unruly, or when they grew real. Regardless of the reason, when books ran, it was a librarian's duty to catch them.

The twisty annex of Assyrian romances, full of jagged words and shadowed hearts broken on unforgiving clay tablets, had a tendency to turn around even experienced curators. The librarian, Claire, cornered the book there. The book had chosen to take form as the character of a pale, coltish girl, and her breathing was nearly as ragged as Claire's was from the run. Claire forced her shaking hands still as she approached. The book was young, and so was its character, back pressed into the bookcase, dandelion-fluff hair fluttering around thin shoulders. Muddy jeans, superhero tee, a whimper like dried reeds. "Please. I can't—I don't want to go back."

Damn. Claire preferred them angry. Angry was simpler. "The Library has rules."

A flicker of color swung around the corner. Her assistant, Brevity, skidded to a stop just short of the book. Her apple-round cheeks, usually a shade of robin's-egg blue, were tinged purple from the run. Seafoam green bangs puffed above her eyes, and she mumbled an apology as she handed Claire a slender bit of steel wrapped in cloth.

Claire stowed the tool in her pocket, where it would stay, she hoped. She considered the cowering figure in front of her.

There were two parts to any unwritten book. Its words—the twisting, changing text on the page—and its story. Most of the time, the two parts were united in the books filling the Unwritten Wing's stacks, but now and then a book woke up. Felt it had a purpose beyond words on a page. Then the story made itself into one of its characters and went walking.

As the head librarian of Hell's Unwritten Wing, Claire had the job of keeping stories on their pages.

The girl—*No, the character, the* book, Claire corrected herself—tried again. "You don't get it. In the woods—I saw what it did. . . ."

Claire glanced down at the book in her hands and read the gold stamp on the spine. The font was blocky and modern, clearly signaling this was a younger book despite the thick leather hide of the cover. It read: DEAD HOT SUMMER. Her stomach soured; this job had ruined her taste for the horror genre entirely. "Be that as it may, you have nothing to worry about. It's just a story—*you* are just a story, and until you're written—"

"I won't make trouble," the character said. "I just—"

"You're not human." The words snapped out before Claire could censor them. The girl reacted as if she'd been slapped, and curled into the shelves.

Claire took a measured breath between gritted teeth. "You can't be scared. You're not human—let's not pretend otherwise. You're a very cunning approximation, but you're simply a manifestation, a *character*. A book playing at human . . . But you're not. And books belong on shelves."

Brevity cleared her throat. "She *is* scared, boss. If you want me to, I can sit with her. Maybe we can put her in the damsel suite—"

"Absolutely not. Her author is still alive."

The character zeroed in on the more sympathetic target. She took a step toward Brevity. "I just don't want to die in there."

"Stop." Claire flipped open the leather cover and thrust it toward the character. "This is only wasting time. Back to the pages."

She looked uncertainly at her book. "I don't know how."

"Touch the pages. Remember where your story starts. 'Once upon a time . . . ' or what have you." Claire slid a hand into her pocket, fingers finding metal. "Alternately, stories always return to their pages when damaged. If you require assistance?"

The scalpel was cool in her palm. It was normally used in repairing and rebinding old books, but a practiced hand could send a rogue character back to its pages.

Claire had plenty of practice.

"I'll try." The girl's hand trembled as she flattened a small palm against the open pages. Her brow wrinkled.

A chill of quiet ticked over Claire's skin. The books weighing down nearby shelves twitched sleepily. A muffled murmur drifted in the air. The wooden shelves towering overhead pulsed with movement, old leather spines shuffling against the bronze rails. Dust shivered in a spill of lamplight.

Brevity shifted uneasily next to her. An awake book was a noisy thing. Returning it, even noisier.

They couldn't waste time. The girl startled when Claire took a quiet step toward her. "I've almost got it!"

"It's all right." Claire spoke through a tight throat, but her tone was gentle. She could be gentle when it was efficient. "Try again."

The unwritten girl turned her attention back to the pages. It was an act of contemplation, and Claire could sense the weaving of realities. The girl was a character; she was a story, a book. She might feel like something even more, but Claire couldn't afford to consider that. She placed a reassuring hand on her shoulder. Then she slid the scalpel between the character's ribs.

Brevity swallowed a squeak. Claire stepped back as the unwritten girl fell. She made small, shocked gulps for air, twisted on the carpet, then began to fade. Within a minute, nothing was left but a small smudge of ink on the floor.

Only books died in Hell. Everyone else had to live with their choices.

"Couldn't we have given her another minute? It's awfully hard to feel like the good guys when we do that." Brevity took the book after Claire snapped it closed.

"There's no good or bad, Brev. There's just the Library. The story is back where it belongs." Claire couldn't keep the resignation from her voice. She cleaned off and stashed the scalpel back in her many-pocketed skirts.

"Yeah, but she seemed so scared. She was just—"

"Characters aren't human, Brev. You always should remember that as a librarian. They'll convince themselves they're people, but if you allow them to convince *you*, then . . ." Claire trailed off, dismissing the rest of that thought with a twitch of her shoulders. "Shelve her and make a note to check her status next inventory. What kept you so long, anyway?"

"Oh!" Brevity fluttered a hand, and Claire was struck by the eerie similarities between her assistant and the book they'd just put to rest. Brevity was shorter than the character had been, and her riot of cornflower blue skin and bright eyes was vibrant with life—not scared, not pleading—but her gaze kept drifting back to the dull leather cover in her hands. "There's a messenger for you."

"Messenger?"

Brevity shrugged. "From the big guy. I tried to get more, but he's wound pretty tight. Swore he can't leave until he talks to you."

"How . . . unorthodox." Claire turned down the row of towering shelves. "Let's see what His Crankiness wants."

◆ ◆ ◆

WHEN THEY EMERGED FROM the depths of the Unwritten Wing's stacks, Claire found the demon sweating holes into her rug. It was a particularly fine rug, peacock blue and intricately dreamed by an artist of the Ottoman Empire. Dreamed but never made, which made it all the more irreplaceable.

The scent of rotten eggs curdled the Library's pleasant smell of sleeping books and tea, scalding her nose. A bead of sweat fell from the nervous demon's cuff and hit the carpet with a hiss. Claire closed her eyes for a count of five. She cleared her throat. "Can I help you?"

The demon jumped and twisted around. He was scrawny, all bones and amber skin in a cheap oversized suit. He appeared human, or at least human adjacent, as most demons did, save for the pinpricks of ears that poked up through an oil slick of springy black curls. He bit his lip, managing to look skeletal and innocent at the same time, and he held a thin purple folder in front of him like a shield. "Ms. Claire, of the . . . Is this the Library?"

"That generally is where librarians are found." Claire sat down at her desk. She eyed the repair work she'd started, while Brevity returned to sorting books on a cart. "You're in the Unwritten Wing. You may read, or you may leave."

"Oh, I'm not here to—" The demon twitched. Claire tracked his movements out of the corner of her eye, giving the text in front of her only cursory attention. The books stacked on the corner of the desk gave a lazy growl, and the demon sidestepped quickly away. His nervous gaze landed on her hands. "Is . . . is that blood?"

Claire glanced down at the hand that had held the scalpel. She wiped her fingers on her skirts and returned to her work. "Ink."

The book open on the desk was one of the young ones, one that still had a chance of being written by its author someday. Brevity had misfiled it with a particularly crotchety series of old unwritten novels. Whaling stories, if Claire remembered right. The impressionable young book now had all sorts of rubbish jumbled in its still-sprouting narrative. Five-paragraph descriptions of food, meditations on masculinity and the sea, complete nonsense for an unwritten tale about teenage witches in love. If its author began to write while it was in this state, she would never attempt another book. It was Claire's job to keep the books ready for their authors in the best possible state. Tidy. Stories were never tidy, but it was important to keep up appearances.

When she didn't look up again, the demon coughed and shook loose another bead of sweat. It hit the rug with a dull hiss.

Claire winced. She pressed her scalpel flat against the book. "You're damaging my rug."

The demon looked down at his feet. He stepped off the rug awkwardly, found himself on an even more complex rug, and shuffled again.

He'd be at that all day, and Claire would be at repairs all night. She reluctantly turned from the book she was working on, pressing one elbow on it to keep it from creeping off. A slow, deep frown pulled on her face as she gave him a better once-over.

Young, Claire assessed—the young seemed determined to plague her today. A junior demon, though young demons didn't venture to the Library often. Most of Hell's residents got reading privileges only after decades of clawing for power. He fidgeted under her scrutiny and combed through his wiry, ragged hair. It made her want to find him a brush. Suspicion tinged with familiarity tugged at her. No demon felt quite right, but there was something exceptionally *off* about hellspawn with anxiety. Claire raised a brow at Brevity, but her assistant just shrugged.

"You're . . . unexpected. I understand you were sent by His Grinchiness?"

He licked his lips. "Yes, but . . . you can't . . . you can't call him that. His Highness, I mean. There's a message. I got the brief here." The demon held it out, eager to be rid of it. Claire didn't move, so he added, "It says a book is missing. I'm supposed to tell you . . . it's . . . ah, one of yours."

Claire stilled. "In what way?"

"Because it's unwritten? Early twenty-first-century unauthor, still living."

Ah. The tension crept off Claire's shoulders. "Stolen or lost?"

The demon pawed through the folder before withdrawing a small stack of printouts. "They suspect runaway. No recent checkouts or invocation alarms . . . whatever that means."

She grunted. "It means my day is shot. A runaway."

A bewildered look spread across the demon's face. "Is that . . . ?"

Claire waved a vague hand. "It means an unwritten book woke up, manifested as a character, and somehow slipped the Library's wards. A neat trick that I will be keen to interrogate out of it later. It is likely headed to Earth. There's nothing stronger than an unwritten book's fascination with its author. But a book that finds its author often comes back damaged, and the author comes out . . . worse."

"I'll pack the scalpels," Brevity said, and received a dark look. Claire rubbed her temple, a fruitless gesture to forestall the coming headache, then shot out her hand.

"Just give the report here." She released her hold on the open book, and it happily snapped shut, barely missing her fingertips.

The demon deposited the paperwork in her palm and quickly hopped out of reach. The books stacked on her desk complained with growls that ruffled their pages.

"The author's alive? Where?" Brevity asked.

He shrugged. "A place called Seattle."

Claire groaned as she squinted at the paperwork. "It's always the Americans."

NAMES WERE A NECESSARY nicety even Claire had to tolerate. The demon introduced himself with a very clumsy bow; this small bit of etiquette helped him to relax and stop sweating acid everywhere. Claire frowned at his name. "Leto. Like the Greek myth?"

The skinny demon ducked his head. "Like from the sci-fi novel."

"So, you're a demon of . . . ?"

"Entropy."

"They sent a demon of entropy to a library wing full of irreplaceable artifacts?" Claire stared at Leto and then shook her head, muttering, "I will kill him. Positively kill him."

Leto twitched. "If you don't mind my asking . . . how, ah, how can you talk about His Highness like that?"

"Simple," Claire said. "The Library exists in Hell; it doesn't serve it. He's not *my* Highness."

Leto paled, and she dismissed it with a wave. "It's a long story. Don't worry yourself. I still follow orders. This is Brevity, muse and my assistant in the Unwritten Wing."

"Former muse. I flunked out." Brevity made a face and offered her hand.

If Leto was a scarecrow teenager in appearance, Brevity was of the sprite variety. Her hair was spiky and short and a dainty shade of sea glass. Beneath the cuffs of a multicolored jumper, propane blue tattoos flowed over paler cornflower skin in a shifting series of script that almost appeared readable, at least until one tried to focus on it.

"Nice to meet you, ma'am." Leto shook her hand shyly, taking care to keep his fingers back from the ripple of tattoo.

"Hey! A demon with manners. I like this one," Brevity said.

"Many demons are perfectly polite to me," Claire pointed out.

"No, many demons are intimidated by the Library, boss. There's a difference," Brevity said as Claire pulled out a drawer in search of tools.

The mundane tools of a librarian's trade included notebooks and writing implements, and the less usual: inks that glimmered, stamps that bit, wriggling wax, and twine. All of them went into a bag that Claire slung across her chest. Pen and paper went into the hidden pockets of her muddled, many-tiered skirts. She'd been buried in some frippery that was dour even for her time, all buttons and layers. She'd chopped the skirt at the knee long ago for easy movement, but Claire lived by the firm moral philosophy that one could never have too many pockets, too many books, or too much tea.

It wasn't as if she had proper hours to maintain. Claire squinted at a squat copper sundial, fueled by a steady if entirely unnatural light all its own, and scribbled a new line in the Library's logbook. It was thick and ancient, crusted with age and the oils of a hundred librarian fingerprints. It also never ran out of paper. Claire flipped from her personal notes to the "Library Status" log and ended an entry with a flourish, and the lights in the hall began to flutter.

The Library is now closed. All materials must be returned to the shelves. A disembodied voice, clipped and dull, echoed through the hall. Claire tapped her foot as the voice continued. *The Library is now closed. Patrons are reminded that any curses, charms, or dreams left behind are considered forfeit to the stacks. The Library is now closed.*

There were not many patrons lounging around the reading area, but the few imps that were reading put down their books reluctantly and began to make their way to the exit, much to Leto's slack-jawed amazement. Creatures of Hell, on general principle, took to following orders as well as one might expect. Which is to say, not at all and with liberal interpretation. Most of the Library's regulars were powerless imps and bored foot soldiers, but one beefy incubus with horns, clad in little more than chitin and scar tissue, handed his book directly to Claire with a grunt.

Claire clucked her tongue. "No sulking. You know we don't do lending. It'll be here for you tomorrow, Furcas. Go on now."

Leto managed to close his mouth before his sputter could ruin another rug. "That— Was that . . ."

"Intimidated. Told you," Brevity said.

Once the remaining patrons disappeared out the great doors, Claire closed the log and swept toward the far wall. Leto clung to her heels, and Claire bit back a smile. The Library was fickle, eerie terrain, especially to demons.

From the main desk, the cavernous space ran back into shadows in all directions, and every available surface was layered with wood or parchment of varying ages. Rows of shelves filled with books ran high over their heads, and larger tomes crouched at the end of each row in quivering packs. Plush rugs of riotous color muffled the floor. Every visible wall space carried an oil canvas, with images in various states of completion. They governed themselves with their own regular rotation and changes. More paintings hung on a monstrous series of pivoting racks at the far back, draped in shadow like a leafy thicket.

Claire's target was the far wall, a large section of buttery pale yellow drawers. Endless rows of drawers that hadn't been there a moment ago. The Library functioned on requirement, shifting and flowing to the needs of the books and librarians. Leto eyed it with anxiety, but Claire shoved the folder back into his hands. She began to scale a ladder clipped to a rail. "Author name and story title?"

"Ah . . ." Leto opened the file. "Author, McGowan. Amber Guinevere McGowan."

Her foot stabbed out at the wooden wall, and the ladder coasted a few feet down the row of drawers. "McGowan. Right. God, middle name Guinevere? What were her parents thinking? No wonder she never became a writer." Claire yanked a drawer open. "Title?"

"Uh, the missing title just says 'Nightfall.'" Leto looked up as Claire let out a snort. "Something wrong?"

"I think every writer, written or unwritten, has some glorified adventure titled 'Nightfall' stuck in their head. Half the residents here were a 'Nightfall' at one point. Even unwritten stories eventually migrate to something more original." Claire danced her fingers over the drawer before snapping up a card. She slid the drawer closed and descended.

Her sneaker-clad feet hit the ground, and Claire headed for the exit. "Calling card says it's definitely still in Seattle. Brev, you up for a field trip?"

Brevity's gold eyes grew to saucers, and she stumbled forward in a little dance. Her voice wasn't quite a squeal but flirted with the idea. "You mean upstairs?" she said breathily. "Always and forever, boss."

2

LETO

This log is a curious thing. Previous volumes appear to date back to early Sumer. Yet I can read and understand every word. Books are a strange kind of magic in this Library.

The reading has been enlightening, no doubt. Though rambling and peppered with a plague of personalities, it chronicles the training and supplemental experiences of every librarian that has helmed the Unwritten Wing.

Ancient Egypt had her Book of the Dead, a scroll buried with loved ones to guide them and advise them on their behavior as they navigated the afterlife. I suppose that makes this our Book of the Dead Librarians. All the proper protocols for navigating but never escaping this place.

Thousands of years of librarians have kept their advice in this book. Somewhere, somewhere, there's got to be a solution for the problem I'm faced with.

Apprentice Librarian Claire Hadley, 1988 CE

HELL WAS A SERIES of hallways. An endless series of hallways, at least to a junior demon. They wound through passages Leto didn't recognize, broad balconies, and whispering broom closets. They passed jagged stairs and alcoves with shadows like wounds, and finally a non-euclidean gargoyle that had a troubling habit of not quite staying in the viewer's spatial perception. Leto averted his eyes from it at the start of a wince-inducing headache.

Each hall was lined with a narrow bay of windows. The first looked out upon wide fields of wildflowers, the next on a dark cavern with end-less pools of starlight, the third, a lava-drenched plain. The conflicting light painted the hallway in a rainbow of bright and dark, yellow after-noons and blue twilights spilling over them as they passed.

Finally, the librarian took a sharp right into a narrow doorway that Leto would have missed. Its wooden arch was decorated with an icon for travel: a small set of interlocking wheels, marred with the claw marks of large birds. He followed the women down a steep set of stairs, watching Brevity's light teal hair as it bounced like a brightly colored flag. They emptied out into a claustrophobic office, taller than it was wide.

Leto stumbled to a stop behind Brevity and turned in a slow circle. The office was tall, he realized, in order to accommodate the dizzying rows of shelves that reached from the floor up into the shadows of the ceiling. Unlabeled jars of various shapes lined each shelf, putting out a faint but steady colored glow that was the room's only light.

Brevity grinned at Leto with ill-concealed amusement. "First time traveling?"

"Yes, er . . ." Leto shot her an alarmed look. "Rather, no. I'm not going with you, am I? I just deliver the paperwork."

Brevity shrugged and turned to tap at a glass jar that swirled with plum and sickly orange mists. Leto stepped toward Claire. "Miss . . . eh, Head Librarian?"

"Not now, kiddo." Claire slapped her hand on a dusty bell sitting on the counter. Instead of a simple chime, a trio of vibrations pinged hard out of the metal and made all the jars tremble on their shelves.

Leto most certainly was not a kid. Demons didn't really have child-hoods. Soul-shuddering inductions, nightmarish hazings, yes; childhood, no. Leto started to form his protest when a walking mountain in a tight tailored suit came trumbling out of the gloom behind the counter.

A pale head, the size and shape of a boulder, floated above a starched collar. Leto quailed. He retreated toward the door as he took in dark pits where the monster's eyes should have been. The creature opened its mouth to reveal a row of jagged red edges that almost, but not quite, passed for teeth. Its voice rumbled in a timbre that shook the shelves around them.

"ABANDON ALL HOPE, YE WHO—"

"Yes, yes, hope abandoned, Walter," Claire cut in. "We need transport."

The creature's face fell, serrated teeth disappearing behind a quivering lip. He straightened his tie and blinked bottomless-pit eyes at the librarian. "Aww, miss! C'mon, let me do it proper-like. Ever since the Reformation, I never get mortals in here no more."

"If you must, but do please be brief. And quieter."

"Bully, ma'am. Thank you." The giant straightened, and his shoulders nearly hit the rafters. He cleared his throat, opened his razor-filled mouth again, and launched into his speech.

"Abandon all hope, ye who enter here! Beyond me lies the city of woe. Before me waits the sleep which ye earn. None shall pass unless the soul be light; none shall pass out of the dark. I am that which stands; I am that which waits and shall not falter; I am that which keeps the fates. Weigh now your soul or turn back to thine sleep."

It struck Leto as a little flowery, but echoed in a howling baritone, it did the job. The jars trembled on their shelves, so that a hundred glass voices seemed to echo the words. The vibration reached in to jostle Leto's organs unpleasantly.

Claire did not appear impressed. She propped her elbows on the counter, her back straight even in the middle of a bored recline. She tugged at one of her many braids, fussing with a stray bangle.

Brevity twisted her hands and risked a shy smile at the beast behind the counter. "I think that was awful terrifying, Mr. Walter. That trembly bit on the end is a nice touch."

"Thank you, Miss Brevity. It took ages to get the acoustics just right." The beast appeared to shrink and glow under the praise. He caught sight of Leto and leaned over with a dagger-filled grin that was something out of even a demon's nightmares. "Hey, I don't suppose you're—"

Claire cleared her throat. "We're here on business, Walter."

The creature turned his sightless gaze back on the librarian. "Sorry, ma'am. How can I help you, Miss Claire?"

"We're on an errand up top. I need one pass for Brevity here and two summoning candles for me and the boy."

Leto bristled, forgetting his original protest about the trip. "I'm not a boy. I'm a demonic messenger of—"

"Yes, yes, two summoning candles for me and this most esteemed and powerful messenger of our fearless leader." She raised her brows to Walter. "White should do. Don't you think?"

Again, Walter leaned over the counter, peering above the librarian's head to scrutinize Leto. Leto squirmed his toes and forced himself not to fidget and definitely not to meet the gaze of those bottomless black holes that threatened to swallow him up.

After a pause that did not seem at all short, Walter nodded. "White summoning should do 'bout right, Miss Claire. Coming right up. Miss Brevity, you've used summat like this before, yes?"

"Yep, I know the routine. Hauling the chief's butt out of Hell is why she keeps me around."

Claire cast her assistant a sour look as Walter thundered back into the halls behind the counter. "I do not get 'hauled' anywhere. You are merely fulfilling your duties, Brev."

"You maybe want to summon yourself, then, boss?"

Leto glanced between the two women, a fresh layer of confusion coating his already stewing anxiety. "I don't understand. Why does anyone need summoning? I thought you were going to Seattle."

Claire turned as if suddenly remembering his presence. "You really are new, aren't you? It's because I'm human."

At Leto's blink, she gave a weak chuckle. "You assumed a mere demon could make sense of the tangled, unfinished dreams of humanity? Not likely. Too messy. Last demon assistant I had ran screaming after one full inventory. No, librarians are nearly always mortals, and nearly always unwritten authors themselves. Brev here being an exception worked out by the Muses Corps."

"When they kicked me out," Brevity muttered.

Leto nodded uncertainly. He had heard the rumors, of course. The whispers about the unwritten works by Hell's librarian. Claire hadn't held the position that long—thirty years was a blink in Hell's terms—but she'd become a whispered name in demonic courts for the stories she'd left uncreated, filling the shelves, worlds unmade. The rumor said there was a whole annex of the Unwritten Wing that housed her works, under lock and key, never visited. Buried under the fog of some old and quite horrible scandal.

Of course, Leto thought, any good rumor always had a scandal.

"Right," he said, attempting to recover, rubbing the back of his neck, and looking anywhere but at the stern woman. "I just . . . Well, shouldn't you be doing your time to get out of here? Isn't that the only reason mortals are here, to, y'know, work through their . . . their . . ."

"We all get the afterlife our soul requires. I've heard the sales pitch," Claire supplied with an impatient cluck of her tongue. "This is mine. Lucky me. The trick they don't tell you is that the longer you're here, the harder it is to remember anywhere else." She paused as Walter lumbered slowly back out of the gloom. "It's quite inconvenient. As are these questions."

"S'why boss needs a summons," Brevity said. "Spirits and demons can come and go on business. But mortals can't leave Hell if their souls haven't freed them yet. But with a bit of ritual magic, library folk get a day pass."

"A day, no more," Claire said. "Not everyone gets access to a ghost-light, but since it's part of the Library's duties, King Crankypants has to make an exception."

Leto couldn't help but twitch every time she did that: refer to Lucifer with a horrific pet name. It was disrespectful. Undignified. Not *done*. He'd begun to suspect that was why she did it.

Walter reached the counter and paused to pat delicately at his suit pocket. He whipped out a pocket square the size of a bath towel and wiped the counter before carefully placing two waxy candles on it. He then heaved one of the large glass jars filled with colored fog and set it next to them on the counter. "Modern-day Seattle area, aye? Where you want t' be set down, Miss Brevity?"

Claire answered instead. "City center is fine. Space Needle, if you need a landmark."

"The *base* of the Space Needle, this time," Brevity added with a scrunched-up face.

"Oh yeah, sorry 'bout that . . ." Walter furrowed his brow and twisted the jar sharply, once, twice, three times. Each time, the swirling mist inside changed color slightly, darkening from sky blue to navy, brightening from forest green to spring. The colors settled into a slate blue and lime swirl, and the eyeless creature seemed satisfied. "That should do it."

Brevity stood on her tiptoes to reach over the counter and inspect each white candle before sticking them in one of the many pockets of her cargo pants.

Leto eyed the swirling jar and edged another step toward Claire. "Pardon me, Miss Librarian, but I don't think I'm authorized to travel. I was just supposed to—"

"Deliver the assignment and assist with completion. This is assisting."

"I don't think I'll be much help—"

"It's just a summons, Leto." It was the first time the librarian had bothered to use his name, and the demon felt irrational heat in his cheeks. She offered him a trace of a smile. "A summons to a relatively boring time and place on a relatively boring errand. If you're new, it'll do you good to learn how these things work. I imagine that's what High Grump had in mind. Unless you want to return to him to check?"

"No! No. I mean, if . . . you're sure, ma'am."

"You have matches?" Claire asked her assistant, and Brevity nodded. "And spares."

"Right. Walter, whenever you're ready."

The giant nodded, rubbing his gnarled palms on his pants once before twisting the lid off the jar. Leto caught what sounded like a whisper of seagulls as Walter set down the lid with a clang. The giant took the over-sized jar carefully in two hands, leaned over the counter, and upended the jar over Brevity's head.

The mists swirled out, not so much in a downpour, but like roots seeking purchase. They snaked around the muse's head and swiftly raced around her, thickening as the room filled with the smell of briny sea and petrol, concrete and rain.

The navy and lime fog seemed to envelop her and then constrict, squeezing the girl-shaped fog into unhealthy proportions. Leto gasped, but Claire set a placating hand on his shoulder. The fog rippled and, in the next second, neatly withdrew back into the jar Walter held. There was a faint smell of ozone and sulfur, and Brevity was gone.

"Thank you, Walter. Now comes the unpleasant part." Claire stepped toward the clear space in the center of the lobby. The giant nodded and set to screwing the jar closed and bustling with things under the counter. Walter seemed to make a point of averting his eyes, which did nothing for Leto's nerves.

"Unpleasant?" Leto stayed close to the librarian and began to wonder why he couldn't have traveled with Brevity instead.

"Well, unless you really love roller coasters."

Claire straightened and locked her shoulders back. The air around them began to take on an odd quality. Leto frowned as the floor tilted under his feet. A heavy sensation pressed on his collarbone.

"What's a roller coas—"

And then the world dropped through his skin.

LETO HAD NEVER HAD his liver pulled through his ears, but he could now imagine the experience. It was as if a force had reached through the walls of the little room, through his skin, through every atom in his body . . . and ripped. Not up, not down, but betwixt, shouldering aside reality as it went. Leto's vision faded and his equilibrium reported movement in one direction, then another, before giving up entirely.

Something hard bit into his knees, and fresh air hit his face. Rather than helping, this reminded his innards that he was no longer dying, and Leto felt the peculiarly mortal need to lose the contents of his stomach.

"He's okay! Too much excitement." A voice chirped to his right. "We're okay—thanks! Have a good day."

Leto forced open one eye and saw Brevity waving off a cluster of humans. The group was clad in loud nylon jackets and showed polite, if flimsy, concern before shuffling off. *Tourists*. Leto found the term in his mind, though he didn't know where the word came from.

They stood in a large outdoor space, paved with concrete and studded with a line of round marble shapes. Milling humans cluttered the area around glass sculptures and souvenir stands. Behind them, dull metal struts rose to form a towering, spindly landmark that disappeared into an eternal gray.

Leto gripped a marble sphere and slowly wobbled to his feet. "Shouldn't we be worried someone saw us?"

"If they did, they'd just as quickly forget," Claire said. "Summonings are tough to remember. Wouldn't be a useful means of transit otherwise."

Leto turned and saw the librarian had fared the summoning just slightly better than he had. She leaned on a concrete bench. Her skin, normally a rich nut brown, was waxy around her flushed cheeks. Her dark hair, once full of tiny and impressively complicated beadwork, was now a thatch of simple braids tied away from her face. Her complex layers of clothes were also simplified into a vaguely Bohemian mix of a blouse, thick skirts, and sneakers.

Brevity, too, had undergone small mortal changes. Her skin no longer held a propane blue glow, her gold eyes were a plain brown, and roiling tattoos had resolved to a generic knotting pattern up each arm. Her hair, Leto was surprised to note, was still pastel green.

Leto glanced sharply down at his own hands but saw little change.

Running fingers over his head revealed a long tide of faintly curled, mostly tangled dark hair, less oily and thornbush-like than it was in Hell, and his pointed ears were blunted to fleshy circles.

He also felt clammy and smelled vaguely of meat.

"Don't worry—it's not permanent." Claire brought him out of his self-inspection.

"I don't know if I like being this . . . squishy," Leto said. It brought thoughts to mind, disquieting feelings, mortality, flashes of laughter and starlight and loss no longer felt. It was uncomfortable, like wearing someone else's suit, but also faintly familiar in the way all the worst things were.

"Confusingly squishy. That's humans in a nutshell." Brevity shooed off the last concerned bystanders and held out a small object to each of her companions.

Leto took the small plastic canister. It was blue, with metal workings on top, and translucent. Inside, a delicate flame, no bigger than a speck but brighter than it had a right to be, bubbled in a clear liquid.

"Your ghostlight candles. They'll last about a day. Don't lose 'em," Brevity said as she saw Leto's puzzled look. "We can't exactly carry lit holy candles around here. Basic camouflage. Candles down below turn into cigarette lighters up here. But don't let anyone borrow a light. It's kinda your passport while you're here."

"You do not want to get caught outside of Hell without your ghostlight. Very bad things happen. Now, then, about that book . . ." Claire tucked her ghostlight into a skirt pocket without looking at it. She paused to dig the tiny calling card out of her leather bag. "We've got some ways to walk."

"Ooh, taxi?" Brevity squeaked. "I've always wanted to ride in one of those!"

"You're a muse—you always want to do everything," Claire said. "If it will save time, I suppose I can fold enough for a cab. Let's go."

To Leto's surprise, the taxi driver paid no attention when what appeared to be a brightly colored rave kiddie, a dreadlocked hipster, and a malnourished teenager in an ill-fitting mortuary suit crawled into his cab. Nor did he blink as Claire spent the entire ride industriously ripping strips of paper out of an ancient-looking notebook and making complicated folds. One more oddity in an odd human world, just passing through.

Claire frowned at the card before directing the cab to drive "downtown" and not stop until they lost "the smell of fish and commerce."

The driver squinted into the rearview mirror, probably rethinking his fare. "Uh, Pioneer Square?"

Again, the librarian consulted the tiny card. "Sure, close enough." Over her shoulder, Leto was surprised to see the neatly printed type moving and shifting across the tiny square card, reorienting with new (poetically vague) directions each time the cab turned.

As the cab pulled up to a curb, Claire finished her folding and held the slips of paper out to the driver. "Keep the change."

The driver frowned. "What the f—"

"You dreamed of a big house." Claire's voice dropped, odd and strangely formal, as Leto slid out of the car after her. She leaned through the window of the cab and caught the driver with her gaze. "With a big porch and a fireplace in the bedroom. Hearth, heart, hurt. You want to take her there and kiss her in the kitchen at the end of the day, food cooking, fire inside. Secure, solid, someday. Steps. This is your first."

The driver watched Claire's face and blinked slowly; then a fragile smile slid over his rough features. "Yeah, the house . . ." He nodded and tucked the slips of ragged paper in his pocket. "Thanks for the tip, ma'am. You have a good day."

Claire straightened and tucked the notebook back into her bag.

"What—" Leto began.

"A story." Claire watched the cab pull away. "I paid him in a story, his story. It's all most souls want, really, so it's easy for them to accept."

It didn't sit right with Leto. "But we cheated him. It's a lie."

"A lie. A dream. Good stories are both," Claire dismissed. "Is it so bad? He'll remember the story, turn it over carefully in the back of his mind, feel the edges of it like he would a lucky coin. A story will change him if he lets it. The shape and the spirit of it. Change how he acts, what dreams he chooses to believe in. We all need our stories; I just fed him a good one."

"But he's got bills to pay. His tally will come out wrong. The money—"

"It doesn't do no harm." Brevity nudged Leto. "Besides, don't get boss started. If there's one thing librarians know, it's stories."

"Still doesn't seem right." But Leto let it drop.

They were no longer in the gleaming tourist center of the city. All around them crowded old brick giants, thick buildings with drooping rows of narrow windows, papered with faded posters of all kinds. The main street maintained an infestation of shops, windows displaying discounted baubles or closeout-sale signs. There were fewer people down here, but there was enough foot traffic that no one seemed to pay their trio much mind.

Claire scowled at the calling card before handing it to Leto. "It's getting vague. Keep an eye on that, and let's look around."

WHEN THE SCRIBBLES ON the calling card finally changed, they evolved into . . . nothing. An inky, irregular period filled the tiny card under the title information. Leto held the card out to Claire for her to see. She nodded and paused on the sidewalk, then began turning slowly in a circle. "It's nearby."

"What are we looking for, exactly?" Leto asked.

"A leather-bound book, like the rest of our collection. It'll think it's being sneaky, but it should stand out pretty clearly against modern-day paperbacks." Claire frowned into store windows as they wandered a few yards up and down the sidewalk. "Or since it is awake and manifested, it could be a person."

"A person?"

Claire frowned into a coffee shop window. "They look like anything, but you can tell by the . . . oh, hell and harpies."

Both Brevity and Leto turned and peered over the librarian's shoulder. The shop was a popular spot, filled with an assortment of creative and business folk jostling for table space and power outlets.

Leto didn't see what had caused the librarian to utter increasingly dark and esoteric oaths under her breath until Brevity pointed. "There. We got ourselves a hero."

Leto followed the girl's finger to a table by the window where a young and attractive couple perched. The woman sipped at a tall glass while she flicked animated, slender hands around in her conversation with what Leto assumed, from the smitten look on the man's face, was her boyfriend.

He was a composition of fine tailoring and good genes. He leaned conspiratorially over the table and offered the woman a practiced smile. The man's fingertips rested artfully at his temple, where bronze hair ruffled in a nonexistent breeze. Leto was no judge of such things, for many reasons. But even he could tell in a moment that the hero was, frankly, perfect.

"Is the woman the author?" Claire had finally exhausted her cursing. "Brev, grab me the photo from the author profile."

Brevity ruffled around in the librarian's bag before flipping open the file. "Yeah, looks like Miss McGowan to me, boss."

Leto suspected, from the stormy look that crossed Claire's face, that the author's presence was a very bad thing.

The librarian heaved a sigh. "Why couldn't it have been a damsel? This is going to make things significantly more difficult. We need to corner it and keep the contact with the author to a minimum."

"Wait—I thought we were here for a book," Leto said.

"We are. *He* is the book." Claire's explanation was peevish as she scanned the shop. "When unwritten books get too wild, too loved, or just too hungry, they get it in their fool heads to be real. They leak into the world, usually in the form of one of their characters. They aren't the most creative lot on their own. That guy is obviously the hero—did you see those cheekbones? All he's missing is a sword and a white horse. That's our character."

"And he's talking to his author?"

"Violating every rule unwritten works have. When I get that book back to the wing . . . Bugger. Why'd it have to be a hero?"

"What's wrong with heroes?"

"*Everything.*"

"Boss ain't exactly fond of characters that decide to wake up, 'specially heroes." A thoughtful look flickered across Brevity's face. "He's just a representation of the story, of course. The physical book still exists. He can't stray too far from the rest of his book, so it must be close."

"Hopefully, Mr. Nightfall here is fool enough to keep it at hand, and we can wrap this up easy," Claire said. "All right, a plan. Brevity, I'm going to need a distraction that gets the author's attention."

The former muse positively glowed. "Wild, public display of drama? That I can do. What did you have in mind?"

"Let's keep this classic." Claire turned to Leto with a smile that made him gulp. "Leto, time to earn your keep."

3

RAMIEL

I'm glad I'm here! I'll be the last librarian, for all I care. Think of it: what is more boring than paradise?

Apprentice Librarian Brevity, 2013 CE

The realms of the afterlife are long-lived, but not static. Realms function off belief, and will change as beliefs change. Realms can die if starved of souls, but more often they morph into something closer to legend than to religion. Eternity bends to the whims of mortal imagination.

I wonder what we would do if we knew we held such power when we were alive. It's an opportunity.

Librarian Poppaea Julia, 51 BCE

THERE'S A FIRST QUESTION that anyone who lived a good life hears after they die. It's a simple question. And it was Ramiel's duty to ask it.

"Anything to declare?"

"What?" The soul was a thin man, his hairline meandering that border between middle-aged and elderly. He was confused, as they always were, wobbling slightly as he stood before the massive gates of Heaven's inbound processing. The Gates, as they were called, stood as representation of Ramiel's own personal angelic duty. And torment.

Rami pinched the thick nub of his stylus between his even thicker fingers and leveled his gaze at the man over the edge of the desk. He did not look at the line of souls stacked beyond him, a shimmering line of heads in every shape and color that twisted as far as he could see into the light.

He did not do a silent calculation of the amount of time the souls would take to process.

Did not feel a cramp in his calloused hands, joints much more accustomed to holding something colder and harder than a stylus.

Did not consider how many ledgers he had yet to fill with notes for judgment.

Instead, the angel took a slow breath and tried again. "Do you have anything to declare, sir? Secrets taken to the grave, yearnings never realized, visions, prophecies, perhaps?"

Rami did not anticipate much of an answer. Souls carried the baggage of their lives under their skin. Undeclared, unacknowledged, and therefore none of his concern. The rare soul ended up in front of him with some deathbed vision or prophecy. In which case, Rami dutifully recorded it for the judgment.

"No, nothing like that. I am an accoun—wait, was. *Was* an accountant." The soul tapped gnarled knuckles together. Rami began marking the log when the voice interrupted him on the downstroke.

"Actually . . . does this count?"

Rami glanced up. The soul had fished a small scrap of parchment out of his suit pocket.

Paper. Real paper.

Not secrets, not dreams. Not soul-type stuff, conjured by a dying soul. Physical, linen-and-wood-pulp and human-ingenuity-type paper.

At the Heavenly Gates, the entrance to a world of souls, that was most definitely worth declaring. Rami frowned and leaned over the desk. "What . . . That's not— How did you get that up here?"

"I'm not quite—" The skin around the old man's eyes knit together like rumpled tissue as he searched around for an answer. "Wait, ah, yes. Black magic."

Rami stared. "Black magic."

"Yes, quite. Enochian, if I recall. Bit of a fuss it was."

Figures it would be Enoch, Rami thought. It was always that bastard. "Right. Black magic. To bring scratch paper to your Heavenly reward."

Rami reluctantly shoved away from the bench and came around. Broad but not tall, he was forced to shoulder aside some blank-eyed souls in line. Each shuffled to one side without complaint, but the contact still left a residual feeling, the psychic smudge of the dead, that made Rami rub his palms down the front of his gray tunic before facing the old man. "Well, Mr. Avery, was it? Just give it here, and let's see—"

The moment Rami's fingers came in proximity of the folded scrap, he heard a loud snap. He jerked back his hand with a grunt. A flare of light slowly dimmed around the paper. For a moment, ink on the inside page had glowed sickly green. It left behind the faint smell of ozone and anise.

It was the smell that alarmed Rami. Nothing at the Gates smelled. Nothing at the Gates had the physical property to smell, per se. An important and convenient fact when dealing with the recently deceased.

The old man smiled. "Well, look at that."

"I most definitely am now." The hairs on the back of Rami's neck crept up as he considered the innocuous-looking scrap. "I need you to come with me, Mr. Avery."

"Oh, did I pass?" The old man was delighted.

"You did. I just need you to hold that—not too close!" Rami veered away as Avery swung toward him with the paper. He opted to steer the lost soul by the shoulder.

"This way. And the rest of you . . . ah, well." He spared one glance for the mass of souls behind him before shoving the old man up toward the Gates.

Mr. Avery was happy enough to be led. For an accountant and an evident practitioner of the black arts, he was an agreeable sort. Rami brought him up short a couple of paces away from a tall figure encased entirely in silver. He took a deep breath and brought his knuckles up to rap on the armor.

An ornate visor pivoted up. A perfectly formed face carried a perfectly expressed sneer. "What do you want, clerk?"

The angel's youth made Rami's bones ache. They seemed to staff the Gates with only the newer caste, just to irritate him. "It's Ramiel, you know."

"I do. I just don't care," the guard said.

"I need to speak with an arch."

"Arches don't speak to the Gate, especially not to you."

"I'm well aware." Rami fought not to grind his teeth. Because he was a fallen Watcher, his position among the angels was complicated and barely tolerated. "There's an abnormality they'll want to hear about."

"Is that so?" the angel said. The old man next to Rami shifted and finally caught the angel's gaze. "What have you got there, mortal?"

It was a question that Rami had forgotten to ask, what with all the glowing and the fuss. The old man looked lost for a moment, gazing down hard into his hand at the trembling bit of scrap. He looked up with a brilliant smile. "It's the Devil's Bible."

The silence that hung between the two angels was louder than all the shuffling of a million souls past the bench. Rami was the first to recover. "If that's—"

"I'll get an arch."

The guard disappeared through the Gates. Effortlessly, as Rami had once been able to do. But instead he was left to wait, occasionally shooting out a guiding arm whenever Avery wobbled too far away.

He sighed at the mass of milling souls that stretched out across the featureless plain. They would be backing up without processing, he knew. It struck him as entirely unnecessary. And tiring. This was Heaven. Souls judged themselves. No one found their way up here unless they were meant to be here. The processing, the Gates, the judgment, it was all a performance someone—likely the only Someone that mattered—had decided was necessary. Once, very long ago, when Rami was allowed past those vast shimmering gates and came and went from the Heavenly court at will, he might have agreed. Now he was just tired.

And he wanted back in.

"Uriel will speak to you." The angel guard appeared at his elbow.

Rami stifled a groan. "It would be her." He ignored the guard's scandalized glance as he pulled the old man along. Avery was busy grinning at his pockets again.

A door appeared in the wall next to the Gates, revealing a narrow pearl staircase. At the top, Rami and Avery stepped out into a nursery of stars.

The dimensions of the room followed the general idea of an office: four walls, a smooth floor, and a high ceiling. But it was as if one had tried to explain the idea of an "office" to an elder god and this was the result. Everywhere, upon almost every surface, clung a thin film of the universe. Stars burst across the floor; an orange nebula cloud of color gestated new suns in the curve of a bookcase accented with brass spindles. It wasn't a painting or a model; the office was molded out of life. It was a miniature, breathing existence that bloomed color and expansion. So much color, so full of texture and movement after the unrelenting sterility, it was dizzying. Rami blinked his eyes against it.

The only mundane surface in the office was a deep oak desk, but even this was held up with pillars of stars. Rami recognized the angel seated behind it.

Quite tall and nearly as powerfully built as Ramiel, Uriel was all light. Her white-gold hair was trimmed short, and her uniform was impeccable, where Rami's was dark and faded. The uniform was not much changed from the last time Ramiel had seen it, despite the centuries that had passed. Outrageous buttons and tassels had been replaced with clean military trim, but it was still a leader's uniform. Still assuredly Uriel. Five seconds in her presence left Rami feeling shabby and mismatched.

Uriel was always as inerrant in her presence as she was with her purpose. Rami had once chalked this up to the confidence of youth. Ramiel was from the original Watcher angels, made before the Fall. Uriel belonged to the batch of angelic creatures made after.

But as the centuries went on, the difference in age became negligible, and he was forced to admit that Uriel was simply better made. Made for power, made for righteousness. Where Rami struggled to be certain of his way, Uriel burned with it.

"Ramiel." No less certain were the daggers of disappointment that edged her smile as she rose to greet him with a powerful handshake. "I was there when the Host voted to allow you to serve at the Gates. A chance at redemption, a great honor." She said this evenly, as if it was a decision she would not have made but could be generous enough to allow.

"Uriel." Rami nudged the old man to sit in an armchair of dwarf stars, cold and lumpy, but stable. "There's an abnormality—"

"You've served well, so far," Uriel continued. "I'm glad you've found your place, my friend."

Rami's jaw clenched. "I don't recall our last parting as exactly friendly."

Uriel dismissed it. "Foolish failure, but one that I'm pleased to see you're moving past."

Rami's cheek twitched. The Watchers, sympathizing too deeply with the fragile mortals in their care, had granted humans forbidden knowledge. The cost had been exile with Lucifer's minions, though the Watchers had not rebelled themselves. Heaven called it justice.

But Rami remembered the impoverished years of war and anarchy among the fallen Watchers, seeing the oldest witnesses to the universe feud and scrabble for survival, soaking men's dreams with enough blood of Heaven to drive them mad. Rami had stayed sane only by walking away.

Being a fallen angel meant he belonged nowhere, but being a Watcher meant he had access everywhere. Somehow, he'd found himself back at the Gates, looking at the one place he no longer could go. It was after an eon of walking that Ramiel realized the only thing he wanted was to be able to call a place home.

It'd taken him another century before the archangels had deigned to notice. Another before he was given a chance. Serve Purgatory, faithfully process the mortal souls entering Heaven, and the unspoken offer had been maybe—just maybe—one day he'd pass the Gates himself.

So he had. So he did. All rather uneventfully, until today.

"What have you got there, little man?" Uriel snapped Rami out of his thoughts as she approached Avery. The soul had relaxed even in the surreal surroundings, no longer hunching over his curious scrap of paper.

Avery looked up at the angel. "A barter."

"And what do you hope to barter for?"

"Forgiveness."

"Well, now." A sharp gleam set over Uriel's eyes. "That's a big trade."

It really wasn't—every soul in Heaven was forgiven. The judgment had always been for show; the only one who damned you to Hell was yourself. But Rami saw Uriel's tactical mind turning that for information. "What would be worth such a trade?"

"Just a piece of paper. From something I heard was valuable." There was a sharpness, an awareness, in the soul's eyes that hadn't been there before. As if the prospect of negotiation had woken him up. "The Devil's Bible."

The same change came over Uriel's gaze that had transformed the guard as well. "Ramiel, I'll need a moment with the human soul."

"YOU CAN'T BE SERIOUS," Ramiel said.

"I am always serious."

"But I'm not even an angel. Not anymore. I'm—"

"Thunder of God. Shepherd for the lost." Uriel marched her hand over the desk as she spoke, and stars eddied around her fingertips. The office was empty, Avery divested of his treasure and sent Heaven knew where. "Well suited to chasing after a powerful artifact. Or you were once."

"Not anymore. I can't . . . I'm not. I am in exile, at best." Rami begrudged even having to say it aloud. It was a barbed twist in his chest. "I can't even enter Heaven, let alone complete its work."

He refused to meet Uriel's eyes. Until her next words snapped his head up.

"Bring the pages of the book back, and that can be changed."

Rami stared. No angel or Watcher that had followed Lucifer had ever, ever been forgiven. Heaven did not forgive. It wasn't its nature—not when it came to angels.

He didn't want to ask, but the words were out of his mouth. "What kind of paper would be worth that kind of offer?"

Uriel stilled behind the desk, but she met Rami's gaze steadily. "It could be nothing more than a remnant. Something left over from the time of Enoch that the Betrayer's people missed." There had been a time of miracles, when the divine had still held an active interest in . . . anything really. That had been a long, long time ago. "But—that paper whispers power, Rami. The mortal named it the devil's. The stories on Earth were thought to be . . . Well, whatever it is, it will be something our Creator would have a vested interest in."

"You've . . . spoken to the Creator about this?"

"No. You know that . . ." Uriel caught herself, clenching her hand around the pommel of the blade at her side. "Or perhaps you don't. The Creator has grown . . . distant during the past age. Even to those in the holy presence."

"Distant . . . how?"

"The divine's attention is turned . . . elsewhere. Not here." A flicker of pain appeared on Uriel's angelic features, quickly schooled away.

Ramiel thought the Creator must have grown distant indeed to withdraw even from Uriel. She was the Light, where he had once been the Thunder. At times, she'd even served as the Face of God. The only one perhaps closer to the divine was Metatron. If their Creator was drifting beyond even Uriel's counsel, much must have changed in Heaven since Rami left.

Yet nothing had changed for the Host, not that he could see. The line of souls processed and progressed smoothly. Every angel he encountered at the Gates was as they always were: confident, golden, glowing with the righteous or, at the very least, the self-righteous. That kind of confidence was inspired only by true leaders. Like Uriel.

The realization hit Ramiel all at once. "You've been running things in Her absence."

Uriel's lips thinned. "Not alone. And only as the divine would have willed it."

"Ruling a realm. That's quite the promotion, Uriel."

"It's my duty. Our duty. The other archangels agree." Uriel averted her gaze. "Until the return. The Creator wouldn't abandon us entirely."

"I see." Temporary absence was frightening in itself. But Rami detected the rising tension in Uriel's shoulders and kept his voice neutral. "And you think this scrap holds enough power to draw the Creator back?"

"Not alone. But if it has a complete book of power on Earth equal to it . . . such a threat couldn't be ignored. The Creator would have to return. We would no longer be—" Uriel rose from her seat. "Am I to assume from your skepticism that you have no interest in my offer?"

"You're saying if I do this, I will be allowed back. Heaven. Does that mean forgiven?"

"That is up to the Creator, upon return. I can only promise you will be allowed past the Gates." Her voice took on a softer note. "It's your chance to prove your worth. Join us. You could come home, Ramiel."

Home. The word stuttered in his chest and traveled down his arms. Rami clenched his hands at his side. To set foot in the land he hadn't seen since the Earth was new. Only grasped in faded dreams during his time in the dark.

But it wasn't just the prospect of returning that drew him. It was not the memory of floating spires and air heavy with music. It was the prospect of stopping. Of truly belonging somewhere again. It was the idea of slowing his steps and turning his eyes to a place that saw him, that recognized him, that claimed him. It was that concept, the cessation of motion, that drove his words.

"I'll do it."

"Excellent." Uriel graced him with a rare smile. "You'll want to start with Avery's life, of course. I've got the brief prepared."

4

LETO

It's uncertain what precise conditions precipitate a book's waking up and becoming a character. Some restless characters must be soothed back into their bindings once a decade; others may not stir for several centuries. Some wake when disturbed with attention; others fidget with neglect. Some ache to be told; others appear to want to escape their own narrative. Or improvise upon it.

The only certainty is a book is most at risk while its author is alive. Like any good story, unwritten books have the capacity for great healing and great hurts. We do not act out of cruelty. The safest place for an unwritten book to be—for both it and its author—is sleeping in the Library, dreaming what stories it will tell.

Librarian Gregor Henry, 1944 CE

THE SLAP TURNED LETO'S chin. He took a step back from where they stood near the counter of the coffee shop, but Brevity advanced on him, hands on her hips. "Did you think I wouldn't find out?"

"I, uh . . ." Leto twisted, meeting pair after pair of blandly curious eyes. They had the attention of the entire shop, whether out of sympathy or annoyance. Claire positioned herself discreetly at the far wall, near the book's table. The hero, as Claire had called him, and his companion were entirely focused on Brevity's display. "You found out . . . ?"

He had just enough warning to flinch before another open hand aimed for his shoulder. Brevity burst into a very believable font of tears. The former muse had mastered the art of crying prettily, and Leto heard sympathetic murmurs drift among the coffee shop's patrons.

He reached out to pat Brevity on the shoulder. "I'm sorry. . . ."

"Don't touch me!"

Although the red-haired author was riveted, the hero began to lose focus as he scanned the crowd. His eyes stopped when they stumbled upon Claire. The two locked gazes with a crackle of energy that went unnoticed by the rest of the shop.

A flash of silver hung from Claire's fingertips, held low at her side like a blade. Her lips moved. The faintest silver script swayed, just a moment, in the air between them. The hero's eyes narrowed and he stood up from the table with a murmured word to his companion.

Brevity cleared her throat, bringing Leto back to their improv.

"Can't you at least tell me what I did?"

The hero and the librarian exchanged a series of hissed words and sharp gestures across the way. Claire seemed to get the advantage when she flicked up the hand holding her tool. The hero blanched and shot nervous eyes toward his oblivious companion.

"It's like you're not even here." A nudge brought Leto around to face wide brown eyes. Brevity gave him an inscrutable look before her eyes welled with tears again. "You don't even see me anymore." Her voice was a stage whisper.

Leto's stomach did a flip-flop, and he hesitantly put a hand on Brevity's arm. He garnered the courage to make his contribution to their little display. "I, ah, always see you. How could I not see a beautiful girl?" He resisted cringing at the line, randomly plucked from his limited exposure to human romance. His voice was not quite as confident as he would have liked, but he frankly had trouble thinking straight in close proximity to Brevity's large, wet eyes.

Past Brevity's shoulder, Leto could see the hero scowl at Claire. He leaned over and whispered something to his author. She made a face, but the handsome man mollified her with a smile. The hero stood and began making his way out of the coffee shop, Claire tight on his heels.

Just in time. The onlookers were growing bored now that Brevity and Leto weren't screaming at each other. Brevity made a melty noise, flinging her arms back for show. "Why're you always so sweet, huh?"

Leto had just enough time to catch a subtle wink from the muse before she caught his chin and pressed soft, smiling lips against his.

"YOU DID GOOD," BREVITY chattered as they popped out of the coffee shop a few minutes later. "I was going for a big, classic breakup fight, but that makeup kiss made most people uncomfortable enough that they wanted to look away anyway. Good idea."

Leto managed a nod as if, yes, of course, that had been his plan all along. He kept his chin tucked into his chest to hide the heat still on his cheeks. He was grateful to find Claire and the bronze-haired man—Leto still had trouble thinking of him as a character from a book—waiting for them around the corner.

Claire had the tall man cornered against the brick building, pinned with a scowl. Brevity and Leto slowed as they approached.

Claire spared a glance in their direction. "It's hidden it."

"The book?" Brevity wrinkled her nose. "Don't suppose he'll tell us if we ask really nicely?"

"He is not an *it*. He's also not an idiot and is standing right here," the man said as he crossed his arms and slouched against the brick wall. "I have no intention of going back to slowly go insane for all eternity on some dusty shelf."

"And I have no intention of letting you hang around here, torturing that poor girl," Claire said. "The difference is, I have a say in the matter. You do not."

"I'm not torturing her!" The hero straightened. "She's . . . she's so . . . I could never harm her."

Claire gave an impatient wiggle of her fingers. "She's amazing. She's brilliant. She's creative and thoughtful and clever and kind. That the gist of it?"

"Yes." The hero's face softened. "You see it. She's perfect. At first I just wanted to meet her, but now . . . we've spent days just talking. If I can just inspire her to—"

"She's your author. Inspiring her to write is not your job. You've already caused enough damage."

"I have been a perfect gentleman!"

An arm shot out and Claire pinned the much taller man against the wall. "You've already hurt her. Just your *being* here has changed her. She's going to be paying the rest of her life for your damn selfish curiosity."

The man started. "I have not! I—"

"Did she argue?" Claire snapped. "When you made your excuses? Did she even notice you were exiting with another woman?"

"I . . . am very persuasive." The hero covered sudden uncertainty with a delicate sneer. "Not that you would understand such an intimate connection."

Claire rolled her eyes. "Yes, yes, I'm an ogre. You wound me. And you're still twisting her mind all up just by being here."

"I can't be. . . ." Color drained from his face. "An agreement, then. I'll show you where I hid it. I'll go with you. Just . . . let me say good-bye to her."

Claire was unmoved. "No. Out of the question."

"It's not a trick! You can even watch me. Please." The hero gave a pleading glance to Brevity and Leto. "I owe her a decent good-bye, at least that much. Wouldn't that help repair some of the damage I've done?"

Brevity spoke up. "A proper good-bye might make him more human, boss. To the author."

Claire's face remained stony. "Are you speaking as a former muse?"

"Speaking as a girl who remembers how hearts work. Since sometimes you forget."

Claire huffed her disagreement and considered. She rustled in her bag. "Fine. Hold out your hand."

"What?"

"Your hand, hero. If I'm letting a book walk around, I want some insurance. You're getting a stamp."

"I'm not . . ." The hero's delicate brows knit together in confusion. Nonetheless, he reluctantly shoved up a sleeve. "This is demeaning. You already have my card. Is this really necessary?"

"Quite." Claire retrieved from her bag a small stamp with a stubby wooden handle. She squinted and twisted one of the gears at the base. With a utilitarian jab, she stabbed the tip of the handle into her own palm. Brevity made a small noise as she looked away.

Leto felt queasy but entranced. Blood pooled briefly on Claire's hand before being wicked into the stamp's handle. Leto swore the wood now had a warmer, ruddier sheen.

In another practiced move, the librarian snatched the hero's palm and planted the stamp's rubber end squarely in the center of his pale wrist.

A red-black ribbon of ink escaped from the rubber circle and twined its way around the hero's wrist, leaving behind a worming knot of threads and shapes. The medallion pulsed on his forearm. Curiosity getting the better of him, Leto leaned closer. A tiny calligraphic font, almost too slender to read, shifted in chaotic patterns across the hero's skin.

The hero yanked back his wrist and rubbed at it tenderly. He raised his chin, regaining some of his initial arrogance. "We have an accord?"

The librarian scowled, but with less force than she'd had before. She was pale, as if she'd lost energy as well as blood. "Welcome to Special Collections."

She stowed the stamp away in her bag without looking at the hero. "Go. Be back here with book in hand in twenty minutes."

THEY WAITED ACROSS THE street from the coffee shop, at a bus stop bench just long enough to accommodate all three of them. Claire had fallen into a quiet that was tense enough for Leto to wish she was yelling at people again.

The librarians kept their eyes fixed on the coffee shop's window. The hero was inside for moments before reappearing at the front table with the redheaded author, just as he'd promised. Leto could see him cradling the woman's hands across the table, their heads angled toward each other.

Leto rubbed the backs of his knuckles before breaking the silence. "So, uh, do you two do this often?"

"I wish. I love it up here." Brevity sighed. "But characters don't often just walk off with their books. And stamping is even more rare." She gave the librarian a side glance.

Leto's curiosity overcame his nerves. "What exactly does that do?"

"Stamping?" Again, Brevity's eyes bobbed to Claire and away before she answered. "A stamped book becomes part of the Library's special collection. It means the librarian can IWL it."

"IWL?"

"Interworld loan," Brevity explained. "Loaned out to or called back from anywhere, basically. Books have a way of going where they're needed, and Hell's Library keeps unwritten art, but it isn't the only library out there—I hear great things about Valhalla's, actually. It keeps all the untold acts of heroism," Brevity said. "Librarians can summon a stamped book back to Hell's Library from anywhere, even if its calling card is destroyed. If it's in Special Collections, it will always return to its originating Library."

"Sounds . . . serious. Why don't you do that to all the books to avoid their going missing like this?"

"There are limits. It . . . takes a little from the head librarian to administer and maintain a stamp." Brevity chewed on her lip.

Leto glanced back at the shop window. "What do you think he's saying? You mentioned something about fixing stuff."

Brevity started to shrug, but Claire made them both jump by answering. "There's no fixing that damage."

"What damage, though?" Leto asked after a moment of surprise. "I mean, he's handsome. I'll give him that. But it seems like just a date . . . ?"

Claire didn't turn her attention away from the couple in the window. She drew in a long breath. "Books don't appear as normal people to their authors. Characters are made of something more to the one who created them. They're made of our dreams, our scars, slivers stuck beneath our skin. You're not meant to meet someone like that. She doesn't know it yet, but she's talking to the most alive person she'll ever meet. The kind of alive you don't find in real life. No one, no great love or her own flesh and blood, will ever come close. She'll remember that glint in his eyes, the twist of his chin, a casual turn of phrase. She'll hold it quietly in her mind like a fire. A fire that will consume everything.

"If she's lucky, she'll walk away haunted. But if she's unlucky, she'll believe it. She won't write him; she'll spend her whole life looking for him." Claire's knuckles were white on her lap. "If she's smart, she'll try to forget. But that brand of memory is always going to be there, seared into a tender curve of her heart, a breath caught in her chest. It kills you eventually."

Cars rattled past. Brevity's expression was startlingly serious, wide-eyed, and silent. Leto stammered for a response, but the librarian cut him off with a harsh laugh.

"You surely didn't think I got duty in the Unwritten Wing by random chance?" Claire's voice was hollow. She glanced at Leto with a paper-thin smile. "You know how they say 'Never meet your heroes'? For authors most of all, *never* meet your heroes. Ruins everything." She shook her head as she continued to watch the coffee shop.

They fell quiet. Brevity scuffed her toes on the sidewalk, while Leto squinted up at the rooftops, trying not to think about what he didn't understand.

The sun was setting fast, and the brick face of the buildings began to bleed shadows, clay turning the color of dried blood. The seagulls echoed from the ferry port down the street, and Leto knew the tour boats would be evicting the last of their passengers, while the ferries took on commuters headed home. He did not stop to wonder how he knew this.

"Please stop looking at me like that, Brev," Claire finally said.

"Like what?"

"Like I'm a soap bubble about to pop. I am perfectly capable. It's just been a long . . . There he is. About time." The librarian shook off the look her assistant gave her and stood quickly as the hero crossed the street.

They intercepted him at the corner, and the unwritten man held his hands up with a taunting smile. "Easy, warden. I surrender to your tender mercies." The hero's tan seemed a bit paler to Leto, and his eyes darker in the fading light.

"Your book, hero." Claire had shed all sense of wistfulness on the short stride from the bench.

The hero reached into a jean pocket and pulled out what looked at first like a small tourist guide. As his hand withdrew, however, the book expanded and shimmered until he was holding a weathered leather tome of the same style that filled the Unwritten Wing. Claire snatched the book out of his hands and ran a finger over the spine carefully before handing it to Brevity to stow away. "You hid it in the coffee shop."

"I did."

"And you made your good-byes to the author?"

"Yes. It was . . . hard. She was upset. Crying." The hero's eyes strayed across the street, searching the windowed front with a shadow of pain. "She thinks I broke up with her."

Claire was unmoved. She pointed down the street as they began walking. Leto and Brevity fell in line behind them. "I hope you were not foolish enough to try to reveal yourself to her."

"No, of course not. Something more subtle had the same effect."

Claire stopped so abruptly that Leto nearly ran into her. She twisted the hero by one arm and diverted them into the closest alleyway. The steamy smell of old rubbish reached out to greet them. The hero wrinkled his nose, and Claire shoved him against a wall. Her heavy braids whipped and nearly caught both Brevity and Leto in the face as she wheeled on the taller man. "What did you do?"

The hero's lips held a smug smile. "You make the most colorful of fusses, Librarian. Is being surly and dramatic part of the position?"

"It's part of having to deal with idiot heroes all day. Answer me, book, or so help me, I will take a cleaver to your spine."

Leto was uncertain whether she was speaking about the book or the man, but Claire repeated her question. "What. Did. You. Do?"

"It was just a hint, really." The hero looked far too pleased with himself. "I gave her my opening pages."

Her mouth dropped open. "You . . ." She swore and shot out her hand. "Brevity, the book."

Her assistant wrestled the large leather manuscript out of the bag. She cast a spooked look at the hero before passing it over. Claire fished out her ghostlight lighter. It filled the darkening alleyway with a faint blue glow. Brevity nudged Leto, and they both shuffled a step to make sure the eerie light wasn't obvious from the street.

Claire flipped open the cover and held the glowing lighter up. Leto craned to see. The title page was intact, thick vellum tinged a buttery color even in the blue light. But as Claire lifted the page, a jagged edge came into view. Several pages, a dozen or more, had been torn from the front of the book. They'd been ripped roughly, in some places torn deep into the binding, exposing dark scarlet veins of thread. The remaining text picked up midsentence, and each word trembled on the page.

Brevity gasped. Leto noticed Claire's shudder only because it made her braids tremble. Claire took in a sharp breath and held the ghostly lighter closer for inspection. Her lips parted, and she muttered words Leto couldn't understand as she studied the grisly remains of the first pages of the book. The hero crossed his arms and slumped slightly against the bricks, unperturbed as she gingerly closed the book. Her voice was pinched with the kind of quiet one used around a terminal patient.

"You ripped out your own pages."

"I did," the hero said.

"That would have been . . . painful."

"It was."

"Self-mutilation." Claire shook her head. "You're a book. What can you possibly hope to gain?"

"Everything." A fine sweat broke out on the hero's forehead, gleaming in the dim light and plastering the tips of his bronze hair to his temples.

His words were fevered. "I can see it in her eyes, Librarian. She's so close to it! She wants to write, she needs it, and she doesn't even know it!"

"It's not your—"

"It's cruel. You say it's cruel to visit my author when I am unwritten. But I find it monstrous how you allow these authors to suffer. And yes, allow their stories to suffer as well. To live these half-lives, stories and authors, wearing holes in their souls that hold the shadow of other worlds they'll never see. When you could so easily help them. Ask your muse here!"

The hero sank more heavily against the brick. "One word, one hint, one familiar face in a coffee shop. If I can inspire her to write and make us real . . . you should be freeing your entire library. Introducing books to their authors, not jailing them. If it gets them to write and gives worlds a chance to live . . ."

He made a guttural sound in his throat. "Who are you to stop them? Or must every author fail so they can be just as miserable as you?"

Brevity gasped as if the hero had struck a blow, but Claire's expression faded from anger to concern. "Hero." Her brows knit together as she watched the unwritten man, who was sweating profusely now. "Tell me what you're . . . feeling."

The hero looked pale, much too pale. Claire gestured, and Leto quickly went to the hero's side, gripping him under one elbow. He was surprisingly light. The hero grimaced at his touch. "I'm . . . fine. It's just damnably hot here, and . . . where—where was I?"

A tremor shot through the man's body. His brow furrowed, then smoothed to distant dismay. "Oh dear. The pages. I think she's burning them."

And with that, the hero fainted onto the concrete.

A stunned silence, then Brevity spoke.

"Well, he did break up with her."

5

RAMIEL

We think stories are contained things, but they're not. Ask the muses. Humans, stories, tragedies, and wishes—everything leaves ripples in the world. Nothing we do is not felt; that's a comfort. Nothing we do is not felt; that's a curse.

Librarian Poppaea Julia, 50 BCE

RAMIEL TRANSPORTED HIMSELF DIRECTLY to the dead man's living room. The rush of air that accompanied his arrival sent up a burst of dust and fluttering papers. Mr. Jonathan Avery had not been a tidy man toward the end of his life. His Seattle apartment perched at the top of a very trendy tower downtown, but inside was a study in crumpled bags and stacks of papers.

Still, Rami thought he could detect a modicum of reason in the stacks lining every available surface of the accountant's apartment, sprawled with the minutiae of a life of numbers and details. Dust came away on Rami's hand as he thumbed open a cabinet.

Avery hadn't given him much to go on, even after Uriel's prodding. Upon arrival in Heaven, souls were frequently fuzzy on the details of their lives. The whole business of death was traumatic, so temporary amnesia often helped new arrivals adjust to their afterlives. It was a testament to the man's desperation that he even remembered what the scrap of paper was.

Which is why Ramiel was on Earth, scrounging around a dead man's apartment for clues. Uriel opted to stay behind and try to draw more answers from Avery. Rami suspected that had less to do with sympathy for the dead and more to do with Uriel disliking modern-day civilization. Rami had the impression that Uriel took the development of human curiosity as terribly inconvenient altogether. She'd never had much use for humans beyond what function they had to please her Creator.

For Uriel, humans were cut flowers for a lover's bouquet, nothing more.

A superficial sweep turned up little but week-old newspapers and sour milk, and a laptop buried beneath a tilting cliff of paper. He understood these sleek devices were the nexus of modern human lives, the modern confessional, but it would not give up its secrets for him. Luckily, he was less interested in Avery's secrets than in Hell's. There were more traditional ways to track nonhuman artifacts. He crossed the apartment to open the sliding door that led to a shriveled excuse for a balcony, then carded his fingers through his feathered coat until he found an appropriate sacrifice. Wincing as it came free, he shielded the feather from the wind in the cup of his palm.

Uriel had said that the scrap came from a book created for Lucifer's realm. Rami did not know this cartoonish "devil" that terrorized modern imagination, but he knew Lucifer. He was a selfish angel and likely an even more selfish demon. If something of his was missing, his servants might have already been dispatched to retrieve it. They would have a head start, possibly in this very city, would possibly even have the book already. If Rami could intercept them, he could keep a powerful tool out of evil's hands and end this before any harm could be done.

Rami withdrew a silver compass from his pocket and brought it up to the feather he sheltered in his hand. He bent, muttering a few sparse words until a faint white light hummed between compass and feather. As with ink seeping from quill shaft to tip, the feather slowly changed into a deep, pitiless black. Tainted, like the quarry he sought.

Rami let the feather flutter off the balcony, then retreated inside to watch the compass in his hands. The next time the demons moved, to or from this city, he'd have them. He just had to wait.

Rami was good at waiting.

6

LETO

Books and stories are the creations of imagination, and that power is just for humans. Take it from me. Gods can will a realm into being, and muses can try to edge things along, but only a mortal can imagine a different way for the story to go. How cool is that? Humans are freaking terrifying. I love it!

Apprentice Librarian Brevity, 2014 CE

"BALLS," CLAIRE MUTTERED.

As soon as the hero collapsed, the librarian instructed Leto to hoist his legs. It was a waddling walk to drag the prone man farther into the alley where no passing tourists would notice. Despite being surprisingly light, the hero was tall, with long arms and legs that Leto found impossible to corral. Leto grimaced as they hit another trash can that boomed loudly in the darkness.

Brevity, hand full of book rather than hero, kept pace with something close to a nervous dance. She flashed Leto a reassuring smile. "Cheer up. At least she's not cursing His High—"

"Lucifer's *frilly, satin* balls," Claire grunted as they deposited the hero against a stack of stained cardboard boxes with a shove.

"Never mind," Brevity said.

Leto flinched. Despite his growing increasingly used to Claire's colorful wording, each blasphemy still sent a tremor of unease through him.

He set the hero's feet down gently on a box. The character's haughty face was still pale. "Is he going to be okay?"

"For now, I reckon." The muse cast glances back to the alley entrance, and pedestrian traffic was slowing as the afternoon waned.

Brevity crouched over the hero and poked at his shoulder. "Tearing out your own pages is one thing; they can be reattached. But his pages were *destroyed*. Anything that was on them is gone forever. Places, plot . . . or characters. You can do a lot with restoration, and boss is one of the best, but you can't reinvent things out of whole cloth."

"Which is why it's time to stop dallying and get him back to the Library." Claire dusted off her hands. "When you arrive, make him comfortable, then be sure to send a message to the muse cache. I'll have to work on him myself, and I'll need fresh parchment and binder."

"Yes, ma'am. You're not . . . ?"

"One more piece of business. I'll be fine. Leto's been extremely helpful so far. Isn't that right?"

Leto jerked his head up. "Uh, sure. I mean, I hope so. We aren't going back now?" The hum of the city streets made his skin itch, and the whole adventure had left his human form disconcertingly . . . sweaty.

"Brev will take the hero and book back," Claire said, as if to a small child. "We have a quick stop before we use our ghostlights."

Claire met Brevity's concerned gaze, and some unspoken discussion occurred between the librarian and her assistant. After a moment, Brevity took hold of the hero by the collar. "I'll take care of handsome here, sure thing."

The muse etched a figure on the dusty concrete faster than Leto could follow. He could have sworn the brick walls wobbled, just a moment, before he was distracted by a hissing *pop*. Brevity and the prone hero were gone in a swirl of dust and paper debris. A trace scent of cotton candy and ash hung in the air.

Which left Leto alone with Hell's librarian. He pulled his gaze away from the swirling air to find Claire scrutinizing him over her glasses. Her lips were cinched up like purse strings. Leto didn't know her well enough to know what that meant, but he was sure it was nothing good. He again suffered the sense of being appraised for something he didn't understand. Claire nodded and took off down the alley at a pace that required Leto to hurry to keep up.

"Do you know the origin of ghostlights, Leto?" Claire asked after they had joined the evening foot traffic on the sidewalk. She guided him around the corner at a brisk pace, stopping occasionally to squint at street signs.

"Not exactly." It wasn't much of an admission. He was a junior fiend at best. He hadn't understood half of what he'd encountered today. They wandered downhill from the business buildings, away from tall towers, and toward squat ferry buildings and shops that lined the pier. Distracting smells and sights filtered his thoughts. They passed a famous chocolate shop, where buttery, sweet cocoa smells wafted out and drove away the briny smell of the bay. Leto didn't stop to wonder how he knew the scent; he just did. He knew if they turned right, they'd run into a flock of taxicabs that swarmed around the Four Seasons and a crusty protester who always stood on that corner, waving a picture of the current president—didn't matter who—with horns drawn on. No one knew what he was protesting.

"The term comes from the theater. Or at least, from days when theaters were more popular. When a theater closed for the night, a single light was left on, usually just a bulb on a stand at the center of the stage. The stage always stayed lit. A ghostlight. It had a practical purpose, of course—that way the first one to enter didn't accidentally fall into the orchestra pit."

"And the nonpractical?" Leto had seen enough today to understand that the nonpractical was usually more worrisome.

"The theater ghosts, of course." Claire smiled and eased to a more sensible stroll as they passed the first trickle of crowds lining up outside dockside restaurants and bars. "Theaters traditionally always closed for at least one day a week, leaving on the ghostlight, to appease the ghosts. To allow them one day on the stage to perform their acts. To live and love and hate and triumph on the stage like the living."

She slid him an unreadable smile as they slowed down at a new corner. "That part's true. In the glow of a ghostlight, the dead all get one day. One day only." Claire looked down the street. "Last time I was here, there was a long pier. Good view, outdoor patio across from a ferry. It should be around here somewhere. . . ."

"Two blocks down," Leto said automatically.

Claire hummed. "Aren't you handy?"

They walked on, weaving through sidewalk crowds until the waterfront came into view. Far down the walk, Leto could just make out the lights of a Ferris wheel flickering on, painting the night's low clouds with luminous pinks and greens. The quiet was amiable, until Claire let out a sigh. "You're a stubborn one."

Leto's stomach dropped. "What?"

"All during this fiasco you've been asking things! Gawking! Mr. Questions! Fussing over taxicab ethics, even." Claire stopped at a railing and tugged at a lock of hair irritably. "But I try to introduce the one thing you're supposed to question and suddenly you're more gullible than a saint."

Leto shifted. "I'm not sure I— I'm sorry if I've—"

"No, just stop." She dragged a palm over her face. "I just finished explaining how ghostlights work. How they allow the souls of dead humans like me a day on Earth. So an obvious question might be . . . ?"

"Yes, ah . . . Do they have something to do with the hero?" A trickle of sweat lined the back of Leto's suit. He felt like he was failing a pop quiz.

"No." Claire crossed her arms and motioned to his pocket. "An obvious question to someone in your situation might be, 'So why does a demon need a ghostlight at all?'"

"Why does a demon need a ghostlight? Well, I thought . . ."

Leto tried to consider it—he did. The stern librarian's approval had swiftly grown important to him. But even as he repeated the words, his mind kept trying to hitch off in a new direction. Surely there were better inquiries. Where *was* the hero now? How did Brevity pop in and out? How were they going to fix the book? Considering all those, his brain refused to waste time on a silly question about ghostlights. Demons didn't deserve the luxury of learning. Leto deserved even less.

But Claire's expectant look made him try. He'd grown to respect the librarians. He liked Brevity and Claire, prickly as she was, and the thought of disappointing her curdled his nerves. He slid his gaze out over the choppy water as he tried to focus. Surely there was a reason he needed a ghostlight. It was obvious.

Because he was new? Because of entropy? Because of the time of year? Because he was such a miserable excuse for a demon?

He felt his stomach tilt as he sorted through each possible reason and discarded it for lack of logic. He felt like he was being tipped over the top of a very tall, steep hill, adrenaline climbing into his throat. He couldn't see the bottom, couldn't stop.

Like a roller coaster.

Roller coaster. A term he hadn't recognized when Claire said it right before the summons this morning. But he could picture it clearly now: the clattering metal track, the thick, foam pads that came down across his shoulders and always smelled vaguely of someone else's sweat, someone else's nerves. The flip in his gut as the roller coaster would start. The feeling of a hand grabbing his, belonging to someone soft and bright and all wonderful things at once. The smell of popcorn drifting up from below . . . human smells. Mortal feelings. Living memories.

Leto did not notice his legs failing until his knees banged against the wooden railing harshly. Claire caught him under one arm, stopping his chin from meeting the wood. She supported his weight with a grunt. "Easy, now."

"I'm . . . I'm not a demon?" Leto's voice was suddenly hoarse. "I'm mortal."

"Well, technically no. You're not mortal, not anymore. Bad term for it. Dead, eternal soul, and all. But you were *human*, once. Up here." Claire hitched him to his feet and waited till Leto's knees worked again. Then she drove him forward, off the sidewalk to the pier. "Onward, now. Walking helps."

Leto's heart was trying to swim out from his chest, but he moved his legs woodenly. "I don't understand."

"You explained it well enough before. When you die, you get what your soul's debt demands. Like what you need to do to atone for what you've done, or to just forgive yourself, to heal, or find justice. It varies. My soul decided I needed to spend a century or two—god, I hope I don't reach past that—as the keeper of the Unwritten Library in Hell. Lucky me. Yours . . . Evidently you needed to be an amnesiac demon. Rather melodramatic, that."

They started down the long pier. It was wide and ringed with cheery lights. Patio restaurants. People talking. Boats groaning. It threatened to overwhelm him. There was a light post at the end of the walkway, and Leto kept his eyes locked on that.

"You don't remember anything, even being up here?" Claire asked.

Leto squeezed his eyes closed briefly, but it did no good. His memories only tasted of bitter anise and shadows. "I . . . know things. Stuff about here. This place. But I don't remember how I know it."

Claire shrugged. "Well, it's a unique sentence for a soul—that's for sure. Must have been a hard end. Not many people see themselves as *literal* devils."

"I'm not—" Leto's hand absently tugged at an ear that was still blunted rather than pointed, here in the human world. "But I remember being a demon!"

"What do you remember? Being summoned for courier duty? What about before that? What did you do yesterday?"

"Well, sure. I was doing . . . demony stuff." Leto faltered. To tell the truth, before this assignment it was all a dark haze he couldn't really put his finger on. He had a fleeting impression of a figure, someone powerful and terrifying, resting a hand decked with cold rings on his shoulder. He remembered a constellation of stars falling through his hands. Bitter chalk on his tongue. He knew things about being a demon, but specific memories skittered away from him when he reached for them. "How did you know?"

"His Grouchiness doesn't usually send a brand-new, full-fledged demon to deliver a file folder, first of all. We're in a library of magical texts. Do you really think we deliver messages by hand?"

"Well. Now that you mention it . . ."

Claire smiled. "And if you're a demon of entropy, you're the worst one I've seen, because you got torn up at the idea of shorting a taxi driver's tips. And then Walter confirmed it when we set up transportation—only human souls need ghostlights. Even if he hadn't, once we got up here, it was all the little things. Human things. Like the cute little blush when Brev kissed you."

"I did not!"

"Ah, there it is again."

Leto buried his face in his hands, but they'd reached the end of the pier. They walked past an open patio where diners nibbled on overpriced oysters, and came to a stop at the railing. Claire nodded at the view. "You know, I had a view of the ocean when I was alive. Not here. England. Colder, harsher, different kind of pretty."

"Was it nice?"

Claire considered. "I wouldn't have the slightest idea. I suppose it would have been, had I noticed."

Leto hesitated. "What will happen when we go back?"

Claire braced her elbows against the railing and faced him. "That's largely up to your soul. You may remain a demon. You could try to speak to Boss Creepy if you want."

"No! No, that's all right." Leto shook his head so fast that Claire chuckled.

"He's not that bad. Well—he is, sometimes. But any good story is half exaggeration. *It's* not that bad. Really, being—"

Claire's words cut off, and her expression went rigid as she stared past his shoulder. Before he could turn, a cold, sharp point presented itself between Leto's shoulder blades. A voice, gritty and sounding of steel and stone, spoke low from behind him.

"Stand down, demons."

"Speaking of exaggerations . . ." Claire had excellent posture. She had relaxed while leaning against the railing, softening as she talked of souls and eternity, enough that she seemed almost human. But she stood straight now, with a hard, chill gaze reserved for the voice behind him. Leto didn't dare turn with something pressed against his spine, but the gaze told him enough.

"We have no business with you, Watcher," Claire said.

Leto didn't know what a Watcher was, but from the curl of Claire's lip, it didn't seem like a friendly thing. He'd never thought to ask what would happen to a soul that got stabbed while visiting Earth. In his human form, he doubted it was anything good.

"But I have business with you," the voice grated. "Identify yourselves, or you will be short one demonic servant."

"If you are as dull as you seem, it appears I must. You're speaking to the head librarian of the Unwritten Wing. The boy you're frightening is Leto, a *human*." Claire held one hand clenched on her bag, as if shielding the trade tools within.

"I know a demon when I see one. And you—a *librarian*." The man breathed the word like a curse, like he was admitting something. "Of course. Then I am just in time." He let up the blade from Leto's back, though Leto wasn't sure whether it was from relenting or that he was now focused on another target.

Leto twisted as he backed up defensively. From the voice, he'd honestly expected something closer to Walter: looming and monstrous. But the man was not much taller than Leto himself, was thick shouldered and dark with strong features. Broad face, olive skin, and sharply angled brown eyes dark with threat. A strange trench coat hung to the ground, slate gray with an odd assortment of dark-colored feathers peeping out from under the epaulets and trailing down the back in a scattered pattern. A short sword clutched in one thick hand gleamed under the pier lights.

Leto risked a glance at the evening crowds on the patio not too far off, but the eyes of the diners seemed to slide right over them as they gazed across the pier. No one saw the madman with a sword. Or Watcher, as

Claire had called him. Whatever the man was, Leto wanted to be far away from him.

Leto retreated, trying to move toward Claire, but the man flicked his gaze at him. "That's far enough." Dark eyes shifted back and the Watcher spoke low to Claire. "He *would* send you. I know what you're here for. Hand over the book."

The corners of Claire's lips tugged into a mocking smile, but Leto was close enough to see the new tension tighten her eyes. "Why, Watcher, patron checkouts are not my department. But if you want something to read, you only had to stop by during library hours. What are you after, some bodice ripper to liven up your dull, immortal exile?"

The mockery slid off the Watcher's stony face without effect. "You will have to try harder to enrage me, I'm afraid. Hand over the book."

"Seeing as I have no idea what book you're referring to, you're going to have to be more specific." Taunt failed, Claire reached for placating. "Honest, I really don't know what you're after."

"Don't waste my time. The book. You didn't get all of it, did you?"

Leto's mind conjured the hero's unwritten book with fangs of jagged missing pages. Leto swallowed hard, and Claire turned guarded. "There might have been an accident. What concern would that be for a Watcher like you?"

The man's hard lips took on a smug demeanor for the first time. The blade in his hand didn't waver as he withdrew a small clear bag from his coat pocket. Inside fluttered a scrap of paper, a corner ripped from some larger piece. As his eyes landed on it, Leto thought he heard a faint hiss, quiet words he could almost make out.

"Because I got there first." The man gave a hard smile.

The whispers swam Leto in vertigo. He shook his head to clear it. "Is the author okay?"

The Watcher paused. "What?"

"The—"

"Hush, Leto." Claire cut him off. She frowned at the paper in the man's grasp. "If those are the pages, that belongs to the Library, Watcher."

The Watcher straightened his sword. "It belongs to Heaven, as everything does. Now, I will have the rest of the book from you."

"I'm afraid you're out of luck. It's already been sent back to the Library. But if you want to come by during visitors' hou—"

"Liar!" A voice like thunder sent the hairs on Leto's neck on end. Claire flinched as if she'd been shocked. The Watcher had cleared the space in a moment and rested his sword at Claire's breast. "I am Ramiel. Soldier of the First Host, the Thunder of God. I'll have the truth."

Light shuddered just beneath the blade's surface, though Leto swore Ramiel hadn't moved. Leto twitched, and Claire shook her head ever so slightly.

"Ramiel . . ." Claire breathed, and for the first time Leto heard fear in her voice. "I wasn't aware fallen angels had such a passion for literature." Leto blinked at the word. Angel.

"Will you hand over the book, Librarian?" Ramiel's shoulder inched down as his lips pressed into a pale line. The clear bag with the parchment dangled from his free hand at his side. Leto found himself listening for the whispers. He wasn't sure if he wanted more to pick out the words or to block his ears. "I will not ask again. I know you are neutral. You were once human. I have no quarrel with your duties. But I must return with the book."

The pause was charged, air before a storm. When Claire spoke, her voice was calm again. "Leto, dear. Remember to blow out your ghostlight." She spoke without breaking her gaze from the angel. "Unfortunately, my duties extend to every book in my care. I cannot help you."

"A pity. I wish it were otherwise." A shutter came over Ramiel's gaze, eyes guarded. His sword arm trembled. The air felt on the edge of cracking, and then Leto knew.

He didn't know what a Watcher was; he didn't know what a Watcher did. Didn't know about fallen angels or books in Hell. Leto barely knew himself. But if he was human, then everything human in him—every teenage, powerless, frustrated human fiber—knew what angry men in power did when denied something they felt they were owed. Leto darted forward and grabbed desperately at the nearest thing in reach: the bag dangling from the angel's fingers.

He'd intended merely to create a distraction, but the reaction was immediate and violent. Ramiel grunted, jerking his sword away from Claire's chest. His arm swung back, and Leto flinched against the railing, waiting for the blow.

Instead, Claire's arm crashed against Leto's chest. They careened backward and pitched against the wood.

"Deep breath!" she ordered as the world spun. The railing dug into his back and then they toppled over the edge of the pier. The Watcher's startled face tilted out of view, sword faltering as a free hand reached out. And then they hit the black cold water.

Ice spasmed through his nerves and the water closed over him. A brackish taste flooded the back of his mouth before he remembered to clench his throat shut. Diffuse light bled away as they sank into the bay. Claire's hand clamped tighter onto his chest as another hand pawed for the pocket that held his ghostlight. Leto got the idea and managed to pull the tiny lighter out with a free hand.

His lungs burned. It was too dark to see, and his movements were turning thick and sluggish from the icy Puget Sound waters. Claire's hand fumbled on top of his, and she thumbed the switch. The ghostlight flared, sparking light into the dark water with an impossible blue flame.

A trickle of bubbles breathed against his cheek as Claire mouthed something. He could not hear them, but he caught the last words as they bloomed quiet in the center of his head, like a half-remembered poem.

"*. . . and I'll drown my book.*"

7

CLAIRE

A librarian has already failed if a book requires repairs. Books will age, yes, even in the Library. Need new binding, a tidying up of revisions. But true damage happens only when a book escapes.

I expect you, apprentice, will never fail so in your duties. But should a book need repair, be prepared to devote all your time and patience. It is simple enough to repair a book's paper form; even its manifested form will mend. But a book in the Unwritten Wing is the manifest potential of a story—the words are the thing. Potential cannot be ripped out and replaced like parchment or leather. You cannot substitute your own words. A story must be fed, encouraged to grow its own roots.

Keep the books from damage, Gregor. Repair those you can save. But beware the stories that find their freedom.

Librarian Yoon Ji Han, 1817 CE

WHEN CLAIRE BLINKED, ENDLESS gnarls of red thread danced on the insides of her eyelids. She groaned, rubbed her eyes, and drained the remains of her cold tea.

They'd landed back in Walter's office, flopping about like fish, and bringing a hearty helping of the bay water with them. Walter had insisted on wrapping them both up in his jacket—it was big enough to practically engulf both Claire and Leto—and escort them personally back to the

Library. The big gatekeeper tutted about the disgrace of such treatment the whole way.

The hero was still unconscious. Claire allowed Brevity to make a tolerable amount of fuss before retreating to the restorations room with the hero's book, supplies, and the scrap that Leto had, miraculously, held on to during their escape. Despite the panic in his wide eyes, he'd demonstrated quick thinking; Claire was forced to revise her impression of the confused teenager.

She'd allowed Brevity in to deliver a hot pot of tea and a clean change of clothes before turning her attention to the process of restoring the book. If Claire was going to get answers as to *why* a fallen angel, let alone a Watcher, was interested in an unwritten fantasy novel, she would need to make sure the hero survived long enough to answer questions.

After hours of painstaking work, she was no longer afraid they were going to lose the book entirely. An unwritten story was fragile when damaged. Pushed too far, it could fall apart, like ice cream on a summer day melting away for lack of authorial intent. There had been no time to do it properly with a full rebinding, but Claire had held the book together with thread and paste. She breathed every curse she knew under her breath as she stitched blank sheets into the wounded front pages, carefully tying the savaged front matter together with tiny red binding threads. The new pages were strong, but it still might all be for nothing if it didn't restore the story. She'd spent the last two hours trying to coax the words, first with soft assurances, then with orders, finally with the blunt end of her quill, nudging the trembling text to repopulate the blank pages.

But they wouldn't budge. The best she'd been able to do was convince some pointless footnotes to spread to the heading of the first page. The rest of the replacement pages remained infuriatingly blank, their text lost forever. Which was going to leave the hero in a predicament. Stories needed a beginning to make sense. Claire had to restore the book if he was going to go back to where he belonged. Something was missing. She turned to the scrap they'd procured from the Watcher.

With tweezers she withdrew it delicately from the plastic bag, turning it over under the lamp. The paper was yellowed and fibrous. Lichen green ink glimmered when the light hit it, and a delicate scent of anise and ash was detectable when it drifted under her nose. There was neither green ink nor such a scent in the rest of the book before her. She shook her head, setting aside the strangeness to try to puzzle out where it fit.

It didn't. It took no time at all to come to the conclusion. No matter where Claire positioned it, no matter which way she twisted the scrap, the book rejected it. Even if it had belonged to one of the missing, burned pages, the book would have recognized it as its own. Instead, it took all of Claire's strength to keep the tome from skittering off the table to flee the tiny piece of parchment.

The book jerked again. Claire lost her grip on the tweezers, sending the scrap drifting off the table for the hundredth time. The book fled to the far shelf in a froth of paper and leather. The librarian hissed a dark curse and bent to snatch the stubborn scrap between two fingers.

And the blood sang in her veins.

The shadows tilted, and her vision swam as a chill shuddered from the paper, up one arm, and down to her toes. A flash. The edge of a shadow, the fault in a rock, the supple joint in the pulse of the world. Tender hollows designed to break. And time, time, so much time, howled underneath. A wildfire of images hit her, burning up all thought, breathing ash in its wake. Undoing. Unending. Unyielding. She came back to herself bent over her chair, gagging for air while the scrap of paper drifted toward her toes.

That was, most definitely, *not* an unwritten book, nor anything imagined or written by man.

Claire clenched her hands, clamping down on the shiver that threatened. Her pulse was still stuttering in her head, but she retrieved the tweezers and carefully lifted the scrap. She could see the age of the otherworldly parchment now, the fineness of the fibers. Not paper, not parchment. There was no way it belonged to the hero's book, belonged to *any* of her books. Impossible that she'd missed it before.

"What are you . . . ?" Claire turned it under the light. Whatever it was, it was old. Powerful. The fallen angel wasn't after the hero's book after all—this was something different. A fallen angel working for *Heaven* sought it. Thought the Library had it.

But it wasn't of Heaven; of that much Claire was certain. Nothing that sang that song could be. It was a song of destruction and endless hunger.

That was Hell's song. But Hell had no literature of its own.

A muffled groan escaped through the closed door. That would be the hero. Claire carefully set the scrap down with a sigh, pushing it away in favor of more immediate concerns. Vague murmurs drifted in through the door, summoning her. The hero would need her attention next; then she could focus on the mystery of the scrap in front of her.

Claire worked the kinks out of her aching hands before opening the door and, likely, answering yet more of Leto's unending questions. The human-demon had an inexhaustible supply, it seemed.

Her gaze flicked again to the whispering page. Questions.

She had a few.

BY THE TIME CLAIRE joined the group in the main section of the Library, the hero was sitting up. He draped a lanky muscled arm over the back of the couch while Brevity clucked instructions at him over her teapot. Leto perched at the far edge of the sitting area, wound tight as a spring.

Leto was returned to his demon features, but Brevity had taken the opportunity of his soggy condition to replace his ill-fitting suit with a more comfortable pair of slacks, suspenders, and a buttoned shirt, arms rolled up, in a vivid blue that matched the muse's tattoos. He looked slightly less cadaverous and more like a high school kid on an internship. Claire smiled. Brevity was in the middle of interrogating him, her hands animated over the caddy of saucers and cream.

Leto caught sight of Claire first and coughed on his tea. Brevity's head whipped around, and she stomped toward Claire. "You were attacked by a *Watcher?*"

Claire cast a sharp glance at Leto. "I see someone's been catching you up."

"Attacked," Brevity insisted. "By a Watcher. An angel from before the world was made."

"Technically, a fallen angel. If I remember Enoch right, Ramiel was one of the human sympathizers." Claire paused. "Though he seems distinctly less sympathetic now."

"Attacked."

"Threatened," Claire corrected, shrugging her off to let the repaired book hit the desk with a thud. "Leto here staged quite a heroic intervention before anyone was attacked."

Leto colored as he looked to the floor. "Well, I just . . . really . . ."

"Why would he be after a character?"

"One emergency at a time, Brev." Claire turned her attention to the hero.

He raised his cup. "Back to the brig already, warden? I was still working on my tea."

Claire narrowed her eyes. The hero was still pale, pale as the maddeningly blank parchments in his book. But his eyes were bright, and his hand was steady enough to mock her with a salute. Stable enough, for now.

"Your story still exists. That means it's time for you to go home." Claire tapped the book. "But you've managed to do far more damage to yourself than I thought possible for any story. At least any sane one."

"Characters can go insane?" Leto blinked.

Claire waved a hand. "Anything long-lived will deal with bouts of questionable sanity from time to time. Unwritten characters included."

"Perhaps if you spent half the energy working with us that you do keeping us contained here, such drastic measures wouldn't be needed," the hero said.

"A hero with a crusade. How unoriginal," Claire said. "How are you feeling?"

The hero gave a sour smile. "Trapped. And famous, by the sounds of it. Perhaps you should let me stick around if I've got Heaven and Hell fighting over me."

"You cause any more trouble, maybe I'll let Heaven have you," Claire said, though it was an empty threat. Even if Heaven wanted him, she had no intention of giving up any of the books in her care. "You'll be perfectly safe back in your story, however. The pages are repaired, but the words won't take." Brevity made a small distressed noise, but Claire kept her eyes leveled on the hero. "I was hoping it might listen to you and repair itself. It's a long shot."

"Long shots are a . . . hero's specialty," Hero said with an uncertain lilt as he stood. He was smooth but not quite as graceful as he'd been hours before. He approached his book and laid a proprietary hand on the cover. "What do I need to do?"

"First, open the book." Claire swatted his hand away to open it to the fresh, blank pages. "Now, talk to your kin, get them settled. Remind them how the story starts. 'Once upon a time,' all that."

"I was thinking 'In the beginning . . . ' had a nice ring to it," the hero sulked. He pressed his hand to the page and fell silent. They all did, librarian, muse, and demon alike. Claire felt the book stop its frantic, minute vibrations, and listened. The remaining words on the pages slowed their skittish mutations, twitching quietly as some private conversation went on. An invisible line pulled tight.

Then snapped.

The book shuddered. The hero's hand flinched off the pages as it snapped itself shut. His brows knit together as he looked up, incredulous. "They . . . The gall! They pretended they didn't know me! Me! Oversized inkblots just—"

"The story didn't recognize you." The sliver of anticipation Claire had held dissipated. She'd suspected as much would happen, but she'd hoped to be surprised. She exchanged a glance with Brevity. "That makes sense."

"No, that makes *nonsense*." The hero's voice was acidic, a barbed accent surfacing with his distress. "I'm the bloody—" He snapped his mouth shut abruptly. "Without me, there wouldn't be a story."

"It appears your book disagrees," Claire said, and the hero glowered up at her. "By all means, make another attempt."

The hero shifted uneasily. "All the better to allow you to put me back on a shelf?"

"Is that fear I hear?"

He shot her a stormy look and stepped up to the book again. He paused to spare a glance and a nod at Brevity. "Thank you for the tea, muse." He winked at Leto before turning a cold look to Claire. "It's been an unmitigated displeasure."

Claire's smile was just as icy. "Always glad to meet a fan."

The hero's lip curled and with a flourish he slapped his hand down on the cover. When nothing happened, the little remaining color drained from his face.

Claire cleared her throat. "Brev, you might want to guide our hero to a seat again."

Brevity helped him stumble back to the couch. The hero's green eyes had taken on a glossy look. "What does this mean?"

"Your damage disconnected you from your own story. Congratulations—that's a feat. That means, at least until your book decides to accept you again, you're a free agent." Claire paused, then amended, "Well, not free. You're still Special Collections, and you're going to be answering to me."

The hero's face froze. His gaze fished around the room before coming to the book again.

"Whoa, our own hero. The damsels are gonna freak." Brevity clapped, only a little awed. "We can't keep calling him that. Hero. Can we?"

Claire shrugged. "Fine. He can rename himself when he comes out of shock. I thought 'Janitor' had a nice ring."

The hero shook his head, subdued. "This isn't happening. . . ."

Claire let that go. It was probably best to let the man work it out for himself. He quite possibly had eternity to do so. "Brev, if you can hold the fort here, I've got an errand I need to run. Leto, I'd like you to come along." The teenager jumped up from where he had been lingering at the edge of the group, twisting his hands together. "You proved so useful before."

Brevity's brow knitted. "You just got back. What now?"

"The Watcher's scrap did not belong to the hero's book. I need to run it past the Arcanist to be certain before I explain more than that." Claire cast a glance toward the restorations room. "But there might be more than one book missing."

8

LETO

The demons have been petitioning for borrowing rights again. The log says they waited a whole three centuries before trying again. This time they got a minor duke on their side.

I know scavengers when I hear them. The Unwritten Wing holds a delicate balance in Hell: neither vassal to nor clearly apart. It's the nature of books that keeps us here, but it's the nature of books that the devils want. They want anything that tastes of mortal mind. An unwritten book is nothing but pure potential, and a soul's potential is power down here. Power, naturally, is all the creatures of Hell care about. They'd descend on the shelves like a swarm of locusts if we let them.

Librarian Ibukun of Ise, 786 CE

A SOUND, MORE GRAVEL than snore, grated from the sleeping gargoyle as they passed the bookcase. Leto gave it a wide berth as he struggled to keep up with the librarian's long strides. Hell's hallways passed in a blur, and Leto had long ago given up keeping track of the path they were taking. He decided to stick to the basics. "Where are we going?"

"The Arcane Wing. The Arcanist, Andras, is a colleague and old friend." The bag holding the page scrap crinkled between Claire's pinched fingers, as if she was afraid it would escape. She accelerated down a wide flight of stairs and forced Leto to speed up again.

"Arcanist. He's some kinda wizard?" Leto asked.

"Not quite. He curates the Arcane Wing. It's part of the Library. The Unwritten Wing is larger and stores the unwritten works, and the Arcane Wing contains . . . curiosities."

"Like a museum?"

Claire shook her head. "Libraries traditionally housed a cabinet of curiosities; I suppose that is why the Arcane Wing exists here as well. It houses arcane artifacts—prophecies, spell books, monkey claws, and soul gems. That kind of nonsense. Things that gain power on Earth become . . . slippery. Slippery and dangerous. They tend to fall through the cracks of reality and end up here, where we can contain them. It's the Arcanist's job to do that, and fetch the dangerous stuff. Messy job, one I'm glad I don't have. Books are much more straightforward."

"So he's your boss?"

Claire's chuckle was not entirely warm. "I'm sure he'd like to think so, since he's been here forever, but no. The Unwritten Wing and the Arcane Wing are allied."

"Allied?" Leto frowned. "Against what?"

The question made Claire slow. Leto had to career into a pillar to avoid running into her. Claire seemed to consider before giving him a serious answer. "Against everything. As long as there have been places like libraries—places attempting to preserve and curate—there have been forces attempting to acquire. The Library makes for a very juicy target for the demons of Hell, even though they're supposedly our hosts."

That made no sense. "But they're just books," he blurted before he could worry about insulting the librarian.

Claire didn't seem prone to taking offense. She just chuckled. It was a dry, crackling laugh that made her sound older than she looked. "They may be just books to you, Leto, but these are *unwritten* books. Pure potential. They're the stuff of something demons don't have: imagination. That's the stuff of humans. The power to create. Down here, that's a decisive power. There are factions here in Hell that would love nothing more than to eat the books whole, for a momentary burst of power. If the Arcane Wing and the Library didn't work together to present a united front, the books would have been burned long ago."

Yet another thing Leto might have known, should have known, had he been the demon he was supposed to be. Instead, he was a stupid human asking stupid questions. He could even fail at *damnation*, and now he was in Hell, surrounded by shadows containing dangers he didn't even know existed. His arms felt chilled. He wrapped them around his middle. He couldn't remember the source of self-loathing that welled up in his throat, but the bitter taste coated his tongue.

They wound their way across a dark foyer. The wide amber floor was dusty and bare and seemed to swallow up the light. Claire halted them before a set of thick bronze doors. The grillwork was cast with figures so encrusted with age and grime that Leto couldn't make them out. Claire's hand hesitated above the handle. "Andras is a friend—he won't harm you—but just one rule: don't touch anything."

"O-okay?"

"Andras won't harm us. But the Arcane Wing . . ." If the smile Claire gave him was meant to be reassuring, she sucked at it. "The Arcane Wing is . . . different."

"Different? Like, compared to the Unwritten Wing or . . ." Leto trailed off as Claire shoved the door open.

The air was chilled and clotted with dust. The first impression Leto had, as he breathed in stale air, was of the shadowy neglect of an abandoned museum vault or perhaps a disreputable pawnshop. *A cabinet of curiosities*, Claire had said. It was an accurate description of the place. Dozens of dusty little boxes lined black wood shelves, punctuated by puddles of shadowy fabric, twisted figures in discolored ivory, a bowl rimmed with sharp teeth and filled with tiny seeds that sparkled like bloody rubies. Some artifacts were left in open air; others were inexplicably bound with chains behind glass. All were stacked and piled with no discernible logic. A staccato grackling noise came from the far wall, and the cold iron bars of a tall stack of cages filled with ravens cast menacing lines of shadow across the floor.

The Arcane Wing was smaller than the Unwritten Wing, and colder. Shadows stretched and reached farther than they should have. There was just enough light to define the shapes of the darkness, not drive it away. Sound pooled and dribbled in murmurs that sounded the way goose bumps felt. It was a palace to shadows and acid ambition.

Unfazed, Claire rapped on a scarred countertop with her knuckles. "Andy? You about?"

The black birds increased in volume as something thudded in the back recesses of the collection. "Is that a pup I hear? No one else is cheeky enough to use that name." The voice was as rugged and distinguished as the gentleman that followed it.

A gentleman with demonic features: sharply pointed ears, and eyes an unnatural shade of liquid gold that set Leto on edge. Leto had the fleeting impression of a tiger caged and pacing. He shivered, blinked once; then the tiger shrank to a house cat. Andras was not an intimidating figure. He was a hair shorter than Leto, and he wore an old-fashioned evergreen doublet studded with glittering brooches and topped with a black satin sash. His hands were folded politely, burdened with silver rings. His hair was a short ruff of charcoal streaked with lines of gold. He glimmered and gleamed attentively in all the ways his wing glowered and gloomed.

"My dear librarian." A smile sprang into place on Andras's lips as he swept across the floor to greet them. Andras touched Claire's cheek and turned it this way and that. His hand looked pale and faded against her teak skin. "You are working too hard, pup. You look thin."

It was the first time Leto had seen anyone touch the prickly librarian— even Brevity seemed to respect Claire's personal space. But the Arcanist swept in with familiarity, and to Leto's great surprise, Claire simply shrugged off the hand. "A trip upstairs does that."

"Of course. Dreadful place. I don't know why you don't just send your assistants."

Claire chuckled. "Some of us prefer to do things ourselves."

"Of course. I taught you no less; shame I don't heed my own lessons.

Speaking of assistants . . ." He turned his attention to Leto, and his gaze was sharp enough to bring a trickle of acidic sweat to Leto's neck. Andras's lip curled in a smile to reveal a pointed tooth as he studied him. Polite, but exacting as a scalpel. Leto felt dissected, and foolish to have ever believed himself to be a demon or any creature related to someone with that kind of keen gaze.

Claire nudged Leto forward with a grand wave. "Leto, meet Andras, Hell's Arcanist and former Duke of the East Infernal Duchy. Andras, this is Leto, my . . . assistant, I suppose."

Leto's stomach did a swooping kind of flip at the introduction. It was a startling warmth, distracting him momentarily from the vague sense of dread that Andras imparted. "Uh, pleased to meet you, sir."

"I haven't seen you about before." Andras gave Leto a shrewd squint. "What legion are you, son?"

Leto stuttered out of reflex, but Claire saved him. "He's human. Made a demon down here for his penance." She gave a not-unkind squeeze where she kept hold of Leto's shoulder. "And he's been instrumental in finding something that I believe you might have an interest in."

"A human, now? Fancy that." Andras tapped his lip. "I assumed you had business. You were never one for small talk. What can I do for you, my dear?"

Claire raised the bag that held the scrap and upended it with care on a nearby table. "I ran across something I was hoping you could identify."

Andras brightened and wiped his fingertips on a pocket square before approaching the table. He snapped his fingers, and a globe of light appeared over his head, bobbing softly and reminding Leto of summer fireflies. "What gift do you have for me today?"

Claire made an impatient motion. "Do you recognize it? It seemed like something of yours."

"It's not an unwritten book—I can certainly verify that. It seems . . ." Andras stilled and flicked his gaze, suddenly sharp and suspicious, between them. "Where did you get this?"

"Leto palmed it off an angel that was trying to kill us. He said he was Ramiel, if you're familiar with the tales. An entirely unpleasant man, absent manners, and present one very sharp sword. He seemed under the impression we had something of his."

"Ramiel." Andras was quiet for a long moment, hands hovering over the scrap. "He's on the hunt for this?"

"And quite insistent that we knew what the hell he was talking about." Claire frowned. "It is from a book?"

Andras had returned to staring at the scrap. "Intriguing."

"Yes, so intriguing, in fact, I thought I'd visit my dear old friend because I was under the impression that he would assist more than ask questions," Claire grumbled as the old demon didn't look up. "Well?"

"Hmm."

"Andras." Claire rubbed her brow. "I've been bled, nearly skewered, and mostly drowned today. Words, please."

The demon shook his head, and a thought moved across his expression. It was a thought with teeth, but then it was gone. Andras smiled again. "It's . . . a very rare piece."

"I gathered as much, considering it tried to blow my circuits when I touched it." Leto let out a startled noise, but Claire waved him off. "What is it?"

"It has the markers of a piece that shouldn't exist." Andras's eyes drifted back to the scrap. "The Codex Gigas. Have you heard of it?"

"Codex Gigas. The . . . giant book?"

"Apt translation, given the original book's size, but it's also known as 'the Devil's Bible.'"

Claire raised her brows. "You have my attention."

Andras's fingertips danced away from the bit of paper every time he attempted to touch it, as if it burned. "A curious piece of antiquary history, to hear the humans tell it. Some sordid drama about a medieval monk signing a deal with the devil to create a holy tome in a single night."

"What nonsense."

"Of course. No proper demon would bother with a trivial deal such as that." Andras shrugged. "But there was a book created, and Lucifer claims ownership himself."

Claire frowned. "Lucifer . . . wrote a book? Impossible. Demons don't create books."

"They don't *write* books." Andras held up a finger. His voice took on a teaching tone. "This wasn't a story; it was an *artifact*. A container. It takes a lot of power to hold a realm like Hell as long as Lucifer has. Power burns out a god as much as a mortal. The oldest beings have been known to siphon off bits of themselves over the years, stash bits of themselves here and there. To remain sane. To hedge their bets. The more innocuous the piece, the better." Andras made a vague gesture to the curios around them. "Something like that should be here, by all rights. But I suppose he didn't trust my predecessors with it. Rather insulting that he thought *Earth* was safer."

Claire's brow furrowed. "That does sound . . . eccentric. Even for him."

"Highly. I always suspected it wasn't just mere power he was hiding away in that thing. Perhaps a secret, a key, something he didn't trust to keep on himself for some reason. Something to be kept far away from the realm. Tantalizing mystery, isn't it?"

"You think everything is secrets and conspiracy, Andy."

"That's because everything *is*, pup. And you do know I dislike that nickname."

Claire smiled. "Almost as much as I dislike being called 'pup.'"

"Quite so," Andras said with an odd tilt of fondness. "In any case, this codex, it stayed unnoticed on Earth for centuries. Then, out of the blue, Lucifer called his Arcanist and librarian to him—our predecessors—and ordered them to retrieve the book and replace it with a mundane replica." The old demon's lip curled with a strong distaste. Leto began to see where Claire might have gotten her opinion of the ruler of Hell. "Something must have spooked him."

Leto found the whole conversation alarming, and unease finally began to work its way into the nervous tap of Claire's fingers on the counter.

"Why wasn't I made aware of any of this?" she asked.

THE LIBRARY OF THE UNWRITTEN

"Why would you be? It's a perfectly written book. Not one of your delicate unwritten things," Andras said. "As I understand it, the book was retrieved during some mortal uprising. A fire made a convenient cover. Our agents replaced it with a harmless mundane copy in the chaos. It disappeared after that—who knows what our benevolent dictator did with it?"

"Not everything got recovered, though," Leto said. When Andras frowned at him as if just remembering his presence, Leto nodded to the table.

"Well . . . yes. There might have been complications," Andras said. "They replaced the book as it was . . . but humans say that precisely ten pages might have gone missing in the fire. We thought it was just the replica that was damaged."

"Ten pages. Of a book made of Hell stuff. Did anyone bother to check the original before handing it over?"

Andras's lips thinned. "The records don't precisely say so."

"And you've not pursued it, gone after these pages?"

Andras snorted. "I'm not daft. I proposed the idea decades ago once I ran across the discrepancy. But I was ordered not to. *Forbidden.* A decree from our great ruler himself. And no further investigation into the book was condoned. Whatever it is, whatever it was, Lucifer didn't trust anyone looking into it."

It didn't make sense. Leto found himself chewing a hole in his lip as he tried to follow. "If it was so important, why would he risk . . . ?"

Andras gave an elegant shrug. "The whole affair went down before my inglorious downfall. Long before I became Arcanist. I was still a duke then. It was all done rather hush-hush, and the court didn't hear about it until much later. One of your predecessors was the one who retrieved it. If anyone has covered up a failure, it was him."

Out of the corner of his eye, Leto saw Claire flinch. The color drained from her cheeks. "Predecessor . . . You mean Librarian Gregor."

"No, no. More than a few back. This would have been"—Andras gave a dismissive wave at the whole idea of time—"the barbarian. Beard. Loud type. Drunk. Stuck around forever. What's his name? I can't keep your people straight."

The tension in Claire's shoulders eased by inches. It was the second time Leto noticed her strange aversion to her predecessor. "Bjorn? Bjorn the Bard. He had the longest tenure, spanning the Middle Ages. Two before Gregor."

"Sounds about right. Your wing's history in any case, not mine."

Claire and Andras fell into warring scowls. Little as Leto knew, he had a sinking feeling that worse news was yet to come. It appeared the librarian agreed with him as she shook her head. "If it's resurfaced, we can't just leave a thing like that floating around."

Andras watched Claire warily. "An order is an order, pup."

"At the very least, we can report this latest appearance and reopen the investigation. Blood and ink, Andras. *Angels* are involved, for goodness' sake. This isn't time for politics."

Andras shook his head. "It's not wise. Not without more information to justify approaching the court."

"Information that we can't get until it's sanctioned. Which it's not," Claire said flatly. "Information he doesn't want the court to hear in the first place."

"That is how Hell works."

Claire crossed her arms. There was a distant *tick-tick-tick* of claws as ravens shifted in their cages. Leto could see a subtle tic in Andras's bearded cheek as he met her stare.

Claire swept up the bag, snagging the scrap before Andras could protest. She turned on her heel and strode toward the doors. Andras gaped, first at Claire, then at Leto. Then he broke into a run after her. "Pup! Librarian! Claire! Stop this instant!"

"Come along, Leto," Claire called, not slowing her pace before she raised her voice to a level that sent the ravens chattering and raced a chill down Leto's spine. "LUCIFER."

"Don't be a fool!" Andras was faster than his gray hair indicated he should be and he bolted after her. Leto had to sprint to keep them in sight as they sped down the hall. If Claire was summoning *him*, then he wasn't really sure he wanted to catch up.

"No, this is ridiculous. I won't tolerate— BELIAL."

"Claire—listen—"

"MORNINGSTAR. GET DOWN HERE."

"Claire!"

"IBLIS. LORD OF—"

"Do you want to start a war?" Andras caught hold of Claire's shoulders at the base of the stairs. He let go just as quickly under Claire's withering glare. "You don't want to do this, pup. We can't tell him this has surfaced in the hands of an angel."

Tension trembled through Claire's jaw and her fingers clenched around the plastic bag. "You have one minute to tell me one good reason why. And *without* using 'girl' or 'pup,' or I'll walk right out of here, Andras. I mean it."

Leto came to a stop a step away. Andras jerked his hands away from Claire's shoulders and raked a hand through his striped hair. "Consider the facts, Claire. Somehow, a book of Hell resurfaced after all this time and found its way into Heaven's hands. They very likely don't know what they have, but they sent nothing less than Ramiel after it. Thunder of God, a bloody Watcher. Fallen or not, unforgiven or not, he's no errand boy. Now think it through. What will happen if you report this to the court?"

Claire sniffed. "They'll send us after it, obviously. Just as they did before. And this time *I* will do a proper job."

"They sent the Library after it when it was merely an embarrassing personal secret of Lucifer's, held by humans. You know your history, Librarian. What happens when you scare powerful people who have armies? What does the court of Hell do when Heaven moves against them?"

"Don't be ridiculous." Color fled Claire's cheeks. "This is a book. They wouldn't—"

"We've gone to war over less. I was *there*." Andras said the word "there" in a way that conjured yawning voids and loss. Leto shuddered.

Claire threw up her hands. "That's unnecessary. This is a book. Lucifer knows we could much more effectively—"

"He might, but the court wouldn't. You know their opinion of the Library, run by a mere human and a washed-up demon?" Andras's tone turned brittle and bitter. "We're pawns, squatters on top of desirable treasures. They wouldn't just not *trust* us—they'd take the opportunity to prove us incompetent, to pillage the Library."

Claire paused, as if losing her footing. "To put the Library above the realm—"

"What about Earth?"

"What?"

"Think," Andras snapped. "Even if the greedy lot can pull their tails out of their arses long enough to follow the trail and do the job, where do you think this will be settled?"

Andras scrutinized Claire for a response. She stilled, flicking a concerned glance toward Leto. Andras looked as if he'd scored a point. "Do you see now why reporting this is foolhardy?"

Leto saw Claire's chin rise almost imperceptibly, the stubborn steel that he'd begun to recognize as the librarian's will coming to bear. "To the courts, perhaps, but if we approached this as a private matter with him . . ."

"The Purge."

Claire stopped. "That was an entirely different scenario."

"The what?" Leto felt his confusion had reached a breaking point.

"A . . . tragedy in Hell's history." Claire scowled at Andras. "A fool librarian challenged Lucifer for dominion of the Library. Tried to claim independence and lost. She . . . Well, the books were preserved, but the entire Library was remade, sealed. It spurred a line of book burnings on Earth—if you've ever heard of the Library of Alexandria, she was born of that time. I suppose he wanted to punish her where it hurt. The muses were in an uproar. It was chaos until the Library had a proper librarian again. Tragic but beside the point, because we are not challenging anyone."

"'Test it if you wish." Andras gave a soft shrug. "But our fool king went to quite a lot of trouble to keep the codex out of Hell the first time around. It wouldn't be the first time he's eliminated his own people to protect a secret. I'd rather not go through that again."

Claire's fingers worked a silent calculation, twitching around the bag in her grasp. "Suppose we don't seek Lucifer's sanction on it. It's still an arcane object, presumably on Earth, and a danger to humanity as well as the rest of us. That's your responsibility to act."

Andras's smile eased. "It can't be ignored. You were right about that. I would be happy to chase this artifact and return it to Hell before it can do more damage. But the last time this book was hunted, the Library did it together, Arcane and Unwritten. Why is that? I wonder."

Claire narrowed her eyes. "We have a dispensation when books are lost, yes. But this isn't one of mine, and *I'm* not a demon. I can't do this unsanctioned. We just returned the only book—"

"Returned with how much time still on your ghostlight?"

"Most of a day but . . . Oh. No. You can't be serious." Leto briefly wondered how the Arcanist had kept such close tabs on today's events, or if it was public knowledge. Claire voiced the larger problem. "We would still need Walter's help to travel."

Andras tapped his lip. "Walter holds transport to the mortal realms, but where would you start looking for the Devil's Bible, Librarian?"

"I would . . ." Claire hesitated as she appeared to give the question the full measure of her attention. "The angel found us in Seattle, but I suspect that's because he was chasing any demonic activity. He seemed surprised to find us. That means his leads ran out. No, the pages might be on Earth, but we would have to start with information on how they went missing. You say Bjorn the Bard was the librarian who retrieved it, but . . ."

Both Claire and Andras went silent, and Leto lost his patience. "But what?"

"Bjorn's not a librarian anymore. Not even in Hell. He did his time in the Library, and his soul found rest. And he was of the old beliefs, so . . ."

Claire raised her brows at Andras. "If we wanted to talk to Bjorn, we would have to find him . . . in Valhalla?"

"In Valhalla."

"Ravens?" Claire was curious.

"Ravens." Andras was certain.

"Ravens?" Leto was confused.

An unsettling smile, sharp and resigned, tugged at Claire's mouth. "I thought you were retired from the game, Arcanist."

Andras chuckled. "I can be induced, for a good cause and a lovely face."

Claire ignored the flattery. "And to sate your curiosity about a secret, I imagine."

"Well, now, that would just be a bonus for an old man's entertainment, pup."

Claire glanced once at Leto, and he gave her what he hoped was a nod of support. She sighed. "Where do we start?"

"With the raven road, of course," Andras said.

A BRIEF ARGUMENT ENSUED, which was settled only when Claire invoked some obscure rule of conduct that Leto had never heard of. Andras threw up his hands and disappeared back into the cluttered shadows of his wing, and Claire resumed her atrociously fast stride up the stairs the way they'd come. Leto found himself winded by the third flight. Librarians were exhausting.

"Miss Librarian? What's happening now?"

"We've drowned together, Leto. You can call me Claire."

"What's happening now, Claire?"

"I believe"—Claire gave the gargoyle a pat as they rounded the corner into the familiar maze of halls that led to the Unwritten Wing—"now I am about to become a very bad role model for you. If you really are a demon, this is the point where you should probably be running off to tattle on us."

Leto reached up to rub the point of one ear. "I don't think I want to tattle after what Andras said."

"Me neither, unfortunately," Claire said with a sigh.

Leto considered the Arcanist and fought back his unease about being around another demon. "You said he was a . . . a duke?"

"Was. Once." Claire gave a tight-lipped smile. "Before I knew him, he was a high duke in Hell's court. Very highly respected, commanded legions, and was Lucifer's right hand. Demon of Confessions, I think. He was ousted in a political coup more than a hundred years ago. Demons love nothing more than their political games; never stand between a demon and a rise to power."

"Isn't that where you said the Library is now?"

Claire made a face. "Yes. Aren't you a fast learner? In any case, Andras survived but withdrew from the court to lick his wounds. He eventually took over the role of curator for the Arcane Wing. He's a demon, yes, but retired from the court. He's always been a supporter of the Library. He . . . ah, he helped me out a good deal when I was a new librarian. He taught me a lot."

A memory, a pain, a regret, all flicked over Claire's face, too rapid-fire for Leto to comment on. He stared at his hands. One claw had a hangnail. He worried at it. "But I still don't know what I'm supposed to— I mean, you said we're going to go after this thing?"

Claire slowed so suddenly that Leto nearly ran into her back. She cast a glance toward the Library entrance, then pulled him to one side. "This isn't like fetching the hero's book, Leto. This is going to get . . . complicated."

"I had a feeling."

"I'll be doing something which may upset the rest of Hell. The Library's always been a bit separate. . . ."

"I understand."

"But you're not part of the Library." Leto's face fell, and Claire closed her eyes briefly. "I mean, you're welcome here, but you don't have to be part of this. It's going to be dangerous. Even if we manage to accomplish what we intend, when we get back, we'll be . . . You should leave while you can."

"Where do I go?" The question sounded more pitiful than Leto had intended, but it was out of his mouth before he could think. Panic began to edge its way up the back of his throat, and he tried to envision what leaving the Library meant. His first real memory of this place was of being a demon messenger sent to Claire's desk. Everything before that was . . . darkness, fear, self-loathing. A coil of despairing acid in his throat. He'd rather do anything than that.

"You could stay at the Library, until we return. Plenty to read," Claire offered.

"You said demons aren't librarians because we can't handle the nature of the books." He looked down at his clenched hands.

"Leto . . . you're not a demon. You're—"

"I was sent to you. And you're the only one who's even tried to tell me the truth. You . . . you're the only assignment I have. Until that changes, I'm staying." Leto tried to sound confident rather than pleading. He chewed on his bottom lip as he saw Claire's normally brittle brown eyes soften. Sympathy, pity. It wasn't what he wanted. He didn't want to be protected, to shield himself from hurtful truths. Not again. It felt the opposite of being human. He wanted . . . "I want to help. Please."

Claire swept her gaze over Leto once before nodding slightly. "Okay. All right. I did say you were a fast learner." She started down the corridor again. "Next lesson: move quickly."

9

RAMIEL

When you consider all the realms of the afterlife, there are aberrations. To a librarian, Heaven is a large aberration. It seems curious that one of the grandest, most belief-fueled realms of paradise does not possess a library of its own.

In the minds of its believers, Heaven must be perfect. Absent nothing, regretting nothing, wanting nothing. It makes sense, then, that Heaven has no wing of our library.

What is a story without want, without desire, without need?

Librarian Gregor Henry, 1896 CE

"THIS IS, QUITE OBVIOUSLY, unacceptable."

Ramiel had, frankly, expected more of an outburst from Uriel. He'd delivered his report of the encounter on Earth, standing stock straight in the center of the archangel's office, bracing for the anger he knew was coming. But Uriel had merely listened, giving him the full measure of her ageless, infinite attention until he fell silent.

In some ways, that was much worse.

"You not only allowed our best leads to escape, but you lost our only evidence and means to pursue." Uriel toyed with a small compass in her hands without looking at it, her stern gaze reserved for Rami. The sharp edges of the navigator's tool flickered and slid between her fingers like a blade.

"We still have leads—"

"What leads?" Uriel interrupted, voice level but knuckles white as the compass stilled. "Do tell me, Watcher, how we can locate these *librarians* when *they* possess the artifact."

There were no ways, not in the magics Rami understood. He held his tongue.

"What's more, the fact that you were bested by a dead woman and a—what? A demonic servant who could mug you like taking candy from a cherub?" Uriel shook her head. "It's a stain on Heaven. Was it sympathy? Your fondness for humans from your time as shep—"

"Souls!" Uriel's glare could melt galaxies, but Rami swallowed and pushed forward. "Hell's librarian is a *human soul.*"

When Watchers had served Heaven, Ramiel had been the Thunder of God . . . and the shepherd. Sent to lost souls to shepherd them to the afterlife. No soul stayed lost under Rami's care. The conclusion lit Uriel's eyes with a strange, sharp glimmer. "You can track her?"

"Not while she's in Hell or another realm," Rami admitted. The *lost* status of a soul was critical. "But if she strays to Earth again or travels the roads between, I should be able to narrow our options. Without a divine mandate, however, it will take some time."

A smile curdled Uriel's expression, a strange and unnatural look. Rami had thought winning Uriel's approval would be satisfying, but instead it felt startling, like a show of claws. "Make your preparations. The fact remains that we must move forward quickly to catch up. We know Hell's Library has it. May, in fact, have the whole thing. I'm not giving the victory to the Betrayer that easily," Uriel said. "In the meantime, we'll start with the other realms she'd be likely to rabbit to. The major ones: Duat, Jannah, Valhalla, Indralok. We have passage agreements with most realms of paradise. If we're very fast and very blessed, we'll catch the scent."

Rami abruptly felt less an angel and more a hunting dog. But one look at Uriel's hungry smile and he held his tongue. "And if we catch up with the librarian?"

"Ascertain whether she has the rest of the codex. Follow and impede if she does not. Hell cannot be allowed to acquire this book. And if she has it already . . ." Again, Uriel twirled the silver compass in her palm. She abruptly flipped her grip and drove the point into the desk. "She serves Hell. She is already damned. If the librarian seeks salvation, then Heaven's justice will purify her."

10

CLAIRE

Of course there are other libraries. The Unwritten is just one wing, though one of the largest. There are wings of poetry, wings of songs, wings of dying words and visions. The libraries maintain a prickly kind of alliance, separated by realms. If one library falls, it could signal the end for them all. The Library stands together.

The only exception to note is the Dust Wing, which houses all the works created and lost to time. But the less said about that dark hall, the better.

Librarian Bjorn the Bard, 1630 CE

It is our duty to maintain a cordial yet professional relationship with the other libraries. If only for the sake of the interworld loan. But one library wing is not like another. Do not trust librarians serving other tales.

Apprentice Librarian Yoon Ji Han, 1791 CE

SOMETIMES, WHEN CLAIRE ALLOWED herself a moment to reflect on the absurdity of her fate, she wished she could find the soul of old Father Roderick. It was one of the few memories she'd kept. He'd presided over her family's parish and instilled in her, at the wicked age of eight, the deep fear of damnation of her immortal soul. She drifted away from it, as many children did, and grew up into a comfortable agnostic, or as much as was proper for the time. But now, literally residing in Hell, she wished to revisit those old conversations with Father Roderick. Father Roderick, who taught her the necessity of good Catholic guilt. In the end, guilt and self-recrimination were the worst sins for a soul.

What would the good father think to see her? Her current position in Hell was entirely due to her own soul's self-imposed judgment. She dealt daily with condemned souls and demons because her own soul didn't believe she deserved better.

And perhaps the most scandalous thing she could tell Father Roderick was, frankly, how comfortable it was. She had regrets, deep regrets, yes, about how she'd lived her life, the time she'd wasted. They were why she'd ended up in the Library. But the *after*life she'd built up was more than acceptable. The start had been rough, and there were the mistakes she made, hauntings she still pretended not to have. She was not completely insulated from Hell here in the Library.

But there was work to do, a purpose to her fate. And she owed something to those in her afterlife. She owed something to the Library, its books, Brevity. Now there were Leto and the damaged book to consider.

Claire found herself well suited for damnation. Sorry, Father Roderick.

By the time Claire and Leto returned, Brevity had put the hero to work trundling carts of books up from the recesses of the Library. The muse tolerated his sulky muttering with more aplomb than Claire would have, patting his slumped shoulder as she sent him off with another cart.

"Truthfully? Those books weren't even due to be inventoried yet," Brevity admitted as he disappeared into the stacks again. "But it keeps him busy. How was Andras?"

"Well-informed. Patronizing. Per usual." Claire began to tick through her head as she calculated where to begin with the disasters on the Library's plate. "How's the hero doing?"

"He's wearing a pout that could curdle milk, but otherwise he's bucked up. He just wants to be called Hero. Like, for a name." Brevity poured a new cup of tea for herself.

"That's . . . quite the literal affectation."

"That's what I told him in less fancy words." Brevity lowered her voice as the cart emerged from a back aisle. "He sure seemed set on it. Said he thought it had a certain *je ne sais quoi*. And *that's* when I put him on inventory."

Claire nodded and waved Leto over. No use putting this off. "Well done, but inventory needs to wait. We have new business. I am going to pull some supplies. Brev, I need you to take Leto here and prepare to shut down the wing."

The muse nearly choked on her tea. "What?"

Claire began dumping the less necessary—and somewhat soggy—books out of her leather bag, and filling it quickly with an assortment of tools from her desk. "The entire wing. All books on lockdown. Nothing leaves. Jot a note to inform the muses. Earth is just going to have to deal with writer's block until we get back."

"But that's—if we—" Brevity made a strangled noise in her throat. "Begging your pardon, boss, but you give an order like that, I need a story."

Claire frowned as she ordered her pens in the bag's side pocket. Brevity was a muse—a former, ex-muse, certainly. But it was the muses that would feel the blowback most keenly if the source of all unwritten stories was suddenly shut off. It was a tricky relationship between the Library of unwritten works and the muses that were tasked to inspire them. If the muses had their way, the Library would be empty, but that wasn't the way creation worked. Sometimes inspiration was not enough. They would not take a closing well. "Get Hero up here, then. I've got no time to say this more than once."

Once Claire had briefed the others on the existence of the Codex Gigas, the danger of the remaining pages, and Andras's plan to seek Bjorn in Valhalla, she took a long draw of her tea, carefully watching Brevity's and Hero's reactions. Brevity's mouth had made a silent "oh" before she schooled her face. Her eyes took on the same intense glint she got when wrestling with a particularly stubborn acquisition.

The newly dubbed "Hero," on the other hand, had snorted at every opportunity throughout the tale, lips curling to express more disgust than concern by the end of it. "Why, again, are you haring off after a myth rather than leaving it to your betters?"

"Because there's a chance that my *betters* would either start a war or make it so that the Library—and all the books inside, mind you—never existed rather than admit the thing still exists in the wild." Claire took a peevish sip of tea. "I have no patience for politics. Whatever game went on with this codex before, we have a job to do."

"We," Hero repeated flatly, but Brevity brightened.

"That means you'll be needing me, right?"

"I always need you, Brev." Claire's determination softened into a smile. "If that's settled, every minute counts. Take Leto and get moving. Hero, you're with me."

Hero sulked silently after Claire through the warren of the Library's storage rooms. Claire measured him in brief glances between checking and locking doors. His color was better, his walk steady and smooth. For a thing that had just been cut out of his own entity like an amputated limb, Hero was doing remarkably well.

Especially for a hero. In Claire's experience, heroes of unwritten stories were often the most fragile. All that destiny and tragic backstory. It made it easier to force them into their books, but it left a sour taste in her mouth. Entirely useless. Nothing folded like a hero without a story. Even damsels were sturdier.

Hero grimaced as she turned a corner deep in the Library, selecting a book here and there. "Here I was thinking I'd be spending my near future developing a nice, boring dust allergy."

"Buck up. There will be plenty of dust where we're going," Claire said. "Tell me, what kind of hero were you? More of a lover than a fighter?"

"Decidedly a fighter." Hero preened his nails. "Never had much use for love in my story."

"With cheekbones like that? I'm shocked." Claire paused at the end of one of the aisles, eyeing the ornate suit of armor that decorated the endcap. Master craftsmen had unfinished works of art too, and the Library had a larger armory than one would expect. They were mostly elaborate work meant for noble showpieces but still well made. "Swords?"

"Rapier, preferably. I'm not a barbarian. But a well-balanced basket-hilted broadsword is comfortable enough." Hero watched with obvious skepticism as Claire rapped on the suit's knuckles. The suit loosened its grip on its weapon, and she grabbed the pommel of the ornate sword. Claire gave it a cursory inspection; it was sharp and covered in excessive filigree—just like Hero, really—but that was as far as her weapon discernment went. She tossed it underhand to Hero.

He caught it, gave it a careful heft, and sighted down the end of the blade. Claire took the moment to take silent stock of him. He certainly had the air of a hero, capable, with confidence that irritated like a hangnail. Still, Claire was more used to shelving characters than trusting them.

Hero cast an unreadable glance at her. "Adequate."

"Excellent." Claire waited until he'd stripped the blade's sheath from the suit of armor and secured the weapon across his back. She started down the aisle again. "We need to get straight on a few things before we leave."

"Is this where we swear to be true and loyal in the face of certain death? Your short acquaintance has already branded me." Hero held up the wrist that had been stamped.

"Which is the only reason I'm bringing you along," Claire said. That and a swashbuckling hero could not hurt their odds if that angel showed up again. Her little group needed him. That was an unfortunate fact he didn't need to know.

"Not worried I'll slip the leash again?"

"Oh, I'm sure you would try. I just trust my leash more." Claire allowed him to catch up as they turned a corner. "I have no doubt you'll do as I say, when I say. But I need you to swear to something outside of that."

Hero sniffed. "No, thanks. I've reached my inconvenient-oath quota for the year."

"I will make it worth your time."

"I doubt that."

Claire stopped. They could hear Brevity's high, clear voice chattering at the far end of the aisle as books thumped around. "Inspiration."

Hero narrowed his eyes. "What do you mean?"

"You wanted your author to write her books. I happen to be on excellent working terms with the muses."

"It seems to me that the Library's relationship with the muses is more adversarial than collaborative."

"Nonsense." Claire waved her hand to cover the fact that his perception was entirely accurate. "We all care about the well-being of authors and books. Serve admirably on this trip, maybe I will suggest more focused efforts for young Miss McGowan."

There was a gleam in Hero's eyes that had not been present before. "What admirable service do you have in mind?"

"Protect them," Claire said. Too quickly, too urgently. That was a misplay when dealing with a hero who seemed as contrary as a tomcat. She picked her next words carefully. "You're duty bound to do as I say, but I cannot foresee how this ill-advised errand will go. If I am not there to command you, Hero, I want your oath that you'll not abandon Brevity and Leto—or Andras, I suppose, though he can take care of himself. See they return safely to the Library, to the best of your ability."

The gazes of both fell to the suit of armor capping the aisle. The hero leaned against it, draping one arm over the knight's shoulder as he eyed the librarian. "Why?"

"Why? Because I offered to inspire your auth—"

"No, I mean, why do your assistant and your puppy-eyed hanger-on deserve my protection?"

Claire chewed on the inside of her cheek. Truth was a gamble, but then all of this was. Claire hated gambles. "Because I'm not the monster you think I am. And I fervently hope, somewhere under that ridiculous coat, you're not the childish brat I think you are. Brev is going to be librarian one day. A muse. First of her kind to run a wing of the Library, and she will deserve every bit of it. She's clever, quick, and has more heart than I do. Maybe she'll even be able to offer the unwritten that better life you seem to be obsessed with."

"And the demon?"

"*Leto.*" Claire emphasized the name. "Leto is human, and may be more than meets the eye."

"A demonic book is on the loose, the world in peril, and you ask me to guard children." Hero shook his head. "What priorities. I would have thought you would make me swear on my life to retrieve the codex pages without you."

Claire's lips twitched. "I hadn't thought of that. Can I get you to do both?"

Hero's snort was a decided answer.

"I'll stick with protecting Brev and Leto, then." She took off toward the end of the aisle. "If you aren't interested in my offer, of course, I could just lock you in with the damsels."

"Damsels? What are—" Hero had to untangle himself from the armor before sprinting to keep up. "Slow down, damnable woman!"

"What, you thought you were the only book to ever wake up?" Claire stopped in front of a frosted-glass door. She knocked once, then ducked in. "You're not even the prettiest."

She shut the door after Hero followed, stopping short just inside the threshold with a confused grunt. She couldn't blame him. The room was a marked difference from the long book-lined canyons of the Library. It was a cozy sitting room; shelves cluttered the walls and overstuffed chairs dotted the corners, occupied by a cluster of animated figures, mostly women. One pored over a microscope at a far table, sleeves of a thick Victorian dress rolled up and stained with ink. A wartime housewife on the couch balanced a magazine on her knees as she showed off pages to a young boy. Near the fire, a fair-haired princess snuggled contentedly with a pigtailed girl in overalls. A captivating alien of no particular gender played a complex, vertical version of chess in one corner. Their entrance had gotten the room's attention, and a dozen pairs of eyes roved curiously over Hero before Claire shooed them off. She'd never allowed herself to learn their names—Brevity had always been better at such things—but they all knew her.

"What . . . what kind of prison is this?" Hero had to drop his voice under the censuring gaze of the pair of ladies nearest them.

"No prison. A sanctuary, perhaps," Claire said. "Most books wake up as heroes like you—sending out their most empowered, admirable characters into the world. Puffed-up peacocks set on making messes and throwing tantrums to get their way. We send them back to their own stories straightaway."

Hero opened his mouth to protest, but Claire waved him off. "And why not? Not that it's my concern, but they're perfectly happy as masters of their own domain in their stories. But sometimes, it's not the hero."

"You called them damsels."

"Stupid name," said the girl in pigtails sitting to their right. She met their looks with a wrinkled nose. "We ain't even all girls."

"It's just a category," Claire said. "Sometimes, a book wakes up as a character that has reason to be dissatisfied with their story. No agency. Flatly written. Just another reward for the hero—"

"Heteronormative bullshit," the girl added.

It would not be proper to be amused right now. "As she says," Claire agreed. "They have no interest in living it out—they're *happy* their story has gone unwritten. We call them damsels because, most of the time, they're women. Wonder why that is."

Hero ignored the look cast at him on behalf of his gender.

Claire continued. "If their authors are dead and gone, it seems unnecessary to send them back and simpler to let them stay, as long as they remain in the Library and entertain themselves. Learn things. Make up their own minds. Some even find families. So the damsel suite was established." She turned to Hero with a speculative look. "Though I'm sure they might let a pretty hero like you join if you would rather stay behind."

Hero eyed the gathered damsels, color overtaking his cheeks as he made eye contact with a rogue with a wicked smile. Beside him there was a slender, pale-haired princess who flashed a charming smile and hesitantly waggled her fingers. The combined attention appeared to be too much. Hero looked down and surprised her with a flustered noise. "You wouldn't."

"Try me." Claire leaned against the doorknob, indulging in a good modest gloat. Hero's cheeks were still pink, and she didn't miss the small interested glances he gave femme and masculine damsels in equal measure. "Frankly, I'd be impressed if you survived five minutes in here. I didn't figure you for the shy sort, Hero. It is almost endearing."

"Whatever." Hero stiffened as a damsel nearby got up and reached past him for a book on a shelf. She winked, which appeared to unnerve him more. He skittered back a step, rubbing a delightfully pink cheek. "Fine. Take me with you. I'll agree to your little promise."

"Glad to hear it." Claire paused to exchange a few words with the damsels. She didn't bother with the details, but sketched a vague reason for the Library's temporary shuttering. She guided Hero out the door, closed it with a click, and took off again. "It was a close call last time. Heaven's not catching us defenseless again."

After they returned to the front desk, Claire and Brevity left the boys to finish packing. Librarian and muse disappeared into the stacks for several long minutes to conduct the arcane parts of shutting down the Unwritten Wing.

Gradually, the Library took on a different tenor. The light spilling from shaded lamps drifted to a cooler tone, fading from amber to blue before dimming entirely. The shadows deepened. The deer that had frolicked in a nearby pastoral painting cast nervous glances outside the frame and disappeared into the oil-painted woods. The air became hushed and heavy.

Claire's last act of business was to pat the gargoyle as they slipped out into the corridor. "Hold down the fort, friend," she murmured. She half turned to look back but abruptly thought better of indulging the guilt that twisted in her stomach. She squared her shoulders and led the party toward the stairs at the far end of the hall. "Hopefully Andras is ready to go."

11

LETO

Stories and books have had many forms over the centuries. Humans have written down words on paper, but also on wood, clay, bone, bark, ivory, linen, stone, and the skin of every creature under the sun. Logic dictates that the unwritten words would be the same. But the Unwritten Wing is filled, shelf after shelf, with sturdy leather-bound books. Proper, civilized books. Even the Librarian's Log refers to current collection materials— books, not scrolls. I suppose the log must have some translation magic worked into it, but the Library itself?

It puzzled me until I came back to the simple truth: stories want to be told. And we, the librarians, are the only readers they have here.

Unwritten books yearn, and unwritten books change. Yet we expect them to remain timeless. I would say that's an accurate description of Hell.

Librarian Claire Hadley, 1990 CE

BOOKS WERE HEAVIER—AND muses stronger—than they looked. Leto had offered to carry Brevity's bag and quickly regretted it. He scrunched his nose as he followed the others down the stairs.

They passed through the Arcane Wing's ornate double doors, and he nearly collided with Brevity as she came to a sudden stop. Claire's back went rigid, while Brevity shuddered. Leto craned over her head to see what had startled the librarians.

He really wished he hadn't.

At the center of the laboratory, Andras conferred with two very large lab coats. The sheer size required to fill these lab coats was surprising enough, but then the lab coats turned. The faces above starchy white collars were . . . not there. Or they were there in the same way that the Library's gargoyle was there—that is to say, in angles and proportions that were only reality adjacent, best not considered straight on. But these faces didn't just give you a headache, like the gargoyle did; they twisted and writhed and broke through your calm, like sanity-fed maggots. Their smiles contained screams.

And there were so many. Leto looked away only to see another half dozen such creatures working the shelves. He was certain they hadn't been there on his previous trip, but now their presence was overwhelming. Leto focused on his shoes and fought the urge to retch. Behind him, Hero made a queasy noise.

Claire alone kept her eyes riveted straight ahead as she cleared her throat. "I didn't know you'd taken on interns in the Arcane Wing, Andras. Let alone such . . . prestigious ones. Wherever did you recruit them?"

The Arcanist looked up from his papers and glanced at the hulking horrors to either side of him with a fond smile. "It is so hard to find reliable help. I've had to devote quite a lot of time to recruitment lately."

Claire shook her head. "And here I thought I was your only mentee. I'm crushed."

"You're still my favorite." Andras gave an indulgent smile.

"What are those things?" Leto hissed to Brevity.

"Horrors, they got a lot of different names aboveground. You don't usually see them outside the lower levels of Hell. Demons use them sometimes to keep a legion in line." Brevity frowned at the lab floor as she hung back.

"They most definitely shouldn't be here." Claire dropped her voice so it wouldn't carry to Andras's very sharp hearing. "The Library isn't supposed to deal in torment. Or tormentors."

"Not for humans at least," Brevity said, catching Claire's gaze with a coded look.

"Not *normally* dealing in torment," Claire corrected after a weighted moment. "This is not normal."

"Maybe they're the runts. Castoffs and rejects of the proper Horrors," Hero suggested. He'd recovered enough to pull level to Claire and sneer at the creatures that towered above them. "Seems this place deals in that kind of thing."

"Either way, it's none of our business." Claire let out a little breath as the Horrors turned away. Leto found it comforting that even she was unnerved by them. She nodded to Andras as she raised her voice. "If you're ready to go . . . ?"

"Absolutely. Just through here." Andras led them farther into the lab, winding around shelves, limned with dust, that held strange artifacts. A rusted ring that glowed black. Spectacles that didn't quite reflect the same image in their lenses. Red gems, black pearls, white bones. And stacks of books, books that were still, not lively like the unwritten ones. They emanated a thick, pulsing power nonetheless. It made Leto long to wipe the goose bumps off the backs of his arms.

The raucous cawing of ravens could be heard all through the Arcane Wing, but it grew louder as they drew closer to the back. Turning the corner of a tall row of shelves revealed a rookery of cages, each filled with a black bird. Ruffled feathers and suspicious eyes turned to meet them. Andras brought the group to a halt and fiddled with a large key ring, occasionally fitting a key to a lock on a cage as he muttered.

"I assume you're familiar with such conveyance," he said.

"In theory, yes," Claire answered, looking about as displeased to see the ravens as they did her.

Andras finally opened the first cage with a flourish and paused to give her a sideways glance. "You're certain you and your people are up for this, Librarian?"

"Capable and willing. Your concern is kind, Andras, but misplaced." Claire tightened the bag across her chest. "We'll have time before there's any cause for alarm. A trip to Valhalla's wing is unusual but still in the bounds of my duties as librarian."

"And then? Surely you don't think Valhalla holds what we're looking for."

"After Valhalla . . ." Claire hesitated, and Leto caught the way her eyes measured him in a glance. "The ghostlights will buy us time once we hit Earth. It'll be suspicious, but His Nastiness won't bother sending Hounds until it's obvious we've flown the coop without permission. I suppose we will just need to avert disaster within twenty-four hours and return before the lights run out."

"A reasonable assumption." Andras did not seem as sure, but he turned back to the caged ravens. "As you say. Demons do not need to worry about such things. But the afterlife would be such a dimmer place without you in it, mind."

"Oh, get off it. You'd be moving the furniture in my wing in a heartbeat." Claire almost but not quite stifled a smile. "Let's get going."

"Right, then." Andras cleared his throat and expanded his address to everyone. "Simple process. Pull a feather, give the bird your treasure, then run like the dickens after it."

"Run where?" Hero asked with a frown.

"Wherever it takes you. All ravens know how to get to Valhalla—they're creatures of Odin. But they're contrary beasts, require a firm hand, from what I can tell. The path between realms is treacherous." Andras settled into a tone that made it obvious he was used to issuing orders and not answering questions. "Ravens have myopic, greedy natures. They can be bought, for a price. You must offer it something you dearly value. The shinier the better, but you'll need to be quick to reclaim it at the other end." He raised his brows expectantly at Claire, who nodded.

"Leto and I have our ghostlights. Hero, you will offer your sword. And Brevity . . ."

"Stupid raven better not claw it up." Brevity was already picking at the skin of her wrist. Leto blinked as the edge of one propane blue tattoo slowly came away from her skin. Brevity kept it pinched between two fingers as delicate translucent lines twisted and squirmed in the air. It glimmered in the low light, like the shed skin of something beautiful and rare.

"What is that?" Leto asked. He tried to keep his voice down but knew he was gawking nonetheless.

Brevity's answer was muttered, quiet enough that Leto barely caught it. "Inspiration." After a moment, the muse raised her voice but didn't risk more than a glance at Leto. "I kept it. Muses are just supposed to transport inspiration to humans, deliver it at the right time and place, help things along. That's it. That's why I was kicked out. I was a good muse at first, but . . . well, build enough dreams for other people, and you start wanting to make something for yourself."

"Inspiration?" Leto repeated. "You mean that's someone else's sto—"

"It's *mine*." Brevity's voice cracked.

Claire cast an oblique glance at where Andras and Hero were engaged in dickering about his sword, then rested a hand on Brevity's shoulder to guide her a polite distance away. She lowered her voice. "Brev, it's okay."

Brevity flinched. She gave Claire an uncharacteristically bleak look before her gaze shied away to her arm again. "Muses aren't supposed to keep anything for themselves. I was sent to the Library for punishment."

"Muses aren't my biggest fans," Claire explained.

"You weren't exactly thrilled yerself, boss."

Claire's mouth twisted. "I refuse to be anyone's *punishment*."

"If we've all got our valuables . . ." Andras cleared his throat, breaking the sympathetic quiet that had derailed the two librarians. His eyes were sharp, though, and Leto had the uncomfortable feeling that no incidental admission made in front of the demon was missed. "I thought you may want to take your companions through first, and I'll bring up the rear."

Claire composed herself. "You're the arcane expert here, Andras. Perhaps you should lead."

The Arcanist and the librarian exchanged a look, held just a second too long to be casual, before Andras nodded. "Off we go, then. Try to keep up."

Andras opened a cage and hauled one of the birds out by its legs, awkwardly enough to make the whole rookery take up complaint. He dodged snapping beaks and thumped it harshly on the side of the head until the poor bird lay still. He plucked a single black feather from its side and offered a tiny silver dagger from his pocket in exchange. A fragmented jewel in the hilt shone and glimmered independent of the light.

The raven eyed it, tilting its head to one side, then another, before snapping up the bauble. Andras had to jerk back his hand to preserve his fingers. He swore, but in a fitful burst of feathers, the raven launched into the air and took off down the aisle.

Leto watched, wide-eyed. "But where's it—"

The raven, with Andras close on its heels, passed through the rocky face of the far wall. The rock shifted, then snapped back into place with a vaguely jelly-like wobble. Leto's stomach swam to watch it.

Claire rattled at the lock on the next cage. "There's your demonstration. Let's get moving. Brevity, you next. Then Hero and Leto."

Claire reached into the cage with far more care than Andras had and came out with a calm—if gravely annoyed—raven perched on her wrist. She passed the bird to Brevity, who took a steadying breath before plucking a feather and offering the bird her shimmering ribbon of light. The bird snatched it up, and they were off, running toward the same rock face at the end of the aisle.

Hero cast a shrewd glance toward Claire. "I don't suppose you'll let me carry my own book. You might get lost after all."

Claire snorted and shook her head. "Your care for my well-being is touching, as always. I'll be along with the book right behind you."

"The connection—"

"I'll risk that it'll hold. Now go, book."

Hero allowed one disappointed curl of his lip before he repeated the procedure. His raven took off, flying with ease despite the large sword clutched in its talons. Leto supposed immortal magic birds were bound to be strong.

Claire turned to Leto. "All right. You've seen how the others did it."

"Right." Leto eyed the wall, which looked worryingly solid. The others hadn't even had the courtesy to flinch. He wondered what happened when you flinched. He wondered what happened when you fucked this up too.

"The running is the easy part." Claire stroked the waiting raven's head. "The vital thing is to keep your eyes on the raven. It can be tricky in there. It's a road between worlds, nowhere and everywhere at once. No matter what you hear, no matter what you think you see—follow the bird. Stay focused. Got it?"

Leto doubted anything in the world could possess him to abandon a magical lifeline, but the creases in the librarian's brow prompted him to nod with more confidence than he felt. "Got it."

"Good. I'll be right behind you." Claire handed him the raven. Its claws were gentle as they clamped around his wrist, dry but smooth and hot. The bird was surprisingly heavy and swayed on his forearm. Dark beady eyes regarded him with a canny kind of judgment. The bird gave only a disgruntled croak as Leto plucked the smallest feather he could manage from its chest. He swallowed hard, then opened his hand to reveal the ghostlight.

It had once again become a white candle upon its return to Hell, though slightly shorter and with a melted pool of wax around the wick. Leto had worried it wouldn't be shiny enough to be acceptable, but the raven gave it a careful once-over, then snapped it up. Hard nails pinched momentarily into his skin as the raven launched itself into the air.

And then they were running. Leto was so concerned about keeping up that they'd passed through the rock face before he'd had a chance to anticipate the impact. The moment they were through, shadows swam up and engulfed him. The world narrowed to only the bobbing bird ahead of him, white candle clutched in its claws like an arrow pointing the way.

Frost ticked up the back of his neck, but he kept his eyes locked straight ahead.

Not so bad, Leto thought.

Then the whispers started.

"BOYS. STOP BEING LITTLE *monkeys and smile for the picture.*"

Leto stumbled. His stomach dropped as he spun in the direction of the voice. It echoed around him, as if the speaker was lost in the cavernous dark. He twisted around and barely caught sight of the black bird disappearing into the fog. He broke into a run again, but it felt slower, as if he was covering less ground than before.

"*You got to check this out.*"

"*That's crazy.*" Leto's lips moved around the response. It was his voice, and they were his lips that spoke it, and they felt like his words, but it was wrong, all wrong. As if he were watching himself from far away. His legs gave out beneath him, and it was a shorter fall to the ground than it should have been. His knees banged against a soft surface that was suddenly slippery and pliable. Leto smelled chlorine and sun-warmed rubber, an inner tube in a shady backyard pool. The laughter that cut up through his constricted throat felt like a foreign presence. "*Did you see the one where he—*"

"*I know, right? We could totally start our own channel.*"

The other voice was young and gleefully confident, just over his shoulder. Out of the corner of his eye, a figure swirled through the deep mist, and it took every inch of self-control not to twist to face it. He shoved to his feet, though he could feel his body changing. The bob of the ghostlight was a speck in the dark. He ran, even as his legs stretched and returned to something like normal.

"*You never got time to chill anymore.*" And now the voices sounded older.

"*I'm just busy. You know.*" The words were frosty with apathy. Leto tried not to say them, but they forced their way out anyhow.

"Yeah. I know."

Everything felt familiar, like an echo. Leto clutched his fist over his chest, where an ache bloomed. The ground swayed, roiling with the mists, and it was becoming increasingly difficult to keep his feet. The raven didn't care. He was swimming after the bird to—where, forward? Backward? Deeper in or farther out? Time dilated, a drip of fatigue in his veins. Like bleeding out. A lulling exhaustion, spiked with dread.

His lips parted again, and there was no fighting this painful script. *"Stop, Darren. I don't have time—"*

No. *Don't*, Leto thought.

"I just thought—"

Stop. Leto tried to bite his mouth closed to keep it in. *You don't know—it ruins everything. Don't say it, don't—*

Pain blossomed over the horror, and Leto's lips bled as they parted. *"Well, don't. Shit, Darren. Don't bother thinking. Just don't."*

The feather crumpled in his fist, and a new pain brought him back. The quill had pierced his fingertip. It wasn't in the script. It was enough. He gasped and stumbled through the fog. The raven's distant form abruptly swerved up. It took a panicked scramble before Leto found where the ground inclined, rising up toward liquid shadows that poured between a gap of nothing that seemed thicker, darker, somehow.

"Who? Darren? God, no. He just always hangs around. . . ."

Again his voice betrayed him, stealing his breath. This time it came with a chill of calculation. Hope. The primal adolescent instinct that pointing to someone weaker somehow makes you strong.

Acid burned up Leto's throat and pooled on his tongue. It tasted bitter, like loathing. Leto hated that voice and hated himself. Maybe he deserved to be lost here. Maybe the others would fare better without him. They would, wouldn't they? Leto twisted to find the voice but stumbled midstep. And then he was falling. Leto's arms windmilled out for something, anything. An alien sound intruded, a digital *ping* that Leto struggled to place in his panic. Then a last voice that hissed out and bounced into the darkness:

"If you want to die so bad, why don't you hurry up and do it, then?"

Leto didn't even try to fight it this time. The voice was cruel and viciously cold. The voice was *his*.

Light. Air. Cool hands pressed on the back of his neck. Grass tickled his hands, and the air filled his lungs with the smell of green, sunlit things.

12

CLAIRE

A librarian exists in service to the books, and takes peace in that. Future librarians, I exhort you: do not meddle in the affairs of Hell or concern yourself with the mortal world. Our time there is past, but the stories we shepherd are immortal. What we do here echoes in eternity.

Librarian Ibukun of Ise, 971 CE

[Scribbled at a much later date in a slightly sloppy hand:]

Bleed that. We got a job to do, sure, but what good's a librarian without a story of his own?

Librarian Bjorn the Bard, 1253 CE

THE MOUNTAINS WERE BLACK and sharp, like the ribs of an ancient giant rimming the field of flowers. The closest peaks were spotted with white snowfall and a sparkle of glacial ice. It was daylight, but traces of northern lights played hide-and-seek against the far clouds drifting like passing thoughts. It was a perfect blend of mythic reverence and dream-like impossibility. It was ridiculous, half-forgotten heroics with changing faces, half mead and belief turned legend turned pop culture. It was Valhalla.

Claire had time to soak it in only after they retrieved their possessions from the ravens, who left in a huff. Brevity had been the fastest, snatching her own glimmering ribbon from her raven and pausing to drape it gently over one wrist. It twitched a protest, then absorbed seamlessly back into the complicated patterns tattooed on her arm.

A strangled cry caught her attention. Leto had arrived last, even though Claire had brought up the rear. That alone wasn't concerning; the raven roads were always changing. Each path was unfathomable and personal. However, the way he crouched in the grass, breath short and hands fisted tight in his hair, drew everyone's attention.

"Leto." Claire dropped to a knee beside him. His shoulders spasmed violently away at her touch, though the rest of him didn't appear to acknowledge her at all. His breath was a fevered, shallow wheeze. She gently threaded his fingers away from his hair before he pulled it out by the roots. "What's wrong?"

Leto stared at his hands in reply, fists clenching and unclenching. Claire could feel his pulse merging into a single fluttering drumbeat under her hand. She was about to try to shake him out of it when Brevity jostled between them.

"He's having a panic attack," Brevity said crisply as she clasped Leto's clammy hands and rubbed gently up his arm. "Leto, hey, buddy. We're safe. Doesn't feel like it, but we are. We're gonna take as long as you need, okay?"

Leto didn't respond, so Brevity dropped to her knees next to him. "You're right. Brains are fuckin' liars. But you got this. No rush. I'm going to count to four; maybe you can breathe for me. Four in, four out." And then, a few moments later, "Want to walk around? No? Good choice—this grass is kind of scratchy, don't you think? And that air—smells like butterfly farts, yeah? Look at those squishy, weird flowers. Wonder if you can eat 'em. . . ." Brevity kept up the words, grounding him, creating a steady, soft patter that, over a handful of minutes, slowly eased Leto's shoulders away from his ears. Brevity produced a small blue bottle from her bag and pressed it into his hands before shooing the rest of them away to give Leto a chance to recover.

"You seemed well prepared for that," Claire said, feeling thrown by her own assistant. Brevity was always surprising her, but then, that was what muses did. In all fairness, Brevity talked so much Claire had learned to only half listen when it wasn't related to the Library. Perhaps she should change that strategy.

"I was a muse. Contrary to popular belief, it's hard to get inspired when you're panicking. Not the first time I've seen someone struggle through anxiety." Brevity gave a careless shrug, not quite looking Claire in the eyes.

"You never talk about your previous work," Claire said.

"You never ask either, do you?" It carried an accusation, but Brevity brightened, only a little bit forcefully. "It's okay, boss. I knew better than to ask about yours too."

The lightness in her tone sang along Claire's nerves, but she was aware they had an audience. Thankfully, Leto had recovered and got to his feet unsteadily. "You didn't . . . didn't tell me it would be like dying." Leto's voice was hoarse and hollow, as if he'd been screaming. His color was faint, skin still clammy, but his chest rose and fell in steady, calm time.

Claire nodded to herself. "It's different for everyone. That path is intended to be a test. It feeds on your worst fear."

"Curious to fear dying, since you're already dead." Andras sounded more amused than sympathetic. It earned him a glare from Claire, but Leto ignored it.

"Is this the place?" Leto took his ghostlight back from Brevity. A distant cheer rose from the west, accompanied by the sound of clashing metal. They turned as one toward the noise, and Claire nodded.

"Oh yes, definitely Valhalla." She struck off up the hill toward the sounds. They picked through the rubble of what looked like a wall built by giants. Huge stone blocks piled on end. Just over the rise, the faint gleam of a rooftop caught her eye. Claire squinted at it. It was easier to keep moving forward. Anything was better than looking back.

Andras caught up with Claire first, lifting his knees high to try to keep the worst of the burs from catching on his fine slacks. He grimaced at his surroundings before giving her a scrutinizing look. "My dear, are you unwell?"

"What?" Claire looked down and realized her hands were trembling, fingers curled into a fist. She took a sharp breath and stuffed them in the pockets of her skirts. "I'm fine."

"The raven road can be trying even for experienced mortals," Andras offered.

"I am quite well, Andras," Claire said, if only to shut him up.

Burning books, blood on an unwritten rug, the back of her head, hunch of her shoulders as she turned away from her. Bile curdled in her gut. Worst fears, she'd told Leto. They were never things she wanted to run to, that tempted in the dark. Just things to run away from. Claire pursed her lips into a thin line. "Just fine."

She cleared her throat and turned her attention to the nearest available target. "And what do fictional heroes see in the dark?"

"Nothing. Just . . . nothing." It took Hero a moment longer than usual to marshal his usual haughty expression, and his sneer was slightly off-kilter. "Your company is nightmare enough, of course. What else could I fear?"

"Should have let go of the feather, then," Claire said, "stayed in the void. Lovely place. The gibbering voices could have taught you some manners."

"As opposed to the gibbering of the present?"

"Mind your tongue, book."

"Mind my tongue? Why, that's my most charming attribute."

"Maybe humility went with his lost pages," Leto muttered, and Hero rewarded him with a sliver of a grin.

"And the shadow gets a sense of humor! I didn't know he had it in him. Your bad influence, to be sure, warden."

THE HALL ROSE INTO view as they reached the top of the hill. A grand longhouse squatted in the middle of a wide training yard. It was constructed of dark timbers, each as big around as Hero was tall. All the wood was trimmed in gold, and dark carvings resolved into sinuous animals that curled into one another as Claire drew near. Lining the roof, gutter to gable, were wooden shields of every color. Their painted heraldry was bright in the late-afternoon sun.

It was the set of double doors at the top of a flight of steps that brought the group up short. A beaten-bronze sun decorated the tops of the doors, caught in the teeth of a giant wolf. Through the carvings that emanated from the sun ran ribbons of gold, dribbling between the wolf's teeth. Every recognizable creature, real or mythical, was represented, and though the carvings were rough, they pulsed with a chained energy. Ravens roosted among the uppermost gables. The roiling cloud of black feathers croaked and chattered down at the group as they hesitated at the base of the stairs.

"So many birds. How unclean," Andras commented as he squinted at them. "What is the term for a group of them? A nest, a colony . . . A murder is for crows. . . ."

"An unkindness of ravens," Claire muttered.

"Apt."

"They seem kinda pretty to me," Brevity offered as Claire placed her foot on the first step.

That was a mistake.

One of the largest ravens erupted from the flock and launched into a bulleting arc. At the apex, it dove, angling directly at the group. Brevity shouted a warning, but it was drowned out by a screech. First sounding avian, then . . . it changed.

A dark blur folded into Claire, and she slammed to the ground. She shook her head to clear it but was arrested when a long, curved blade came to rest lightly under her jaw, tip prodding her skull behind her ear.

"Squishy thing. Weak thing," said a woman's snarling voice. "You're no warrior."

Claire squinted in the sun to make out the figure straddling her. She was tall and broad shouldered, with dark leathers covering her and smelling vaguely of fire and sweat. Lean, hard muscle covered what leather did not, and she had a sharp, beaklike face with dark, kohled eyes. The sides of her head were shaved, and a frill of jet-black hair and feathers on the top of her head twitched as she leaned forward.

"Warriors go to Valhalla. Cowards to Hell. Intruders go to the flock." The woman's lips curved into a smile to match her knife.

"Hero—" Claire croaked out, but the blade tightened against her skin.

The chuckle was so smug she could *hear* the smirk in it. "Sorry— didn't catch that command, warden. Need something, did you? I am ever ready to assist a lady in need. Would you like a cup of tea?" She heard Brevity hiss something, which seemed to make Hero only laugh louder.

She really would kill that damned man.

The raven woman's companions joined her in human form, surrounding their party. Claire grimaced and crept her hands up, open at her sides. She might not die in Valhalla, but being skewered and sent back to Hell was not in her plans. "We mean no harm."

"You could do no harm even if you meant it, squishy woman."

"Excuse me, bird lady?" Brevity's voice brought Claire's attacker's attention around. "I'm afraid I need you to let go of my boss. Or I'll need to hit you. With very large books."

"Is that so, little worm?" Claire felt a warm trickle as the knife pressed harder. She began to wonder if her assistant was after a quick promotion.

"Who comes, Arlid?" A new voice sounded from somewhere beyond the steps. "They might have difficulty announcing themselves with a cut throat."

The raven woman, Arlid, made a disgusted noise, but the knife came away from Claire's throat. "Intruders, Ragna. My flock brought word. These are the ones holding our fledges in another realm, wicked things. Now they try to enter the halls, slinking in like cowards."

"We're not cowards. We're librarians!" Brevity protested, but the flat silence said the guards did not see the distinction.

Claire pressed her hand to the nick at her throat, wiping the dribble of blood as she sat up. A thickset woman, layered in furs and old scars, stood at the top of the stairs. She had a warrior's ease, but her arms were crossed, and she held less hostility in her gaze than Arlid.

"We are members of Hell's Unwritten Wing and we're here to see Bjorn the Bard." Claire got to her feet, knocked the dust off her skirts for what seemed to be the tenth time today, and assessed the situation.

Arlid loomed over her, knife angled so Claire didn't think about moving too fast. Brevity stood with the others, and still had her bag hoisted over her head, trembling arms waggling it threateningly at the nearest guard. Hero was content to stand to one side with a complete lack of concern. Useless book.

The powerful woman at the top of the stairs made no move to help or hinder. "And what would bring Lucifer's folk to see our storyteller?"

Storyteller. Claire had never thought of librarians like that, but then, Bjorn was before her time. "Library business." When the warrior raised her brow, she clarified, "*Confidential* library business."

"We respect the work of your storytellers. They may pass, Arlid," Ragna said, and the raven woman stepped to one side with a grunt. The party began up the stairs, now warier of the ravens overhead. "I'm sure Bjorn will speak to you after you pass the trial."

"Trial?" Brevity echoed.

"Valhalla is the field of heroes. You didn't die in worthy battle, so you'll have to prove your worth if you want our hospitality."

Claire shook her head. "But we're just here for a visit—just a moment is all—"

"You still must prove yourselves warriors to enter Valhalla," Ragna said.

"And if you don't . . ." Arlid skipped up the stairs after them. A feral smile crossed her hooked face, and she motioned to the ravens above. For the first time, Claire noticed bits of bone and unidentifiable lumps strung up amid the eaves. They clattered along with Arlid's singsong croak. "Intruders are consigned to the flock."

◆ ◆ ◆

"WHEN YOU SAID YOU knew the way to Valhalla . . ." Claire's eyes were quickly adjusting to the light inside the hall. It appeared even bigger inside. The long hall of Valhalla comprised a disconcerting mix of ancient myth and the exaggerated flux of modern influence. The roof rested on rafters made of thick spears, and shields and carvings decorated the walls that seemed to run on forever. The inhabitants were every age, shape, and size, not the uncouth giants that the decor indicated, but the interior of the hall bristled with an aggressive mix of song, wine, and a jovial sort of violence. Sweet smoke and mead were heavy in the warm air. "I assumed you had a plan for this part."

"I *knew of* the way. I don't get out as often as you do, remember." Andras slid aside as a warrior with a spear staggered past him toward the keg. "The rumors might have . . . left out a few details."

He had to raise his voice to be heard over the boisterous drumming that issued from an assembly gathered in one corner. Claire's gaze was drawn to an older man at the center of the circle, drumming a skin basin as large as a table. He used his hands, sticks, whatever fell into his grasp, and had his head thrown back, lost to the howling rhythm. He was not the largest warrior in the hall, but the energy that poured from his sinewy arms drowned out practically every drummer around him.

Claire found herself frowning at the unnecessary exuberance. "Andras, you've been a dear mentor, but if your theoretical knowledge gets us killed, I will be withdrawing my professional acquaintance."

"Understood, pup."

"Who will your representative be for the trials?" Ragna finished conferring with another Norseman and turned back to them. "You should pick your finest warrior. Today's battle master is Uther, wielder of the guardian maul named Widowbane."

"I suppose we just missed the wielder of crumpets and tea." Claire pursed her lips and looked to her companions. Wordlessly, all eyes slid to Hero and the sword on his back.

Hero jerked, pulling his thirsty gaze away from a line of silver goblets and possibly the lean warriors attached to them. "You can't be serious."

"You are kinda the only one with a weapon. Or any idea how to use one," Brevity pointed out.

"Also, the only one with enough sense not to get anywhere near someone named Widowbane!"

"Actually, that's the maul's name," Andras said. "Interesting human quirk, that—Norse only named their blades when—"

"Fascinating," Hero snapped, reserving a glare for his companions before looking at Claire. "Surely you have a better plan than sacrificing me to the natives."

"If you have ideas, I'm open to suggestions." Claire was not happy about the way things were going, but she kept her face neutral. "We can't continue until we prove ourselves, and we can't leave until we've found Bjorn. You heard what's at stake."

Hero's frown faded, and he held Claire's gaze levelly, trading anger for a quiet that made her skin itch. He appeared contemplative. She found she rather preferred him sullen and angry. "And is that an order, Librarian?"

"Duels are honorable combat. They must be entered into voluntarily," Ragna said.

If Claire couldn't order Hero to satisfy the duel, that shot down any hope they had. Claire glanced around the hall, searching for a new plan. She racked her brain for Nordic culture, wondering what the reaction would be if she made a run for it and attempted to find Bjorn on her own. Corner and threaten him if she had to. There had to be protocols, protections. Surely they would have to respect the gravity of the . . .

"Fine."

Hero stood stiff as the blade on his back, dark eyes glowering at Ragna. He'd managed to imbue an acid disdain into the one word. "As the only *hero* present, trials of honor fall to me. I'll participate in your barbarian sport." He grumbled, "Might enjoy hitting a few things, actually. . . ."

Ragna, if she even noticed it, was immune to scorn. "You may choose your weapon."

Hero gestured to the filigreed sword on his back. "Broadsword. Unless you have a rapier about."

"Sword it is." Ragna turned toward Claire. "And you, storyteller. What weapon?"

Claire choked. "I beg your pardon?"

"You are the leader of these . . . people." Ragna motioned over the Library's host with a broad hand. "Leaders do not allow their own to bleed alone."

"Who said anything about bleeding?" Hero interjected unhappily.

"You must forgive me, Ragna." Claire chose her words with care. "Arlid was right, outside. I am not a coward, but I am not a warrior either. I'm a librarian, a scholar—my only skill is with words. I'm afraid I would put on a very poor show for your hall."

"Not so!" The voice that boomed from the pit brought all the music to an abrupt halt, which caught the attention of the rest of the hall. Talk ground to a murmur as a scrawny man, nearly as leathery as the wide drum in front of him, stood.

It was the same man Claire had seen earlier, hooting and drumming like a creature possessed. He leapt around the oversized drum and made his way out of the drum pit with a few pats and shoulder slaps for the warriors he passed. "I believe we'll be in for a grand treat. And it's been far too long since I stretched my jaw."

Ragna's hooded eyes lit up. She clasped the man's arm. "You will do us the honor, storyteller?"

"Storyteller?" Claire gaped. "You're Bjorn?"

"That's what they say." The man wiped a sweaty hand over his impressive beard. "I hear you've come from the Library."

He did not look much like a proper librarian, but Claire was relieved. Perhaps they could yet avoid this foolish scene. "Yes. We have questions about—"

"How is the gargoyle?" Bjorn asked suddenly. "Still got that chip on the right wing?"

"Probably. I try not to look too closely." Claire shared an exasperated glance with Andras. "It's of the utmost importance that we speak—"

"And we'll discuss much, Librarian. After our duel."

"Not a warrior. No time." Claire clipped her words to keep from being cut off a third time. She gripped her bag of books more tightly. She was familiar with the outlandish nature of Viking tales, but this trip was quickly spiraling out of her control.

"There's always time for a story," Bjorn said. "Surely you know your stories, Librarian. Let the best verse win."

"But—"

"A battle and a tale! A treat," Ragna crowed, clapping Claire on the back hard enough to send her forward a step. "To the ring!"

13

CLAIRE

My dear apprentice, as a librarian you'll undergo strict training under my somewhat unworthy tutelage. It can take decades to learn to wield words properly. But you need only look at the hungry demons at our door to know the power of inspiration. As we are unwritten authors, yes, some of that work is our own. Words may call to you, but it is important to maintain a healthy respect for that power. I know you grieve your lost life, but have patience.

There is much I have yet to tell you.

Librarian Gregor Henry, 1987 CE

THE POLISHED OAK OF the staff seemed to glow in the thick warmth of the longhouse. It was a beautiful construction. Claire knew if she ran her fingers along it, she'd find joints of birch, yew, hawthorn, and the other sacred woods of the north. Her thumb worried at the gnarl of amber trapped in its tip.

The hall had reacted quickly to the prospect of a duel. Claire and Hero were evidently to fight simultaneously—a dual duel. The wordplay made Claire roll her eyes, but she had to admire the way the hall had quickly reorganized for the occasion. Bjorn had swept her away to the far end. The tables were pushed clear, revealing a hard-packed arena in the center of the lodge. She stopped her pacing at the side of the ring. "Librarians are not warriors *or* wizards. Is this really necessary?"

Bjorn rolled his shoulders as he selected a staff of his own. "Have some sense of showmanship, lass. We may be a rough lot to you, but we appreciate a good performance. You've dueled in our way before, yes?"

"My predecessor taught me." Claire stared at the staff in her hand as if it were a snake. "But more for . . . recreation and training, not death by combat."

"Oh, I would never kill you, lass." Bjorn turned with a smile. "Just mightily embarrass you in front of all these fine, handsome Viking men."

"No loss. I prefer my partners slightly less hirsute."

"Like your pretty lad, there?" Bjorn gestured to Hero, who had his back to them. He was allowing Brevity to fiddle with the straps on his armor. He had abandoned the jacket and waistcoat for fine-scale mail that hung lightly on his chest and gleamed the same burnished bronze as his hair.

Claire turned back. "I also prefer my partners slightly less fictional. He's a character. A *book*."

"Looks real enough for me. But then there's no accounting for taste." Bjorn was in no hurry to turn his appreciative gaze away. Claire didn't have time for the antics of a lecherous old bard. She located the notebook in her bag and pulled it out. She had begun making notations when Bjorn cleared his throat.

"No books in the ring."

"I beg your pardon? I'm a librarian. You asked for a story, and this is where I keep my stories. I'll carry your silly staff, but I'm keeping my notes."

"That's not how stories work here, lass. You're not in your library anymore—here, the word is your voice. And your voice is your tale." Bjorn flashed a grin. "The spoken word was the first kind of library, after all."

Oral storytelling. She should have expected as much. It was awkward, dated, and entirely unreliable. Messy in every way she couldn't stand. Unreliable narrators, the lot of them. In her opinion, there was a reason humanity had invented the written word, and that reason was progress. Claire ground her teeth. "That is a loose interpretation."

"Is it?" Bjorn mildly met her glare. "Once, people memorized books' worth of spoken words, songs, and sagas that contained all their history, traditions, stories, survival. The Arrernte called it their Dreaming."

Bjorn knew his stuff. Claire was forced to remember that, for all his wild appearance, he was a former librarian. And had a longer tenure than her. She ceded the point. "I'm not a *storyteller*."

"Then you can go back to your library." Bjorn shrugged.

The crowd was increasing. Someone had procured a war horn, and its bleat was seeding a headache. Claire tossed the book on top of her bag in a huff. "You're crude."

"And you rely too much on those bits of paper. This is how it all started, you know." Bjorn handed Claire a mug of a dark frothy liquid. When she bent her head, she caught a vague whiff of fire and chocolate. "Drink up."

Up close, the smell nettled her nose with iron and honey. "What is this?"

"Mead of poetry," Bjorn said a touch too lightly.

Claire searched her memory of half-remembered myths. Nothing in Valhalla's stories was as simple as mead, and this place seemed exaggerated past even the original myths. "This isn't . . . Kvasir's blood?" The Norse had a tale about the *mead of poetry*. Blood extracted from a keen, all-knowing, and thoroughly murdered god. She gave it a repulsed look before taking a tentative sip. She could feel the magic begin to seep into her tongue. It tasted like bitter chocolate. "If I recall the lore right, a simple vial of this is adequate."

"But then ye don't have an excuse to drink." Bjorn downed his portion in one gulp and wiped his beard. "No books, just a saga, a staff, and a swig. I'll make a Norseman of you by the end of this, Librarian."

"Just try not to fall on your head when I beat you." Claire finished her mug and handed it back to him. "I still need answers."

Bjorn's laughter was as warm as their drink as he led the way into the arena.

◆　◆　◆

BJORN ABANDONED CLAIRE AND Hero in the middle of the ring and disappeared to fetch Hero's opponent. The tables and stands were already filling up with curious faces. Word of their spectacle had spread, and Valhalla's residents were always ready for a fight. The arena bubbled with spilled mead and a lazy kind of bloodlust.

Claire ran her gaze over the crowd, locating Hell's contingent at the table nearest the ring, easy enough to pick out by Brevity's seafoam green hair. Brevity stood on the bench in order to throw Claire an exuberant thumbs-up sign. At least one of them was confident about their chances.

Claire's toe found a divot in the packed dirt. She glanced at Hero. "You're quite prepared, then?"

"I'll do my heroic best not to embarrass you, warden." Hero's voice was dry. He shifted on the balls of his feet and didn't move his gaze from where Bjorn had disappeared. "I'd see more to yourself. You don't strike me as the battle-maiden type."

"Librarians have their own way of competing. Though I admit . . . it's been quite a while." More than quite a while. More like since she became librarian three decades ago.

It's not as if she'd had anyone to spar with. Brevity, being a muse, didn't have the interest in classic literature most human unauthors did, and no assistant before her had progressed far enough in the training to make dueling relevant. Claire had been lax, and she wasn't looking forward to Bjorn reminding her of that fact.

She pushed that thought away before it could unravel her nerves more than it already had. "I have to ask, Hero. Why?"

Hero appeared ready to force her to draw out the question—why had he volunteered? why was he risking this?—but his eyes slid past her face, and he shrugged. "It's what I'm made for, isn't it? Figured I might as well agree while I could still *pretend* you honored me with the choice. Besides, you're not the only one with a reason to see this foolhardy mission through."

His author. She was alive and would be caught up in this if Heaven and Hell truly decided to go to war. Claire put it together quickly, but

Hero offered it with a smile just scraping the line of loathing. "Pure self-preservation."

"Selfish heroism, then. I expected nothing less," Claire said.

The ground began to shake. Hero's grip tightened on his sword, Claire saw in her peripheral vision.

Out of the gloom swung a wall. Or what had to be a wall. A wall in the shape of a man. No, men didn't grow that tall. A giant. Uther.

He was easily as large as Walter back home, Claire estimated. His shoulders were bare and as wide as Claire was tall. The warrior's scarred face was occupied by a long yellow beard, knit with bones and feathers, below a gnarled nose. In one boulderlike hand, a wrecking ball of a maul lazed. The weapon glowed with a dark red stone.

Bjorn was dwarfed beside him and could only give the giant a pat on the elbow before separating.

Hero had gone very still beside her, and Claire glanced up. His face was blank and held the dread of a goose only now vaguely aware it was about to be made dinner.

She cleared her throat. "He's not wearing much armor." The warrior, in fact, wore more war paint and feathers than clothes from the waist up.

"Oh, good. I would hate to cause him a laundry bill when I inconsiderately die all over him."

"What I mean is, if you're fast enough, you have a good chance."

"I don't need tactical advice from an academic, thanks," Hero snapped, and he glared steadily at the beast lumbering across the ring rather than look at Claire.

"Fine, be a fool. Heroes are good at that." Claire turned with her staff to where Bjorn had taken up position. "But I've already stitched your life together once today. I've got the hand cramps to prove it, and I'd rather not do it again. So . . . just don't die."

If Hero had a reply, she didn't hear it as she strode away to face her own test.

✦ ✦ ✦

THE RING WAS LARGE enough to separate the duels by several yards—far enough that she would not be swept up in the first swing of Uther's grand maul.

Claire positioned her back to Hero's match. She would have to keep moving. This was not the stand-and-deliver type of duel that she was familiar with from the Library. But as she wrapped her fingers over the soft grip of her staff, she settled on a grim certainty. Whatever the outcome, she was not leaving the realm until she had her answers.

"Seeing as you're our guests"—Bjorn raised his voice so it carried over the watching crowds—"we'll allow you the first attack."

"Grand." Claire heard Hero's dripping sarcasm behind her.

There was a shuffle and a thundering step as Hero initiated the attack, and Claire could not stop from twisting around as the crowd began to roar. Hero had opened with a testing swing, darting forward and aiming for Uther's unprotected side. But the giant easily avoided it, batting aside Hero's sword as if it were a gnat. Hero grunted and recovered, cautiously maintaining his distance.

"Well, Librarian?" Bjorn's voice brought her around.

She would have to stop worrying about Hero's fight if she was going to survive her own. A duel between librarians was a duel of words. Not just any quotation from a poem or other passage would do; it had to hold meaning for the audience. It was the meaning that carried the weight. The opposing librarian would have to identify it, take away the audience's meaning, and redirect it to defuse the attack. Claire tightened her grip on the staff and considered her audience. This was Bjorn's audience, not hers. She would be operating at a disadvantage. The encounter with the ravens at the steps came to mind. "'Cowards die many times before their deaths; the valiant never taste of death but once.'"

Her voice rang out, and she felt the silky shudder on her lips as the magic took hold. Fine silver script flowed through the air, etching the words in a glowing ribbon. A flare of figures formed around it, tiny points of light in the shape of faeries, fine ladies, jesters and daggers, moons and men. It whispered as it flew sharply at Bjorn's face, and the crowd murmured approval.

The old man grunted and whipped his staff to the side, catching the words from the air. The silver script tangled and scraped at the wood, tendrils whipping like a lash toward his face. He spoke just one word to make them disappear into nothing. "Shakespeare." Bjorn snorted as he named the author. "Starting with the Bard, Librarian? A beginner's move. I hope you have more than that."

"It seemed fitting, considering." Claire began to circle as Bjorn moved. The tumult from the crowd was growing. Out of the corner of her eye, she registered swirls of movement as Hero and Uther began to trade blows in earnest. Claire forced herself to stay focused on the bard in front of her.

"'It's much better to do good in a way that no one knows anything about it.'" Bjorn's words were gold and old stone runes, tiny marching men and snowflakes, all sharp edges as they snapped toward her. Claire's mind spun along with her staff, and she stumbled back a step as she barely avoided being sliced by the tail end.

"Tolstoy." The words disappeared, and she stifled a sigh of relief before she began to circle again. Bjorn was faster than an old man had a right to be, his words too sharp. She needed the space to react.

"Out of practice, Librarian?" Bjorn took easy strides around the ring. "'The sun himself is weak when he first rises, and gathers strength and courage as the day gets on.'"

She aimed the words lower this time, forcing Bjorn to dance away lest the gossamer script tangle his boots. "Dickens. Wasn't he a contemporary of yours? Or would have been if you'd written."

"Low blow."

"Not low enough, it seems." The old man narrowed his eyes at her before forming a return volley. "'He knew everything there was to know about literature, except how to enjoy it.'"

Claire caught the gold words at the center of her staff. She found the quotation but took a fraction too long. The gold script managed to slice at the back of her arm before she could dispel it. "Joseph Heller," she gasped. Blood welled up in thin lashes up to her elbow.

So they went, back and forth, trading blows up and down the written words of history. Bjorn staggered when an Austen escaped his guard and landed a blow to his knee. Claire found herself diving to the ground to avoid an Eliot as it lashed for her head. It was when she was rolling to her feet that she first noticed the blood staining the other side of the ring.

Hero moved like a dervish, darting into the larger man's reach only as long as it took to aim the edge of his blade along Uther's flank. Striking a blow, then flinging himself out of the way of the maul again. Both men were bloodied, though Hero bled black, pitiless ink. They both breathed heavily; Uther favored his side, while Hero held one injured wrist away from his opponent.

Claire took a deep breath and faced Bjorn again with a long attack. "'Be men, or be more than men. Be steady to your purposes and firm as a rock. This ice is not made of such stuff as your hearts may be; it is mutable and cannot withstand you if you say that it shall not.'"

A boisterous approval came from the sidelines. "What soldier wrote that?" came a call from the crowd.

"Mary Shelley," Bjorn said grudgingly. With more bravado than she felt, Claire bowed, and the gathered crowd laughed.

Bjorn shook his head. "'And the rest is rust and stardust.'"

"Nabokov," Claire said with a grunt as she spun and dispelled a marching line of script and meteors. "God, Russians."

Bjorn chuckled but did not dispute her sentiment on the literature. Claire paced a few more steps to catch her breath. This needed to end soon. "'We lived in the gaps between the stories.'"

"Atwood." Bjorn returned with a line from Tolkien, which Claire dispelled before he commented, "Your soldier looks tired, Librarian. Blows like that . . . he's not standing much longer."

Claire allowed her eyes to stray to Hero. Uther had gotten lucky. She'd missed the blow that had sent Hero sprawling, but its impact must have been tremendous. He'd risen from his knee but held heavily to his sword with his one good hand, ink dribbling down one cheek. He reserved all his energy for a glare at the moving mountain in front of him.

Claire swallowed hard and forced her attention back to Bjorn. "'Logic may indeed be unshakable, but it cannot withstand a man who is determined to live.'"

"Kafka." Bjorn dismissed it with a wave of his staff before returning a volley toward Claire. "'The weak man becomes strong when he has nothing, for then only can he feel the wild, mad thrill of despair.'" He aimed the volley for Claire but was grinning at the other combatants in the ring.

"Arthur. Conan. Doyle." Claire gritted her teeth, searching for a line that would wipe that smug, blood-mad grin off the Viking's face.

But it was then that Hero made his move. He regained his feet and swung, lithe bronze figure glinting as the sword arrowed toward Uther's ribs. The giant turned, fast, too fast, and a crack reverberated throughout the hall as maul met blade, and both sword and swordsman were flung away.

Hero sprawled on the dirt, groaning. Black liquid flowed freely from the cut on his temple now, and his movements were slow. His sword came to rest several yards away. Weaponless, Hero clenched his teeth in a death's-head grin as he gained a knee and turned toward Uther. The Norse warrior inclined his head and brought his arms back to deliver the winning blow.

"'War is cruelty, and none can make it gentle!'" The words were out before Claire could think them. But they were not aimed at Bjorn; her gaze was locked on the other fight. Silver words flew, and sharp serifs struck deep across a monstrous, scarred face. Uther stumbled midswing, bellowing in pain as his maul dropped, and the giant man clawed at his face.

Bjorn stared, mouth gaping. Hero, to his credit, knew an opportunity when he saw one. He scrambled for his sword and took a hobbled leap at Uther, growl in his throat.

"Parker! Gilbert Parker!" Bjorn shouted, and the silver words wound around Uther's face dissolved. But Hero was faster. The broadsword pierced his ribs deep, and Uther's bellow became shrill, then silent.

The giant man convulsed, landing a grip on Hero's shoulder. But it began to loosen even as they fell back to the earth. Hero twisted the blade with a snarl, and it struck Claire that his features were beautiful, even more so in fury. A purity in the hate that she recognized. She hadn't thought books could truly hate.

"Clever. No honor, but clever." Bjorn was solemn as Claire turned back to face him. There was a dark regard in the old man's eyes, but he spoke before Claire could open her mouth to explain. "'And hope buoyed like a flag, fragile on the wind. Death was the only freedom.'"

The gold words curled in the air and furled out, thick and unstoppable. The words were unfamiliar, even as they triggered something that burned at the edge of her brain. But they were strange, accompanied with dizzying shapes, birds in flight, cathedrals, and cobblestone streets. White cliffs and sunsets. She had no defense. She managed to retreat two steps before the gold letters slammed into her chest and drove her to the ground.

A thick, buzzing weight twined hungrily around her arms. She squeezed her eyes shut and waited for the ensuing pain, but it never appeared. After a moment, Claire carefully cracked one eye open. The words had wrapped her up neat as a present, and they thrummed warningly against her chest, but they did not cut unless she struggled. Bjorn stood over her, dark eyes regarding her with a mixture of disapproval and amusement. "No response, Librarian?"

Claire took a short breath—all she was capable of with the words twined so tight around her chest. "You have me at a loss, Bjorn. I must cede. Who's the author?"

"Claire Juniper Hadley," Bjorn said, and the crowd roared.

14

CLAIRE

Everything went wrong. Gregor is gone and I am still here. But I won't apologize. Not to god or the devil, not when souls are trapped here, left to wither and dry like flowers pressed between the pages of the books we keep.

Andras says I'll grow into the role. I suppose I will. It's the only path you left me.

I won't apologize, but I won't forgive either.

Apprentice Librarian Claire Juniper Hadley, 1989 CE

"YOU CHEATED."

The room, like everywhere else in the lodge, was uncomfortably warm, and Claire picked irritably at the bandage on her arm. She sat on a cushioned bench, grudgingly sipping tea Bjorn had brewed to restore her strength and "put hair on your chest." She'd insisted on bandaging her arm herself, freeing the healers to tend to Hero, who had been quickly whisked to an adjoining room after the fight.

"Do explain, lass. I'm in the mood to laugh." Bjorn rubbed his bruised knee from the opposite side of the small table. They were in his personal study. The walls were lined not with books but with rows of *capsae*, hat-boxlike containers that held scrolls and wooden slates of every shape and size. A fire roared in the fireplace that took up the far wall, and the study was as cozy as it was chaotic.

Claire shuddered to think what the Valhalla library must look like, if this was a tidy personal collection.

She took another sip of the tea and made a bitter face. "You quoted an unwritten author. That's specifically against the rules of the duel. Worse, you quoted *me*. That's not just cheating—that's dirty."

Bjorn raised a brow. "Would that be more or less dirty than turning your words against a noncombatant?"

"Uther was about to *kill* my character. He most certainly was a combatant."

"Not *your* combatant."

"Close enough." Claire smacked the mug on the tabletop with a peevish frown. "He may be disconnected from his book, and he's most definitely a pain in the ass, but Hero is still mine."

"Well, you and your boy certainly set Uther straight on that."

Claire remembered the mule they'd had to bring in to haul Uther's body out of the arena, and she diverted her eyes to the table. "Yes, well. Sorry about your champion."

"Don't be." Bjorn gave an airy wave of his hand. "He'll be right as rain tomorrow."

"I beg your pardon?"

"We're in an afterlife for warriors, Librarian." Bjorn leaned back, and his chair let out a long creak as he grinned. "Any who fall in battle today wake up fresh as springtime tomorrow. He'll never wield Widowbane again—he's been proven unworthy. But he'll continue on. We do love a good fight, and Valhalla sees to its own."

"Well, that's . . . convenient," Claire said. "Tell me, would it have been the same for Hero if he'd fallen?"

Bjorn raised his brows, considering. "He didn't die a warrior of the halls, so . . . ah, probably not."

"Good thing I cheated, then."

"Good thing," Bjorn relented. "Up until then, you did comport yourself well enough to pass. The hall will have you."

Claire was quiet a moment before saying, "The book you quoted. How did you . . . I mean, have you read—"

"I was the librarian of the Unwritten Wing before your grandfather was a twinkle in anyone's eye." Bjorn's lip curled as he toyed with the edge of the table, running a rough thumb back and forth. "I had time enough in that place to get familiar with lots of books. Including yours."

"My books were there before I was even born. . . ." A queer feeling flipped in Claire's stomach, and her mind could not settle on a proper question to ask out of the hundred that bubbled up. She'd helmed the Library for thirty years, and it still felt like a mercurial kind of impossibility. A story was more immortal than its teller. Time had no play there, only potential. Claire had failed both. She looked up to find Bjorn studying her carefully. "They were readable?"

"I wouldn't call them Shakespeare, but they were passable, yes," Bjorn said. "You do have quite the collection."

"Well . . . not that it matters now." Claire's eyes dropped, and she abruptly found an excuse to stand. The hearth needed poking; irresponsible to let the flames die down.

Bjorn followed her to the fireplace and rubbed a sore arm before glancing at her. "I heard about what happened, of course."

The fire twitched behind the grate. Claire found her breath tripped up in her throat before she could let it out again. "There were a hundred tales about my ignominious rise to librarian, Bjorn. You'll need to be more specific."

"The rumor that goes against the tale. The one that says Gregor didn't retire to his greater reward. The rumor that says he was attacked. Attacked by something with the power to unmake a human soul. Your mentor disappeared under . . . unusual circumstances, we shall say." Bjorn said it calmly, as if recounting last night's dinner. "And the attacker was never found, of course, so the retirement line was the one that took. Left you to take on the mantle far too soon, by most folk's estimates."

"That is one of the more fanciful ones. Did you hear the one where I sold my soul for the promotion, danced naked with Cerberus? Never mind how I would sell my soul when I was already in Hell, but . . ." Claire trailed off as Bjorn failed to take the joke. She rolled her shoulders in a weary shrug. "Gregor . . . He was more than a mentor. He was my friend and I would have never wished him harm."

It was true enough, Claire thought carefully, in a certain kind of light.

Bjorn was quiet for a moment, as if testing the edges of that statement. Then he turned with a grunt. "Ah! Where's my mind? They'll already be at the feast. Hero too, if the healers have done their work."

"Feast . . ." Claire's voice was flat. "Bjorn, I can't tolerate another delaying tactic—"

"A feast for our angelic guests."

"Angels?" Claire's eyes widened in alarm. "Here? But how—"

"They arrived shortly after you. Because of what they are, the hall already recognizes them as warriors. They were welcomed in, think they even caught the last of the fight." Bjorn hooded his eyes as Claire began to pace. "I suppose you know why they're here."

Claire twisted her hands, wincing as doing so pulled on her bandage. "You said there was more than one?"

"Two. One formidable lass all in white and a man in gray who frowns too much." Bjorn paused. "I don't hold with that lot, but they seemed a capable pair."

"Capable and problematic. We'll need to leave right away," Claire muttered. "*You* know why they're here?"

"Let's see. Hell's librarian and two hunter angels visiting a simple storyteller on the same day, muttering disaster and all hackles up about something." Bjorn snorted. "Even a dumb old Viking has to get the idea."

Bjorn held up a hand as Claire opened her mouth. "Easy, lass. I am loyal to the Library, but listen. Even if I answered your questions now, worst thing you could do is go tearing out of here with the angels watching the gate. They'd be on you faster than a raven flies. Feast. Rest a while. I'll give you your answers, and you may slip out in the morning when half the realm is still sleeping off the drink."

Claire's mouth shut slowly. "Do angels even drink?"

Bjorn chuckled and took her by the arm. "All warriors drink in Valhalla. Come! I'll prove it."

ALL WARRIORS DID, INDEED, drink in Valhalla. The arena had been invaded, lined with additional long tables and benches to accommodate the revelers, who were several drinks in already. Claire could barely move through the crowd without having to dodge sundry blades and axes strapped to backs. Valhalla's citizens did not believe in leaving their weapons at the door, even for a party.

In truth, Claire found it maddening, the chaos, the cheer, the swells of mood and passion that roiled over the pressed bodies like a wave. She'd never cared for crowds. Crowds were messy; crowds were not predictable and not reliable. After she'd spent thirty-plus years in the quiet of the Library, dealing only with the trickle of Hell's patrons and recalcitrant books, Claire found the chuff and churn of Valhalla's festivities incomprehensible. It made her head hurt and her joints ache. Mercifully, Bjorn guided her to the table her companions had staked out, before he drifted away, muttering about proper drink and song.

"Oh, try the little blue ones!" Brevity had been busy in her absence. A stack of small pastries and dainty twists of meat, far more ornate than Claire would have guessed the Vikings capable of, was set out in the center of the table. She smiled despite herself. Trust Brevity to find the sweets at any party.

Claire allowed Brevity to shove a mug of something sloshing and foamy into her hand. Hero was still absent, but her assistant succeeded in coaxing Leto and Andras into sipping at their drinks. Judging by the empty mugs and the bearded grins sent their way, she had passed the time warming to the warriors at the adjoining table. Excellent work. It couldn't hurt to win the goodwill of Valhalla's residents.

"You did great, boss," Brevity said.

"If you say so." Claire kept her eyes on Bjorn and set down the mug the moment he disappeared into the crowd. "There are angels here."

Andras choked on his drink, flecks of ale dotting his beard as his gaze darted around. "Already?"

"It seems so." Claire recounted Bjorn's news as quickly as she could. Leto, having run into an angel once already that day, began to exude panic, acid sweat forming on his temple and sliding down to his collar with a hiss. Frankly, Claire couldn't blame him. Brevity pivoted in her seat to scan the crowd, covering the gesture by ordering another round for the boisterous table next to them.

"You're *certain* there was no way for them to track the scrap in the afterlife?" Claire asked Andras.

"Absolutely not. It's a piece of Hell. They could detect general demonic activity if they were in the area, but not across realms. They must be searching anywhere we were likely to seek help."

"Which means they have an inkling of how important it is. Brilliant."

"If so, we need to leave, pup. Sooner rather than later." At Claire's look, Andras's brow furrowed. "Surely we're not *staying* here while there are angels looking for us."

"Of course not," Claire said. "Bjorn may trust in the hospitality rules of Valhalla, but I don't. We will just need to get around them carefully. Do you see them yet, Brev?"

"Only one, ma'am. Tall lady by the entrance, all shiny and terrifyin' lookin'. I don't think the Vikings care for her much."

Claire raised herself from the bench just enough to spy what looked like a pale, walking storm cloud over the heads of the crowd. The crowd, despite the increasingly rowdy tone, did its best to flow away from her general vicinity. "Well, she's not doing much to hide herself."

"Heaven never was much for subterfuge," Andras said with a touch too much demonic pride.

"Then that's going to have to be our way out."

Claire toyed with the foam on her drink, trying to develop a plan that balanced meeting their goals with getting out with their skins intact. "Brev, Leto, go extract Hero from the healers, assuming he's not run off, and get him up to date. Then find Bjorn and get him alone in his office. I don't care if you have to tie him up by the beard—we're getting our answers tonight. I'll meet you there."

Brevity was already springing from the bench. "A rescue and Viking-napping sound fun. What're you going to do?"

"Go find our other angel."

Leto paused halfway out of the bench. "Pardon me for suggesting, but you don't want to wait to take Hero with you? Last time that angel was kind of . . . angry. And violent."

"I'm sure Hero will just be thrilled you volunteered him for mortal peril again," Andras mused.

Claire remembered the lightning crack and smell of ozone from their first encounter with Ramiel. The point where the blade had rested on her chest tightened a little, but she shoved it away and shook her head. She'd risked the book enough for one day. "No. I'll be fine. We're all guests in Valhalla, correct? I just want to talk."

"I'll come, then," Andras said.

Claire frowned at the old demon. "I'm not sure that's a good idea. This one seemed to have a hair trigger even around Leto, and he was in human form then."

"He *really* doesn't like demons," Leto confirmed.

"You said it yourself: Valhalla's safe." A calculating look flickered through Andras's red-gold eyes. "Don't worry about me. I've dealt with more than my share of Heaven's pests in my time. And this one, Ramiel? He's not even part of the Host—a fallen angel. I want to see why such a creature is after us, and how they came to possess the pages of the codex after all this time. I might be able to detect something from what he says."

It was much the same reason that Claire was taking the risk herself, so she couldn't find much fault. "I still don't think it's a good idea."

"Then it's a good thing I'm not one of your apprentices. I'm coming." Andras's smile was mild, but Claire knew when the demon's mind was made up.

"Stubborn."

"A requirement when dealing with humans."

"So it seems."

Andras had a demon's care for order and justice—that is to say, none at all. For the first time, Claire wondered exactly what his real motivations were for setting her on this path, let alone coming himself. Andras could have just as easily advised from the Arcane Wing; in fact, staying behind the scenes, subtle and withdrawn, was just Andras's preference. A tactic he'd tried to impart to Claire, but she'd always preferred doing her own work.

She trusted Andras, despite his being a demon. He'd protected her, taught her, cared for her. She would not have held on to the Library if he hadn't stepped in and guided the way thirty years ago. Still. She trusted him, but she didn't pretend to understand him.

Perhaps exposing him to the angel would shake loose more than just clues about the book. She forced a smile. "All right, but I will do the talking."

Ales barely touched, the group disbanded from the table. Claire ducked toward the back with Andras while Brevity shoved cakes in her pockets and began a loud round of drink buying and shoulder slapping to cover their exit.

15

RAMIEL

On the subject of angels: be not afraid.

Oh, hush. Let an old crone have her fun.

No, really, kiddo. Don't mess with 'em. They're all hopping mad as the English. And twice as dangerous.

Librarian Fleur Michel, 1762 CE

THE FROTH ON THE ale was good. By rights, a pour that resulted in a head like that should have flattened the taste of the beer, but the drink was a crisp relief beneath the soft foam. Like Vikings, angels had a good appreciation for an excellent brew. There was a reason monks brewed ale to supplement their monasteries.

Ramiel was surprised to find he enjoyed Valhalla, though he was certain enjoyment wasn't part of Uriel's plan. The plan, of course, was to bust down the doors of the realms, find and confront the librarian, and get out before an interrealm grievance could be filed. The paperwork for that would be atrocious.

They'd been lucky to find Hell's representatives so fast. They'd been unlucky, however, to find them in the arena, fighting with cleverness and heroics, two things that were certain to endear them to Valhalla's residents immediately.

Uriel had threatened to start glowing, a very bad sign, until Rami had coaxed her into a back corner and explained they needed a new approach. It'd taken some talking to make her see the logic.

Contrary to Uriel's speech, Heaven was not set above Valhalla, Hell, or anywhere—all the after-realms maintained a careful, if grudging, balance sustained by the fuel of belief and the flow of souls to each realm. Realms of similar purpose were often most harmonious, but all of them were sovereign. An incident here, between two paradise realms, could upset all of it for centuries. Thankfully, the Light of God had eventually calmed down enough for them to formulate a new plan: gather information on Hell's activities and apprehend its representatives the moment they isolated themselves from the realm's warriors.

Uriel, of course, had taken up a very visible and glowering guard by the front entrance. She'd made no effort to fill in Valhalla's master of the guard, an old warrior named Ragna, on what brought them there, declaring Heaven's business was no one else's if they were acting within the rights of the treaty. Even a formal stance couldn't hide the repulsed looks Uriel cast at the Vikings.

To be fair, the residents of Valhalla appeared to quickly develop the same sentiment toward her. Rami saw how companionable smiles quickly fell to suspicious frowns over their ale. Uriel had never had patience for the souls that chose other realms, worshipped other gods, and once again Rami wondered why she'd left Heaven for this. Hunting was primarily a game of information, and there would be no information to be gained without the goodwill of Valhalla's denizens.

She did, at least, serve as an admirable distraction. He had told Uriel that he would sweep the hall for other exits and then promptly left her to her self-righteous watch.

It hadn't taken long to find out where Hell's servants gathered. The librarian and her champion were still missing, but Rami recognized the bewildered-looking young man who had accompanied her on Earth. He was with a pair of companions, a demon and a spirit he couldn't identify but who radiated curiosity and sticky fingers.

But it was the boy who seemed the oddest of the group. He was changed, now with the pointed ears, red eyes, and sharp pale cheekbones of a minor demon, not the harmless human he'd presented himself as before. It riled Rami—further proof that all souls in Hell were liars—but he made no move to confront them. Patience was also a virtue in Heaven.

Which is how he found himself in a publike room near the rear exit of the longhouse, virtuously enjoying a mug of dark ale. It appeared to be a keg room, one of many, considering Valhalla's infinite supply. But in front of the old barrels a high table had been set up, with several stools to form a makeshift bar. The crowd was small, an eddy in the greater raucous sea of the main hall, but it appeared even Valhalla had introverts. It was a welcome pause from the chaos of the party.

In a strange way, he felt comfortable here. These mortal souls were strange with their hairy bodies and unfamiliar gods, but they were *soldiers*; Ramiel could understand soldiers. He had quickly gone to work plying them with just enough ale and cheerful aggression to justify conversation.

According to the others, the visitors from Hell had arrived shortly before the angels, and with no treaty recognized, they'd been immediately challenged to combat. They'd been forced to oblige, claiming they sought audience with the storyteller. That was good, because it meant they likely did not yet have what they'd come for. Rami didn't have a clue how Valhalla was tied to that dangerous bit of paper, but it bought him time.

It was simple to survey the impression they'd made—most had been impressed with the champion's courage and skill, if not necessarily his appearance. "Too smooth. He'll freeze his chin off," one soul with a particularly impressive red beard had grumbled.

Rami also discovered, to his surprise, that even more admiration had begun to coalesce around the librarian.

"Not a bonny lass, course. Someone should tell her t' smile," grunted a bald and tattooed man with an ax strapped shoulder to torso. "But she got good and bloodied. And put down Uther with a word, imagine! Handy trick, that."

"Sommat a Freyja-touched in that one. Good thing the naked babe they called a champion had her to mind 'em," another said, bringing about another rather telling round of speculation about the fighter's looks.

"If you say so." It was hard not to let judgment lace his voice. The librarian seemed just as arrogant and unrepentant as every other servant of Hell he'd encountered. He could not parse the idea of honor being attributed to anyone consigned to that realm.

"Puts a man in mind o' what stories a teller like that could tell," added the squat, walking beard on his other side. "Or what she could do with a proper weapon. Mark my words—lass like her's got spirit. I'd love to get her in the ring."

"Or in bed, eh, Holfad?" And both warriors devolved into an entirely inappropriate exchange about the relative bed-warming merits of both the librarian *and* her champion.

But that had been two ales ago. By now the small barroom had emptied out as the more sociable warriors flowed back to the halls and the less sociable ones went to sleep. Rami took the opportunity to process his drink and his night.

Their prey had obviously made too big an impression for Valhalla to look the other way when Heaven confronted them. He and Uriel were warriors, and therefore respected in Valhalla, but from the way the Norse storyteller had taken the librarian under his wing, it seemed Hell had friends in Valhalla as well. The trick would be catching them alone.

The reflection of his frown abruptly dissolved into ripples in his drink. A fresh mug careened against his, spilling a generous portion of the contents of both across his knuckles.

He jerked his head up. The curse on his lips died as his eyes landed on the woman at the other end of the bar. She had one arm bandaged, poorly, and her braided hair was in some disarray. But that coin-flip smile was just as unreadable as on the pier. The librarian had the look of someone caught perpetually midsecret.

She raised her own mug at him. "Sorry—I'm a poor shot. Bars weren't places for a lady when I was around. Or, at least," she amended after a pause, "not the kind of lady my family allowed me to be."

Instead of responding, Rami gave the room a sweeping glance. The pub was but not quite deserted, with a few inhabitants drinking by the fire. The keg master in the corner gave them a shrewd squint before turning back to his cups. A silent warning not to start any trouble.

"Librarian." Rami felt caught halfway between a grunt and a sigh. The woman had the knack to wear him down in a blink.

"Claire," she corrected. "It's Claire, by the way. If you're going to be hunting us, threatening destruction of our immortal souls, all that, personal names seem like the proper thing."

Rami bristled and found new fascination with his drink. The weight of her gaze on his shoulders was nearly intolerable until she pushed herself from her stool and slid down the bar. She stopped one seat away, just out of arm's reach. So she wasn't entirely stupid.

"What brings an angel to the halls of Valhalla?"

"I imagine the same thing that brings Hell's servants."

At the corner of her mouth there might have been a flutter of irritation that was quickly smoothed away. "Tenant. Not a servant."

Rami snorted, though he found his tongue considerably looser than he liked. He was not like Uriel, disdaining every soul not Heavenbound—he of all people knew the many paths that led everyone astray—but the librarian's manner set him on edge. A creature of Hell that didn't consider itself a servant was either dangerous or a fool. It was beginning to strike Rami that the librarian might be both.

Rami must have muttered that thought out loud, because the woman laughed. "A fool. That might be fair. From time to time." She surprised him by taking the insult with a shrug.

Rami tried again. "Where's your pet demon? Tired of pretending he's human?"

"Leto *is* human. Though . . . I suppose convincing you of that story would take too long for one drink," she said. "But my other pet demon is here, so I don't disappoint you. Say hello, Andras."

In a blink, a figure dressed in fussy silks sat where no one had been before. Sharply pointed ears and pupils the color of blood gold marked him as, indeed, a demon, and a powerful one at that. Black-striped hair glinted like a pelt in the dim light. The taste of sulfur slicked the back of Rami's throat and burned his tongue. The handsome demon looked harmless and familiar, in the way of the worst childhood nightmares. He gave a mild smile that was too well crafted to be sincere.

"'Hello, Andras,'" the demon mimicked politely. "I am not a pet, by the way."

"Apologies, Arcanist. I was merely speaking his language. We're less than animals in some eyes," Claire said with a cool look at Rami.

"So I hear." Andras swept his eyes over Rami with a look that felt surgical, claws hidden in a velvet glove. *A predator behind those glasses,* Rami felt in an instant. He recalculated his estimation of the creature.

The Library had brought force. It seemed an odd way to show their hand. Rami shifted to keep an eye on the demon, though found he much preferred looking at Claire. "I take it you've found what you seek here?"

"Not yet," she said easily and, Rami thought, a bit too promptly. "But travel is taxing on our kind. We intend to enjoy Valhalla's excellent hospitality. Price of admission was high enough, so we might as well get our money's worth. Leave tomorrow evening."

Rami doubted it. "And I suppose this visit means you don't intend to surrender the book."

"What book would that be, again?"

"You obviously know of what I speak. You stole it from me."

"The scrap, you mean. A misunderstanding, really." Claire shook her head. "You know, if you'd been just a little more patient and a little clearer when we met, you'd still be in possession of it. Here I thought angels were supposed to be forgiving and kind."

"I'm not that kind of angel."

"I know very much what kind of angel you are, Ramiel, Thunder of God, Watcher of the World. Question is, why is a *fallen* angel helping Heaven?" Claire tilted her head. "Why are you here?"

Rami fell silent. He knew there was nothing to say.

The abomination wrapped in a gentleman's skin didn't help matters. "Ask him what Heaven's offered him," Andras said.

Claire frowned. "I wasn't aware that Heaven was in the dealmaking business."

"You'd be surprised." Andras shrugged.

"All right, I'll bite. What's Heaven offered you to jump-start a war, Ramiel?"

"Again, not your concern—" Rami paused. "What war?"

Claire exchanged a look with the demon, but only Rami saw the look that crossed Andras's face as Claire glanced away. Eyes narrowed, lip twitched up. Pleased. Possessive. Predatory. While Claire sat with the creature at her side as if it were a favored pet.

For the first time, Rami wondered if the librarian knew what kind of creature she had at her back. But his speculation was cut short by Claire's sniff.

"Are you telling me you're hunting a book whose purpose you don't understand?"

"And what should I know, Librarian?"

The librarian's brown eyes gleamed with amusement. "I'll give you one thing for free, though I know you won't believe me: what you're after is not anything Heaven has a right to. And your interference here could cost the mortal world dearly. More than that, you'll need to ask your terrifying partner."

"Uriel has told me all I need to know about your sins." The creeping, hollow unease in his chest made Rami toss out the first rebuttal he could think of. Harsh and untrue, but he knew better than to admit that to servants of Hell.

Both Claire and the demon fell silent.

"The angel out front is . . . Uriel?" Claire asked.

Rami cursed himself for rising to the bait. He pushed the still half-full mugs away from him as he stood from the bar.

"Surrender the artifact and give up this errand, Librarian." Rami's jaw tightened. "Don't risk your eternal soul."

"I find myself already damned, but your concern is noted. I'd watch the threats. We're guests of some very nice hosts with very large axes," Claire said, gaze falling to where Rami's fingers brushed the hilt at his side.

Rami made a slow show of measuring the room. "You've found yourself some privacy, Librarian. What if my good friend the bartender decides to step out?"

The librarian looked scandalized. "My goodness. Someone is desperate. Whatever will we do? I suppose that depends." She cleared her throat and raised her voice. "What exactly *is* the protocol for handling aggressors in Valhalla, Arlid?"

Rami stifled the urge to jerk back as a leather-clad raven woman dropped from a shadow in the rafters. The woman squinted her kohl-heavy eyes, none too happy at being called out. "Aggressors are fed to the flock."

"And am I the aggressor in this scenario?"

"No." Arlid's lip curled. "But the night is young."

Claire turned to Rami. "There, you see. The raven captain has been keeping an awfully close eye on me and will be making sure the only one who gets to rough me up is her. You are welcome to test that, of course, but I think you'll find she likes her duty even more than she loathes me. Isn't that right, Arlid?"

"You have no honor," Arlid muttered.

"Something you two agree on," Claire agreed. Her eyes dropped to his coat. "It's a shame that your feathers are the wrong color for her flock."

Rami worked his jaw but said nothing. It was the second time tonight he had been surprised by Hell. He found he didn't care for it.

Claire shrugged and slid one of the abandoned drinks to Andras, though Rami noted she'd never touched her own. "The bottom line is this: the book is under the protection of the Library now. It belongs in Hell. Heaven should mind its own business."

"Not when the safety of humanity is at stake," Rami said.

"Funny, that's why I'm here too." The woman gave a rueful smile that was so human it made the backs of Rami's hands itch. He wasn't used to interacting with human souls from other realms. He'd spent plenty of time among souls on Earth during his stint as a guide for the lost, not to mention his time in exile among mortals during Earth's earliest history. But a human soul that chose an eternity in Hell? He couldn't understand that. Especially a soul that seemed so . . . practical. He half wished she'd be as sinister as her demon attendant. It would ease that wrong feeling at the back of his head.

Rami shook the thought from his shoulders and stood. "You work for the Deceiver."

No one followed as he left, though Rami thought he heard a long sigh at his back before it was swept up in the increased noise of the hall. Rami hit the door hard enough to make it rock on its hinges as he waded into the sea of revelers. He needed to clear his head. He needed to form a plan.

He needed information for a plan. Answers.

Uriel was in deep conversation by the time Rami found her again in the main hall.

Or, rather, the broad-shouldered creature with a pair of double axes on his hip was in deep conversation. Uriel looked distinctly unamused. Not that Uriel was in the habit of being amused ever, but she held a glare for the Viking man that she usually reserved for improperly tempered blades and disappointing reports.

"No. I am not interested. Thank you."

"But a maiden like yourself—"

"Move. On."

"Trouble?" Rami asked as he slid to fill the space vacated.

"Humans." Uriel grunted the word like it left a bad taste in her mouth. "It defies logic that their base interest in reproduction lasts beyond death. And the entitlement to it! Arrogant, all of them."

"Hmm, yes. The arrogance. Imagine." Rami guided Uriel into a quiet corner. "I encountered the librarian and her people."

Uriel raised a brow. "Demons?"

"At least one. I don't know him from . . . before. But powerful, danger-ous."

"What did you learn?"

"They do not have possession of the artifact, but their hunt led them here, and the librarian considers it under the jurisdiction of the Library."

Uriel waved that away too easily. "Heaven's claim supersedes that of any other realm."

"She also implied that there's more to this artifact than powerful magic." Rami said it with a dismissive air but watched Uriel's reaction carefully. She tilted her chin but looked out over the crowd, hiding the pull of her expression.

"Is that so? How curious."

"Is it true?"

"Acquire the artifact and we'll know." Her answer only seeded the doubt in his gut. Uriel turned back to him. "Their plan?"

"I gathered that they were waiting for something they needed here. She said they would be leaving tomorrow," Rami said. "She was lying, of course."

"Glad to see your time in the wild hasn't made you entirely soft." Uriel narrowed her eyes and searched for something in the crowd. "We will need to intercept them."

"Any attempt to confront them will get us expelled from Valhalla. Or worse," Rami said, thinking of the raven captain and her guard.

"Not if they stray someplace where Valhalla isn't watching. First rule of demons, Ramiel: you can always rely on servants of Hell to be where they shouldn't."

16

CLAIRE

It's not magic, what we librarians do. It's the same as what our imaginations tried to do when we were alive; the realm just takes a more literal interpretation of it. The pen and paper are a librarian's tools of office. With them, we can weave stories back together by force of will. Guide lost ink, draw a plot back to its true north.

Without 'em, we're just exceptionally long-lived busybodies.

Then again, sometimes busybodies are the only ones to get anything done.

Librarian Fleur Michel, 1735 CE

THE FEATHERS FROTHED AND churned like a small storm cloud clinging to the Watcher. Claire kept her eyes on it until he disappeared through the swinging door. Then she allowed herself to let out a long breath.

"Well, that was bracing." Andras drew a fingertip over his lip, amusement ill concealed. He took a neat sip of ale.

Claire, on the other hand, was too much on edge to drink, unlike the demon and the damned angel. Ramiel had been in easy conversation with the warriors when they'd found him, forcing Claire and Andras to hang back until his drinking companions had left.

He was comfortable here, Claire realized as they'd waited. Comfortable and with a stronger natural connection with this place than Claire or even Hero could hope for. If it came down to forcing Valhalla to choose a side, Bjorn's allegiance to the Library wouldn't be enough. Brevity's charm wouldn't be enough. If the angels pushed, it was only a matter of time before Valhalla's hospitality showed cracks.

"We need to get out of here." The conclusion brought her up out of the chair.

Andras nodded as he followed. "We should have time if they think we're staying the night."

"He didn't buy it." Claire had seen it in the angel's eyes. All angels had keen eyes, but Ramiel seemed particularly tuned to reading mortals. At any other time, she would have found it interesting, a deviance in the angelic personality type, but right now it was a significant threat. She would need to avoid revealing too much next time they crossed paths. "We need to leave as soon as we speak to Bjorn. Before they have time to plan."

"That necessitates that we act without a plan." Andras was displeased. "I'm a very big proponent of plans. Ardent fan, even."

Claire waved a vague hand as they left. "Can't be helped. We'll be doing this the human way: quick and improvised."

THE MAIN HALL HAD progressed beyond boisterous celebration and into clusters of dedicated drinkers industriously working toward a stupor. This worked in Claire's favor, as the path had eased and the largest warriors still blocking her path had become significantly less mobile. She and Andras wound their way through the stifling hall toward Bjorn's study.

Claire touched her hand to the handle but paused when raised voices trickled through the rough wood.

"Showman like you, thought you'd appreciate admirers."

"You're not admiring, lad. You're molesting."

"Merely partaking of the simple joy of fine literature. I was bravely wounded in battle, you know."

"Don't think I can't finish the job!"

Claire gave a sigh and pushed through the door. The study was still a picture of clutter and warmth, but this time a very agitated storyteller paced in front of the fireplace. Hero perched in an armchair and shook a partially unfurled scroll as a greeting. "Warden! I do believe I've found our host's weakness. Had you merely rumpled his manuscripts in the ring, this whole nonsense would have resolved itself."

"I see you're feeling well enough to be a nuisance again, Hero."

He was pale, but his wrist appeared restored, and the cuts on his face were gone. He didn't rise from the chair, which could indicate some stiffness, but he seemed in one piece.

Hero chuckled. "The healers here are marvelous. I suppose they get some practice."

Claire made sure the door was firmly closed before approaching the group. Brevity and Leto were present, the latter a dark shadow positioned closer to the door, having obviously taken the "keep Bjorn there" order with teenage seriousness. He gave Claire a tight nod as she entered with Andras. Darkness pooled under his eyes, and Claire made a mental note to enforce a rest when they had a chance. Demons didn't need sleep. Human souls didn't either, technically, but every human psyche needed a break. Mental breakdowns happened in the afterlife just as easily as they did in the world above, and Leto had been through more than enough.

"Brev, please see if Bjorn can point you in the way of a decent teapot." Claire had her own ways of shoring up her psyche, after the interrogative game with the angel. Brevity wiggled her way free of couch cushions, and Claire turned her attention to the still glowering storyteller. "Problems, Bjorn?"

"He doesn't like me reading his books . . . scrolls . . . things," Hero offered.

"I don't mind if you read. I mind if you *converse* with them," Bjorn snapped, finally succeeding in sweeping the scroll out of Hero's hands. He turned to Claire. "Who leaves a hero unattended in a library?"

"I watched him!" Brevity protested as she hung a small pot of water—

no teapots in Valhalla, but it appeared Brevity had improvised—over the fire.

"Great lot of good it's done. He's been chatting up every tale he can get his hands on."

"I'm a story. They're a story. I was simply being friendly," Hero said with an elegant shrug. "Besides, I learned a few things. Lots of strategic texts around here. Might help me keep my head on my shoulders next time I'm forced into the warden's service."

"Must you persist in calling me a warden?" Claire asked.

Hero's smile was a calculated dazzle. "Would you prefer jailer? Or shall I curtsy and call you mistress?"

"Nuisance."

"Warden."

"Ass."

"It's not right!" Bjorn interrupted, leathery face creating even more wrinkles as he drew a hand over his long beard. "Learning changes a character. Changes a *story*. This is irresponsible."

He was entirely correct, and a twinge of regret nagged at her. Claire knew Bjorn's concern as well as any librarian. Hero was a character. He came out of his book with certain skills, certain knowledge, a personality, even, all based on who he was in his story. The longer he remained separated from his book and unable to go back, the more likely that would change.

If you considered Hero human, it was a good thing. But if you considered Hero what he was—a living portion, only one small part of a larger book—it was making him something other than his original character. It would be harder than ever to fit him back into his pages. It was why when books woke up, excepting the damsels, they were quickly put back to sleep again. But Claire was the one who'd dragged him along. She told herself it was necessary.

It was his choice if he wanted to change. It came with a strange, guilty foreboding, the idea of giving a character a choice again. Of making that mistake again.

"It can't do any more harm than has already been done." Claire finally settled on an adequate response.

"Bah!" Bjorn threw up his hands. "Sorry excuse for a party, this is. Just tell me why your apprentice hauled me out of my cups before dawn."

"Answers, Bjorn. You owe us some, and we don't intend to wait while you sleep off a hangover." Claire fished in her pockets until she came up with the Codex Gigas scrap. "You've guessed why we're here."

Bjorn hissed, shrill like a teakettle. He shoved Claire's wrist back into her pocket. "Don't bring that thing out here." Claire raised her brows and trailed her gaze down to his hand. Bjorn released her with a sigh. "That thing's brought me nothing but trouble."

"And yet you seem to have done a shoddy job of ridding the world of it," Andras observed. Bjorn wheeled on him.

"Destroying it was *your* predecessor's job, demon. Not mine. Direct your bellyaching to him. I was just supposed to find the bloody thing," the storyteller said. He paused to fetch his half-empty mug of ale before continuing. "You must already know about the missing pages, then."

"Yes," Claire said before Andras could cast the acid she saw brewing on his lips. "It appears they've turned up in the world again. It's very important that we locate them before any other . . . interested parties."

"You mean Heaven, eh." Bjorn did not phrase it as a question, and no one bothered to answer it. "That lot never did understand books. Well, I tracked the book the first time just as you would. The Arcanist brought me in because it was a book. It wasn't part of *my* library, but she and I collaborated and created a calling card for the task. Tricky bit of magic, if I do say so myself."

Claire was desperate enough to entertain hope. "You still have this calling card?"

"Why would I do a fool thing like that?"

"Call it a hunch." Claire flicked her free hand at the catastrophic clutter around them. "You don't seem like the type to get rid of anything."

Bjorn's fist tightened in his beard and he sighed. "Something wasn't right. The way the old skinflint was acting about it. Hiding a thing like that on Earth. I mighta held on to a scrap, but it will do you no good. It's too damaged to give a location."

Claire's hopes fell. "There's no other way to track it?"

"Not by Library means, no." Bjorn frowned into his mug. The logs in the fire ticked before he seemed to decide something. "But it's not a book of the Library, not unwritten—it's a book of the realms. There are *means* outside the Library."

Brevity handed Claire her tea and crinkled her brow. "How's that possible?"

Bjorn chuckled. "Which do you think came first, little apprentice? Books or tales? It's like I told your senior before. The first library was a song. I daresay I've learned more about the sound of a story since I came to Valhalla."

Claire could tell the old man was dancing around something he wasn't exactly eager to share. "So, there is a way to track it. Out with it, Bjorn. Please."

Bjorn pressed his wrinkled lips together. "There's more to a story than just its pages. Yes, put together with my fragment, if that little paper of yours cooperates, you might have a way to go. But you're not going to like what it takes."

"The best stories are bled," Claire muttered, almost like a chant, before shrugging. "I'll do what's necessary."

Bjorn's eyes dropped to the bag on her hip. "You have to give up your books until you find it."

Claire nearly snorted into her tea, and she set the mug down carefully. "I beg your pardon? Not more of this duel nonsense—"

"Not for a duel, Librarian. Until you locate your quarry, you have to leave your books. It won't work otherwise."

"The notes I brought are the only tools I'll have in the mortal world. You're asking us to continue on completely defenseless. With two violent representatives from Heaven at our backs." Claire narrowed her eyes. "You're going to have to explain a bit more than that."

"The voice of the book. The music—the song of the tale." Bjorn paused with a glance toward Leto and Andras. "Every book has it—you know, the book's way of talking, the words it uses, the rhythm of the speaker in your head as you read. Its voice. Each one a bit unique to the author and the tale. Before the written word, it was even more important. Every storyteller worth their salt knew how to create their own voice, mimic others, and find the beat that wove it."

"Well, obviously not *every* storyteller." Claire was droll. "You're talking about an actual . . . narrative voice . . . of books. A sound. A song. That's ridiculous."

"Says the woman accompanied by a muse, two demons, and Prince Charming," Andras added.

"I've been librarian for three decades and never heard of such a thing."

"A whole three decades? Goodness." Bjorn didn't hide his disdain.

"It . . . makes sense," Brevity said slowly, drawing Claire's attention. She fidgeted, fussing with the cooling pot of tea before looking up. "Muses see more parts of a book than librarians do. They got these colors, these— Well, it wouldn't surprise me if they got a song too."

"Just so," Bjorn said. "The Library wouldn't have bothered with it much. Too many books, too many restless tales coming and going. I didn't know about it till I got here. Things are . . . more sedate here."

Hero snorted.

"You learned how to work with these 'songs' here in Valhalla," Claire guessed. "And you think you know the voice, the . . . song . . . of the codex?"

"I don't." Bjorn gestured a knobby hand at her skirt pockets. "But if that paper will tell me, I know how to listen. Coupled with the calling card, we might be fixed to jigger a clear tune. A book of the realms won't be sharing a song with any other book, so it should lead you right to what you're seeking."

Claire considered. "You still haven't explained why I have to leave my books."

"Too noisy! Too loud. You're already going to be tryin' to pick out a who-knows-how-old song out of a million stories in progress in the mortal world. There are ways of sorting that out—written stories, existing stories, simple enough to mute and filter out. But those unwritten books and personal notes in your bag, Librarian? Coupled with your own words? Unwritten stories are like ink in water. You'll never follow the thread if you're distracted."

A disquiet began to creep up Claire's back. She flicked an unsettled glance at the rest of the group, and Brevity shook her head emphatically. Abandoning her books was antithetical to every duty a librarian had. The only powers she *had* were with the tools of her office. Even trusting them in the care of another librarian felt . . . wrong.

Without them, she'd be more vulnerable. She'd be more . . . human. Claire dropped her gaze for the first time and studied the fraying edge of the bandage that wrapped around her left arm.

It all came back to finding the lost pages of the codex. Hero's return to his book, Brevity's training, Leto's mystery, even her own duties as librarian of the Unwritten Wing, had all taken a backseat the moment she'd decided to close the Library and follow a raven out of Hell. She was responsible for those that followed after her, though.

It had changed the moment Andras painted a future where the Library could be destroyed for doing its duty. Where Heaven was willing to wage war for a secret. The archangel and the Watcher outside were nothing compared with what that would look like. And if she and Leto, as human souls, got caught outside Hell when their ghostlights went out, even worse things would be after them. She was risking all of them, in various ways.

Abandoning her books would open her to more risks. But it was the only clear path ahead for any of them.

"Teach me this 'song' of yours, and I'll consider leaving my books. *Consider* it." Claire paused. "Except one. Hero needs to keep his book nearby, for obvious reasons. Unless Hero believes he's found his kin in Valhalla?"

Hero let out a mirthless laugh. "Stay with this bearded mayhem? I'd rather eat my sword."

"See, he's warmed right up to us. Like family, we are," Brevity chirped.

Bjorn shuffled his feet, slanting a disgruntled gaze at Hero, before nodding. "It'll be better if he can keep it quiet, but keep him at a distance when you're listening, and it might work."

Claire felt the gathered eyes shift back to her. It felt like a weight settled on her shoulders. She stood, slinging the bag from her grasp. She first dug out Hero's book, newly replaced pages still gleaming glaring white next to their faded yellow cream brothers. She held it out to him with one hand. "You're still in Special Collections, mind. Don't make me regret this."

"As always, your faith sustains me." Hero found an inside coat pocket, and the book diminished slightly to fit.

Claire carried the bag over to Brevity and slung the strap over her assistant's head before she could protest. "Hold these for now."

Brevity's nose crinkled as she took the bag. "What are you thinking, boss?"

"Just hold them. We're not leaving quite yet," Claire said, dodging the question. That part could wait. Rid of her possessions, she turned again to Bjorn. In her chest there was a lightness that was unexpected. Hollow, vulnerable, but it was done. The act of doing had a decisive power in itself. "Ready when you are, storyteller."

Bjorn nodded and turned toward the bookcase near the fireplace. He shuffled the scrolls on the middle shelf for a moment before there was a thunk. The shelves melted into thin air to reveal a night full of stars behind it. "We'll need to get away from my collection as well, if we're going to be proper about it."

17

BREVITY

❡

[An entry barely legible through a halfhearted attempt to blot
and scrape the parchment clean:]

I've been through the records. Each apprentice in the Library
can expect, on average, at least a couple decades of education
before the sitting librarian retires to wherever they go.
   Decades.
   . . . I had three years.
   I can't do this. Gregor, I can't do this. Please.

[Entry followed by a much clearer addition:]

Arcanist Andras has politely offered to assist in the Unwritten
Wing until I can brief myself on the full log of instructions. He's
been efficient and helpful, and not asked any more questions
than necessary. He's a godsend, as blasphemous as that phrase
may be in my present situation. More than that, he's been kind.
He brought me a new teakettle the other day. God knows where
you acquire such a thing down here.
   I suppose I'll have all the time in the world to repay the kindness.

Librarian Claire Hadley, 1989 CE

VALHALLA WAS A CANDY jar to a muse. Brevity's fingers traced the carved wood handle of her mug and she grinned into the fizzy drink, a little drunk on the feeling of it. Valhalla was as full of art and beauty as any afterlife, but what set it apart was *passion*. Strength and survival and unbridled passion, not anchored to a single song or story but lived. Knit in the blood flow. Salted in the sweat. Simmered in the saliva.

Hmm. Yes, it had definitely gone to Brevity's head. Not that she could be faulted; if inspiration was the trade of muses, passion was their fuel.

After Claire had foisted her bag onto Brevity and followed Bjorn, Hero had announced he needed to drink, and Brevity followed under the guise of making sure he didn't disappear with his book. That had been nearly an hour ago. Now Hell's contingent took up a table at the far side of the hall and sat—human, demon, book, and muse—avoiding one another by contemplating their drinks. It struck Brevity that Claire had picked them all up, for one reason or another, like toy soldiers. Without her abrading presence, they fell apart.

Brevity, at the very least, could fix that. "Whatchya got?" she asked, perhaps a bit too loudly, pointing to Leto's drink.

He nearly choked on his sip. "Cider. Hero found it for me."

"From the kids' table," Hero supplied with a wink.

"Not sure Valhalla would have that," Brevity said.

"With these savages, it wouldn't surprise me if there was. Can't you see it? Murderous children! Slaying toddlers for honor and other useless virtues . . ." Hero managed to get his bandage wet as his drink sloshed. He pulled a face. "At least there's liquor."

"No desire for honor?" Andras joined in, which surprised Brevity. In all the years she'd been in his acquaintance, the Arcanist had possessed excellent manners but also a low tolerance for small talk. Now he looked at Hero like he was a particularly novel new artifact.

"Honor is nothing but cold pity for the dead. Better not to fail at staying alive. Or avoid the conflict in the first place," Hero said.

Andras's eyes narrowed. "A rather unorthodox position for a hero to take."

A tic appeared in Hero's jaw and was just as quickly tucked away. "I'll choose to interpret that as a compliment. There are plenty of ways to be . . . heroic." His brow knit, and he frowned into his drink before changing the subject. "Does it bother you that we seem to be left waiting around like useless lapdogs?"

"I don't know. You did get to star in that duel," Leto offered, and Hero snorted.

"The next call we have for a sacrificial lamb, the honor's all yours."

"Could you have really died?" Leto asked, betraying more curiosity than he seemed ready to admit. Brevity had noted the way his eyes had brightened as he watched the fight, much more interested in the deadly slaughter between Hero and the giant than in Claire's battle of words. He was a teenage boy, so some excitement might be expected, but she didn't like the way Leto had finally seemed to perk up at violence and cruelty. Demon things, not human things, in Brevity's opinion. Claire insisted Leto was human, but Brevity could see more. Leto was a human, but a hollowed-out human. Someone had scooped out his human life and filled him all up with darkness and demon stuff, like tar inside a candy shell. Brevity worried that unless they drained it out soon, the tar would stick. And that'd be a tragedy. Leto was sweet, and there was nothing more amazing than a human, in Brevity's book.

"I mean, being a book or . . . a character from a book and all," Leto finished weakly.

"I'm sorry—was my bruising not realistic enough for you? Prefer a little more ink on the sand? Did my wrist not crack in a convincing manner? Really, what more heroics do you expect of me?" Hero arched a brow. "Without a welcoming book that I can return to and escape damage, I am just as destructible as anyone else. More so, even, since I don't have a soul like a human. I'll crack and burn and fall to ash easy as anything." Hero's lip curled. "You saw for yourself—just because a book can be fixed doesn't mean it can't be ruined."

He'd done that damage to himself, but Brevity wasn't about to rouse his irritation by saying so. Leto tilted his head. "But it's not as if any of us are mortal—"

"There are worse things done to a man than death," Andras mused.

There was a tone in the way he said it, academic and contemplative of potential. Hero's disdain turned toward a new target. "That sounds like a threat, Arcanist. But you're the cheapest puzzle out of all of us, I think."

Andras's smile grew indulgent. He reclined in his seat. "Please, go on."

Hero didn't need the encouragement. "You're a demon, and demons seek power. You're a former duke, so I am guessing you never shied from ambition. Yet you're dusting trinkets in the Library. The Arcane Wing— and the relationship with Claire—what's it get you?"

The light of the longhouse had shifted as the celebrations had wound down, flickering torches and thick lanterns swaying under the jostling tremors of hundreds of Valhalla's residents. The shadow that slid across Andras's face could have been that, had it not pulled his features with it. Eyes darker, smile sharper, skin the color of old bone.

"Perhaps it gets me left alone," Andras said before Brevity could attempt an intervention. "Most learn after a brief period of my acquaintance to leave me alone. In case you haven't heard, I'm retired."

"I was under the impression demons never retired," Hero persisted.

"I was under the impression that heroes weren't impertinent fools."

"It appears we both exceed expectations," Hero allowed. Brevity thought perhaps he would drop it, but of course not. "And what do you want with Claire?"

"The librarian and I have a long history. You should remember that. She trusts me much more than she trusts you," Andras said, acid sweet. "Does that chafe, young hero?"

"Hardly." Hero let out a dignified sniff. "I'd expect wardens to plot together."

"D-don't take it personal-like!" Brevity was too happy to latch onto the insecure underbelly of Hero's words. Her stomach was already tied up in knots. Hero and Andras were frowning at each other, trading feints to reveal a hidden weakness. It struck Brevity as pointless—of *course* they all had secrets, regrets. It was what Hell was for. She stole Hero's attention by slapping him on the back. "Boss is really a softy underneath. She didn't care for me much either when I showed up."

"That woman doesn't have a caring bone in her body," Hero said dismissively.

Brevity's smile pulled tight. "It's a mite more complicated than that."

Understatement was something she'd learned from Claire. Brevity remembered cold tension, ashen skin, orders simmering with resentment, secrets tucked in the shadow of her eyes. The questions and library shelves Claire avoided. Muses were naturally drawn to humans, but Claire was an unwritten author. Brevity still caught her, now and then, staring at the inspiration on her skin, thoughts locked and far away.

Muses loved humans, authors doubly so, but the relationship with authors was always more complicated. Brevity had broken through Claire's hostility, in the end, with aggressive friendliness. Humans couldn't see like muses—they were practically blind, relying only on what things looked like on the outside. So Brevity had shaped her outside to what Claire needed. A cheerful teenage girl in need of guidance. Her apparent age, her personality, the way she talked. Muses had a knack for understanding what an author needed.

Claire had needed a friend. Maybe Claire still did.

"Give her time. She'll warm up to ya. You'll see," Brevity insisted, and put her full force of will into believing it.

"Mmm, no doubt you'll be eating out of the palm of her hand in time," Andras said. "Characters are fools for authors."

"She's not *my* author." Hero sounded positively horrified by the idea. "Your whole library can burn for all I care."

Instead of taking offense, Andras smiled so that it reached his eyes for the first time. "You are such an *interesting hero*, aren't you?"

Hero came to an unnatural stillness. Before Brevity could figure out a new distraction, the door to Bjorn's office boomed open.

Claire slunk through at a simmer, shaking her head at a parchment in her hands. Bjorn followed, and made an injured sound when Claire rolled up the paper and slapped it at him. "Well, this complicates things."

"We know where the codex pages are, then?" Leto asked.

"Bjorn's trick doesn't pinpoint a location, even with the paper shaving he has generously titled a calling card." Claire pointed to the carefully folded map in Bjorn's hands. "We can track it as far as an island in the Mediterranean. My educated guess would be Malta. We'll have to hope that the so-called song is clearer when we get there."

"You'll hear it. *If* you clear your head of other books." Bjorn unfolded the map and Claire leaned over his arm as they made notations.

Brevity took the chance to assess Claire. Her skin was waxy, shadows smudging her eyes and lips pressed thin. A pang of guilt washed over her, and she wondered if Bjorn's method would have been easier if she'd accompanied her. There'd been a moment, as they prepared to leave, when Bjorn had cast a silent glance at her inspiration gilt, a question in his eyes. Claire could leave behind her books, and Brevity would follow her anywhere. But there were things Brevity could not leave behind. Blue lines itched and twined against the soft skin of her wrist.

"The bigger question," Claire said after they were done, "is how to get there. I suspect ravens don't work both ways?"

"Ravens travel the realms freely, but only go to Midgard on Odin's word. If you think the ways of proving yourself to Valhalla are tedious, you don't want to try to seek the All-father's blessing."

"Fantastic," Claire muttered. "I assume you're about to suggest an alternative."

Bjorn grinned. "There's always the boat."

Claire rumpled her braids wearily. "Trust Vikings not to leave a simple road in and out of their own paradise."

"Where would the fun be in that?"

"*Fun* is not the primary—"

Hero cleared his throat and gestured. "Pardon the interruption of what I'm sure is about to be a fascinatingly dry debate, but you may wish to continue this on the way out." The mead-soaked chatter had shifted in the hall. Between bobbing heads and walls of armor, the two angels at the door had begun to argue. The tall woman in white—Uriel, Claire had said—turned abruptly and began to shove through the crowd. Her progress was hampered by the drum pit, but her gaze hunted through the crowd before locking on them.

"I don't think she wants a drink," Brevity murmured.

"So much for keeping the peace and slipping out quietly." Claire turned to Bjorn. "I assume there's another exit?"

"Valhalla hosts a door to each site of battle," Bjorn said grandly before adding, "and a couple to a nice picnicking spot or two." He shoved open the door to his quarters. "This way."

Brevity made to follow but stopped when Andras caught Claire's sleeve. They traded whispered words, and Claire looked displeased when Andras winked and stepped back into the crowd. Bjorn shoved the door behind them when they caught up. "About time that creature made himself useful."

Claire bristled. "Andras is a good—"

"Oh, I know precisely what the Arcanist is," Bjorn muttered grimly. He fished a tiny ivory tube from his pocket. It looked like a quill, but when he brought it to his lips, it let out a tritone trill. "Arlid, I got a task for your folk."

"I am sure she's close by," Claire said dryly.

Not waiting for a response, Bjorn led them through a new door in his study that opened to one crowded hallway. A tuneless hum cut through the low roar of voices. Brevity realized it was coming from Bjorn, causing Valhalla warriors to shift as they passed. Once they were through, the crowd seemed to redouble their celebrations, creating a rowdy wall between them and the angels pursuing.

"That's a neat trick," Brevity said.

"Storytelling." Bjorn gave a sly wink. "Try it sometime, lass. I bet you got a fair hand."

They shoved through a final door, and cool air swept some of the tension from Brevity. The wide meadow behind the longhouse was still and empty, painted indigo by starlight.

Shadows untangled from the eaves above them. Arlid, captain of the ravens, rose out of a crouch and dusted her leathers. "You called, storyteller?"

"We have some guests taking undue advantage of our hospitality. Not them." Bjorn waved his hand as the raven women wheeled on Claire. "The angels are getting twisted about in the halls behind us. I reckon it might be time to show them the way back to Heaven."

"With pleasure." Arlid's mouth curved into an unpleasant smile. "But what about them?"

"They are taking a different road," Bjorn grunted. "Just find and escort the two angels—they're likely getting into an illegal tiff with a hapless demon."

"One more, if I may," Claire said, drawing their attention. She had her hands folded in front of her in that rigid way that she always had when she was pretending to be harsher than she was. "One of my companions will also be returning to the Library in Hell."

A wilted sound came from Leto. He stepped forward, already entreating. "Please, I can do this—"

"Leto—"

"We're going to Earth. I've got a ghostlight and can help! I—"

"You will," Claire cut him off. Leto stopped and tilted his head like a confused puppy, and Claire squeezed his shoulder. Then she turned. Her eyes sought out Brevity, and Brev's stomach dropped. "You have the books."

Brevity's hand clenched around the bag she was still holding, then started to try to disentangle itself from it. "Me? No—boss, you need me." Her voice cracked, threatening to show the start of a panic she was too proud to admit to. Claire more than needed her. Of all the people she thought Claire would set aside, it couldn't be *her*. Brevity was her assistant. She was supposed to *assist*.

She wasn't quite sure who she was if she didn't assist. Failed muse, now a failed assistant? No. The thought felt like a fist clenched around her gut. "You need— Well, you need all the help you can get. I'm—"

"You're a librarian of Hell." Claire's voice was steeled, unforgiving. She stopped Brevity's movements and shoved the bag back into her possession. "I can't take my books, and we can't leave the Library unattended. I need you to return and take care of the books. This scavenger hunt may take longer than planned."

Her eyes were burning. Brevity tried to blink the despair away. "But— what changed?"

"Angels. Secrets. Too many coincidences. Something about this is not right." Her gaze flicked significantly over Brevity's head before returning. "I'll feel better knowing there's someone responsible taking care of the books."

Claire's compliments were rare things. In other circumstances, Brevity might have flushed under the praise. Instead, Brevity's throat felt tight. "I'm your assistant."

"And you're a librarian. I trust you." The honesty in Claire's voice stepped Brevity's panic down to a simmer. Honesty from Claire was also a gift, when not wielded like a weapon. Her smile was weak, so instead Claire swiftly reequipped herself with a frown. She squeezed Brevity's arm. "I'm just going on an errand. Don't be so sentimental."

Anxiety still twisted tight against her ribs, but she forced air between her teeth. "You can count on me."

"Good." As usual, Claire misread anxiety as eagerness. Brevity could barely enjoy the rare, warm smile that was there and gone. "Now, listen. Go back with the ravens. Wake up the Library—it will listen to you. I'll send messages if I can—you can have Walter help you do the same. Business as usual, but if anything troubling occurs, you have full authority to lock it down. Got it?"

"Lock it down? But I don't—"

"You can do this." Claire swept her up into a smothering hug that was almost as alarming as her orders. Things were truly serious if Claire was *hugging*. "I expect tea when we get back."

Brevity felt like she'd swallowed a slug. "Don't have any fun without me."

Claire made a dismissive noise. "No books, no annoying assistant, Mediterranean island. Going to be a vacation. Might not come back."

"Don't you dare." Further words were cut off by a disturbance of wood and steel coming from the longhouse. Arlid glanced at Bjorn, and he nodded.

"If yer goin', now is the time."

"We are." Claire released Brevity and nudged her toward the raven woman. "Make sure she gets back safe."

"That's up to her soul." Arlid gripped Brevity by her shoulders, jerked, and then the meadow disappeared in a smothering rush of frost and feathers.

18

CLAIRE

Books have songs, songs have stories, and then there're humans at the heart of the jumbled mess. I've come to the conclusion that you just can't subtract a human from the story, no matter how hard you try. Even death doesn't do that.

Librarian Bjorn the Bard, 1712 CE

BJORN LED THEM ON a serpentine path across the field, hiding their escape in a churn of lavender that tickled and tugged at Claire's skirts and suffused the air with flowers. The day had passed twilight into the kind of crystal night seen only in the after-realms. There was no wind to carry sound, but no one spoke, and for once Claire was happy for an absence of words. Leto's concern fluttered at her back like a wounded bird.

She wasn't running away, precisely. She was fulfilling her responsibilities, sending Brevity back to the Library. She'd waited too long to give Brev more responsibility anyway. Even if this all turned out to be a fool's errand, it was good for Brev to get a feel for running the desk. Brevity was competent, talented. The Library would mind her, and nowhere was safer. She would be fine.

She would be fine.

"All aboard." Bjorn broke into her thoughts as they stopped at the edge of a lake.

It was the same shore that they'd arrived on, cold and barren. There was no dock, just a stone-mortared embankment jutting out into the dark water like a tooth. A shabby weapon stand and a coil of rope were the only things that marked any official status. A small, open wood boat swayed, half-anchored on the sand. It was larger than a canoe, and the lip of the thin wood was painted a cheery green that didn't reassure Claire in the slightest.

Thick gravel churned under their feet, and the water sent a shock of ice through Claire's feet where it lapped at the toes of her shoes. She climbed aboard and Hero and Leto followed with significantly more reserve.

"We're sailing to Earth?" Leto asked, as if, after the day he'd had, that would be the logical conclusion.

"Just till we get out of the realm." Claire tossed Bjorn the rope that anchored them and passed an oar to Hero.

"I hope you know more of sailing than I do, warden." Hero eyed the oar with reluctance but positioned himself to row.

"Head toward the mists, fast as you can." Bjorn braced a foot on the bow of the boat and gave a shove to dislodge it from the gravel. "I'll handle the rest."

"Right. *You've* got the hard part." Claire caught herself as the boat began to hitch and bob beneath her.

"Just find those blasted scribbles before Heaven does."

"Beat an archangel, divert war, save our souls. Simple as that?" Claire called.

"I still got my bets set on you." Bjorn raised his voice to be heard as the boat drew out into the lake. His grin was a spark of white against the dark.

They cleared the shore, and Claire snapped up the second oar, earning a surprised nod from Hero as she bent in to row. They fell into a quick rhythm and were nearly to the mists when a noise rose up from shore.

Two figures—one tall and vengeful, one short and stony—appeared at the rise. Andras was nowhere in sight of the shore, which Claire hoped meant he'd escaped according to plan. The tall angel, Uriel, gave a cry and stormed down to the shore. Bjorn flourished a longbow from the weapon stand on the sand.

"Does the old kook really think he can fight a . . ." Hero's murmur turned to a squawk when the tip of the nocked arrow caught fire. "Wait. He's going to fire on us! *Us!*"

Claire redoubled her rowing and kicked Hero's ankle for him to do the same. "Technically, he's only supposed to fire on the boat, but I suppose it depends on his proficiency."

"You *knew* he was going to . . . to what end?" A yellow flare arched through the air, and Hero yanked Leto back with a grunt as the arrow struck the bow of the boat. The boy's eyes widened, and he flailed away from the flames.

"At least there's no kindling to . . ." Hero trailed off as the fire caught, leaping from arrow to boat hull with an unnatural ease. "I'm beginning to have a grievance with your plan, warden."

"Duly noted," Claire said. She shoved Leto behind her and grimaced as the fire began to lick around the edge of the boat. Cheerful green paint curled into smoke. "Just keep rowing."

"You're mad." Nonetheless, Hero turned his back on the fire to pole his oar into the water.

"The logic of most of these realms is that the way out and the way in are usually the same."

"Oh. A pyre at sea." Leto paled.

"Someone was listening during history class. Yes. A Viking burial. Full marks." Claire cast a quick glance to the shore. Through the smoke, she could see that the angels had waylaid Bjorn, and there was a furious argument under way.

Uriel had a great glowing sword out, and Bjorn stood, lean and proud, arms crossed over his chest. Ramiel, his squat and gray outline just barely visible next to Uriel's incandescent form, appeared to be trying to keep the calm.

But Uriel's shoulders were thrown back and even at this distance, the threat was visible and strumming. Claire had not expected the concern that gripped her chest. *Be careful, old man.*

"Will it hurt?" Leto asked.

"Hmm?" She pulled her attention back to the fire that was quickly eating at the sides of the boat. "Oh no, we're not required to burn, necessarily. If we can reach the mist by the time the boat goes, and I can keep hold of that trace, we should theoretically—"

"Claire," Hero interrupted. "Your skirts."

"Bother." Claire stamped her hand where scorched edges threatened to catch fire. The act scalded her palms, focused her attention. The heat was seeping through her shoes, and with a calm she did not feel she directed Leto to move toward the middle of the boat.

Hero eased his rowing as they reached where the fog grew thick at the center of the lake. "To think I'm beginning to miss the ravens . . ."

"What—" Leto's question was drowned out with a rush of air.

The fire consumed the boat whole in a flare of magical heat. Claire had just enough time to squeeze her eyes closed before the wood turned to ash under her feet and glacial water rushed over her head.

And for the second time in a day, Claire began to drown.

19

BREVITY

❦

A library without its librarian in residence is vulnerable as a bleating lamb. Librarians serve as the readers the unwritten books never had. It anchors them, quiets them, and assists in keeping them asleep in their binding. Walk careful in the long shadows of abandoned stacks, for you walk footpaths of restless dreams.

Librarian Ibukun of Ise, 991 CE

THE DOORS OF THE Unwritten Wing were not as foreboding as the Arcane Wing's. The Library veered away from Gothic wrought iron, and instead toward polished brass and light oaks. Brevity hadn't often had occasion to see the doors *closed*, though, and they loomed over her. Her hand hovered over the brass pulls, but she couldn't quite bring it to land.

The ravens had deposited her in the transport office, startling Walter into nearly dropping a jar. He'd been too flustered, and too kind, to ask questions, but she'd seen the way his gaze shifted over her shoulder, searching for Claire to appear behind her. The real librarian, not the clumsy excuse for an assistant. Claire wouldn't be coming—not for a while at least—and the tasks she'd hoisted on Brevity along with her books now felt like iron weights pressing on her ribs.

Brevity began to feel the cracks. Open the Library, run the Library, protect the Library. That's what she needed to do. That's what she'd done with Claire for years, but it was always *with Claire*. Claire had no idea what she was asking. Muses enabled, supported, inspired; they didn't *act*.

But muses also didn't stand around hallways looking foolish and green at the gills. At the corner of her vision, the gargoyle had begun to stare. Brevity pushed open the doors.

A locked-down library was a space of ink and whispers. The darkness was absolute; the blue glow of the inspiration on her wrist barely lit the gloom in front of her face. The light from the hallway behind her was immediately drunk up by the shadows pooling at her feet, so tangible that Brevity nearly tripped as she made her way in.

"It will listen to you. It *will* listen to you. It will *listen*. To *you*." Repeating it enough tamped down the flicker of apprehension in her chest. Brevity let the door close behind her and raised her voice. "Lights."

Even to her own ears, her impersonation of Claire's confident command felt quailing and swallowed up too fast in the dark. Brevity clenched her fists and tried to make her way to where she knew the front desk was. "Library . . . lights."

Her hip collided with a hard corner. A stack of books avalanched past her shoulder. "Oh, tit-eared motherfuck."

Muses didn't act, but they could cuss with the best. She continued her grumbles as she crouched to grope for the books. "C'mon. Lights . . . please? I *know* you can hear me!"

With an almost sullen slowness, a dim glow blossomed in the table lamp. It eased, unfurling light until it spread to the next sconce, then slowly began to light up the stacks. The Library responded with a resigned sigh, fluttered pages and sleepy shadows.

"You don't gotta be a jerk about it, you know." Brevity finished scooping up the books and surveyed the facing stacks. The light was too grudging to be bright and cheery like it was for Claire, but the glow was enough to make out the books still on their shelves, muted and sleeping, their trails of color dim and still.

The Unwritten Wing was a world of color to Brevity. Each book a whipping, seeking coil of light when it was awake. As a muse, she could see them. Books desperately wanted to be written, and were constantly sending out tendrils, hoping to catch and find purchase in a fertile mind. It had been nearly overwhelming when she'd first arrived, rejected and unwelcome. Claire had resented everyone back then, and she had been open about her feelings toward her new assistant. To be honest, the years hadn't made her much less brittle. Brevity often wondered, if Claire could see the books like she did, would she have more sympathy for the stories in her care? Brevity tried to care enough for them both.

Asleep, the books were withdrawn, tucked within their borders and emitting only dull pulses as Brevity passed. She picked a row at random and slowly walked the stacks, checking as she wrestled with her unease. These were books. She was a muse. This was the Library. This was *home*, or as near as Brevity could make one. She'd thrown her whole heart into making this home. There was no reason for the hairs on her neck to prick, for the inspiration gilt on her skin to coil and flutter anxiously.

But shadows gathered a little too deep in the corners of shelves, and books slept fitfully under her fingers as she ran them along the spines. Dust hung suspended in the light thrown by sconces, as if someone unknown had just passed through and left the Library unsettled in her wake. The gloom increased as she ventured farther into the stacks. The air became so still it suffocated. And as she turned a corner, cold hands landed on her goose-bumped skin.

A shriek, and probably several years of her immortal life, escaped Brevity. She spun, hands in front of her face though they couldn't quite decide whether to make a fist or shield. It took a moment for her heart to restart when she recognized the blue-skinned girl in front of her. "*Aurora!* Are you trying to kill me?"

Aurora was a damsel from a space thriller—likely from the late 1960s, if you judged by the skimpy miniskirt and midriff that she had arrived in. She'd built up more of a wardrobe over her years in the damsel suite, and now she worried at the edge of her cotton jumpsuit nervously.

She'd been mute at first—probably some author's idea of a doe-eyed-alien reward for his space hero—and while she'd learned to speak over the years, she still kept words to herself like rare pearls.

Her response was to look penitent, then curl her arm around Brevity's. Her hair was a mass of white curls, studded with silver tentacles, which twitched just at the ends. Brevity sighed and allowed her arm to be captured. She drew a soothing palm over Aurora's knuckles. "What are you doing out here? Did you hear something?"

A nod. Brevity tried to ignore the way it fed the disquiet in her gut. "It was probably nothing. Just me stumbling around. Or the Library reorganizing."

"No." The certainty was enough to warrant a word. Aurora's voice was less human and more synthesized bells. It sent a chill down Brevity's spine. The book-heavy shelves swallowed the sound, but Brevity had to resist the urge to hush her. She thought she heard a shuffle, which could easily have been a painting relocating, a rug fluffing itself, or a book turning in its sleep.

But it didn't feel like it was. Aurora's nails were filed down from sharp claw ends to rounded little fingers, but still managed to scratch as they tightened on Brevity's arm. She winced, found she had been leaning into the damsel unconsciously. She extracted herself and tried to think. Perhaps the Library was just trying to test her, perhaps she was letting her fears get the best of her sense, or perhaps something really was wrong.

In any scenario, hiding in the damsel suite until Claire returned was not the way for a librarian to behave. But that didn't mean Brevity was going to make any moves without good reason. Aurora was watching her with skittish silver eyes. Brevity sighed and headed back for the front desk. She wasn't surprised to hear the clip-clop of Aurora's space-fawn feet shadowing behind her.

Nothing seemed disturbed on the desk. Brevity let Aurora keep a wary eye on the stacks as she located the midnight blue ledger at the bottom of a drawer, buried under gnarled thread and tea cozies. Claire pretended to be rigidly organized, but really she just hid her clutter well. She dropped open the book on the table and cleared her throat. She placed one finger to the blank page.

"Execute inventory: full."

If there was something out of place in the Library—or something missing from it—she'd know soon. Or, if she was lucky, the others would return before she had a chance to screw this up. Nerves singing, Brevity clutched an empty teacup to her chest as the book began to hum.

20

CLAIRE

We expect books to attempt to force change, but not the librarians. Dead things are not supposed to change, to grow. But here I am, a century into this role, and . . . I don't recognize myself anymore. Maybe it's best to say I don't recognize the Library. Not knowing what I know now.

I wonder if there are other places for us. But I won't abandon my charges.

Librarian Poppaea Julia, 48 BCE

CLAIRE WOKE AS THE sun began to bake the moisture off her skin. She opened her eyes to a dazzling world of sunbaked dust and aquamarine. She also woke choking on seawater.

"Ma'am? Oh, thank . . . well, ah. Thank *somebody*. You all right?" Leto crouched on the stone, a trembling hand on her shoulder as she coughed her lungs clear of the taste of old glaciers and burning pine.

She wiped her watering eyes. They were in an alley paved with pale squares. Sandstone, Claire decided, feeling the grit under her fingers as she pushed herself up. She waved off Leto's concern and took a moment to orient herself.

It was Earth. Claire could tell that just from the air. The air in afterlife realms like Valhalla and Hell was thinner, brighter almost, each lungful colored with the realm's spirits. Valhalla had smelled of wildflowers, ice, and steel, while Hell left the taste of ash and anise in her mouth.

But Earth was not so simple. The air was weighted by the contradictions and messy complexities of its inhabitants. She could smell stone and warm earth and a dozen trace scents of a living, breathing city. And the sea. The faint salty and green notes of the water in the quay stung her nose. They were in an old port city, then. Hopefully in Malta.

The codex. Alarm jolted her fully alert, and Claire furrowed her brow, trying to call the narrative song of the book to mind like Bjorn had taught her. She rifled around in her soggy skirt pockets until she came up with a pale scrap of parchment.

It was small, smaller even than the codex remnant they had. It was the remains of a calling card—the calling card that Bjorn had destroyed . . . except for this ashy tendril of paper. She closed her eyes to listen. It was not an entirely unfamiliar sensation, Claire had decided.

It was like when she'd been alive. Whenever she read a book in a binge, cover to cover in a day with little break, she always found it stuck in her brain like a haze. The narrative voice stuck with her, and for a bit after, it was always like a waking dream, living someone else's thoughts. The book haunted like a ghost in her head, coloring moods until she shook herself from it.

Tracking a song, like Bjorn had taught her, felt like that. Only instead of a vague feeling, it was a pulse she could hear if she listened close enough. The codex's song was not a pleasant one. Dark and bottomless and splintered, broken glass and tremors in the deep, like corrupted Latin and whale song. But it was there, stronger now that they were on Earth, and she could trace it.

That, at least, was reassuring. She brought her attention back. Leto was staring at her with wide brown eyes. He did look rather puppy-dog-ish as a human, all teenage gangly. She remembered, abruptly, his rough trip to Valhalla. "Are you all right?"

Leto blinked, then rubbed his nose, not quite meeting her eyes. "Oh. Yeah, that one . . . wasn't— It didn't feel as . . . real."

Drowning, apparently, was preferential to whatever he had seen on the raven road. Claire sighed and started wringing out her wet skirts, grimacing as she touched her tangled hair. "Andras will be along soon, if all went well. Where's Hero?"

"He was going to go look for a towel and something to eat."

Claire stopped midtwist. "You let him leave, alone, on Earth, with his book?"

"Yes?" Leto suddenly looked uncertain. "You weren't waking up, and we were worried, so—"

"Oh, I'll *bet* he was worried." Claire struggled to her feet and spun in place. They were in an alley. "Which way did he go?" Leto pointed and Claire ordered him to stay put before she pelted into the street.

The roadway connected to the alley was wider but not by much. The thick walls, built to hold back the ocean and the invaders that traveled it, were composed of sedan-sized blocks of sandstone, as were the dust-choked streets. Many of the older buildings rose out of the same sandstone, though she could see newer constructions, bright plaster and steel cobbled and clinging to the parapets of the thick walls like barnacles on a pier. Everywhere, the architecture blended the most outrageous features of a dozen cultures together to spit out medieval walls and minarets with fairy-tale abandon.

The street was busy and forced Claire to waste time weaving between pedestrians. She shouldered her way downhill toward what looked like a port. The nearest form of transportation was a good bet for a book on the run, and Claire cursed herself for giving up her tools. She couldn't easily locate, let alone call, an IWL outside the Library. That had to be what Hero was banking on. She would chain him to his shelf if he . . .

The road dumped into a square plaza. Claire had to boost herself up on the edge of a fountain to see over the crowd. She zeroed in on a flash of bronze on broad shoulders and dove into the throng again.

She found Hero at the back of a line for the taxi stand. He was slouched into his jacket, but said jacket was velvet and satin in a sea of denim, so it did little to hide him. Claire cleared her throat. "Food and towels? Really?"

Hero startled, but when he turned his head, he already had an inno-cent smile on his lips. "I am simply being solicitous about your health. I have it on good authority that the next village over has positively the *best* kebabs. . . ."

His face was handsome, symmetrical, and enticingly punchable at the moment. "Your consideration is overwhelming. Taxis, really, Hero? I'm insulted," Claire said. "I thought when you decided to abandon your word, you would be a little more creative."

Hero crossed his arms and looked down his nose to consider Claire. "Taxis are too simple, I agree. Let's revise. What if I'd decide to run? How's your stamina, warden?"

Claire was already winded from the run over, but she attempted to bury that fact with a deep sigh. "You're already IWL'd."

"And you're without your tools of office. How long would it take you to get back to Hell with the little errand you're on?"

"Quite a while. But when I did, you would *still* end up in the Library with much to answer for. Unless you think I'll never make it back because Heaven's the surer bet in this little race. Is that your wager?"

His eyes were grass green, sunny and sharp, as he studied her. She thought for a moment he was going to take that bet and run. But the smile on his lips faded and he glanced down with an awkward cough. Claire thought she saw color drift across his cheeks as Hero grunted, "I was never a good gambler."

"I knew you were a clever one." Claire let out a breath she hadn't known she'd been holding and made sure that Hero walked in front of her.

He made an offended sound. "I just find Heaven's agents interminably dull."

"Well, long as you quit trying to hare off, I'll endeavor not to bore you."

"Now, *that* you'll never do." Hero stuffed his hands in his pockets as they headed back up the street.

✦ ✦ ✦

WHEN THEY RETURNED TO the alley to retrieve Leto, Andras was fussing at the boy's waterlogged curls.

"That was fast," Hero grumbled.

"Walter isn't the only one who deals with artifacts like ghostlights. You're easy to find." Andras shrugged.

"Did the angels give you any difficulties?" Claire looked over the demon carefully for any signs of abuse.

"Child's play. I left when the tall one threw a tantrum. All's well in Hell, by the way."

"What is *this*?" Hero made an injured sound that drew her attention. He dangled a large handgun pinched between two fingers. His lip curled like he smelled a dead animal.

"It's called a pistol, Hero. Your sword would have been a little obvious in streets filled with cell phones. The sword changed to fit, like our ghostlights." Claire rolled her eyes. "Or do you need me to show you how to use it? It's like a sword. Just aim the pointy end and—"

"I know how to use a gun," Hero said archly, sniffing one more time to ensure the full measure of his disgust was felt. He checked the weapon over with surprising dexterity, then stowed it in his coat pocket. "The muse foisted all sorts of combat manuals on me for instruction before we left. But that doesn't mean it isn't an insulting choice. Guns are all noise and bluster. Nothing intelligent about their use."

"You'll get along fine with it, then," Andras said.

"Oh! A sarcastic demon. How original!"

"Uh, did mine change too?" Leto came up with a familiar blue lighter and held it up to the sun. It still glowed faintly, but it was markedly dimmer.

The pool of light had dimmed to a sliver of a thumbnail, sending a shiver across Claire's shoulders. Measuring ghostlights was imprecise, but Claire had never been out long enough for it to matter. Usually, when out on an errand, she took note of when she left Walter's office and entered Earth. But between trips to and from Hell, plus the hours spent in

Valhalla, time had gotten fuzzy. Claire couldn't do more than vaguely guess how much longer they had.

"It's fine," Claire said, voice grim. "Let us proceed, if we're all done complaining?"

Claire motioned to the street. Leto exchanged a humiliated look with Hero but declined to say anything about his detour. Claire trusted they'd work it out themselves. She focused on the codex's song, the snip of card pinched between her fingers in her pocket, and began guiding them up this alley, then down another. They finally paused outside what appeared to be an apex of the tourist district. From a map on the wall, Leto identified where they were. "Valletta. That's in Malta?"

"Yes. The island was a British trading port in my day," Claire said.

"It appears to now be a stronghold of old men with poor taste in footwear." Andras frowned as a portly gentleman trundled by, flip-flops smacking against the ancient stone streets.

"Regardless . . ." Claire leaned against the wall. "The codex pages aren't here."

"I thought the point of this expedition was to locate the thing?" Andras asked.

"I *can*." Claire's hand waved vaguely to the northeast, where past the city walls they could see cobblestones falling away to rolling, dry countryside. "It's that way, but we can't exactly set out cross-country without knowing how far. I still can't understand why the path couldn't get us closer."

Leto's attention had turned back to the tourist board. A map was printed in bright colors, dotted regularly with saccharine-cute icons of desirable landmarks for tourists. His fingers drifted away from the "You Are Here" mark. "Could it be Mdina?"

Claire squinted over his shoulder. "Possibly. Or it could be anywhere in the countryside. Impossible to say without getting closer."

"There's a tour bus that goes that way." Leto pointed to a thick blue line.

Claire cast a wary glance at the stable of buses that roosted along the street farther down and spared an aggrieved thought for her missing bag. "As much as you'd like to play tourist, Leto, you forget—I don't have my books anymore to fake a fare or spin a story."

Sure enough, a steady line of dawdling tourists was purchasing paper stubs, which they handed to the bus attendant as they got on. Claire could feel Leto's mind turning as he searched over the crowds before stopping. "Maybe we still have something. Ma'am, may I borrow Hero?"

"Borrow me?" Hero echoed.

"Not all of you." Leto gave him a positively cheeky grin and tugged him by one arm with growing confidence. "Just need your smile."

21

LETO

There are cracks in the world. It's how artifacts fall through to the Arcane Wing. It's how muses slip through on strains of half-remembered songs. The world is permeable, and so is the mind.

There are small cracks in the world, and there are large ones. I hope you found one to hide you, B. To hide you completely.

I never want to see you again.

Librarian Claire Hadley, 1989 CE

"THAT WAS HUMILIATING," HERO muttered.

"Look at it this way—you made her day." Leto swayed with the rock of the bus and felt a grin threatening to escape. It felt strange, made his cheeks hurt. He couldn't remember, of course, but it felt like something he hadn't done for a while. A buoyant feeling tugged up inside him, smothering the other stuff—the demon stuff—for a moment. It had helped him start to remember things, human things. Like teenage girls and the internet.

Which was handy in forcing a flustered Hero to sweet-talk the ticket vendor. He'd helped Claire, and more important, it was *fun*.

Leto was having fun. He was pretty sure that wasn't something demons were allowed to do. It was a satisfying kind of scandal.

"She propositioned me!" Hero wailed. "As if I would like to go for a tumble like some cheap—"

"She asked if you were on *Tumblr*. You should take it as a compliment;

girls never want to share their Tumblrs with guys. Jeez, relax." Leto paused with a thought. "Maybe when we get back to the Library, we should find you guys some unwritten books on the internet. There's got to be something Doctorow didn't get around to, maybe. Wait—does the Library even get Wi-Fi?"

He turned to Claire for an answer, but the librarian was hunched in her seat, staring out the window at the hard clay furrows that rushed by. Leto wasn't precisely sure where Malta even was, besides on Earth, but it was sweltering. And that said a lot, since he'd come from Hell. Heat split the roadway, and the tour bus's sad excuse for shocks transmitted every pothole into a teeth-shattering bass line. Leto, and everyone else on the bus, clung to his seat for dear life.

Everyone except Claire. The "song" she was tracking appeared to be giving her trouble. She swayed with the bus, eyes closed and lips pressed in concentration. After she nearly toppled for the third turn in a row, Hero muttered something sharp under his breath. He shoved her into a free seat, neatly ignoring the death glare Claire pinned on him.

They passed more hard-baked fields, dusty war memorials, artist enclaves, before finally curling around a hill toward an ancient walled city. Claire let out a short breath and her eyes flew open again. "Here."

Andras squinted at the sign lit up over the driver's head. "Mdina, just as the stray guessed. You're certain?"

"The stray has a name, you know," Leto said.

Claire nodded as her eyes roamed out the window, unfocused. "It's here."

They piled out of the bus with the rest of the tourists. They were in a flat green park that filled the space between a modern—if something built within the last three hundred years could be called modern—suburb of town houses and the thick, ancient walls of the city. As on every tourist stop, they had to fend off numerous offers of special tours and "today only" deals from street peddlers as they wound their way through. A modern city had sprung up around the old establishment, brightly colored plastic and metal around a dusty stone center.

Leto consulted the brochure the tour guide had passed out. "It's called the Silent City. It was entirely walled in to protect from raiders and . . . Huh, think that was a moat once?"

He leaned over a low stone railing to gawk at a deep ravine of green that ran around the base of the walls before Hero hauled him back by his collar. "I could throw you down there to check it out."

Leto grinned. "Heights make you nervous, Hero?"

"Of course not. Now stop leaning over the gaping, death-inducing abyss." Hero lied elegantly; Leto had to give him that.

A squat stone bridge spanned the former moat and led into the city. With Andras at the midway point, Claire stood frowning at the thick sand-colored walls. "This is problematic."

"We don't have time for problems, pup," Andras said.

"We don't have time for a great many things that we've been forced to contend with," Claire said peevishly with a glare at Hero that Leto was glad not to be the recipient of. "It's not— It's just odd. I can still hear it. The codex pages are somewhere here in the city. But it's all muddled, muted. Gone indistinct."

"Maybe it was called the Silent City for a reason?" Leto offered.

"Nonsense." Claire made an involuntary grab for where her shoulder bag should have been. She stuttered midmovement, appearing to remember its absence, and sighed. "This is ridiculous—no one could do this without proper equipment. I should have never—"

"Might I be of assistance, madam?"

Leto startled at the voice. A small olive-skinned man appeared at Claire's elbow, having apparently wandered up from the wide entrance to Mdina. As if he'd been waiting for them.

That was impossible, of course. He didn't seem suspicious. He looked like most of the locals, wearing a faded tee and jeans, which were a friendly sort of juxtaposition with the ancient bridge he leaned on. He had an open face, the kind that would have made Leto comfortable asking him for directions, or help with homework.

Huh. Homework. That was another thing he'd forgotten.

"Have you come to see our beautiful and fabled city?" the man asked, ducking his shoulders just so.

Claire made to dismiss him as she had every vendor she'd encountered. "No, thank you. We're not—"

"Scholars, yes? You have the look about you," the man interrupted. He tilted his head and something knowing colored his next words. "Can I suggest a tour of antiquities?"

Andras turned. "What makes you say that?"

"No offense, sir. No offense." The small man wiped a baseball cap off his head and bowed. "They instructed me to wait here for visiting scholars. You seem to fit the description my employer gave."

Claire narrowed her eyes. "And who is your employer?"

"Ms. McAllister, ma'am," the man puffed up. "Best antiquarian in the country. From England, she is. Deals in the rarest books and antiquities that come through from east, west, anywhere."

"Anywhere." Claire pressed her lips together in the kind of suspicious look she gave Hero regularly. "What kind of books, exactly?"

"Ms. McAllister tends to a very rare collection. One-of-a-kind artifacts of the written word."

Oh. That was handy. Leto's hopes rose, but Claire exchanged a look with Andras. "We don't have any means to pay."

"Not a difficulty, ma'am. Ms. McAllister believes in the free trade of information for all and—"

"This is entirely suspect," Hero hissed under his breath.

Andras shrugged. "What's the risk? They're merely human. You could take a fragile thing like him, couldn't you, Hero?"

Hero at least knew enough to ignore Andras's prodding. Leto chewed on his lip. They were right; it *was* probably suspicious, but it wasn't as if luck hadn't been screwing them over every which way up until now. Maybe they were due some good luck. Seemed only fair, to Leto.

"It's not as if we have many other options, considering," Claire said, evidently coming to a similar conclusion. "All right, sir. I would like to speak to this Ms. McAllister about her collection. If you'll just direct us . . . ?"

"Oh, ma'am. One such as myself would never allow a lady to wander the city without an escort."

Leto dearly wanted to see Claire put the man straight on what he would or would not *allow* a lady like Claire to do. But before that could happen, he'd taken her by the elbow and guided her over to a strange, old-timey carriage drawn by a single horse. He kicked out a small step for the carriage and executed a deep bow.

Hero and Andras seemed reluctant to follow, so Leto gave in to temptation and walked up to the carriage and hesitantly petted the horse. Its hair was delightfully sleek under his palm, and Leto suspected he'd never been this close to a live horse before. He must have grown up in a city, then? He filed that information away for later.

After a moment, he turned away and found Claire shaking her head at him with weary amusement. Andras and Hero had evidently overcome their objections and boarded the carriage already. Leto sheepishly climbed into the middle seat.

With all aboard, the guide snapped into action. He clipped a flimsy velvet rope over the doors, all the while muttering courtesies that sounded like a song: "You're welcome and honored guests to Mdina. The Silent City welcomes you." Over and over. Leto supposed it was the kind of act that tourists paid extra for, though he didn't see the point of it. A little creepy, really. They clattered over the bridge toward the great entrance to the walled city.

A massive stone seal sat at the top of the giant arch. It was surrounded by scrollwork and bore circles and crosses, each slashed through with negative space, upon its crest. Leto thought the shadows it cast looked jagged upon the scrollwork, like daggers spearing the pages. A chill raced up his back as they passed under it, and Leto suppressed a shudder. Tourists passed unawares, streaming into and out of the city like a gentle tide.

The gate spilled out onto a courtyard, hemmed with stone buildings nearly as tall as the walls and just as old. Nothing was new here. Half a dozen alleyways spindled out from the courtyard, though visitors mostly contented themselves to mill quietly between shops.

It was *eerily* quiet; the Silent City had earned its name. There was a hush that settled heavily over the city the moment they passed under the arch. Even the hub of vendors and buses outside failed to leak in; all sound was buffered out by the looming, thick stone walls.

Leto was about to say something—anything—to break the silence when Claire twitched beside him. She looked sightlessly toward the south walls as the carriage took them deeper into the hive of stone buildings. Her hand fidgeted with the pocket that held the calling card scrap. "It's here."

"The codex?" Andras asked. He sniffed. "If we can hear it again, let's dump the guide. He is obviously up to something."

"Exactly what I said five minutes ago," Hero said.

"No, he's still leading us in the right direction." Claire lowered her voice. "As long as he's taking us toward it, we'll tolerate whatever foolishness he's about. It may be this McAllister is in possession of the codex pages."

"And what part of that doesn't scream 'terrible trap'?"

Claire ceded that point. "You're awfully cautious for a hero sometimes."

"The living ones usually are."

Their guide led them down a series of progressively smaller lanes that offered little shade. The sun had reached high in the sky and was unflinching. Andras picked at his increasingly damp shirt with a grimace. "Is Earth always this . . . unpleasant?"

"You've never been above?" Claire sounded surprised.

Andras's look turned sour. "Rarely and only when I can't help it. Not during daylight. Subject to dreadful summonings back in the day, before I rose to power. Artifacts usually come to me agreeably enough, not the other way around."

"That must be nice," Claire said.

"Heard that," Hero said.

They came to a stop in front of a narrow structure. It was not so much a storefront as a warren of windows and balconies built into the surface of the outer wall itself. Andras craned his neck up and shook his head. "Strange place for a book collector."

"Ms. McAllister will be waiting for you in her study." Their guide reached a small door and bowed low enough for his hat to practically scrape the sidewalk. "My colleague inside will show you up."

Hero tilted his head. "You're not seeing us in?"

"Alas, I am not. This one must see to new arrivals at the gates. Please to have a pleasant day, my friends."

The strange little man swept back a step and hurried down the street. They watched him disappear around the corner before they turned to stare at the door ajar before them. Hero gave a weighty look to Claire, but she held up a flat palm.

"Don't even say it, Hero."

Past the door, they stepped into a small, tidily appointed kind of foyer. Leto blinked for his eyes to adjust to the dim, while breathing a sigh of relief after escaping the heat. The thick walls served a purpose: the interior was much cooler than the sweltering street.

He'd just started to relax when an intimidating wall of muscle stepped forward. The bodyguard introduced himself as Murdock but made little effort to communicate exactly who McAllister was or how they had come to be chosen for the honor of a tour. He instead gestured to a cramped staircase and politely requested they follow, as if there were a choice.

The staircase was crooked and narrow, made for someone of a much smaller stature than anyone in their group. They spilled out onto a landing, where the floor was composed of the same stuff as the walls, pale sandstone and painted plaster.

"Ms. McAllister will see you." Murdock stepped to the side at the wide double doors at the other end of the landing. The walls were smooth and windowless, leaving the doors in a smudge of a shadow. The air tasted a little stale, of paper and salt. The absence of sunlight, which had been a cool relief before, suddenly ticked an ominous feeling up Leto's arms.

"Well, so glad this doesn't feel at all like a trap." Hero crossed his arms and his fingers played at the pocket where he'd stuffed his gun.

"Which part, the deserted mansion or the big goon?" Leto said.

"Be that as it may, the song does lead here," Claire said, "trap or not. We're going in for the codex."

Hero snorted. "Well, as long as we have a plan, then."

Claire straightened her shoulders and strode forward. Her hand rested on an antique doorknob just a moment before pushing one of the doors wide open and advancing through.

Leto followed close at her heels, not willing to be left behind with Murdock. Beyond the doors, the space opened onto an expansive, brightly lit study. Exactly the opposite of the landing. Sunlight pooled in from numerous tall windows and fell over walls of glass-covered bookcases holding what looked to be very old and very expensive leather-bound manuscripts. Oversized leather chairs were grouped in corners, and a desk much like Claire's massive station in the Library was positioned at the center of the wall of windows. The air still carried traces of a recent pot of tea.

Leto released his held breath. It was a cheery kind of clutter, books and comfort. Perhaps this collector would be a friend. Things would work out.

The collector in question stood by a window, evidently absorbed with the book in her hands. She was as tall as Hero but rich and solid, where Hero was pale and light—walnut and oak rather than ivory and bronze. She was dressed in simple slacks and a button-up shirt, rolled up to reveal forearms speckled with faded ink. There was something familiar about her sharp face that Leto couldn't place, but her narrow gaze was softened by what seemed like warm brown eyes.

Hero brushed past him, drawing Leto's attention, and stopped just shy of Claire's shoulder.

"Warden?" Hero's question was barely a whisper, and Leto saw why. Tension snapped along her back, and the muscles in her jaw clenched into a snarl as she focused on the collector. It was a fury tinted with shock and fear, and suddenly Leto knew nothing *would* be okay.

The woman collector made no effort to move, but her soft smile tightened. "Hello, Librarian."

The silence stretched, long enough for Leto's nerves to sing in confusion. There didn't seem to be any threat. A quick glance said Andras and Hero were as confused as he was. Claire drew a jagged breath, and Leto turned hopefully for an explanation, a rationale that would—

Then Claire yanked the pistol out of Hero's coat pocket and pivoted to aim, and all hell broke loose.

The gunshot deafened everyone in the room. A flower bloomed on the stranger's throat, not red but impossibly dark—blood was supposed to be bright, Leto thought distantly—and she made a single quivering entreaty with her hand before she hit the floor. Everything was suspended in the moment of that gunshot. It was thunder and silence. All Leto could hear was the wheeze of shock that got tangled somewhere in his throat.

The black blood began to seep from beneath the collector's ear, reaching into the dusty carpet like pitch fingers. Grasping for his feet, rooting him to the floor. The book that the woman had been reading had landed near her feet. Its pages were twisted and bent underneath its spine, like broken legs. It felt indecent, to Leto. He wanted to fix it. His feet wouldn't move.

Claire tossed the gun back to Hero and turned away. "The pages are here. Lock the door and search."

22

RAMIEL

You'll miss the world. That's fair; it used to be yours. But there's a reason we don't get to travel freely among the living, even as librarians. The Earth is not meant for someone who can't treasure it. Time makes us clumsy, dulls our senses. Live too far past your tombstone, and you turn a bit stone yourself.

Nothing burns up humanity as thoroughly as eternity.

One supposes that's why librarian is not a permanent position. We need to retain ourselves, retain our souls, if we're going to be any good to the books. My apprentice has an abundance of soul. That'll make her a good librarian. That will also make her an unhappy one.

Librarian Gregor Henry, 1986 CE

THE TIDES OF THE lake sloshed and shoved against the shore. The grinding churn in the air might have been the wear of water against gravel, or Uriel's teeth. "You can track them," Uriel gritted out. It was an order, not a question.

Rami nodded. "I can. I got a measure of her soul in Valhalla. If she's lost anywhere on Earth, I can find her." It wasn't hard to judge where the librarian and her hellspawn would have gone. They'd taken the mists, the burial roads, and there was only one place those went—though usually in the opposite direction.

"Do it," Uriel had said, already turning away from the shore. "I have business to attend to."

"Business?" Rami blinked. "What business could be more important than the codex?"

The Valhalla sun was setting. Soon the realm would resurrect its dead, beginning the whole dreadful cycle again. The light hit Uriel askew as she turned, brightening her cap of white hair but turning the rest of her features into jagged relief. Her smile was slivered with shadow. "An opportunity for the bigger picture. You think too small, Ramiel."

IT TOOK TIME AND cost to trace a soul: a sacrifice of cold stars and the ashes from his own flight feathers. But in the end, when the knowledge surged through him, it felt familiar, like slipping into well-worn shoes, tracing the weave of lifelines to find the one dropped thread. As he took on the role he had been cast away from, it felt comfortable, and right, so right that it hurt when he released the power. Its departure left empty rivers in Rami, like indents on a violinist's fingertips, useless when away from the strings.

But he had a location. He sent word and when he arrived in Malta, Uriel was already perched on a tumbled pile of sandstone outside the city. She paid no mind to the humans that occasionally filtered by below her, and though she was invisible to them, Rami was relieved she had moderated her appearance somewhat: a sparse cream-colored coat with a military cut instead of a robe, and her shining white hair dulled to a mortal blond. She'd shrunk a bit so she towered only a few spare inches over most humans. But the passing crowds still veered a wide berth around her. Nothing could hide her presence: she was the Face of God no matter what skin she wore, and right now that face was an intense, grit-teethed snarl.

Fists clenched at her sides as she stared at the entrance, as if she could bring the walls down with simply the force of her gaze. "They're here?" she said as Rami stepped up and followed her eyes.

"Yes. The librarian's soul is in Mdina."

"With the *demons*," Uriel bit out. Rami assumed she meant the librarian and her companions. The way she growled it made cold form in his stomach.

He picked a careful reply as he tried to suss out what plan Uriel had in mind. "Well, I'm surprised you waited for me, then."

"Not as if I had much of a choice." Uriel finally dropped her gaze away from the walls and sighed. "It's warded against us."

Rami blinked. "What, the whole city?"

Uriel nodded. "I'd heard tell of it, but never had need to see it for myself. The entire city, warded. Something left over from one of the humans' petty wars. Nothing not born of humankind—not angel or demon or claimed by another realm—gets in without invitation from its residents."

Rami glanced at the thick sandstone walls with new interest. "Then how did the librarians get in?"

"That is a very good question," Uriel said. "If the Creator were receptive, we could have found a way in through the churches."

That startled Rami. "The Creator is removed from the *faithful* as well?" A stroke of unease stirred at the back of his thoughts. The state of a realm was tied—to belief, but also to the godhead that ruled it. If those two become disconnected . . . well, Rami wasn't certain of the repercussions.

Uriel waved a hand as if to flick the irritation away. "It's no matter. I've made arrangements. They will come to us."

Rami frowned. "I very much doubt that. Why would they—"

"I have made arrangements. Second rule of demons: they always want something." Uriel, smug and almost smiling, raised a brow at him. "They'll come to us. I have it on good authority that they'll have no other choice."

23

CLAIRE

My dear apprentice, you learn so quickly. Though it will be years yet before you learn all that is necessary to serve the Library, I see the librarian you will become. Fierce, strong, and yet with enough feeling heart to treat the books under your care kindly. Perhaps even to bring much-needed change to the Library, and the secrets it holds. The Library needs you, Claire.

So I can only beg your forgiveness for what I must do.

Librarian Gregor Henry, 1989 CE

SOMEWHERE, SOMEONE HAD A pot of Earl Grey on. Earl Grey with *citrus*, Claire corrected, detecting the lemon drifting through the air. Her favorite, when not mixed with the smell of death.

It soured her stomach. An old clock on the desk ticked, but otherwise there was no movement behind her, near the body. Claire clenched her fingers, which were absolutely *not* trembling, and pretended to sort through the stack of books by the window.

"May I ask why we just shot our only source of information for the pages of the codex?" Andras broke the silence, his voice mild.

"Come to think of it, why isn't the well-armed guard outside rushing in at the sound of a gunshot?" Hero said.

"You need a body to need a bodyguard," Claire mumbled under her breath. The help around here probably had strict instructions not to enter no matter what was heard.

"Is she dead?"

Leto's panic finally brought Claire's head around. The teenager looked even more pale than usual, if that was possible. He crouched over where the book collector lay, eyes wide as saucers as he extended a finger.

"Don't touch, Leto. She's . . . fine." Claire scooped up a few books at random and gave them an underhand lob. "Flip through these. We're looking for loose sheaves of very old paper."

The books fell to the floor with a clatter—Leto had made no move to catch them. He turned a look of horror on Claire. It was earnest with a cutting edge. "Fine? You *killed* someone!"

"No, I didn't. I—" Claire forced her jaw not to lock with tension. "Just start looking. Gentlemen, please. We don't have much—"

She was cut off by a cry. Leto stumbled back, flinging himself away from the empty rug. An empty rug where, but a moment before, the prone body of the book collector had lain. A tacky pool of black blood and a slight impression in the crumpled carpet were the only indications left.

". . . much time," Claire finished.

"She disappeared." Leto stumbled to his feet. "She just disappeared."

"Disappeared rather like a character from an unwritten book." Hero held an increasingly suspicious glint in his eye as he turned toward Claire. "Now, why would a body do that, warden?"

"As I said, we don't have much time." Claire moved toward the desk and studied the drawers. Locked, of course. She began rifling through the detritus for a key.

"Perhaps a very succinct explanation would speed things up," Andras said.

She found the key resting in the bottom of a cup of pens. Exactly where she would have hidden it.

"Pup. Claire," Andras prompted softly.

Claire's lips thinned, and she let out a hard breath, staring at the key rather than at the others. It was dented; tarnish discolored the grooves between the teeth. "Because she *is* a character. That's why I shot her.

Characters retreat to their books when damaged—assuming they aren't unable to do so like Hero here. It buys us time to find the codex pages while it's busy recomposing itself."

"So you didn't kill her." The relief was evident in Leto's sigh. Claire looked up and wished she hadn't. Color had drained from Leto's face. He was trembling, given away by the twitch of the coils of hair shadowing his eyes. He had the unsteady look of someone desperate to believe the best of people.

Claire wished she wasn't going to disappoint him.

"How'd you know she was a character?" Hero asked, mercifully drawing her attention away. "Not that I don't respect a display of gratuitous violence."

Claire straightened. "Why wouldn't I? I'm a librarian."

"And I'm a character *and* a book. I know how these things work."

Andras made a noise of agreement. Claire didn't dare look at him. She could take anything but pity from Andras. Instead, she picked up the key and worried at it. The teeth were dull, but made a pleasant sting as she rasped the pad of her thumb against them. There had to be a way out of the story she didn't want to tell, a twist that would send them on to a happier story. She came up empty.

"Because she's mine." Her voice came out a whisper. She grimaced and cleared her throat. "She's—she's a hero from one of my books."

The book in Leto's hands slipped to the floor with a thud and a likely crack of the spine. Claire didn't chide him to be careful.

"I wasn't aware there was an outstanding book missing from the Library, present company excluded." Andras gave a nod at Hero.

Claire felt it when the careful, bleak part inside her unlocked and the familiar guilt tumbled out. She studied the key in her hand. It was tarnished, impossibly dull. Claire rubbed at it with her thumb, but it didn't come clean. "There isn't. I removed her from the Library inventory. After I helped her escape."

The words fell on the ensuing silence like lead.

"Well. Finally, the warden gets interesting," Hero muttered.

"You helped a character, but when would you . . ." Understanding glanced into Andras's voice like a spark of fire. "Gregor."

A single word that Claire had avoided for three decades. It called up Claire's best memory of her mentor, tinged by fondness and guilt. He'd been somewhat young when he'd died the first time—much older when he died the second, but then, years in the Library never showed. Not on the outside. A paunchy, scholarly man, American, and, god, had Claire resented him at first. Acid slaked her throat. "It wasn't planned."

"But it did occur."

The accusation in Andras's tone was obvious. Claire squeezed her eyes closed. "Gregor was—"

The world tilted and swallowed Claire's words. She nearly fell over the desk as the floorboards bucked beneath her feet. A long, echoing groan shuddered through the air, as if the earth had torn itself open, followed quickly by a distant, deep howl.

Claire's eyes flew wide, all explanations forgotten. It wasn't the howl of a dog, or even a wolf, of wild things and forests. No, it was a howl of deeper places. Dark pits and tears that tasted of anise. "No—"

"What was that sound?" Leto was the only other one to sway as the room bucked again. He dug into his pocket at the same time Claire fished out her lighter. She muttered a useless prayer before opening her palm.

The lighter sat cold and dark. No flame bobbed in the liquid; no glow warmed her skin. An unnatural cold settled over the little lighter. A quick glance said Leto's lighter was the same. Claire's voice was weak as all the air seemed to have left the room. "Not— I thought we had more time."

"Warden?" Something about Claire's expression must have made Hero's hand stray to the gun in his coat pocket. He and Andras showed no sign of feeling the shuddering of the floor, though Claire and Leto could barely stay on their feet.

Claire wheeled in place once before deciding on what to do and snatching Leto by the shoulder. He made a startled sound as she forced him into the gap between the bookcases in a corner and backed up in front of it. It was pointless. It was doomed. She did it anyway. Leto's breath wheezed past her ear as he caught on to her panic.

"Claire, what's going on?"

It took a moment to realize Hero had been repeating her name. Not "warden," but her actual name. She closed her eyes and tried to shove her drumming heartbeat back into her chest. It took another try to wet her mouth enough to speak. "Andras . . . I don't suppose you brought anything that—"

"Nothing that would stop them, pup." Andras's face was not made for compassion. The pitying look was disturbing on his sharp features. Her ears thundered again with howls.

"I know that," Claire snapped. Her eyes flickered over the room. The door led down the stairs to the street. But what good would descending them do? "Doesn't mean I have to make it easy for them."

"For *who*?" Hero raised his voice, nearly drowned out.

The floorboards shuddered beneath her feet, as if something impossibly large had slammed into the building. Claire braced herself against the wall for support. She squeezed her eyes shut, swallowing down the bile that rose in her before answering.

"Hellhounds."

Hero's frown froze, and their collective gaze turned toward the door.

Creatures had to be terrible to escape Hell, and the hunters sent after them had to be even more terrible. Hellhounds were not made to retrieve, for Hell gave no second chances; they were made to destroy. Hellhounds didn't stop to listen to reason or defenses. Their jaws tore through not just flesh and bone, but soul and spirit. They could rage through the world unseen, and neither time nor space nor reason would placate them. Once they'd been loosed, they'd stop only once they had you in their jaws. They were made to eliminate, they were made to be tireless, and they were made to be ruthless.

When their ghostlights expired, Claire and Leto had officially become lost souls. And lost souls were within the Hellhounds' purview. They would hunt their prey to the ends of the Earth.

The room rocked again, but though the howling had become nearly incessant, it didn't sound any closer. Her pulse pounded in her throat once, twice, three times. But nothing came through the door. Hellhounds could ghost through wood, stone, steel. When on the trail of an escaped soul to destroy, they were relentless. Nothing stopped them—nothing *should* have stopped them.

Andras was the first to move to the window and he stilled as if transfixed. "Claire, you might want to see this."

Claire glanced at Leto, wide-eyed and panicked behind her. She was unsteady as she pushed away from the bookcase and joined Andras at the window. "What—"

"There."

The apartment they were in was built into one of the tiered walls of the city, which gave the window a clear view of the grassy moat and sunbaked fields beyond. She took in the massive walls, the bridge with a thinning stream of travelers flowing through, the way the afternoon sun's light was syrup and honey across the fields dappled with old buildings beyond.

She looked down.

Directly beneath the wall, darkness moved. Creatures, large as lorries and composed entirely of smoke and jagged shadow, prowled the thick city wall. Howls like cudgels and bodies like secrets. There was a handful of them, and they swarmed like airborne sharks, drifting over the empty moat that surrounded the city. Each took a turn throwing its massive body against the walls, and each time one did, the floor shuddered, and Leto and Claire flinched.

"It appears they're stopped," Andras said.

"Nothing stops Hellhounds. What in the world is holding them?" Claire wondered.

"The Treaty of Mdina."

The voice was low, too low to be Leto's, too human to be Andras's, too serious to be Hero's.

Claire spun. The collector stood very still a few steps from Claire, familiar enough to make her heart clench. The deep brown skin at her neck was smooth, showing no sign of the gunshot wound. Dark twists of hair curled neatly over a strong, composed face.

"What the hell—" Hero already had his pistol leveled, but Claire held a hand up. The collector's eyes were deep and calm, and though Claire stared, she couldn't quite bear to meet them. She studied her mouth instead. Her lips were parted on words Claire wasn't sure she could stand to hear. But she had to.

"Talk," Claire said.

The book collector's shoulders dropped a little, as if she'd been expecting a warmer greeting. "During the last great war, there was a treaty, sealed with wards. This city has been warded against anything not of mortal make for years. It means you and your people are safe."

Claire shook her head. "Hellhounds are too powerful to be stopped."

The woman—woman, because even Claire couldn't pretend she was just a character—shrugged, shoulders rolling in such a graceful, familiar way Claire found it hard to breathe. "They've tried before, but the wards have held for decades. No demons, no angels, no servants of any realm can breach it."

The quaint little greeting that their guide had performed at the gates. It'd been a ritual. An invitation. Claire said, "You knew we were coming. You let us in."

The woman nodded. "Anything restricted by the wards needs an invitation from a resident. When I realized what I had, I'd hoped . . . I set one of my people to watch for you."

"And you are . . ." Andras waved his hand impatiently. "I'm gathering McAllister is not your true name."

She hesitated, eyes straying to Claire. There was uncertainty in the gaze, and it hurt. It *already* hurt. There was no salvaging it. Claire jerked a nod, and the woman inclined her head to Andras, though it was not a warm look. "You can call me Beatrice."

"How Shakespearean." Hero lowered his gun slightly. "Now that imminent doom isn't upon us all, explanations are in order."

Claire scoffed. "We absolutely don't have the time to—"

"Actually, if your character is telling the truth, we have a great deal of time. Which we will need, since she has yet to reveal the pages, and we have yet to figure out a way to deal with the Hounds." When Claire turned, Andras had a narrow look for her, as if he were trying to make a particularly bothersome puzzle piece fit. "It is relevant to our interests."

Claire's gaze fell on Leto, who looked trapped between terror and confusion. And he was trapped. Caught in the mess that Claire had made of her own past. If nothing else, she owed it to him. She drew a small breath and faced the window again. Staring at the Hellhounds was the cowardly option, but she took it as she considered where to begin.

"I wasn't even the librarian yet. Newly dead. It might have been . . . what, 1989? Only a few years working in the Library under Gregor, the former librarian. I loved the Library at first. Yes, I was distraught at the idea of being dead; Hell is an alarming thing to wake up to. But the Library itself was . . . magical. I loved books when I was alive. And the idea that they were preserved there was . . . beautiful. Beautiful, but lonely."

The quiet pressed and prodded at her shoulders. It almost made Claire grateful for the howling Hellhounds. "Librarians have always been unwritten authors. And it's natural for unwritten authors to be curious about their own books. It wasn't hard to find them. At first, I spent my free time merely walking the stacks, staring hard at the spines with my name on them as I walked by. That progressed to touch. I knew better than to read them, but . . . I found any excuse to work in the shelves, moving books around them. I suppose it was the attention, the curiosity, that did it."

"Your book woke up," Hero supplied grimly.

"One of them, yes."

A low sigh wisped behind her. "Oh, pup," Andras said.

Claire flinched at the pity. Her shoulders had crept up with tension. But she had to barrel on. If she stopped, she'd never get through it. "Frightened the holy hell out of me one day while I was straightening the shelves. She was just . . ." Claire resolutely avoided looking at the unwritten woman in question. Resolutely avoided remembering how seeing her for the first time, there in the Library, so immediate and so familiar, so *alive* in a place of dead things . . . She did not remember how that felt. Did not remember the twist in her breath, the sharp thrill of wanting. Did not feel the old hurt. "I recognized her instantly. She was . . . part of me. One of the parts of me I would have written into a book, if I'd written one while I was alive."

"You said this was in the Library, though. She escaped?" Leto asked.

"Not then. She didn't need to, at first. I hid her." Her voice had become quiet, clipped, as she tried to get through the tale with the fewest words possible. "The Library, by necessity, is infinitely vast and always changing. Even a tenured librarian can't locate a single book without a calling card. That's why we have the systems in place to avoid missing books. There were plenty of places to hide a hero."

"Why?"

"I wasn't as big on rules back then as I am now." Claire gave Leto a tight-lipped smile. "For what reason? Foolishness or loneliness? It doesn't matter now."

"It mattered to me," Beatrice said, almost too soft to be heard. Claire's throat tightened.

"In any case . . . librarians hold the reins of their libraries. Soon hiding wasn't enough. I concocted a simple plan to get her out. I would get her past the wards, delay the alarms' triggering. The idea was that I would go with Gregor to 'assist' hunting for her. Then I would slip away with her calling card. There would be the matter of outrunning the Hellhounds, but we would have a ghostlight for a head start and . . ."

"And no one would stop Claire when she put her mind to something." Beatrice's comment made Claire finally look at her, giving an unreadable shrug.

"Something obviously went wrong," Hero said.

Claire hesitated, but Beatrice took over. She spoke haltingly, with a slight velvety accent. Her words weren't measured or polished but had a steadfast certainty that felt like a lifeline. "We got caught. Librarian Gregor found out somehow—I suspect he knew the whole time. Never was certain. But he was waiting there for us the night I planned to leave. He had my calling card in his hands and . . . he intended to enslave me in that place. Stamp me to Special Collections."

"Stamping. The monster," Hero said with a look of mocking horror.

"Claire stopped him," Beatrice said firmly, and a recoil of disgust shot through Claire.

"Stop. Just stop." Claire found it difficult to press the words between clenched teeth. "At least do him the honor of telling it accurately. I *murdered* him."

The pronouncement came out louder than she had intended and hung, suffocating, in the air. Claire didn't care to see how it landed with anyone, the looks they were giving her. A cauldron of memories, hurts, fears, bubbled up in her chest, and it took a great effort to lower her voice. She dropped her eyes and said it again, testing the truth on her lips. "I murdered Gregor."

Leto let out a wounded sound. "But that's impossible. In the Library—"

"In the Library, there are . . . words, fail-safes," Claire explained evenly. "Words taught only to librarians, for the defense of the Library. Words that will unravel a soul like the Hellhounds do—it doesn't work on things native to Hell, of course, not on demons like Andras. But on human souls or creatures of other realms, it evicts them. Unmakes and banishes a soul, like waving away a puff of smoke. They don't die, of course, but it can take decades, centuries, for a human soul to reassemble.

"Gregor had just taught me those words, warned I might need them someday when I was librarian." Claire spoke through bile rising in her throat. "*Someday*, he said. And the words just . . . came out. I hadn't even thought they would work. I mean, he was the librarian. *Why would*—"

She stopped herself. Her gaze dragged up, against her will. Leto's mouth hung open in abject dismay, while Hero's face was blank. Andras, bloody Andras, actually smiled. It was a soft thing, a proud thing. The next howl of the Hellhounds she felt in her bones.

"I saw his face when I did it. He'd been calm, so calm, up to that point. Gregor was always so infuriatingly at peace with his work. But then I invoked the words. There was surprise. Pain, confusion. Then there was an unquenchable terror. And he was gone."

There was a silence that was difficult not to fill with a scream. Claire had screamed, quite a bit, in the horror-torn hours afterward.

"Why don't I know these words?" Andras said.

Hero made a disgusted noise. "Really, Arcanist? *That's* what you're getting from this?"

"Maybe Hell doesn't trust you as much as you thought." Claire plowed ahead, barreling toward the end of the story now. Not as if it had ever really ended, for her. It just echoed on and on. Beatrice's presence proved that. "I couldn't leave after that—too much chaos to clean up. I removed any record of Beatrice, of my book, from our inventory. I buried the rest of my books in the stacks so it would never happen again. I let everyone assume I'd been promoted. That Gregor's soul had gone to rest. There were rumors, of course, but Hell prefers rumors to investigation. I . . . became librarian. Andras helped with that." She tilted her head, considering his reaction. "Did you suspect?"

"That you banished your own mentor in a pique of infatuation? No." That unpleasant smile formed on Andras's lips again. "I suspected something tragic had occurred. You were . . . you were not as you are now, my girl. I wish you'd told me."

"Wait." Hero held up a hand and shot a look at Beatrice as if he'd just tasted something sour. "She did all that for you, killed for you, sentenced herself to Hell, and you still just . . . left?"

Beatrice's gaze didn't waver. "Yes, I left."

"Such valor, such *heroism*." Hero's lip curled, something akin to real anger sharpening his gaze. "You obviously cared for her a great deal."

Beatrice's demeanor chilled. "Don't presume to speak about things you don't understand."

"I understand perfectly a coward who—"

"Enough. It's past." The last thing Claire needed was two snarling heroes giving her a headache.

"You're a murderer." The pure venom in Leto's whisper jolted the air in the room. Claire turned to find him staring at her with an alien look of disgust. "You killed someone who trusted you. For what . . . for a crush . . . for *her*?"

Claire's mouth fell open. She expected judgment—deserved it, even—but not from quiet, thoughtful Leto. "It's not like—" She reached out a hand, but the boy jerked back.

"Liar." He said it with a cutting softness. His lips trembled, opening and closing around his disappointment. Leto turned and stalked out of the room. A moment later, there was the sound of the front door snapping shut.

"He's . . . upset." Hero stated the obvious, though it seemed to perplex him. "Shall I go after him?"

Claire shook her head. "No. He's not wrong." And, she thought bitterly, they had nowhere to go anyway.

She raised her face, looking at each of the remaining men in turn. She saw herself reflected in their eyes, changed. Respect, disgust—it didn't matter. It was a grotesque kind of mirror. But when no one else stormed from the room, Claire straightened her shoulders and turned to Beatrice. "You became a book collector."

Beatrice took a breath, a smile warming her serious features. "I did. Antiquities dealer, technically. Turns out, my previous experience as a protagonist didn't leave me with many marketable skills besides tenacity."

Claire made no effort to return the smile. "A book collector with pages of the Codex Gigas in a magically shielded city."

"That does seem to be *quite* the coincidence," Andras said.

Beatrice's smile faded. "I found Mdina shortly after I escaped. If you'd come wi—" She stopped herself. Started again. "The codex find was a recent turn of events. I'd become a book collector, yes. I found a partner,

Avery, with an interest in the obscure and arcane. I had gleaned just enough understanding from the Library to feed him bits of trivia to seem useful. I'd been chasing the rumors of the missing pages for years, only found them in the possession of an unaware French farmer's family a few months ago. Avery got a lead out of nowhere. Tried to steal from me, before he passed. I should have seen it coming. Cancer riddled, at the end. Obsessed with gods and demons, immortality. I'd thought they would probably end up to be fakes, or copies, but I—I admit, I'd held out hope that if they turned out to be authentic—"

"You kept them here," Andras interjected, eyes glittering and keen. "Did you read them? Do they really contain . . . ?"

"Not the issue at hand, Andras," Claire said.

Beatrice risked a penitent look. Her hand hovered, as if her mind had a thought to reach out to Claire, but the rest of her knew better. "I knew if they were authentic, there was a chance . . . I knew someone from the Library would be after them. As I said, I had a man watch the gates."

"For what purpose? To trap us here?"

"You're not trapped. Just . . . shielded." Beatrice faltered. Her hands were calloused from use, but just as slender as Claire remembered. They raked helplessly through her hair, once, and her curls came away softly mussed. "You are free to leave if you wish, but in the meantime, nothing can get in without an invitation. And I doubt the Hellhounds have the social graces to communicate with anyone."

"As grateful as I am for invisible monsters, I—" A terrible thought struck her. Claire took a step forward. "Does the ward guard against angels?"

The unwritten woman frowned. "Like, from . . . Heaven? Yes, I suppose it would."

"And if they got a mortal to invite them in?" Hellhounds were mindless, but angels had every social grace, when properly motivated.

"That would . . . grant them entry."

Angels. If the angels found them here, they would be cornered without an escape. The codex would be lost and, likely, so would they. It was ridiculous, but focusing on a danger she could address helped her ignore the Hellhounds thrumming doom into her skull. "How many gates are there into the city?"

"Four main gates, not counting the catacombs, but those haven't been used in—"

"Andras." Claire turned.

"I needed to stretch my legs anyway." Andras stood and cracked his neck. He furrowed his brow at Claire. "If you're certain."

"Watch for them and secure an exit. We'll need to figure out a way out of here, Hellhounds or not."

Andras nodded and sauntered through the hall. Beatrice waited until the door shut again. "Not necessarily, you know."

Claire had turned to confer with Hero, but she narrowed her eyes. "I beg your pardon?"

Beatrice gripped her arms, as if anchoring herself. Her voice was quiet again. "You don't have to find a way out. You could stay. As long as you wanted."

You could *stay*. The words Beatrice said struck Claire in the chest. And then what she hadn't said: *with her*.

And what they meant together: to leave Hell behind.

The prospect snagged her breath, and she had to work her lips a few times before the proper words beat out the longing ones. "Where's the codex, Beatrice?"

"You could stay. That was always the plan, wasn't it? To—"

Claire gritted her teeth against the words. "Where are the pages?"

"I'm not asking anything of you. You don't have to be with me. You could stay anywhere in the city, and Hell couldn't—"

Claire felt heat overwhelming her eyes, and she spun, instead focusing a furious scowl that startled Hero into taking a step back. He'd been silent through the entire exchange, a small miracle. Claire found it easy to ignore the muddled questions on his face. "It's here somewhere. Watch her. I'm going to go fetch Leto and form a course of action." She heard Beatrice make a sound of protest behind her. "If she tries anything, shoot her."

Hero gave her an uncertain version of his standard cavalier smile. "As you say, warden."

Beatrice tried another entreaty, but Claire spun and stormed toward the door.

24

BREVITY

I would never dishonor my elders, but there were times when I thought Fleur was a frivolous old woman. She held my leash, as I was her apprentice, and she made decisions that seemed so effortless—thoughtless—to me. I judged her for it. But I understand now. The leash gave me something to pull against. To argue. To form my own opinions, but never bear any of the risk of the choice. It's easy to be brave on a leash.

Now the muses argue and whittle away at me. Demons salivate over books. The Arcanist questions my every judgment.

It's hard to be brave alone.

Librarian Yoon Ji Han, 1799 CE

ALL WORKS ACCOUNTED FOR.

Brevity had run the inventory twice, just to be certain. Three times, to verify she was not hallucinating. It'd taken long enough that Aurora had retreated to the damsel suite to sleep. But the third inventory matched the first two. The blue ledger printed the results in neat, spidery ink that bloomed across the page: no oddities, and all unwritten books accounted for. There was Hero's book, of course, which was listed tidily as "out on loan," but all other books, paintings, and other uncreated art were secure in the Unwritten Wing.

Aurora had been insistent that there'd been someone in the stacks. Claire might have dismissed it as a figment of the damsel's imagination, but Brevity knew imagination. It hadn't been imagination that'd driven Aurora to speak, or the shelves to shiver. But it made no sense, someone creeping into the Library and not removing anything. The only ones that could enter the Library when it was closed were its current residents, books and artifacts, and those that took care of them.

Those that took care of them. The Arcane Wing's pet Horrors, clawed hands drifting over shadowed gems. Brevity suppressed a shudder. She tried to think of any rationale around it, anything that would let her just shake the whole thing off and brew the herbal teas Claire hated and binge on the damsels' baked goodies until the whole thing was settled.

It wasn't what Claire would do. Claire would stare down a Horror and solve the whole mystery with the power of superior disdain. No, Brevity amended, perhaps she wouldn't, because she'd never believe there was a mystery in the first place. Brevity wasn't Claire, and never could be.

Brevity stood, head briefly turning toward the damsel suite. She spared a thought for Walter in his office. Someone would surely be willing to accompany her, give her a reason to be brave as she checked on Horrors. Brevity had always been better at being brave for others than for herself.

But the damsels couldn't leave the Library. Walter had his own duties. And Claire had told Brevity to care for the wing.

Brevity stowed the ledger, abandoned her tea, and locked the doors behind her as she wound her way down to the Arcane Wing.

The monstrous doors of the Arcane Wing should have been barred and locked, since that was what Claire and Andras had agreed, which would give Brevity the nice excuse that, hey, at least she'd checked.

But the doors were not barred and locked. Aftrer Brevity skipped down the last steps, she skidded to a stop on the dusty hardwood, just short of the reaching shadows cast by the wide double doors of the Arcane Wing. Which stood open.

She wound seafoam hair around her finger and gave it an anxious tug as she took a step over the threshold. The Arcane Wing felt much as it always had, a slithering, hostile composition of shadow and steel. The air was weighted with cold, clinical things, dust and formaldehyde, rubies and neglect. The Arcane Wing had never been a bright place, but even the domed work lights were dimmed, throwing the cavernous space into thick eddies of gloom. Brevity hesitated in the island of light created by the hallway, not quite prepared to dive in.

"H-hullo? Is anyone—" Her voice and courage failed as the ravens unleashed a series of shrieks from the rookery. Otherwise, the Arcane Wing was silent. She didn't have to venture far in to be certain of it: no demons, no Horrors, nothing. It should have been reassuring, not having to face the monsters she went looking for, and Brevity's shoulders disengaged from hugging her ears until the thought occurred to her: *If they're not here, then they're somewhere else.*

The breath stopped in Brevity's throat, and her leg muscles seized.

It was the unknown that did it. It was an easy mistake to make, thinking fear was the ultimate domain of demons. They looked the part. Or mortals, they had such fleeting things to lose. But humans were constantly changing, and demons were creatures of certainty. The truth was no one, *no one*, knew fear like muses. Fear was an operation of the imagination, the ability to see an empty space and *imagine*. Imagine what might be there, the possibilities filling in what reality left blank. To be afraid was an exercise of self-inspired suffering, and Brevity wore inspiration in her skin.

It burned now, the edge of the blue tattoo writhing against the fine bones of her wrist and hungry to be peeled loose. In Brevity's mind, black sickle claws raked over gems and artifacts one moment, her skin the next. Plucking the soft strings of her veins, shredding her. In her mind, the Horrors reached out so surely from the dark she could *hear* them. It didn't matter that they weren't there, couldn't be there. If she released the inspiration gilt in her skin, pure potential, it would *make* it real.

A raven shriek brought her back to her senses. Her hand hovered halfway over her wrist. Brevity didn't try to calm the shuddering heart in her chest, didn't try to fight the panic that washed over her. She knew from experience that was no good. Instead, she released it, turned her back on the unseen claws, and ran.

She should go to Walter. She *would* go to Walter. She would be safe with Walter, and she would send a message to Claire on Earth, and Claire could come back and deal with it, and Brevity could be brave for someone else again. That's what she needed to do. She just needed to navigate down the hallways, avoid the Horrors and her own fear long enough to make it to the transport office and summon Claire. She could do it.

She didn't remember throwing open the doors of the Unwritten Wing, but she must have locked them behind her. Her knees hit an unwritten rug, and the disappointment she felt was a distant, muted thing. She was devoting too much effort to trying to stop her short, rabbit-quick breath.

Of course, she hadn't made it to Walter. Of course, she'd not warned Claire, had run instead to cower and hide. Muses could imagine anything, inspire anything in an author, but for themselves? All Brevity gave herself was fear.

She was here now, but even her mounting anxiety wanted her to do something. Her hands trembled as she dug through the drawers and came up with a small silver box. Brevity squinted at the words inside, cursing Claire's cramped handwriting. Eventually, she sorted out three squares of translucent vellum, one violet, one red, one black. Dreams. Blood. Ink. The fibers burned her fingers, and Brevity forced herself to focus on the pain as she uncovered the flame of a gas lamp. One paper, then another, went up in a shriek of smoke as Brevity mumbled the written commands. Her voice was hoarse, words dragged over broken glass, but the Library understood her anyway. The air tightened, then snapped in a hiss of anise and ash. One, two, three wards, sealing off the Unwritten Wing from the rest of existence once again.

The air took on an unnatural silence, the taste of Hell fading from the roof of Brevity's mouth. She fell back against the desk, thinking for a moment she could summon up a feeling of silliness, of shame. If the silliness came, that would mean she was wrong about the shadows, wrong about the fear. It would still be a failure, having run back here instead of investigating further, but at least that would mean that she hadn't lost her chance to summon help in the face of an actual threat. Claire could get back and scold her for sealing the Library, and they could laugh about it. Brevity could take her scolding and make it into a joke and—

Dust fluttered from the shelves. The papers on Claire's desk rippled as if an errant breeze had shivered by. Brevity's breath stuttered, clenching when a barely audible boom vibrated. Far away, like a soft finger plucking strings. Nails dragging along glass. An outer ward, being probed by a curious hand, too weak to knock properly. Whoever it was should give up, go away, realize the Library was closed and—

The next shudder reached in between her ribs, jostling her chest as the whole wing creaked. Again, increasing in frequency and strength until it was a war drum. Because that's what it was, not a knock, not an idle curiosity of a passing demon. Someone was knocking, and would keep knocking until it was granted entrance. Brevity's resolve shriveled in her chest, strangling her breath along with it, and she sank to the floor alone.

25

LETO

I tried writing it down, my life, so I wouldn't forget it. Where I was born. My parents. My friends, my loves. My husband, my child. But every time I try to write down something from my mortal life in the log, the words melt into the paper like watermarks. Gone as soon as the ink dries. The log is a record for librarians, not people. I can feel its judgment.

But what happens when the inevitable occurs? When the world forgets me, so I begin to forget myself? What do I become, when I am nothing but a librarian?

Apprentice Librarian Claire Hadley, 1986 CE

MDINA DIDN'T SEEM TO be a natural habitat for the young. Bored teenagers and young children peppered the steady stream of tourists at the entrance, but the farther Leto wandered into the city, taking narrow stone-walled alleys at random, the fewer people his own age he saw.

Fewer people in general, really. The buildings and streets were built out of that same worn island stone. Thick flagstones swallowed his footsteps as he took corners without a destination in mind. Stern signs hung at residential intersections, declaring that the city residents took the name Silent City seriously. As long as he was quiet, no one questioned what a bleary-eyed American teenager was doing so far from the tour buses.

It was probably fortunate, as his head felt like an oil slick just waiting for a light. Thoughts black and toxic, coiled with hurt. He'd felt these black thoughts invade before, more often when he was his full demon self in Hell, but this didn't feel like an artificial nastiness. When he had felt the demon thoughts before, they'd been like a computer virus, infecting and corrupting but originating externally. The anger simmering in his chest now, he couldn't understand, but it felt natural, close to the skin.

The winding alley dumped out into a small courtyard. The fountain at the center hadn't held water for a while, but the sun-warmed stones felt nice under his fingers. He slumped against them and closed his eyes to breathe. The farther he got into the city, farther away from the echoing Hellhound howls, the less fear gripped him, leaving him with just the thoughts he brought with him.

Lashing out at Claire had been more instinct than choice, but feeding off her shame had been unforgivable. Claire had been kind to him, more than she needed to. He hadn't meant to hurt her, but then he'd been glad he *had*, because he was just so *angry*. It was a living thing, boiling in his gut. He was so tired of being disappointed, being hurt. And this cut deeper, somehow. He knew, logically, that everyone in Hell was there because of their own failings. He knew Claire wasn't just an unwritten author, and she could be hard and merciless.

But there was sin and there was *betrayal*. The idea of betraying someone who trusted you—images flashed through his head: a death for lack of well-placed trust . . .

Leto gripped his head to stop the throb. It was unforgivable. The worst sin. It welled, a searing and familiar hurt, and he immediately wanted to *hurt* anyone who'd do such a thing. To make them suffer, as they deserved to.

That'd be what a demon would do, wouldn't it?

He'd pressed the heels of his palms to his eyes hard enough to feel his pulse. Light flared and the pain was real, despite his temporary form. Leto wasn't sure which was the real him anymore, the demon or the human. He wondered if he'd have to choose at some point, and which was the better choice.

"Easy there. Those eyes are expensive to replace." Claire's soft voice nearly sent him tumbling into the empty fountain.

She stood at the other side of the stone ring, diminished somehow. Her shoulders were hunched and her arms wrapped around her, pale knuckled, holding on or holding in. It was a fragile pose, human. Irrationally, that made anger lance back up Leto's throat. He turned away. "I bet you could stitch me up just like your books. Demons are easy enough to replace."

"You're *not* a demon."

"And you're not a liar." Leto hated the bitterness in his own voice.

Claire sighed. He could feel her looking around, gauging the emptiness of the square before speaking. "Leto, listen, you shouldn't run off—"

"Or what?" He was being petulant, but he didn't care. He reached for what he instinctively knew would hurt. "You'll banish me too?"

"Those words only work in Hell," Claire snapped before grimacing. "What I mean is . . . No. Leto, I would never—"

"Never? Sure, go on—tell me everything you'd *never* do as a dead person. You've been so good at keeping your word so far." His hand wound a fist over his chest to quell the clenching feeling. It was irrational, this black *bleak* feeling lodged in his lungs. He didn't want to wield it, especially not at Claire again, but it felt like the infection had reached his tongue. He hurt. "What's gonna happen now? Are you going to turn against us too? I bet you could figure out some way to sell us out, trap us here, hide your secret."

"Don't be ridiculous! It's not as if— I never *lied* to you. I just didn't—" Claire stopped, and from the look that crossed her face, Leto didn't need to say anything to crucify her. She was doing it to herself.

"I'm not saying I don't deserve it, Leto," Claire said softly. "I deserve everything you're feeling. But we're stuck here together, for now, and contrary to what you think, I would never leave you behind. So if you want to sit here forever and hate me, that's okay. Or if you never want to speak to me again—"

Something of the acidic feeling withered in Leto's throat and turned to ash that left an awful feeling in his mouth. He heard the whispers from the raven road again. *We never talk anymore.*

"No," Leto said instead. "I just . . . I followed you. Because you seemed . . . different, better. I didn't know where else to go, and you seemed to care."

"Seemed." Claire repeated the word, half-rueful. She made a cautious approach around the fountain, slow and wary. And weary. Exhaustion bruised her eyes. "You can care and still cause harm. Feeling, *caring*, for someone else is the worst kind of weapon, in my experience. It allows you to do things you never thought you could do and things you never thought you *would* do. All for the love of someone else. It's a trap I'd avoided on principle since Beatrice, up until recently."

There was an earnestness, an entreaty, that softened her face when she looked at him. The librarian of Hell's Library wasn't ever soft, but Claire, occasionally, was. It was what eased the last of Leto's anger. It drained out of him like an oil spill, leaving him suddenly hollow but stained feeling. He wasn't sure whether he wanted to hold on to it or let it go. His shoulders slumped. His voice felt more lost than angry when he found it again. "How do I trust you?"

Claire sat down beside him and considered his question seriously. "I think it'd be disingenuous to ask you to. Let's make a deal."

Leto rolled his eyes. "Give me a break. Adults only say 'Let's make a deal' when they need something they can't justify."

Claire's frown inched up into a smile at one side of her lips. "It appears your teenager memories are coming along nicely."

Leto gave her a dull look. "That's also insulting."

"Fair enough. I'm sorry. It's been a long time since my—" Claire slouched her shoulder against his. It felt comforting. "You don't have to trust me. Just work with me. Give me the chance to set right all the wrongs I've done here. I *need* to get back to the Library. There's something off here, this whole situation. The codex, Beatrice just happening to be here, even you—"

"I already knew I wasn't right."

THE LIBRARY OF THE UNWRITTEN

"You are *perfect*," Claire snapped, and the protective fierceness made Leto smile, just a little. She was wrong—everything in his screaming heart knew it—but it meant something, that she believed it. "I mean all of this happening at once. Coincidences don't happen, not in Hell. Brevity should have sent word by now too, if the Library was in rights. Something else is going on, and of all the members of our little family right now, I trust you at my side the most. I *need* you."

Leto turned and found himself blinking to process that. Claire was a wielder of words, prone to confusing speeches like a teacher, ingrained with librarian authority and scholarly control. But this request had an unvarnished, raw grain to it. Honest and easily bruised. Leto felt the world silently resettle around him to account for that. It confused him, and he was so very tired of feeling confused.

Claire was wrong about him. Wrong about the humanity he had left inside. She cared, and she hurt people with that caring. But she *tried*. She was trapped, perhaps even more than he was. The Library and Hell were tethered to her, like a cuff around her neck, but she never stopped trying. She never looked back. Leto desperately wanted some part of that. "When can we leave?"

Claire's lips twitched at the plaintive note in his voice. He supposed it was ridiculous: the idea of a soul *eager* to leave Earth and go to Hell. She didn't see that every time they went to Earth, he seemed to feel more confused, more tugged in two directions. He worried one more good tug might rip his seams entirely. Only the Library held him together.

"You want to go back?" Claire asked carefully.

Leto shrugged. "I didn't think there was a choice."

"Our ghostlights have run out, and Hellhounds are after our souls. It's going to be difficult, to say the least, to set foot outside the walls without being obliterated. I'd say desperation has broadened our bartering position." Claire made a vague gesture: to the courtyard, to the fading twilight above. "What do you really want, Leto?"

He had a hangnail. His thumb worried at it as he thought. It was a question no one had asked him—not in Hell and, Leto felt relatively certain even without memories, not often when he was alive. The choice was a little unnerving. "I want . . . to make a way forward. And I guess I . . . want to know. I can't stand not knowing. These feelings I get, I don't know which part of me . . ."

"Hell may not help that. We send our souls there for various reasons but . . . you should know," Claire said quietly, a complicated look furrowing her brow. "Realms enjoy stasis. The longer you're there, the harder it is to see yourself anywhere else. It has a way of seeping in."

That didn't sound comforting. Leto gnawed on his bottom lip. "I just want to know who I was. Who I am. I won't find that here."

Claire tilted her head as if absorbing that, then nodded. "Fair enough. We'll just have to outsmart the Hellhounds."

She stated it like a simple course of action, but made no movement to get up. The silence was companionable as they gave the flagstones more contemplation than they probably deserved. Leto felt his chest unwinding and said, "So. You like girls?"

A smile tipped onto Claire's face and she chuckled. "I like . . . interesting people. Everyone has their charms. The details never mattered much to me."

"So you're pan?"

"Pan?"

"Pansexual," Leto explained.

"Is that the term now?" Claire asked, and it took a moment before the realization fluttered into Leto's gut. Another word, another memory. Claire studied his face and relaxed. "I remember loving, a few times. I was married to a very nice man in life. We had a daughter, even."

"A daughter?" Leto was caught off guard by that.

"She was . . ." The ease fell off her face. Claire frowned. "Damn. I can't remember her name anymore. My own daughter." A kind of grief flickered but was just as quickly tucked away. She cleared her throat. "Memories are another casualty of Hell. The more you're forgotten on Earth, the more you forget yourself. It can be a blessing or a curse."

The light in Claire's gaze had faded, dark as the twilight clinging to the square now. "Well, I've already got that problem," Leto said, hoping it would cheer her. When it did, it felt like a small victory. He rocked to crouch on his heels. "Not that I'm likely to forget all this. Should we be getting back, ma'am?"

Claire heaved a deep, grumbling sigh at that. "Oh, blast, we should. The heroes are likely at each other's throats again." She fluttered her hand and Leto helped haul her to her feet. "And I still haven't gone over how I need your help. Let's talk on the way."

THE FRONT ROOM OF Beatrice's apartments was already in disarray from the search, and now appeared to be the scene for a very lazy duel. Beatrice perched at the edge of her desk, feigning interest in the paperback in her hands. She appeared entirely unaware of the half-lidded glare Hero maintained. He was slouched against the wall near the door, and straightened as Leto returned with Claire. The Hounds picked up again as their targets returned closer to the walls. The intermittent growls shivered through the floor at Leto's feet, sending a chill over his skin. At least they were no longer throwing themselves against the wards.

"You're wasting time refusing," Hero pointed out, seeming to continue some line of debate he'd engaged in with Beatrice while they were gone. "The warden is very persistent when it comes to her books. I should know."

"You're too cliché to be one of her books." Beatrice licked her thumb and turned the page of her paperback. "Frankly, I'm surprised you let another of us out and about, Claire."

"She didn't 'let' anything. I freed myself. *Without* help," Hero said.

"How clever of you. And they say we heroes aren't smart." It was Beatrice's turn to squint. She placed an ink-stained finger to her chin. "Curious thing, though. Calling you *Hero*."

Leto knew Hero enough now to tell that ruffled him. A tic started in his jaw. Hero's gaze flickered to Claire and back. He didn't challenge Beatrice with a look again. His hand brushed at his hair in short, jerky movements. "Good a name as any."

"Really?" Claire had waited out the pissing match with a bored expression that made Leto stifle a grin. She straightened now. "If you two are really quite done . . . Any word from Andras yet?"

Hero shook his head and Claire pursed her lips around a sigh. She crossed the room and plucked out of Beatrice's hands the paperback, which she'd hidden behind like a shield. "The codex, Bea. Time is of the essence."

"Time is exactly what I'm considering." Beatrice was quiet, but she folded her arms in a motion that mimicked her author perfectly and she held her gaze. "I won't send you back."

"I'm going back to the Library either way. I'm needed there. The only thing we're debating is whether I have to take you with me or not."

Beatrice's slouch stiffened into stubbornness. "I won't go back. I'll give it to your angels first."

Claire's smile chilled. "We'll see about that."

There was a beat of silence that threatened to freeze over. Leto coughed. "I'm hungry. Is the kitchen okay to use or . . . ?"

"Down the hall. Help yourself." Beatrice didn't break her glaring match with Claire, but she waved a hand vaguely behind her.

"Come on, Hero. Should eat something while we still got human taste buds," Leto said.

"Oh no. This showdown is too good to pass up." Hero, recovered from his earlier mood, danced a look between Claire and her hero. "Like a bull and a brick wall."

"I'll assume I'm the bull in this scenario," Claire said.

"Not even for little cakes? You said you liked cakes with frosting," Leto said.

Hero finally allowed himself to be distracted. "Maltese cakes?"

"Little Debbie, actually. I think I saw a box earlier while we were searching. C'mon." Throughout the exchange, neither Claire nor Beatrice had moved. They'd barely blinked, locked with a divide of hurts between them. So Leto was relieved when Hero allowed himself to be led from the room. They wandered down the hall and left the librarian to face her hero.

26

CLAIRE

How much easier it would be if everyone knew their role: the hero, the sidekick, the villain. Our books would be neater and our souls less frayed.

But whether you have blood or ink, no one's story is that simple.

Librarian Gregor Henry, 1982 CE

IT WAS A SLOW-MOTION earthquake, the lurch and shiver of the ground beneath her feet, perfectly timed with the deep, bottomless howl that reached through thick city walls to stroke goose bumps over her skin. The Hellhounds were not tiring. Claire knew they wouldn't, but there was a difference between theoretically understanding an immortal, indefatigable, undeterrable monster from Hell and having it shake plaster dust into your hair.

The interminable shuddering as the beasts flung themselves at Mdina's wards, the way the air in her lungs seemed to vibrate each time they howled, the way her pulse rose and fell with their growls—it all rubbed her nerves raw. Her sanity might break before the Silent City's wards did. The unrelenting rhythm of it was dizzying.

It was why she was simultaneously relieved and annoyed when Beatrice broke the silence.

"I have something for you." She hefted from the desk a familiar book, leather bound and weathered, like all unwritten books. Beatrice held it gingerly, her face full of vulnerable uncertainty—an alien expression for a hero. She watched Claire like she was an animal she might startle with fast movements.

Claire crossed her arms. "Unless that's the codex pages, you and I have nothing to talk about."

Ink-stained fingers curled reflexively against the book. "I was under the impression that a librarian had a duty to her books." Beatrice kept her voice neutral. "I was hoping you would be willing to look at mine while you were here."

Claire's anger faltered, despite her best efforts. "Your book is damaged?"

"Just loose binding. Thirty years on Earth is hard on a body. I don't want to risk losing any pages."

Claire pursed her lips at that. A shade of the old guilt and duty tugged at her. "I'll work on it in exchange for the pages of the codex."

"The Claire I knew would have done it out of kindness."

"The Claire you knew killed her only friend for an infatuation. Let's hope a lot has changed since then." She tilted her chin. "I'll do it for a favor, then."

"We both know it was more than an infatuation," Beatrice pressed. She shook her head. "I just wanted to talk."

"Then it's convenient that your needs and desires don't concern me anymore." Despite these words, Claire snatched the book from Beatrice's hands and picked at the disintegrating thread. Something in her twisted at the sight of a damaged book, especially her own. "I suppose you don't have any traditional linen thread in this day and age."

"You can get anything in Malta if you simply know who to ask." Beatrice waved to her recently tidied desk. "Scarlet dyed, hand drawn, just like you prefer. Bottom drawer."

Claire sat down behind the desk and began shuffling through the drawer, pulling out a tidy bunch of red thread, thick needles, and other bookbinding materials. The familiarity brought a strange stab of comfort.

Beatrice drew near her, leaning on the edge of the desk. She felt the unwritten woman's dark-eyed gaze follow her hands as she pulled out a particularly sharp-looking scalpel and needle. Color drained from Beatrice's cheeks, her shoulders stiffened, and she faced straight ahead.

Books were squeamish patients sometimes, but that suited Claire. She turned her focus on the book and began inspecting the tension in the binding. Stress slowly edged out of her shoulders as she set into a rhythm of running her ink-stained fingers over each line of thread, progressing quickly through her inspection with long practice.

It was calming, after a fashion. Books were always easier this way. Mere paper and leather. Simple, physical, containable. But, like people, books rarely stayed that way. Stories never lived only in the ink.

Beatrice kept her eyes forward, but long, calloused fingers drummed on the desk in a patient rhythm. "You seem to have made friends. They're . . . nice."

"A demon, a broken hero, and an amnesiac. If you want nice, you should meet my assistant." Claire adjusted the desk lamp for better light. "You're in luck. It appears the headband is frayed and just needs tightening. Good. I didn't have the time or resources to do an entire rebinding." She began to work her tool carefully between the leather cover and the spine.

Beatrice flinched away at the creak of leather. "You trust them enough to travel with them."

"Trust born of necessity." Claire finished working away the leather cover, leaving a thick stack of sturdy vellum pages fused together with thread and glue. She ignored much of the binding and focused on the delicate line of frayed thread at the top of the spine.

Snipping sounds filled the heavy pause. Beatrice's voice was barely louder than the pluck of thread. "You really won't consider staying?"

The question was so plaintive, but the answer was so obvious. Claire shot her a frown, but the unwritten woman was too busy studying her shoes to notice. She turned her attention back to the book. "It's out of the question. If I stay, worse things will come. Either the Hellhounds will wear down the wards, or the angels will con their way in. You're sitting on a time bomb. There's no use."

Out of the corner of her eye, she saw Beatrice's shoulders bunch. "We planned to face down worse things once. Together."

"Well, we didn't exactly run away together, did we?" Claire's voice turned acidic and harsher than Beatrice deserved, but she opted to focus on the colored knots of thread rather than see her reaction.

"And that was my mistake."

"Yes. Seems to have worked out well enough for you." A vicious feeling spiked up her chest. Claire struggled not to overtighten the thread, forcing her hands to relax as she worked. It helped if she imagined she was stitching Beatrice's mouth shut.

Beatrice was quiet a moment, so quiet that Claire wondered if she'd disappeared into her book again. "You don't know who you're traveling with."

"I think I know them better than you."

"Do you?"

The way Beatrice said it made Claire's brow furrow. When she looked up, Beatrice had her chin tilted toward the light, was watching her in profile. "If I can't convince you to stay here, then you should know the creatures you're calling friends."

Claire hesitated. "If this is about Andras, I—"

"The character."

Confusion brought Claire up short. "What about Hero?"

"Has he said anything specific about his story? The role he plays?" Beatrice studied the desk, purposely not looking at her own book. "He's not typical, is he?"

Claire scowled and turned back to her work. She lacked any patience for petty jealousy, book or no. "He's maddeningly annoying. I'd say that's a prime heroic trait. That and the cheekbones."

Beatrice coughed and shook her head. "I forget how librarians have only the external to go on. He's fooled you by looking the part."

Claire narrowed her eyes. "What are you driving at?"

Beatrice's mouth tightened as she considered her words. "Looks can be deceiving. The prettiest ones are. Outside and inside his book."

In his book? As if that mattered: characters were true to how they were written, at least at first, and granted, Hero had begun to display unusual quirks of personality, but that could be attributed to corruption. It made sense that the damage would warp him. Make him less kind, more cruel. Less noble, more grasping. Vain, self-preserving, unreliable, sarcastic—yes, Claire could list all his many flaws. His attitude was more self-serving than . . . Claire stopped midstitch and laid down the needle. Oh, she'd been a damn fool. She considered, turning the thought over in her mind, lining actions and memories up against it.

Then carefully, thoughtfully, pragmatically, she folded the implications up and tucked them away for later.

Beatrice watched her with obvious pity. A hand reached out, briefly skimming over her shoulder in a way that made Claire tense. "Do you understand the danger? You can't trust his nature. Grant him the slightest opportunity and he'll turn—"

And carefully, thoughtfully, pragmatically, Claire lost her patience for concerned ex-lovers.

Leather clapped under her palm as she slammed the book cover in place, and Claire found herself standing. She leaned over the desk with enough force to make Beatrice startle.

"You have precisely *zero* room to lecture me on trust. Listen to me and listen carefully, because though I shouldn't have to explain this to my *own creation*, I am only going to say this once. I am not a damsel in need of saving. You aren't the hero in this story, and you sure as hell aren't my knight in shining armor. No—" Claire snarled as Beatrice made to speak. "You never were! Look at yourself and use your inky brain for once! The same hair, same eyes. I bet you even love oysters and hate salads. I don't know that because I'm your author. I know that because when I dreamed up your story, you weren't the woman I wanted to love; you were the woman I wanted to *be*."

A chill blanched the color from Beatrice's face. Her mouth fell open. "That can't . . ."

Claire didn't stop. It was a wound, and Claire *wanted* to wound her, someone, anyone. If only so she wouldn't be the only one hurting. "Me, as I wished I could have been, once. Independent, competent, educated, and wealthy, above the constant expectations of family, and, most of all, free of society's rules. Why wouldn't I have wanted that? I should have made you a man while I was at it."

The moment the words were out of her mouth, Claire regretted them. Beatrice recoiled as if struck, lip curling into a startled scowl as she shoved herself away from the desk. She stumbled backward a step, losing her natural grace.

"Bugger." Claire chewed hard on the inside of her cheek as she berated herself. Her hands stilled on the book. "Bea, I didn't mean it like that."

"I know how you meant it." Beatrice's voice was brittle.

"No, I meant—the way the world was when I was alive, the way my family was, I just meant—"

"I get it." Beatrice's jaw worked, and she refused to meet Claire's eyes. "But the woman I loved wouldn't have said it."

The hurt simmered in the air, as bitter as ash. Guilt, oily and cold, settled in Claire's stomach. She sighed, rubbing her nose a moment before pressing forward. "That's the point exactly. I'm not that woman anymore. I'm not even the lonely soul that you enchanted in the Library. I am the librarian. I don't need your protection or concern. It is unwelcome."

Beatrice frowned down at the book on the desk between them, as if she suddenly found herself in a different story than she'd thought she was in. "It doesn't matter who you are now. You said yourself Hell is—"

"If I decide I want to leave the Library, I will exit under my own resources. This is not a rescue. I am not your quest. I'm sorry." Claire wasn't used to trying to sound kind, but she tried for Beatrice.

She felt a mirrored hurt as the unwritten woman's shoulders dropped. Beatrice turned away, sitting heavily on the edge of the desk. Tension sang in her back as she turned blank eyes out the window.

Claire waited a breath until she could be sure her voice would be steady before pushing the point. "*My* quest is the lost pieces of the codex. Your repairs are nearly done—you can glue the cover yourself. Now, will you tell me where they are before all of Heaven and Hell falls down on us?"

Beatrice was still for a long moment, long enough for Claire to begin to doubt she was going to respond. Then she tilted her chin down in an imperceptible nod. "Check the back."

Claire parsed the words a moment before the meaning dawned on her, and her mouth fell open. Her gaze dropped to the old unwritten book in her hands. She flipped the book over and thumbed through the back pages until a folded sheaf of even older papers fell out. "You kept them with your own book. So when you asked me to repair—"

Beatrice gave a cold, airless chuckle. "Even a fool knows where such dangerous things belong. You're the only one I would trust with them. And with me."

Like heat roiling off a fire, power whispered in the air around the pages, whispers of dark things, undone things. Claire stared a moment, then very carefully wrapped the edge of her skirts over the remaining pages of the Codex Gigas.

"What will you do now?" Beatrice asked quietly.

The pages felt heavy and warm in the pocket on her hip. Claire wiped her hands as she finished stowing them, but the residual dread didn't come off her crawling skin. Her lips fell into a hard line. "We leave. But first I need to talk to a hero."

27

CLAIRE

Librarians are wisely advised to stay out of the business of realm politics. Nothing good comes of the powers of realms meeting. There's no clear answer, between paradises and damnations, which are stronger. It depends on the time, the place, the tilt of the world and the spin of the stars. Mostly, it depends on the mortals involved.

It seems blasphemous. In a constant war of immortal forces, ancient demigods, good and evil, the most powerful piece on the board is the fragile pawn of a human soul.

Librarian Yoon Ji Han, 1802 CE

Stay out of politics? Ridiculous! When has a writer ever managed to avoid politics? Every story is political. Tell a soul a story they want to believe, and you can change the world.

Librarian Gregor Henry, 1932 CE

CLAIRE FOUND LETO AND Hero in the kitchen, conferring over a woodblock table. Despite being seated, Hero had to stay at a perpetual hunch to avoid knocking the shiny copper pans overhead. The room was small, cluttered, but cozily appointed in line with Claire's own tastes, like every other part of Beatrice's flat. Leto and Hero had a pile of prepackaged cake snacks on a platter between them, and Hero's frown deepened as he scrutinized one still in its cellophane. "This does not look at all like cake."

"It is. Try it," Leto said.

"It's hard and shiny."

"That's just the frosting. It's soft inside. Well, softish. Try it. Everyone loves them."

Hero gave him an arch look and finally took a sizable bite. A moment to chew, and then cake sputtered across the table from an explosive cough. Leto broke into a giggle as the other man doubled over. When he finally recovered, Hero's eyes watered with a withering look. There was a smudge of cream hanging from his offended frown. "You neglected to mention the toxic filling."

Leto bit his lip. "What? It's sweet!"

"Sweet? No, honey is sweet. Freedom is sweet. A pretty boy or handsome girl is sweet. That? That burns." Hero took a large gulp from his mug of tea. "Such nonsense. This is worse than the other place."

"I don't know. They seem to bathe more here," Claire said.

Two faces looked up. A familiar, crooked look of disdain righted itself on Hero's face. A bit of chocolate frosting clung to his upper lip. He gestured dismissively to the cakes on the table.

"That's only because you haven't tried what passes for sweets here yet. Help yourself. Or can we finally leave?"

"I have the codex pages. We just need to find Andras and prepare to leave." Claire held out her hand. "May I see your book a moment, Hero?"

Hero unfolded himself from the chair and wiped his hands. He reached into his pocket as he rose and handed his book over to her. "I've been perfectly behaved. Is there some—"

The flat leather of the cover connected with his jaw, along with the full weight of the tome and Claire's swing behind it. Leto startled, scattering the snacks on the table as he stumbled to his feet. Claire silenced his squawk with a raised hand, never taking her eyes off Hero.

Hero leaned over the table, massaging his jaw. Canniness and caution flooded his eyes. "What was that for?"

"You never told me." Claire ran her fingers over Hero's book, tugging at the blank pages she'd sewn in. "What exactly was your story like? A name like 'Nightfall' and looking as you do, I suspected high fantasy. Do you miss being a brave knight, Hero?"

Hero's brows inched together. "Less than you might think."

Claire swung. This time, Hero anticipated enough to lean away, deflecting the blow. He came up and backed against the wall. A hanging pot clobbered his head. He grimaced and raised his hands. "Peace, woman!"

Claire held the book over her head again.

"What's *wrong* with you two?" Leto stumbled between them, holding up his hands though he didn't seem certain who was a threat to whom. He visibly relaxed when Claire lowered her arm.

"Lesson time, Leto. It's important to know your archetypes. You know the difference between a hero and a typical villain in a fight?" Claire said, pinning accusing eyes at Hero over the teenager's shoulder. "Heroes are optimists. Ambush a hero, and you'll get shock, anger. Retaliation at the injustice. But a villain, a villain, now . . . they know how betrayal works. Strike a villain, they expect it. Villains get cautious, not angry."

"Oh, I can be plenty angry," Hero said.

"Don't." Claire clenched her hands and had to remind herself not to twist the book in her grasp. She shouldered past Leto and shoved the book hard into Hero's chest. "You lied."

"It was more of a . . . failure to correct." Hero grimaced down at his book. "You were the one that started calling me a hero! I didn't think I'd be around long enough for it to matter, but then . . . well."

"You're a villain."

"And you're a murderer!" Hero snapped. "If we're going about handing out titles. Were we supposed to forget that?"

"Don't try to deflect this—"

"Like you did?" Hero leaned into his space, a harsh sneer coiled and ready to strike. "Perhaps we should be talking about what is going to happen when the whole of Hell's court hears about what you did, hmm? When we get back, I'm going to have such *fascinating* stories to tell."

Claire held her expression still, despite the self-doubt and misgivings curdling through her anger. "I'm the librarian."

"For now," Hero said. "What would you do to stay that way? Maybe you could lose track of another book, warden. Let's talk about that."

"Like. Hell." She held his glare, the only sound in the kitchen Leto's nervous shuffling. She would hide, she would obscure, she would mislead, but hell if she would ever fail the Library again. She couldn't stand more ink on her hands, stains that wouldn't rub out. Claire shook her head. "You were never a hero."

"Figured that out on your own, did you? Here I thought I'd been the perfect gallant." Hero's lips thinned into a line before his eyes moved over her shoulder. "Or was there a little bird?"

Beatrice lingered at the kitchen door. Her arms were crossed and she held herself tall and tense, like an arrow pulled ready for a target. "Some of us care about the truth."

"Oh no." Claire whirled on Beatrice. "You don't get to say a word about the truth."

A nerve twitched in Beatrice's haughty face. "I'm not the one who—"

"I don't trust either of you. At least he"—Claire practically stabbed Hero's chest—"knows it's a lie. He pretends to be a hero—but you think you're *being* heroic."

Beatrice's expression became injured and glacial. She said nothing before withdrawing again. Claire waited until the unwritten woman had disappeared down the hallway to release her sigh between pursed lips. She turned and caught Leto's look, which was part judgmental teenager, part injured puppy.

"You are very good at driving people off," Leto said.

"It's a gift." Claire's smile felt forced, but she offered it anyway.

Hero lost his bravado after the outburst and wilted against the wall. "It appears we both have secrets to keep—"

"Don't." Claire cut Hero off. "We will discuss your future—at length—when we get back to the Library. But for that to happen, we must get out of here. I do have a way you can help redeem yourself. Call it an act of goodwill."

"How fortuitous for me." Hero narrowed his eyes. "Why do I feel I am not going to like this?"

Claire merely smiled and gestured them both toward the table. "We need a distraction."

WHEN CLAIRE EMERGED FROM the kitchen into the study a short time later, Andras was lounging on the couch with a cup of coffee and already deep in discussion with Beatrice. He rose when he spotted her entrance, and gripped her shoulders tight in a hug. "I'm sorry, pup. I tried."

His hands lingered on the tension in her shoulders. It was supposed to be a comfortable squeeze, but felt more like a measuring of meat.

Claire ignored the quiet alarm in her gut. "The angels are already here?"

Andras ghosted a nod. "Roosting like vultures on the outskirts. They aren't in yet, but it's only a matter of time—an hour, if we're lucky."

"Hell," Hero muttered as he and Leto emerged from the kitchen behind Claire.

"Heaven, if we're being precise."

"They're watching the main gates, but I was discussing our options with Beatrice just now. There's a road that leads out to the farmlands. Only used by the residents. The bridge looks unguarded. I don't think they know about it," Andras said.

"The Hellhounds will smell us the minute Leto and I step outside the wards. How far is this entrance to the nearest realm gate?" Claire shot a sharp look to Beatrice. "There is a gate to an afterworld here, yes? Malta has too much history to be barren."

"There is . . . of a sort." Beatrice's stiff frown fell into uncertainty. "It's not active, as far as I know. There are some ruins connected to the catacombs—old, very old. There's a gate there, but I don't know what it connects to. Could be a dead realm. A lot of beliefs have lived and died here."

"It will get us out of Earth, which gets us away from the Hellhounds. At this point, I'll barter passage with the tooth fairy if I have to."

"The tooth fairy is real?" Leto asked.

Andras's grin was malicious. "Not the sort you're thinking, child."

Claire ignored them both as she considered, rapping her fingers on her crossed arms. "How far from the gates?"

"On foot, at a dead run?" Beatrice sounded doubtful. "It's close. You could make it in a couple minutes."

"There's no outrunning Hellhounds, pup. You step outside the ward, they will be on you." Andras's gold eyes softened. "Perhaps you should consider your hero's offer and stay here."

Claire raised a brow. "The *demon* wants me to abandon Hell?"

"The *demon* doesn't want to witness his dear friend's demise. Or that of her stray." Andras nodded to Leto. "You've been through enough. You could stay safe here, just for a while. I can think of something to tell the royal cuss when I get back. Maybe even get him to call off the Hounds."

A sour huff escaped Claire's lips. "Even you don't lie that well, Andras."

"I've accomplished more in my time." Andras pressed a hand to his lips. "Please. Stay here. Live a long, ridiculously human life. Several lifetimes. Read books, feel the sun, get happy and fat. You've done your time; your soul deserves it. Give this pretty idiot a chance to redeem herself."

Claire shook her head. "There's too much at stake right now."

Andras's eyes strayed to Claire's pockets. "Send the codex with me. I will take care of it."

It was tempting, even now, even with Claire knowing what she knew. Perhaps Andras saw that. He saw the way Beatrice had created a home— their home—the one that they'd imagined. There, by the window, where Claire could read within a pillar of sunlight. There, an alcove where her typewriter could go—maybe even the modern equivalent—and she could finally try to write all those stories that had festered and burned cinders into her brain. The quiet streets, the charming locals, the distant sea. The coats by the door, perfectly matched.

Of course it was tempting; fantasy always was. It was terrible and it was beautiful and it *was*. Claire's chest felt tight, possible futures clenched in a trembling breath. If she risked looking to Beatrice now, it would be all over. "You've been a mentor and a good friend, Andras. Always looking out for my best interests. But you taught me to be a better librarian than that—don't insult me by asking me to give up my duties now."

Andras's smile was strained; a shadow passed over his eyes. "Forgive me, Librarian."

Librarian, not *pup*. Claire inclined her head, and turned to find Leto looking at her with sad eyes.

"I'm staying," he said.

Claire swallowed, still shaken. "That's not unexpected."

"I can't leave, ma'am. I won't die again." Leto's voice sounded flat. "And even if I don't—I don't want to be a demon anymore. I'm human here."

Claire dropped her gaze. She understood; of course she did. And the understanding built to a weight in her chest. She squeezed Leto's shoulder once, and then there was no more putting it off. She turned to find Beatrice watching her. "You will help him?"

"He can stay as long as he wants. Just as you could." A quiet had overcome her. It was ridiculous how quickly it came back to Claire, how easily she read Beatrice's moods. She knew every tell, the way the soft skin at her temple twitched when she was carrying an injury.

The air was dry; that had to be why it hurt when Claire took a breath. "You know I can't."

"I know, and I know you." She made an aborted gesture with her hand, as if she'd reach for Claire but wasn't certain if she was allowed to. Beatrice's dark, serious gaze never left Claire's face. "I'll always be here. If you ever lose your way again."

Claire refused the heat at her eyes. No use allowing such a thing now. "I'm never lost."

Beatrice's mouth broke into a glittering, sad kind of smile. "That is true." She sighed. "And I know people in town who can set Leto up with whatever he needs."

Claire swallowed and forced her chin up and down in a nod, and nothing more. "Thank you." She glanced back to Leto. "You're sure?"

"I'm sure." Leto's tone wasn't at all believable.

"You can do this." She gave him one fierce hug, patting down the disarray in his bushy hair, straightening his collar. Then, and only then, she turned to Andras. "You know where this gate is?"

"I do."

"And you're certain it's clear?"

Andras nodded, eyes sad.

Claire drew a quick breath. "All right. Then let's run for it."

THE SILENT CITY EARNED its name when dusk fell. As tourists fled on taxis and buses, the city eased into a domestic quiet. The sun sank below the tall stone walls, painting the streets in lavenders and grays. The streets were nearly empty as Claire, Hero, and Andras made their way quickly through them.

Beatrice had wanted to guide them herself, but Claire insisted she stay with Leto. The angels were still trying to get in, and if they made their way to the flat, they would discover Leto. From what she'd seen, she wouldn't count on the serenity of Heaven keeping the peace.

Claire was counting on Heaven's wrath instead. She flicked an irritated glance at Hero. Somehow, he'd found the time to wash up at Beatrice's, and his nails looked freshly manicured, hands soft. He also had his gun out already, which was an added source of Claire's annoyance.

"We'll never escape if we get stopped for brandishing weapons."

"There's no one around. Besides, I'm not dying without getting to shoot *something* with this bloody gun," Hero said.

"The Hellhounds will have no interest in books," Claire pointed out. "You should be thrilled. You might get a chance to bob off during the carnage."

"Until Brevity decides to IWL me, yes. And when that time comes,

I'd rather not suffer the tedium of heartbroken recriminations that I abandoned you."

"As if you know anything about heartbreak," Claire muttered.

"You have no idea."

Hero said it lightly, and it almost, but not quite, masked the jagged edge to his voice. She glanced up, and Hero cast her a measured look out of the corner of his eye. They walked down another alley before the silence got too much. "Fine. I'll bite. For instance?"

Hero seemed to search for words before diverting. "I know that it takes a rare heart to break and leave behind such a sharp, cutting edge."

Claire found herself with no response to that. She chewed on the inside of her cheek as they followed Andras down another alley. "It doesn't matter, you know."

"What?" Hero met her eyes again.

"Being a villain. It doesn't matter, out here." In the fading light, Hero's eyes were dark, the green of old earth. Distant lands she'd never see. Claire turned away to keep from being distracted. "Don't get me wrong—I should have damn well known. But it doesn't matter. You saw the damsels. It doesn't matter what you're made to be, only what you do."

Hero's step faltered to match hers. "For one who calls me 'book' when she's cranky, you're affording me an uncharacteristic amount of humanity."

Claire snorted. "Well. Considering my own story may be coming to an end quite soon . . . I can afford to be a little flexible."

"This is it," Andras announced as they came to a stop just short of the arch of the outer wall. It was a smaller entrance than the grand bridge they'd crossed entering the city, more just a door in the sandstone wall, with a narrow stone bridge spanning the grassy moat. Andras stepped across the threshold first, craning his neck in both directions before giving a nod.

Claire took a deep breath. "Ready to run?"

Hero grimaced. "This is truly the safest course of action?"

"Fairly sure it's entirely dangerous and foolhardy, actually."

"Then yes, I am very ready to run."

Claire stepped through the door. As soon as they were past the shadow of the arch, there was a palpable snapping sound of the ward coming up. The air at her back hissed, and an unpleasant feeling of static shock sizzled at the hairs on her neck. There was no going back that way.

Howls shattered the quiet. Impact thrummed the stones beneath their feet. Claire had thought it impossible, but it was even louder outside the wards. Her heart vibrated in her chest with the earth-deep, bone-deep noise. Claire gripped Hero's shoulder, and they burst into a sprint for the bridge.

Shadows lunged together on the other end, and the Hellhounds broke into the twilight. Fast, so fast. Dark and large as lorries, two of the beasts turned, locking on to Claire with their blood-jeweled eyes. They charged.

Claire didn't have time to react. She didn't have time to slow down. She didn't even have time to flinch. The leading Hound leapt. She and Hero hit the ground in a pile. Hero reflexively threw an arm over her head, as if that would stop a creature with teeth like long swords. *Fool book.*

Something harsh struck stone. Then something large struck something harsh. It sounded like a car crash.

Then a silence that thrummed the stones.

When the ground stopped shaking, Claire opened her eyes to stare into Hero's bewildered face. They untangled themselves. Adrenaline turned her knees to jelly and she leaned on Hero as she stood.

Hellhounds stalked the bridge, just spare meters from where Claire and Hero stood. Barreling sledges of fur threw themselves in their direction; muscle and teeth hit the air with a jarring impact that was hard enough to make even Claire's teeth hurt. She shuddered again until she realized what held them.

In the middle of the bridge, imposed between them and the Hellhounds, was an angel clad in fire and fury.

Uriel's sword had sunk deep into the stone of the bridge, and Uriel stood anchored over it. A shimmering, barely visible wall sprang from the blade. She verified the wall was holding before turning her full attention to Hero and Claire.

Uriel advanced on them. Claire stumbled back. She spun toward the gates, then stopped.

Andras stood, waiting for them with his hands clasped calmly in front of him. Ramiel stood at his side, making a strange pair. Ramiel was much as he'd been in Valhalla, brooding and worn at the edges. A workman's build in a shabby gray coat that trailed dark feathers at his back. The angel regarded her with pitying eyes, but Claire saved her gaze for Andras.

"This was all your plan?" Her voice was dull.

"I did say to stay in the city. I begged you to avoid this." Andras's words might have been sad, but he stood straight, easy with the angel at his side. "It was the only way, pup."

"The only way to achieve what, exactly?" Hero stiffened next to her, and Claire could feel Uriel advancing on their backs. An approaching storm.

"To return things to how they ought to be."

Claire's thoughts rabbited in circles. Andras had been a duke, royalty in Hell's court once. But he'd been thrown out, long ago. He'd . . . been tired, he'd said. Claire wasn't stupid; she'd always known Andras, like all demons, was dangerous. But he'd also been kind. Kind enough to pick her up off the floor after Beatrice left, after Gregor . . . after Claire had been left alone. She hadn't been alone, because Andras had been there. She'd clung to that. She knew he was cruel, but to other people. He was kind to *her* and that was supposed to mark the difference.

It appeared to be the day for being proved foolish.

"You need the codex," she finally said.

"I need the Library," Andras corrected. "Each one of those books is a little battery, a bite of souls locked up in a book. Even an archdemon would do much to taste that. Alone they're nothing, minor bribes, but together . . .they're leverage on the court, and leverage is just what I need. There are demons that could be made to see things my way for a nice, steady supply of dreams. The remaining pages of the codex are powerful, an excellent weapon to wield. But the Library, that's where the opportunity lies. The Library is valuable. It was never going to stay isolated. You have to see that."

The realization came upon Claire like a punch to the gut. "You would . . . *use* the books as a bartering device? The Library isn't currency!"

"And the codex pages were not a matter for the Library," Andras said. "But here we are."

"The codex belongs to Heaven," Rami interjected, brow furrowed as he looked with obvious suspicion at the demon. "You agreed to deliver it. In exchange for . . ."

"In exchange for me," Claire surmised. A deadweight had developed in her chest. It wasn't surprise, or even betrayal. It felt too inevitable for that. "Are you so certain you can walk in and take it? I am not the only protector the Library has."

"That matters little with the power of the codex. I won't kill you, pup. It's why I'd hoped you'd stay—I may be a demon, but I've lost the stomach for it. Your charms have grown on me." Andras's wistful smile made Claire's hand bunch into a fist at her side. "Your assistant's haven't. She will be little challenge for those that follow me."

"You have it?" Uriel's question was more like a demand, coming from close behind them. As one, Claire and Hero judged Uriel as the bigger threat and turned.

For the first time, Claire got a close look at the Face of God. She was tall and pale, like a deity carved from stone. Broad shoulders, pale cropped hair, and a narrow nose just below eyes that would simmer judgment for eternity. Her ivory suit flowed, revealing no distinguishing features but perfection. Claire knew the look of a zealot when she saw one, unearthly or not. Uriel's wings were not a shabby feathered cloak, as was Ramiel's, but a shattered, fragmented ray of light that splintered from her back and seared eyes if considered too long. Claire briefly wondered how on Earth

that translated to a mundane appearance in the eyes of the mortals milling on the bridge.

Beyond Uriel, Hellhounds roiled like a black tide. They were close
enough to see now, masses of muscle and matted shadows, eyes a dark red
that reminded Claire of Walter's teeth. They continued shuddering in
and out of visible light, jarring like a glitching video, throwing themselves
at the shimmering wall that flickered from Uriel's blade. It seemed to
extend far in either direction, for anywhere the beasts tried, a snap of
light threw them back. Unlike the wards of Mdina, it showed no signs
of failing.

Claire was uncomfortably aware that all that stood between them and
her was the fleeting goodwill of Heaven.

Andras made a vague bow to the angel. "The pages and the librarian,
as we discussed. Show the angels your little prize, Claire?"

Claire didn't move. "Introductions first. We've not had the pleasure.
You must be Uriel. I'm Claire, librarian of the Unwritten Wing." She
jerked a chin toward Hero. "This is Hero, unwritten book of no importance. Bit of an annoying barnacle, really. You might want to send him on
his way before he latches on."

"So immune to my many charms," Hero said, but Uriel was not amused.

"You are all prisoners of Heaven. Surrender the codex."

Claire glanced toward the angelic barrier again. "Exactly how long
will your party trick hold against Hellhounds?"

For the first time, Uriel smiled. It was a smile that made the human
parts of Claire's brain recoil and shudder. "Nothing from Hell will overcome a blade of Heaven."

Hero leaned over with a mock whisper. "I'm rusty. Was that a threat
or a guarantee of safety?"

"Hard to tell with angels," Claire said.

"I can confine the human and her companions while you do what must
be done, Uriel," Rami rumbled. He spared a glance for Claire. "Though I
will only confine. No harm will come to them."

"Unless she blasphemes the will of Heaven," Uriel added.

"Well. I feel reassured," Hero said.

"Would you just *stop?*" Claire hissed.

"What? Betrayal, enemies, certain death . . . I'm not a hero, remember? The bravery was just for show. All I have left is weaponized wit and my good looks."

Uriel made a disgusted noise. "I'm eager to be done with this distasteful business. Produce the pages of the codex."

Andras took a step toward Claire and she flinched. Repulsion coiled in her throat and felt very much like panic. "Don't touch me."

"Pup, don't make this harder—" Andras started, but Hero had his gun out. Claire was pleased to note that he did not step in front of her in some idiot heroic gesture but kept angled to her side so she could move. Perhaps there were perks to maintaining a villain in her service.

"Call me pup again and Hero can shoot you." Claire's lip curled, but a hand came down lightly on her elbow. She twitched and turned to see Ramiel. She reached to throw him off, but a wave of chill passed through her. All the strength left her grip. Not just her grip, though—left *her*. Her shoulders dropped. Her mind momentarily blanked, and it took a hard scrabble to remember her present concern. It surely had been trivial, not worth her time. It'd been so long since she could *rest*. Her chin fell.

Andras moved forward and began gently digging through her pockets. She could not have fought him, even if she'd been able to form the compulsion to. Some part of the back of her mind began to snarl against it. Claire turned a horrified stare at the angel.

"I apologize for taking liberties, but it's better this way." Rami's voice was reserved. "Mortal souls. It's part of my gift."

Hero made to move, but Claire shook her head dully. A gun would do no good against angels. She tried to maintain a steady thought, but it was difficult with the cloud of calm that Ramiel had wrapped around her brain.

Andras finished turning out her pockets. "It's not here." He met her eyes with a sudden anger Claire hadn't seen before. "Where is it?"

"The other?" Ramiel nodded to Hero.

"She wouldn't trust it with the pages." Andras's eyes narrowed. "What have you done, pup?"

"Between the Hounds and the angels and this peculiar feeling I got whenever you talked about the pages . . ." Her voice was airier than she liked. Claire shrugged with as much will as she could wrest from beneath Rami's suppressing touch. "I'd hoped I was paranoid. You're the one who taught me to be cautious."

"You . . ." Andras's eyes turned sharp, and he scrutinized her face. He jerked with a sudden certainty. "The stray."

A grin twitched on her lips, a little wild and unhinged as she felt Ramiel's grip ease. She glanced to Hero. "I'd say we distracted the Hounds long enough for him to get to the gate by now, haven't we?"

Suspicion distorted Uriel's marble features. Her hand shifted, straying back to the pommel of the sword buried in cobblestone behind her. "Is there a problem, demon?"

"Not for me." Andras studied Claire's face with something like admiration, which made her stomach churn. He patted her cheek, once. His fingertips were leaching heat. "But I'm afraid I have a stray to catch. Our business is at an end."

"Andras . . ." Claire found her voice just as the demon stepped away. The sad smile on his face was the last thing to disappear as a ground spout of shadows swallowed him into the earth.

"Shit," Hero said.

The Hellhounds bayed, distant in the silence that followed. Then Uriel's face transformed. "Betrayal."

"First rule of demons," Ramiel said, unimpressed. "We might have anticipated this." He released his grip on Claire, and she realized he was watching his partner with rising caution. "Uriel, what do we do now?"

"Now?" Uriel's furious voice nearly cracked with a hysterical note. No—that wasn't the only thing cracking. A flare shimmered over her face, like lightning under clouds. Claire blinked, sure she'd imagined it, but the angel's blue eyes looked ignited. The shards of light on her back appeared to split and scissor into blades. Claire flinched despite herself.

The angels presented themselves as mortals on Earth, but she remembered the stories of an angel's true form, vast and wild enough to break human comprehension. That form played close to the surface now, and Claire's heart stuttered. There was a reason the first words out of an angel's mouth in the stories were *Be not afraid*.

"Now I will shred Hell itself, let every demon know that I will not—that the *Creator will not*—tolerate such insult. That worm dares—"

"But our . . . prisoners?" Rami pressed, having backed up a step himself.

Uriel frowned, turning to Hero and Claire as if she'd just noticed a buzzing gnat. She calmed. Her voice was distant and preoccupied. "They are of no import."

And with that, Uriel reached for her sword.

"Uriel!" Rami suddenly had his blade out and was charging forward. Whether toward Uriel or the Hounds themselves, it was uncertain. Claire and Hero began backing up instinctively.

Uriel withdrew her sword. And the barrier fell.

The Hellhounds had faded to prowling ghosts when they could not cross Uriel's ward. But with the barrier gone, shadows lurched from beneath the bridge, gobbling up the air. Hero raised his faltering gun at the nearest wraith. A gun, even a gun that started its life as an unwritten sword, would do nothing. They both knew that.

"Back!" Claire grabbed Hero by the shoulder and tried to yank him toward the gates.

"You can't pass the walls."

"The point is, *you* can!" Books were made by humans. The Mdina wards had to recognize them as such after all. "Get going."

"Still not taking your orders, warden," Hero said.

Claire snarled the filthiest oath she knew. Now, of all times, was not the moment for a villain to get ideas about heroism.

Rami jabbed at the Hellhounds with his blade while exchanging heated, indistinct words with Uriel. Rami's sword produced enough lightning to dissuade the beasts, but did not have the same stopping power as Uriel's wall. One Hound kept him busy while the others shuddered, blinking through existence to burst onto the bridge. An approaching Hellhound lurched, paws landing on the cobblestones with an oily, lethal grace. Claire jerked back but was forced to stop when a crackle of pain danced against the back of her skull. The ward sparked at her back. An echo sang in her mind. A song.

Claire prayed that Leto had carried out the rest of the plan. That Leto had made it. Would make it. That what she felt at the edge of her senses, a glimmer of a sound, was true and not wild delusion.

She licked her lips. They had seconds, not minutes. "You have to trust me, Hero."

Hero moved to position his tall frame a breath ahead of her, pressing her back hard enough to bury her face in his soft velour jacket. She felt, more than saw, his brittle amusement. "Why start now?"

A chill ran up her spine, and she curled a hand into Hero's jacket. "It's what humans do."

The nearest Hound, teeth dripping oblivion, leapt. Hero's shoulders dipped and braced. Claire swung her arms around his waist and held tight just as the ward behind her crackled. Another set of hands latched onto her shoulders and yanked.

Claire had a momentary view of the darkening star-touched sky filled with the Hellhound's red dagger teeth before she fell backward through the Mdina wards, Hero toppling in after her.

28

RAMIEL

I wasn't a storyteller in life; that much I remember. No matter the stories in me, my people needed strong arms, not words. Scholars and soldiers are natural allies, though few ever recognize it. Both worship at invisible altars, one of knowledge, one of duty. It takes a certain kind of soul to protect the invisible, to protect an idea.

Librarian Ibukun of Ise, 886 CE

HELLHOUNDS, DESPITE THEIR CANINE appearance, were not deterred by thunder. The air crackled all around Rami, and the blade grew heavy in his hands as he moved, extending his sphere of reach ever farther to drive the creatures back from their prey.

Then a reprieve. The moment Claire fell back through the ward, the Hellhounds stopped. They sniffed the air, ignored Rami's feints completely, and melted back into the night. Their absence underlined the stillness of stone, rapidly cooling in the evening air. Rami glanced behind, but the librarian and her rescue had disappeared into the city.

Rami leaned on his long sword a moment, breathing heavily. It had been a long time since he'd needed to raise his sword against anything, let alone against a foe like a Hellhound. He drew another staggered breath.

When he finally turned, he could see only Uriel's back. She was hunched over the crumbling stone railing that marked the end of the bridge. It was crumbling more by the moment, as she slowly ground her fist into the cornice.

"What. Was. That?" The words growled out of Rami's chest, and he found himself having to stop, take another heaving breath, and clamp down on the frozen horror sitting in his chest. Uriel still hadn't turned, so Rami tried again, pleading this time. "Uriel! That was cold-blooded. You've gone too far."

That brought her around. The archangel lurched toward him. The anger on her severe face didn't surprise him; the tears did.

"Don't talk to me about 'too far,' Ramiel of the Fallen. Not when you practically leapt to defend a demon—"

"The librarian is *not* a demon! That was a human soul you just unleashed Hellhounds on for no good reason. They were under our protection! You—"

"They *have* their god. Why *should they be protected?*" All confidence and command were gone, leaving the jagged edge of misery behind. "Why should they have anything? The Creator is gone. *Gone.* She has abandoned us and that *snake* has the only means to bring her back." Uriel's ragged voice bounded off the stone and broke.

A shriveling feeling crept under Rami's lungs. The collar of Uriel's coat fluttered; a smear of dust flinched up one side of her cheek, stopping just short of the glow of fury-banked eyes. Uriel was fastidious. She would never have tolerated dirt on her face. But her hands came up not to wipe it away, but to knot in agony in her hair.

Uriel was the Face of God, to all. But to Rami, she'd become more: she'd become the face of *home*. The face of hope, the hope of returning. The hope of welcome. The hope of rest. She was shattering, bleeding violence at every jagged edge, and Rami's hope bled with it. The cost was too high. He couldn't follow this. An angel with a thirst for vengeance . . . no. Not again. He'd already seen the devastation that caused. He couldn't go down that path again.

Even if that path was the only one that led him home.

He would say it was like a closing door, but the Gates of Heaven had never been open for him. Instead, a dull certainty welled in his chest, and with it a realization. Rami found himself reaching out a hand, but the tremors marked Uriel's shoulders like delicate earthquakes. He dropped his hand. "Why do you really need the codex, Uriel?"

"For the Creator, you fool. For . . ." Uriel stopped, glaring sightlessly at the warded city through her tears. The archangel went quiet. "I can't do it for much longer, Rami. None of the Host can. I don't know why we ever thought we could. Running things . . . It's all falling apart."

Fear deepened Uriel's flawless face, lines etched where none had been, not in the ages since the birth of the world. Shadows in a being of light were far, far out of his experience. All of this was. Rami was used to falling, to running, to wandering. Not this.

"I don't know what else would bring Her home," Uriel whispered.

There would be no answer that way. The Creator was a god, not a lost house cat. She would not be tempted back by a bit of warm milk left outside the door. Wherever She was, *if* She even was, She was exactly where She wanted to be.

The Creator was lost, and so was Ramiel's way home. But he wasn't as strong as the Creator; he couldn't turn away, even now, not without another path presented to him. So instead, his mind numbly reached for what it knew best: duty. The codex was an obvious danger, and they couldn't risk it in the hands of a demon like Andras, especially with the Creator absent. He sheathed his sword so as not to look at her. "What would you have of me now?"

Duty, service. It was an all-curing elixir, for angels. Especially angels like Uriel. The tracks on her face dried. She seemed to sew the broken edges of her mask together, piece by piece. She drew up straight, and her gaze came to rest on the spot where Andras had disappeared. "Our prey has split. The demon is intent on taking the pages to the Library, so I will make the necessary preparations for Hell. You will track the humans. It's what you're best at. The Hounds will leave a wide enough path; perhaps they will lead us to the codex."

Rami strained to keep the uncertainty off his face. "And then?"

"And then . . ." Uriel paused to marshal her own sword. She stared at the blackened spot where it had been planted in the cobblestone. "Then all of Hell will have its reckoning."

29

LETO

Earth is freckled with belief, positively pockmarked with it. No great idea fades from the planet without leaving a mark, and we dwell in the craters. We rely on these old lines and cracks to conduct our business. But watch out; belief changes, and so do the doorways. Walk through the wrong one and it won't want to let you go.

Librarian Claire Hadley, 1994 CE

LETO WAS REMEMBERING THINGS about his life.

Mostly he was remembering that he hated running.

His side had stitched up, morphing into an angry, hot pinch that twisted his lungs every time he inhaled. His pulse thudded, fast and thick in his head. His feet were numb from slapping bare stone, and that made him clumsy as he clambered up and down the broken tunnel passage.

Catacombs, Beatrice had said, and Leto had imagined some stately mausoleum. Perhaps a stone building, statues artfully crumbling here and there, coincidentally lit with a mysterious torch like they were in the movies. But this was something entirely different. It was a hole in the ground that forgot to stop. It was a crooked path daggered with roots and stone and other objects that Leto tried not to consider too closely as he tripped over them. Bare crevices had been cut out of the dirt walls and held scattered bones and bits of cloth. All of this was illuminated not by thoughtful torches but by his single flashlight, splashing quivering light around as he ran.

It was a place, most important, that Leto very much did not want to die in. So he ran, scrabbling at dirt and stone and cowering every time a shower of dust fell from overhead.

The others had set out to create a diversion outside the ward to draw off the Hellhounds long enough for Leto to get to the realm gate via a second path. Claire assured him she would be fine and would catch up with him later in the realm beyond the gates. All Leto had to do was keep moving.

Leto hadn't believed a word of it. He'd been around the librarian enough by now to see her fear. But it was his own fear, his own shameful, crippling terror at the sound of the Hellhounds, that had made him nod. It was his fear that agreed to the plan. He'd meant to follow her. Follow her *forward*, he'd said. But instead his courage had failed him yet again and left him here, hurtling through the dark.

He hadn't told all that to Beatrice. The unwritten woman had not been happy when Leto finally relayed Claire's plan. She'd been distressed enough when Claire and the others had left, but when Leto explained that Claire had been suspicious of Andras and had asked Leto to carry the codex pages to Hell, Beatrice had flown into a barely contained panic. She'd stormed around the apartment and seemed quite ready to bolt after the others until Leto had added something: that Claire had said to get him through the gate, then check the outer ward for the others. Just in case.

Well. He'd *said* that was what she'd said. He'd improvised, ashamed of leaving Claire and Hero to do the hard part. The least he could do was send Beatrice as backup. Beatrice hadn't needed convincing. She had regrets too. Hanging around unwritten authors had taught Leto a lot about the words one didn't say.

They'd gotten to the cramped entrance, hidden in the sewers not far from the fountain he'd seen earlier, when Beatrice's conscience caught up with her. She stopped abruptly at the door. Her hands flew to her head and she grunted.

"I can't. I *can't do this*, not again."

"But Claire said to get the pages to the gate first—"

"I can't leave her to face the consequences alone. Not again." Beatrice's hands fisted in her hair before dropping, still clenched with tension. She seemed to come to a decision. "I'm going after her. You can make it from here. Now, listen closely."

Leto repeated Beatrice's instructions in his head. *Follow the tunnel, veer right when it splits, keep going, no matter what.* He'd been going for a while now and was surely outside the walls, outside the ward. But being underground, among the dead, would confuse and slow the Hellhounds, Beatrice had said.

Not long enough to save him, if it came to that, but long enough for him to run, which was the important thing: to run. When Leto reached the end, Beatrice said, he would see the realm gate.

If there was an end, Leto hadn't found it. He began to worry he'd missed a right turn somewhere in the dark. He took another aimless corner and was about to consider turning back, when a stone outcropping caught him on the shoulder.

Stone in the shape of a fist.

A hand slammed Leto against a wall, and his flashlight flew out of his grasp. Leto's head jolted against hard-packed dirt, and stars briefly dazzled the dark. When they cleared, he couldn't see anything—at first. Slowly, two pricks of gold light resolved out of the darkness. A gem-shaped light flared, stabbing painfully at his eyes, and Andras's face melted into view.

"Hello, stray."

The demon had shed all previous pretense in the dark, keeping only gaunt features, harsh and cutting edges. A sharp-toothed smile split a skull-like face, and the shadows danced wildly as he adjusted his grip. Cold, bony fingers squeezed Leto's throat closed.

The fingers constricted again and slammed Leto's head against the wall. Pain flickered from a spark to wildfire. Everything went gray this time. When Leto could open his eyes again, Andras was shuffling through his pockets.

He had located the folded sheaves of parchment in Leto's suit. There was no more explanation; Andras simply took what he wanted. Leto struggled even as the world tilted hazily around him. But Andras batted his hand aside easily and tucked the codex pages in his own pocket. He made a tutting noise under his breath.

"'This is mine. As is this. See?" Andras held up a thick gem, set into the small dagger that he'd offered to the ravens. That seemed like ages ago. It glittered, matching all the other gems and ornaments pinned to Andras's clothing. Leto had assumed it was for show, some old-fashioned vanity, but now he saw how wrong he was. Each bauble glimmered independent of the light. *Relics from the Arcane Wing*, he realized. In the dim light of another gem—Leto couldn't make out the color or cut—the dagger handle in Andras's palm pulsed with energy. Something moved and bubbled beneath the stone's surface, like a predator in deep water. Leto recoiled without thinking, earning a chuckle from the demon.

"A simple soul gem. Perhaps you recognize it. It's a cousin of the ghostlight. It also latches onto a dead soul, but this one consumes."

Leto couldn't tell if the movement in the stone was increasing or if it was just a trick of the wildly flickering light. He tried to pull away out of instinct. A clawlike thumbnail caught under Leto's throat, pressing until the skin was taut. A pleased chuckling sound came from the demon. "I could have used this against you, against all of you, at any moment during our time together. I didn't, for Claire's sake. I want you to tell Claire that. Give my pup a message. Tell her to stay away from the Library."

Leto bit his teeth together to stifle a whimper as Andras drew a thin line of blood on his neck where he pressed down. Leto worked his throat, holding himself still as he tried to speak around the claws in his skin. "You won't win. You aren't a librarian. You're not even human."

"Of course not. I have no intention of *administering* the Library. What would be the point?" Andras's tone turned silky and dark. "But the court is always hungry. That will secure what I *do* want. I'll have it all."

"You can't—" Leto cut off as a claw broke the skin at his neck again.

"Now, now. Lesson time is over. None of this needs to get messy if you remember your message for Claire. But I need to ensure it carries the proper . . . gravitas. It would be wise to hold still, child."

The medallion in Andras's hand burst into sickly orange light. Leto began to struggle, ignoring the claws sinking into his neck. And then he began to scream.

"MERCIFUL JESUS."

The oath floated through Leto's sluggish head. He couldn't place the low feminine voice. His eyes fluttered open, and he momentarily panicked when he saw only darkness. Then a light flared, and it came back to him: the catacombs, the tunnel, Andras . . . the codex. Leto jerked, but a cool hand stopped him.

"Easy, Leto. Hero—give me a hand here. Help him up. We have to keep moving." Claire's voice hovered somewhere to his left.

Larger hands gripped his arm, and there was a grunt as he was hauled to his feet. "Up you go, kid."

The movement brought the sensations of his body flooding back to him. Hot pain shuddered up his limbs, pulling a jagged sound from his throat, and Leto would have collapsed again without Hero's support.

"*Gently* help him up. Did I really have to specify that?" Claire's voice was sharp even as a cool hand checked his cheek and ran down his shoulder, inspecting wounds. "Bea, a little more light."

The flashlight swung around and seemed to pierce Leto's skull. But he was finally able to make out the faces above him. Hero and Claire clustered to either side, and Beatrice was a tall, dark shape hovering behind them. Claire scowled thunderclouds at Hero, who was keeping him upright.

"You *said* we were in a hurry." Nonetheless, Hero loosened his grip slightly and glanced at him. "You all right to walk, kid?"

"I think so." After the initial wave, the pain faded to a bone-deep ache. Most of the pain, that is. Leto winced. "I think I broke my arm."

Claire's hand drifted to the injured arm. Leto managed to make only a mangled squeak as she probed it. Her voice was taut. "I doubt *you* broke it. You'll be all right, just as soon as we get to the Library." She hesitated. "Andras did this?"

Leto nodded. The glint of claw and gem came back, in a rush. The loss. The crush of codex pages in a jeweled fist. He found a lump had developed in his throat and he had to swallow hard. "He got the pages. I failed. . . . I—I'm so sorry."

Claire started waving her hand before he even got the apology out. "Not unexpected. We can deal with it. I'm just glad you're alive. We'll just—" The earth walls around them lurched, showering clods on their heads. Baleful howls vibrated from afar—but not far enough. Without a word, Beatrice began shoving Claire down the hall. Hero hauled Leto into a stumbling pace.

"We'll just *run*—that's what," Hero finished. He shot a grim look at Beatrice. "How much farther?"

"Nearly there."

Every step made his arm shoot with electric bolts of pain, but Leto forced his feet to keep up with Hero. They turned another corner. Leto heard a strangled yelp, and Beatrice brought the flashlight up to show Claire backing away from a dark ledge. The tunnel emptied out onto an abrupt precipice. The light did not reach far, but wind whipped at the edges of Claire's skirts. Leto could feel the enormous space in front of them.

Claire snatched the flashlight from Beatrice's hand and craned her head. The light disappeared into aimless darkness above them, but when Claire swung the beam down, it hit on something white. Leto leaned forward as far as he dared to peer over the ledge. Far, far below them, the light bounced off dull ivory surfaces. Like seashells, an ocean of seashells.

It took Leto's brain a moment to accept that the shells were, in fact, the human kind.

"A mass burial," Claire breathed. She swung the light up into Beatrice's face. "A dead end. Is there a way across?"

"In a manner of speaking." Beatrice looked uncomfortable.

"What . . ." Claire's eyes widened. "*This* is the realm gate?"

Beatrice opened her mouth, but her explanation was drowned in another hail of dirt. A clear howl came from the depths of the catacombs now. Closer. *Much* closer. The Hellhounds had their scent, and though the ancient catacombs had slowed them down, it wouldn't be for long. Leto edged nervously toward Claire.

Beatrice leaned over the ledge. "You have to jump. Right here." She indicated a spot in the air square off the precipice and somewhere below them.

"The hell I do!" Claire muttered.

"It's a burial rite, Claire. The path to the afterlife. The religion might be long dead, but still—we don't have time to debate!" Beatrice practically shouted, and stepped forward as if she was going to push them both. Claire brought up her flashlight like a club, and Hero drew his gun. Beatrice stopped. "You have to trust me."

Claire's lip curled. "Oh no. I made that mistake once."

"I'll do it." The words were out of Leto's mouth before he thought them through. He could feel the immense weight of the Hellhounds as they materialized in and out of the tunnel, shoving waves of air and dust in front of them. He ached everywhere the air hit him, and he just wanted it to stop, wanted not to feel as broken, as useless as he did in front of Andras.

He wanted the fear to stop. And he wanted to make a difference. "I'll jump first."

"Absolutely not—" Claire reached out for his good arm.

But without debate, without fanfare, without even permission, Leto walked into open air.

And the darkness had him.

30

LETO

Realms can die. I said that before. It's rare, because humans love nothing more than holding on to an idea, worrying it in their teeth until it's shaped into something else. But it happens, occasionally. When a realm loses access to dreams and imagination, it starves. It's not a gentle death. A realm will attempt to preserve itself, feed itself on any unwary dream, any stray soul that wanders into its maw.

Librarian Gregor Henry, 1980 CE

SAND CLOGGED HIS TONGUE and rasped against his teeth. He couldn't breathe. Panic flared. The sand reached into his throat and threatened to draw bile. Leto came to consciousness coughing and then bolted into a sitting position. He doubled over, forcing a startling amount of silt from his mouth. When his eyes stopped watering, he found he was sprawled on a wide shore. Silty gray sand stretched in either direction as far as he could see, salted with a scruff of reeds and dunes that sloped down to a flat, strangely still sea.

Not a sea, Leto thought as his eyes adjusted to the light. The water was a dusty mirror, still but streaked with brown and algae. He squinted across to just make out a skim of pale gray that indicated land on the other side. A river. A dead river.

To his right was a particularly starved patch of reeds, and it was from this that Claire rose with a squawk. "No warning about that impact. I will murder her. I don't care if she's my own book. I will—" She stopped, frowning as she picked tiny seeds out of her skirts. "Can I not stay clean for *one* hour?"

Leto grinned despite himself, but there was a groan behind him before he could respond.

Hero rolled up and with grim distaste retrieved his boot from a puddle. He shook it out and glanced toward Claire. "At least a nap seems to have returned someone's sense of spirit."

Claire was getting better at ignoring Hero, it seemed. She turned a critical eye on Leto. "Everyone all right?"

"I think so." Leto rubbed the back of his head. The moment when he hit the invisible gate had been a queer jumble, rattling his senses around like pebbles in a can. His arm was still broken, protesting movement, but he could wiggle his fingers, and his aches were less painful in this realm. Bodies were distant things. "Where are we?"

"Very good question." Claire stopped fuming over her dress long enough to survey the area. "Not a realm I'm familiar with. River, sand, reeds . . . an old pagan culture. Not Greek. Egyptian? Oh, please let it be Duat. We'll have fast passage back to the Library with help from the librarians there. And they have an excellent poetry collection. . . ." Claire's eyes lit up, and she began to mutter what sounded like a bibliography to herself as she inspected the waterline.

Behind them, a strange dark arch loomed across the interminable sand. It was as if a circle of obsidian had been buried there by a wayward giant. Leto approached and leaned closer to inspect it. A flicker of white in the black material made him jerk back. The interior of the arch wasn't opaque, he realized. It was the darkness of the underground chamber they'd just left. The other side of the gate.

Leto ran a hand experimentally over it, but the surface was solid and unforgiving. The sound from the other side was muted, but he could still hear the howling of the Hounds. Nothing stirred in the dark frame, though. No light, no gleam of Beatrice's aluminum bat.

Leto said lowly to Hero, "Beatrice?"

Hero winced and shook his head slowly. Leto's stomach did a flip-flop. He cast a nervous glance back. Claire turned her head down. The curtain of her hair didn't hide the injured curl of her shoulders.

"Dead?" Claire's voice was hollow.

Hero hesitated. "I don't know. The Hellhounds . . . should have stopped when you dragged us through."

The distant sound of barking from the other side of the arch said they hadn't gone back to Hell, at least. Claire stared sightlessly at the sand a moment, then nodded slowly to herself.

The pinch of concern on Hero's face deepened. "There's a chance that she . . ."

"Enough." Claire cleared her throat and straightened to look toward the water. "Let's figure out our way across, then, shall we?"

Claire wasn't heartless. Leto knew that well enough by now. But as unflinchingly practical as she was to everyone else, she reserved the tightest reins for herself. Leto wondered if anyone else bothered to look closely enough to see the strain. He could see it now, the tic in her jaw, the way her shoulders trembled, just a flicker, before setting themselves hard against the world.

She'd been taking care of Leto all this time. Caring for him like a lost child. He ached to do something to ease the way for her. Something. Anything.

Hero exchanged a long look with Leto before following her down through the reeds. "Not to put a damper on the day at the beach, but what happens if we do manage to return to Hell? Andras already has the pages and a head start on . . . whatever."

Leto remembered Andras's words. "He wants the Library."

Claire seemed unsurprised. She crossed her arms. "He wants more than that, I suspect. He wants the court."

"The court?"

"Hell's court of demons. Dukes, princes, the whole pit of vipers." Claire made a face of distaste. "Andras was a duke of some influence, once. He was overthrown in a coup centuries ago. Infernal politics. I thought time had healed that insult, but I was wrong. I knew he was unusually interested in the codex. I thought it might lead to some pissing match over its curation. But I could deal with that easily enough when we got back. I never thought . . ." Claire kicked a reed, abusing it with the toe of her sneaker.

"But why the Library?" Hero asked.

Claire frowned down at the plant. "I'm not certain."

"He said something about . . . ah, you know who," Leto said.

"Lucifer's our ruler, not a dark wizard, Leto. You can say his name," Claire muttered. "He said he wanted to use the books as collateral, to buy his way back into power. But he has to assume that Lucifer will not tolerate that. Even if he has the codex, I can't see—unless he knew something he wasn't telling me—" Claire stopped with a growl in her throat. "Demons, angels . . . politics ruins everything."

"Right. Sorry. I just . . ." Leto waited until Claire left her tormented reeds behind and met his gaze. "Andras had something—a soul gem, he called it. He said he could have used it but didn't. If we stay away."

It hung in the air a moment—the possibility of retreating. Leto saw that twitch again. That strain under pressure ignored. Claire shook her head and his chest ached. "The old man never did understand."

"Leto might have a point," Hero spoke up. "He could already have won and have something unpleasant waiting."

"He won't have the books. Brevity is there, and the Library is not without its own humble defenses. I won't risk the books—or Brev—to Andras's plans. We'll get back the pages." She kicked a broken reed into the water. "Assuming we can leave."

The reed barely cleared the surface when a froth of sound drew their attention. Claire leapt back from the bank as the water churned, turning from slate to muddy black. A knobby, elongated skull the size of a small island broke the surface. Green and silver veins mottled the skin, contrasting with the flat, black, bulbous eyes embedded at the top of a long snout. It reminded Leto vaguely of a crocodile, but he didn't remember the creatures on Earth being so monstrous.

The creature regarded them, the only movement coming from the filthy water beading down its snout. Claire glanced at Hero and Leto before clearing her throat and stepping forward. She drew up her dignity, and it almost obscured her bedraggled hair and sand-caked legs. "Greetings. We are envoys from—"

BE JUDGED.

Leto nearly startled off his feet. It was not so much a voice that had spoken but an assault of concept. Something had ripped open his skull and shoved the essence of the words directly into his brain, jumbling all thoughts of his own. The words had no voice, no tenor, no personality. Just the power of age and a hunger that was never refused. They pulsed through his head for several breaths until finally easing into a thudding headache.

The shudder that whipped through Hero and Claire said they'd received the same treatment. Hero's hand flew to his side, where his gun had returned to its form as a fine sword. Claire shot him an alarmed look and shook her head until his hand dropped away again.

Claire straightened into her librarian demeanor: shoulders back, spine straight, chin tilted so she could fix her gaze on whatever held her disdain. But she eyed the crocodile creature with new caution, and Leto caught her fingers making nervous little taps at her skirts as she tried again.

"You mistake me. We are not the dead seeking judgment. I am the head librarian of the Unwritten Wing in Hell's Library. We happened here while on Hell's business. Can I know what realm we've entered?"

BE REFUSED.

Claire flinched. "Then may I speak to your master?"

BE REFUSED.

"Then what god or pantheon rules this place?"

BE LOST.

"You have no god? Or no god currently?" Claire asked. Pain jabbed Leto's head with each answer. It was becoming the worst game of twenty questions he'd experienced.

BE LOST.

"Your god is the god of loss or . . . oh." Claire fell quiet. "Your gods died with their believers. I hadn't thought a realm could remain after that."

Leto considered. They'd seen Valhalla, and the only things he associated Norse gods with were superhero movies and those racist assholes on the internet. But Valhalla survived by evolving into something more in line with the legend than with the religion. It existed, if skewed slightly by the pop culture fantasies. If Valhalla thrived and these gods had died, then this had to be a place older and more forgotten than he could imagine.

He swallowed nervously, and the very air tasted different on his tongue. Different from Valhalla or Hell or anywhere previous. No smell, for one. Not the anise and ash of Hell, nor the pine and stone of Valhalla. It felt . . . empty.

It echoed across the empty space inside Leto, and he shivered. He'd felt better, inch by inch, since talking with Claire. The time in Mdina had been a human time, for all its horror. He'd felt the empty blackness shrink, but it wasn't gone. Perhaps it never would be. It was one thing Claire couldn't protect him from.

But maybe he could protect her.

Claire tried again. "We simply need passage to Hell. Or the closest realm to it. We can leave you in peace."

BE JUDGED.

"We are not in need of judgment! Some of us aren't even human." Claire flung a hand in Hero's direction, but the crocodile did not so much as blink. Though it quieted a moment before responding.

BE PASSED.

"Yes, passage. Finally." Claire crossed her arms. "I assume there is some price for passage?"

Waves shuddered up the beach as the head suddenly moved. Reptilian skin flexed, and the head rose slightly as its great jaws opened, sending them all backing up a step. Leto flinched, expecting great rows of teeth or even the bloodred spikes that filled Walter's mouth. But the contents of the creature's mouth made him blink. Suspended between its jaws, held by no support that he could see, was an oversized metal structure. It was dark bronze and consisted of two platforms connected by a lever. A tiny puff of white sat on one platform. A feather. A bronze chain shifted slightly with the sway of the wind, producing a tinkle that sent a shiver over Leto's skin.

"Are those scales . . . ?" Hero identified it under his breath.

Claire stiffened, staring at the construction as if she would have preferred a jaw full of teeth and snakes. When she glanced back at them, Leto saw that all warmth had drained from her brown face. She turned her head again and shook it hard enough to send the tiny braids in her hair flying.

"No," Claire whispered. Then louder: "No. You have no authority to judge us. Our souls—"

BE JUDGED.

"No." Claire's voice couldn't match the command of words in their heads, but the tremble in her shoulders said she was trying. Leto didn't understand what was significant about the scales. They'd had to prove themselves in Valhalla, and Claire had been willing, if reluctant, to comply to gain entry, but this was different. It was a difference that unnerved Claire and sent a well of foreboding through him. There was no time to ask as Claire spun, heel digging into the sand. She scrambled back up the beach toward them.

"What—"

"Burn this place. We're leaving."

"And going where, exactly?" Hero asked.

"Back to Mdina. We'll . . . get back inside the walls. Figure something else out."

"Back to the Hellhounds' teeth, you mean." Hero's voice was harsh.

"At least we have a chance with them. Better than— Piss and harpies." The oath came out with the force of surprise. Claire jerked to a halt as they approached the black arch. It was no longer dark. The cavern they'd just left was lit by strange globes of light. The field of bones was now fully illuminated, like ghastly cobblestones. And at the center of the arch, just on the other side of the flat, dark surface, was the angel in a gray trench coat. Ramiel.

Claire, rather than concerned, was incensed. She accelerated, stalking up the sand, leaving Hero and Leto no choice but to follow. She got her nose up to the arch. Ramiel watched her expressionlessly, and Claire gave a mockery of a smile. "Trouble with the lock, angel?"

"Some." Ramiel stepped to the side and motioned with his hand. "Perhaps you could come across and show me the trick of it."

Claire cast a glance back at the waiting monster and the scales behind them before responding, "After which, I'm sure you would offer to hold off the Hounds and allow us to be on our way."

He shook his head slowly. "I'm sorry, Librarian. Uriel . . . My superior acted in haste. But my duty is to ensure you do not interfere."

"Do you always do your duty, *Watcher?*"

Ramiel gave no reaction. Claire turned away abruptly to confer with Hero and Leto a few paces away.

"He won't be getting through. Beatrice had me to pull Hero through, so if I don't miss my guess, you need a mortal soul to enter. But we need a way past him."

"I could challenge him," Hero suggested, but Claire shook her head.

"He's a Watcher, one of the originals." She raised her eyes to the crocodile scales again. "Our last hero may have died getting us this far. I won't have any more foolish sacrifices today."

"What do the scales do?" Leto asked.

"They weigh the purity of a soul." Claire's face was grim. "This realm must have had influences from Egypt. Maybe a splinter cult, or even a predecessor. It's not Duat—if it were, there'd be a bunch of other monster-headed creatures here ready to record judgment, and be *much* more sensible. There were rules about these things. But the symbolism is easy enough to assume. The feather represents goodness, purity of spirit. If your soul does not shift the scales, you can pass into their realm. If it's heavier . . . the crocodile god will likely consume you."

Leto frowned. "And you, what . . . die again?"

Claire shook her head. "I know this is a hard concept to wrap your head around, but there are worse states for your soul than death. It's like the Hellhounds, or the words I told you I spoke to banish Librarian Gregor. I don't know what the scales do, but it would be nothing good. A soul may not die, but cease to exist."

"That's not so bad," Leto muttered before he realized he'd said it. He looked up to see Hero and Claire staring at him with matching alarm. "I mean, no! Not us, of course. I meant . . ." He stopped, not sure what he'd meant, but the terrible thought had come to him too fast to be one he hadn't had before. An echo of a memory tugged at him, chalk white stars, exhaustion and despair. He'd made this choice before. Cold pooled in his stomach.

Claire scrutinized Leto before shaking her head. "It's beside the point. I suspect the creature has no real interest in finding us worthy. Without a god to rule the realm or believers to nourish it, it likely hasn't had a good meal in eons. It's half-dead and starved. We are not going to be the ones to feed it. I'm going to go see if I can make the cursed angel see sense. Stay put, both of you."

They nodded and watched the librarian stalk back to the arch. Hero clasped Leto's shoulder and squeezed as he looked up and down the featureless beach. "We'll figure something out, kid."

"We will." Leto nodded.

But his eyes were reserved for the dark bronze scales. He thought of the promise he'd made to Claire, the debt he owed her. The darkness in the pit of his stomach that would never quite be banished. He thought of the feeling of falling through the gate, the weightless way the world turned quiet. It had felt welcome; it'd felt familiar. He'd already made this choice.

It made sense. Death was the way you traveled between realms. The echo of the raven roads had never really left him, but he wasn't panicking now. Like the tumblers turning in a lock, everything fell into place inside him. He studied the glimmering sheen of the platforms, the whiteness of the feather, and the shadowy hollow of the crocodile's jaws beyond.

31

RAMIEL

First of all, realms are proud. Realms are proud and vain creations—never forget that. Realms are too proud to bow to your wee ideas of physics and common sense. A realm doesn't have to make sense to its inhabitants. Do not expect a realm to conform to your logic, not if you want to escape with your mind intact.

Realms are beholden to one thing, and one thing only: the inertia of their belief. Anything can happen in service to a story.

Librarian Bjorn the Bard, 1673 CE

What is a story without want, without desire, without need?

Librarian Gregor Henry, 1896 CE

THE LIBRARIAN APPROACHED.

Ramiel raised his brows at her, though his eyes made sure to track where her two companions wandered, just at the edge of the gate's vision. It was a disorienting thing; the portal was built into the floor, superimposed over the pile of bones. He had to crouch over it, but Claire walked toward him straight on, as if it were simply a doorway on her side. The effect made his neck stiff.

The Hellhounds had departed by the time he ventured into the catacombs, though the deep claw marks on the stone signified some struggle had occurred. He noted the librarian was missing the mysterious fourth companion who had pulled her through the ward at the Mdina bridge. He saw no sign of a body. He could only wonder what the price of their escape had been.

That she and her remaining companions had passed through an un-documented afterworld gate was obvious. Uriel said she'd known the gate to every surviving realm on the island, but as soon as he entered the ruins, following the Hellhound trail, it was obvious this one was not accounted for.

He located the gate at the bottom of the mass grave fast enough, urged on by the scent of death and loss that swamped the entire cata-comb. It resisted as he approached, repulsed by his foreign presence. His vision had allowed him to thin the barrier enough to see and hear, but whatever ritual was required to satisfy the ancient gate was unknown to him. He knew these ruins belonged to a long-dead water god, but the worshippers had died out long before.

As long as he had them cut off from escape, he was doing his duty. If the way out of the strange realm was barred in front of them, they would have to come out soon enough.

"So. Your duty." The librarian crossed her arms. "Your duty to 'ensure we don't interfere,' meaning that the moment we cross back over, you de-tain us—in one piece if we're lucky?"

Rami raised his chin. "I can swear you'll be treated with the mercy and justice of Heaven."

"Is that the same justice that turned the Hounds on us once we were no longer a bargaining chip? I don't believe I have the stomach for your justice, Ramiel."

Damn Uriel and her madness. "You can trust—"

"You've given me no reason to trust." Claire cut him off with a sharp hand wave. "How can you simply stand there and do *nothing* while de-monic forces overtake the Library?"

It was a disingenuous argument at best. Rami shrugged. "It's in Hell. Aren't demons always in the Library?"

"You don't know what chaos Andras is willing to unleash to get his title back." She shook her head. "Haven't you ever heard the saying 'better the devil you know . . . '?"

"I have tried not to know more than I have to."

"Strikes me you had more occasion to know the man in charge than I have," Claire said.

Rami bit down hard on a curse.

But she knew her history. He'd followed Lucifer when they'd fallen, abandoned Heaven. Not because he agreed with him or believed in the cause—Rami was not as ambitious as that. But because he was a Watcher, one of the old ones first sent to aid and teach the Creator's fledgling creation on Earth. He'd taken that duty seriously.

And when man suffered, when Rami's charges were dying in droves for lack of food or an abundance of disease that they lacked the knowledge to resist . . . the Watchers had taught them how to survive. The Creator had deemed it "forbidden knowledge." And so the Watchers had followed Lucifer when the Gates of Heaven shut forever behind them.

It had been the first time he'd seen what the madness of angels could lead to. Rami had never regretted the cause of the Fall, though the result had not sat well with him. He'd lingered, watching Lucifer bandy his forces and establish a domain of his own. But he wasn't an empire builder. He wasn't a leader. His heart was still with his duty, the humans on Earth. Not as pawns in a futile war with Heaven, but as creatures with budding potential that could be protected. He hadn't always done a good job of it. Doubting, wandering over the next millennia. But it had been the only path that made sense to him.

Until Uriel had offered him the position in Purgatory.

Until a strange little accountant had walked up to his bench and dropped in his lap a problem that caught Heaven's eye.

Until Uriel had revealed her bloodlust. Until a librarian decided to show a stubborn sense of honor and complicated everything.

Rami almost found himself wishing for the Purgatory desk again.

But then, he knew he would not be returning to the Gates, no matter how this played out. Rami had only his duty left. "I am no friend of the Deceiver. Do not look for sympathies where you will find none."

Rami noted that Claire's companions had stopped in front of the scales in the creature's maw. A furtive argument started. The gangly demon with wild curls—Leto, he remembered; Claire insisted he was human— gestured wildly at the handsome swordsman, motioning past the mon- strous creature in the water. The man appeared upset, a crinkle appearing on his perfect brow. He could have been an angel, were it not for the calculating way his gaze flicked to the arch and back. The swordsman shook his head hard, and the argument continued. Rami could not hear the words spoken, and Claire's intense displeasure was focused entirely on him, which meant the librarian was not aware of the discussion occur- ring behind her.

Curious.

She tapped her fingers on her crossed arms. "What if we offered to leave one of us with you, a hostage? A guarantee that we are striking no offense to Heaven. Your sadistic partner did seem to enjoy terrifying those she had in her grasp, but if you swear no harm would come to him, I could allow Leto to stay while I set things right." The woman's eyes went distant, concerned. "That might actually be the safest place for him."

Rami ignored the offer and the opinion of Uriel, but picked up on the worry in her eyes. "Are you certain you're fighting a battle you can win?"

"The books need protecting. It's my library, and I won't relinquish it. But . . ." Determination drained out of Claire with a breath, leaving be- hind something gentle and tired. "I'm old enough to know the costs of any victory."

Behind her, the argument had met a begrudging standoff. The swords- man had resorted to pleading, shaking his head, but the teenage boy seemed set on something. They traded quiet words and shook hands. The teenager asked something, and the taller man, after a long silence, nodded. Then the teenager looked toward Rami, gaze lingering on the librarian's back. It was a look so filled with unspoken ache that Rami was surprised

Claire didn't feel it. And then the teenager turned and walked toward the mouth of the beast.

He was climbing to the scales, Rami realized. He knew what scales in an afterlife meant. He could read a realm as well as Claire. The boy was submitting his soul for judgment. Rami had seen enough war, enough strife, to know the shoulders of defeated men. The exact line of the down-turned head of someone who knew his fate and had given up fighting it. The boy knew what the scales would find in his soul.

The librarian was not the only one who understood costs, it seemed.

"What are you . . ." Rami must have betrayed something with his face, because Claire followed his gaze over her shoulder.

The teenager had one arm bent against his stomach but held out his other in supplication. The crocodile spirit brought the scales closer. The boy placed his feet carefully on the reptilian lips and left the shore.

Claire made a sound as if she'd been struck, then breathed a word. "Don't . . ."

Claire pelted down the beach, but the swordsman took three wide steps to intercept her, whipping his arms around her waist. She was practically lifted off her feet as she scrambled at the man holding her back.

"Stop! Don't do this!" Claire's voice was jagged, more shattered than Rami had ever heard it. The swordsman bent his head and muttered into her ear soft words that were entirely unheard.

The teenager paused, one hand on the scales, as he looked behind. From the distance, Rami couldn't make out his precise expression, but the boy raised a calm hand.

And then he stepped on the scale.

An inhuman howl, half fear, half fury, welled up from the librarian as the scales started to dip. She twisted and dragged them both to the sand as the crocodile god's jaws started to close. The boy held tight to the bronze chains of the scale and seemed to shiver as the shadows of the crocodile's jaw passed over him. Darkness wrapped over his face. The bronze scale glimmered once, twice.

Then the scales and the boy were gone.

In the silent moment that drew out, as the crocodile god closed its mouth and sank its head back beneath the muddy waters, Rami realized his mouth had dropped open. His chest had gone cold.

A thin keen carried over the sand, and Claire collapsed in a mess of skirts and braids, shoulders trembling. The swordsman kept a tight grip on her shoulders as he crouched next to her, as if afraid to let her go lest she attack the crocodile god itself. He made awkward attempts to pat Claire's shoulders, then resorted to drawing her forcibly to her feet.

Rami saw why. The crocodile had reoriented upon resurfacing. The boy's soul must have satisfied, for now the great creature surfaced with its closed snout touching the shore. Its body extended, just breaking the surface, until it bridged the entire width of the waters and its impossibly long tail rested on the far shore.

The swordsman tried to guide Claire toward it, but the librarian broke free of his grasp with an explosive jerk. She strode back to the arch with a furious speed.

Her usual clay complexion was pale, her eyes red from unshed tears. Her cheeks were stubbornly dry, but the grief and the fury that limned her face gave it a fire all its own.

Rami clenched the pommel of the sword at his side, half expecting her to burst through the gate and launch herself at him.

But Claire stopped just short of the gate, chest heaving. "You did this." Her words were rough as gravel from crying. "He was innocent, and he died because of you. And for that . . . for *that*, Watcher, I will remember you. And one day I will bring all of Hell upon you."

The swordsman caught up to her and hesitated at her back. Claire didn't wait for a reply. She twisted past her companion and stumbled, taking her broken warpath toward the crocodile bridge.

32

BREVITY

War has always followed libraries, my apprentice. History has made no effort to hide that truth from us. Look at Rome; look at the Crusades. Vanquishing an enemy and taking his books was just as strategic as taking his cannons. Books are knowledge weaponized.

And what weapons you cannot steal, you must burn.

Librarian Gregor Henry, 1986 CE

DURING A PANIC ATTACK, time takes on a liquid nature. Stopping and rushing on at once. Feeling like each struggling breath stretches out forever like taffy until the bubble bursts and the present cascades down on your head. Cold and immediate.

Brevity was surrounded by the soothing smells of oak and dust when she came to. A carpet twitched under her toes and the dribbles of tea stains eventually helped her place the underside of Claire's desk. Big, heavy, secure. There were worse places to hide forever.

"She's dead."

"She's not dead. She's a muse; they're immortal."

"Maybe it's a *short* flavor o' immortality, eh? It's her name, innit?"

"Hush, Libby. Aurora said . . ."

Three pairs of feet clustered at the opening of the desk, none of them seeming to go together. Combat boots, scuffed buckle shoes, and one pair of dainty blue hooves. Brevity buried her face in her hands and swallowed a groan.

"See! She's alive!" A mop of red curls upended itself over the edge of the desk, and a damsel gave her an upside-down grin. "Welcome back!"

God, was *that* what she was like when Claire complained she was inappropriately cheerful? Brevity might have contemplated hiding, but the bubble had already burst and time pulled her forward again. She allowed the trio to drag her to her feet. Conversation was a shock of water to her senses, not clearing the panic, but compressing it. Freezing it up into a tiny bundle that caught between her ribs and held, for now. Brevity reached for the first words she could think of that sounded vaguely librarian-ish. "Wh-what are you doing out of the suite?"

"We were going to complain about the noise. It's been going on for hours," the red-haired damsel said. Charlotte, Brevity remembered, taking in the patched dress and scuffed buckle shoes. Probably from one of those puritan moral historicals, where girls were more symbols of . . . something . . . than characters. Purity. Sin. Life. Death. Puritans never did seem to make up their minds about it. Aurora, blue hooves toeing the carpet nervously, hung over her shoulder.

"What noi—"

The question answered itself in a creaking shudder. The Library trembled. The lights flickered, though there was no reason for them to—perhaps just to express the Library's displeasure with the situation at hand. Books twitched uneasily in their stacks, and the damsels looked wide-eyed at Brevity.

Helplessness, sharp and familiar, welled up again, but Brevity had an audience this time. Audiences helped. Brevity put on her best smile and pretended to find something on Claire's desk that urgently needed straightening. "The wards are up—just . . . just a precaution until Miss Claire gets back." Her smile was guttered by another violent thunderclap that hung in the air. "That there is probably just annoying ol' demon roughhousing. You remember Valentine's? Ain't nothing compared to that."

"If the wards are up, doesn't that mean we're cut off—"

"S'not like we're gonna get written anyway," the second damsel interrupted. This damsel was short and angry, like a wet cat wrestled into a leather jacket. Her once-long blond hair had been haphazardly shaved, perfect ingenue features pinched into a frown. "Our authors been dead for decades."

"It's nothing to worry about," Brevity jumped in before Charlotte could be hurt by that remark. "Just librarian business. M-Miss Claire will be back any minute, and wouldn't want to have her catch ya outside the suite, yeah?"

She shooed the damsels off, ignoring the way Aurora trailed after the other two, a quiet blue shadow that cast long, questioning looks back at Brevity as she went. They'd believed her; of course they had. It was what the Library did: distant librarians going about their business, keeping the books in their care well and at arm's length. It was the norm Claire had set, and if anyone noticed that it was Brevity—social, flighty, trivial Brevity—trying to fill those shoes now, the damsels were too sweet to say so.

The empty spaces between her ribs quivered, but held. Brevity pressed her palms to the desk, feeling the vibration as another impact hit the wards. It was a steady drum now. Something was trying to invade the Library. Whether it was because Andras had lost control of his Horrors, or it was some demonic plot to pull the Library into the tug-of-war games of Hell's court, Brevity had no way of knowing and didn't *care*. From inside the wards, the Library was alone.

Alone. The word made Brevity want to crawl back under the desk, but instead she pressed her knuckles into the wood until they stung and the gilded lines of inspiration on her skin stilled. The capacity for fear was still there, because the unknown was still there. But the damsels had reminded Brevity that imagination wasn't just a weakness; it was a tool. Anxiety could fill up the darkness with all the monsters it wished, but if

Brevity tried very hard, maybe she could squeeze in one monster of her own. She was cut off from the world, but she still needed to protect the damsels, keep them in the suite, protect the books. All she needed was an audience.

Care for the books, Claire had said. There was at least one book not yet home in the Library.

33

RAMIEL

The strange thing about souls is they're damned resilient. I mean, look at me. Librarian for six hundred years and counting. According to the log, that's a record! You'd reckon I'd be worn thin around the edges by now. I won't pretend I'm not filthy tired of looking at these same walls. But I'm going to keep on, not fade away. Think of the stories I'll have to tell!

Mark my words, souls are made of tougher stuff. You can wear one down, tear one apart, unspool all the thread, shave a piece off even, but destroy one? I imagine there's an end, somewhere. Or states of being that are as good as an end.

But even an end is just where you run out of book. Stories change, and stories go on. Maybe souls do too.

Librarian Bjorn the Bard, 1598 CE

RAMI HAD WATCHED UNTIL the librarian and the book had disappeared across the crocodile beast's back.

He'd waited while the creature churned the water and disappeared again, leaving behind only a gentle foam that melted into bright blue waters. The abandoned stretch of beach stilled, waters turning idyllic instead of frothy. As if none of it had ever happened. As if a human soul hadn't just been sacrificed to satisfy some pagan thirst. As if the needless sacrifice hadn't been because they feared the justice of Heaven.

Because they feared him.

Fear not. The voice in Rami's head was sour, mocking, and too similar to Uriel's timbre for his taste. Angels were supposed to be feared. By evil, by forces of chaos. They were made to be feared to drive the darkness back. Not to drive suffering young souls into the mouths of hungering beasts. That, Uriel and Rami had done on their own.

The ruins were cold. Rami turned away from the arch and rubbed the gooseflesh out of one forearm, staring sightlessly at the bones churned to dust at his feet. None of this sat well with him. They'd drawn blades against mortal souls. They'd made a deal with a demon, and as a result, the armies of Hell would be arraying against one another. If demons were at one another's throats, even if—and Rami felt it most unlikely—Lucifer himself got overthrown, surely it would result in a stronger position for Heaven. He could return to Uriel and get orders on how to proceed next. The petty losses and trials of those who would serve Hell were none of his concern.

And yet, he couldn't get the image of the boy on the scale out of his head. Couldn't forget the broken noise that shattered from Claire's throat as the jaws descended.

A lost soul, she had called him. Lost souls had been Ramiel's duty once. All the Watchers had owed their services to humanity, once, before the Fall. Rami's responsibility had been the guidance of the lost.

Rami hadn't felt competent to guide anything in a very long time.

But the look he'd seen on the boy's face hadn't been lost. His eyes had been clear, and his chin had been set. Even broken, he'd stood straight as the shadows closed. That kind of calm, that kind of peace, didn't deserve oblivion in a dead god's realm.

It took Rami only a thought to return to Heaven from Earth. He arrived at the Gates practically before he realized he'd made a decision. The Gates felt smaller, the light less bright somehow. He cut through the cattle line of dead souls, ignoring the sputtered cries of the lesser cherub that had filled his place at the desk. He strode past the guard, not toward the Gates but toward the tower. He hesitated only a moment to be surprised that the door was unlocked before he shoved his way in.

"Ramiel." Uriel raised her brow from where she leaned over her desk, archaic maps spread before her. "Report."

He paused, clasping his hands behind his back as he considered how to approach the plan shaping in his mind. He opted for formality. "The adversary escaped through an undocumented gate."

Uriel stiffened. "Hell?"

"No. Some afterlife of a local dead religion. Worshippers long extinct. Water worshipping and sacrifices. I didn't recognize it."

"Continue."

"I stationed myself and observed their progress. They lost a b . . . an ally. It's now just the librarian and the unwritten book. They proceeded deeper into the realm. I believe they will seek a direct exit to Hell. They won't come back to Earth again."

"Good, very good." Uriel seemed preoccupied with her maps. "That will buy us time for our next plan."

Rami squinted, but couldn't make out the gibberish scrawled across the maps between them. "Sir?"

"Hell." Uriel looked up, and Rami nearly stepped back at the bright, hungry gleam in her eye. The archangel made a fist on the surface of the map. "You heard the demon. That's where he'll take the codex pages."

Rami held very still. "You want to infiltrate Hell."

"Not infiltrate, invade."

"That means *war* and the Creator has forbid—"

Uriel's fist thudded against the desk. "The Creator is not *here* to forbid! Think. The point of getting the codex was to decrease Hell's power and return our god to our realm. Why settle for a piece of paper when we could present our maker a *kingdom*?" Uriel looked up and the zeal roaring in her eyes diverted as she studied him. Her shoulders relaxed. "But you, of course, are not part of my forces anymore. You need not concern yourself with it."

Rami felt off-balance. "Sir?"

"Yes, of course. We had a deal. You didn't succeed in procuring the codex, and I should point out your commitment wavered at times, but . . ."

Uriel made a dismissive gesture. "You acquitted yourself well. I will speak to the Host as soon as this whole library business is behind us."

The fuel in Uriel's fireplace cracked as the silence drew out. Galaxies burned and grew cold.

The Host. He'd thought he'd made up his mind, but Rami's resolve wavered. In his mind's eye the Gates opened for him, the first time in millennia. It'd been so long he could barely imagine what lay behind them, but he could feel it. He could *taste* it, gold and warmth, peace and absolution. He would be allowed to go home.

But even in his imagination, his step paused at the threshold.

Rami sought for some footing, some words to say. He was being dismissed. And he discovered, somewhat to his surprise, that success left him hollow. He frowned down at the carpet. He didn't care for Hell. The whole realm could fall into the abyss for all he cared, the Library with it, though a twinge in his chest said that wasn't entirely true.

The Gates in his mind whined on their hinges.

Uriel's vengeance would lead to war. Her zeal would lead to fire and scorched earth. But realms would always war against realms, and Rami wasn't made to care for realms. He was made, from the core of his being, to care for souls.

The Gates shut in his mind. And then the words were out. "Their ally they left behind. I want to try to secure him and bring him back here as an asset."

His skin was cold, hollowed out with the first chill of his decision. His nerves pricked, but Rami looked down at his hands and found they were steady and clenched into fists. Uriel looked up with a mild frown, as if she'd already mentally dismissed him and was annoyed her office was still occupied.

"Value being . . . ?"

"Information. He was working closely with the librarian. Might be able to tell us what to expect." Rami saw the skepticism in Uriel's eyes. He felt a stab of reluctance but added, "He also could grant us access—he was one of Hell's, and he may be able to get us in or draw their forces out."

That did it. He saw the shift as Uriel's gaze thawed from skeptical to calculating. She considered Rami for a long moment. "This is a tactical mission?"

"Yes, sir," Rami lied.

"Fine." Uriel waved vaguely at the door as she turned back to her maps. "The guards outside can procure your old equipment for you. See that this lead bears fruit for Heaven, Ramiel."

For the first time in ages, Ramiel left to rescue a soul.

34

CLAIRE

At some point you just get tired. Is it possible for a soul to get tired? It has to be. I was young when I came here, and my skin never ages, but I feel the creaks inside. The poorly settled joins where time whistles through my thoughts like a sieve.

It's not a sad feeling. I know what I'm about. I know what's important. I know the weight and feel of my life in my own hands. I'm a rock, ready for the sling. I'm tinder, ready to ignite.

They'll send me an apprentice one of these days; I'm sure of it. I can't drag another soul into my fight. If I'm going to act, it has to be soon.

Librarian Poppaea Julia, 49 BCE

STORIES SAID GRIEF WAS heavy. Stories lied. If grief had a weight, had a mass, Claire could have ground the crocodile god's bones into the bottom of the river. She could have sunk her heel into the knobs of chill scale and felt a god break beneath her toes for what it had done.

But grief did not have a weight. Or if it did, it was counteracted by another force. Rage. *Rage* had an upward lift, was a superheated force that crawled up her throat and wanted to do all the things Claire couldn't. Punish the crocodile. Punish this realm. Punish Ramiel. Punish Hero. Punish herself.

She'd felt it, when the scales had tipped. The crocodile's jaws had closed, and her screams had hitched as she had *felt it*. She shouldn't have.

This was not her realm, not where her soul was tethered, but she had felt it like a tear in her lungs.

Had she heard a scream? Had she heard a tear of flesh? Or had she just heard the staccato sigh of a soul unraveling, winking from the universe? She couldn't tell. Her mind was a muddle, and the only thing she knew was that Leto, the one being she'd encountered in thirty years she thought she could actually *save*, was gone. For her.

Claire did not fancy herself an optimist. She had been in Hell too long for that. She saw things clearly. But somewhere along the way, what she'd seen most clearly in Leto was hope. Hope for him had become hope for her, and she'd believed. Believed he was a good soul and that good souls would not be punished by realms. Believing was supposed to be power here, power to protect him. It hadn't.

She hadn't.

It felt like she was walking on Leto's bones. But nothing of Leto remained here, not after the crocodile had judged him. She was walking on his ending, and for that, she walked lightly, calmly. For Claire was not one to throw away her life rashly for vengeance. She respected vengeance. Vengeance deserved time.

And she was already contemplating ways to return to this blighted, half-dead realm one day and burn every inch of it to the ground. She didn't care if she burned with it.

The instant their toes touched the sand of the opposite shore, the creature began to sink. By the time Claire had gotten her bearings enough to turn around, all that remained was the dark froth of churning water.

Claire stared ahead. The beach on this side of the water was very like the beach they'd left behind, but instead of endless sand, the shore rose to a great wall of bone pale stone that staggered a dozen feet over their heads. It terminated in what looked like the craggy ruins of a temple, long in decay. Nothing but gap-toothed bits of wall and column remained.

Hero's gaze was a physical thing, heavy and insistent like a hand on her back. She had said nothing, not since cursing the angel at the gate. No words as they walked the crocodile's back, no commentary or speculation on the realm they were in, no orders for what they would do next. Claire felt his silence deepen, first into pity, then into worry, then judgment.

She couldn't find the energy to care.

They struggled up the beach and stopped in front of the impenetrable wall. Without discussion, they took a right and followed its edge, trudging through sucking, wet sand. It swallowed any chance of conversation. Hero asked no mocking questions; Claire offered no confident explanations. They paused only once, when Claire's low sneakers filled with sand, and she bent to kick them off. She tied their laces together and instinctively went to loop them over her bag. When her hand met open air, she came to a stop with a sharp, halting breath. She swung them over her shoulder instead.

Hero observed the error with quiet pity.

The sand dug grit into the tender skin between her toes. A break in the wall appeared behind the curve. It wasn't a proper doorway. Instead its arches were shattered like a splintered bone in the ribs of the ruins. Inside, the ground turned from sand to smooth, hard-packed earth. It ran straight with thick walls rising on either side, open air above.

"A maze?" Hero ventured.

"So we've reached the Minoan part of our tour." Claire wiggled her toes into the sand. It should have been warm from the sun. Instead it was cold enough to make her bones ache. "It's a labyrinth. Souls were meant to wander until they met their demise at the center of it. Lucky us."

"Every maze has its exit."

"You obviously haven't read enough Greek tragedies," Claire said. Still, it was the only gap they'd encountered, and the sun had begun to creep down in the sky. Claire didn't fancy the idea of spending the night on the beach, so close to the crocodile. She shook the sand from her toes and stepped onto the unforgiving dirt.

They followed its turns until they came to the first intersection of two paths. The pavers were wet with mildew and thick with identical shadows. At least Hell had the occasional gargoyle, Claire thought dully.

Hero hummed. "Left or right?"

"Left. If we keep following the left, we'll find the exit eventually. If there is one. And if something else doesn't find us first."

"Read that in a book, did you?" Hero's smile faltered as he received only silence. He twisted a hand through his hair and muttered dark nothings to himself as he followed.

Claire became aware of a distant noise, a low groan that ground out the spaces between the sound of their steps. It slowly resolved into a gutted howl; somewhere there was an animal in unbearable pain. Claire almost felt a kinship with it. It took another half dozen turns before Hero reached the limit of his patience. "He insisted it was our only chance."

A flare of heat broke through her calm before she could ruthlessly tamp it down. *Maybe. But not a chance I wanted.*

Hero took silence as a sign to propel forward. "I argued. I said he shouldn't be hasty. You might convince the angel to let us back through. Aid us, even, the way you like to talk. He said he saw the way they looked at us, and there was no chance. He . . . he said he blamed himself, for the ghostlights, for losing to Andras. For doubting."

Claire's bare toe tripped over nothing as she sped up.

Hero caught up with Claire and released a helpless sigh. "What would you have had me do?"

"*Stop* him." It came out like a hiss, but caught on its own jagged edges. Claire's eyes burned and the path began to waver ahead of her.

Hero shook his head. "I think he wanted to make the choice. To ensure you got back to the Library. He was so certain, so at peace, and then . . ."

The calm inside her shattered. Claire whirled on him. "What? Then what? The nine-stone-soaking-wet teenager overpowered you? You should have *stopped* him. Held him to the bloody ground if you had to! He was just a child. He didn't know—"

"He was a man who made a choice. You don't get to take that away from him." Hero's voice was hard. It brought Claire up short. "He made a choice, and you're doing his choice a disservice by calling him a child.

Leto wasn't a child. He was a human, a young person who'd had everything taken from him, yet he deserves . . ."

Hero pursed his lips, as if stopping himself, and seemed to jump to a
different train of thought. His tone cooled to clipped edges. "I am a book.
A creation. A possession. As you are so fond of reminding me, I am
bound to go only where the Library allows me and will spend all my
foreseeable eternity having decisions denied to me." He held up the wrist
that Claire had stamped when she'd cornered him, what seemed a life-
time ago.

"But Leto, Leto was a human, and he had a right to his choices. You
helped him remember that." Hero lifted his shoulders. "I might have dis-
agreed with his choice, but I would not steal his right to make it, because
I know how that feels."

Words caught on her lips, clotted just under her tongue. Claire dis-
liked the taste of guilt that came with it. The swoop of regret in her stomach. She'd stamped Hero, bound him to her will, and doomed Leto.
Claire struggled with the impulse to deny the rage, and the grief that
drove everything like a flood in her head. Instead, she turned away. Took
another left. "Let's just keep going."

THEY KEPT GOING.

Claire lost track of time, lost track of the number of lefts they took
as the sun sank lower. It became a blur of stone and distant moans that
threatened to burrow into her skull. Until they came to the stairs.

Labyrinths didn't have stairs.

They were set into an empty expanse of wall, worn, but sufficiently
intact to look as if they'd bear a person. The uneven steps were hemmed
by more stone and quickly twisted upon themselves, a curved staircase
that didn't reveal more than a few steps before disappearing upward.
Claire tilted her head up. The walls were high but open to the perpetual
twilight. Not high enough for a second floor, not high enough for the
stairs to lead anywhere, despite the strange new light that dribbled down

them, just around the bend. The stairs couldn't lead anywhere, couldn't exist, no matter how she twisted the physics.

If this place had physics.

"It could be a way out," Hero suggested.

"More likely it leads directly to the creature we've been hearing for the last few hours."

"Probably. But . . . it is on our left."

That, against all reason, decided it. Claire swallowed her doubts and ascended the stairs. After three corkscrew turns and a dozen steps, they broke upon the landing of another long, tidy hall. Unlike to the ruins they'd left behind, this hall was well maintained.

The sky was still open above them, but the darkness was lit intermittently by torches ensconced at regular intervals along the hall. Hero swept up one of the torches that kept the deepest shadows at bay. "Just in case," he muttered a bit sheepishly.

As they turned another corner, they could see a new break in the wall up ahead. A soft light rippled out of an arch and pooled on the stone floor. A chill danced up Claire's neck, and Hero had tilted his head. "Do you hear music?"

Claire listened, but there were only the constant far-off rumbles. "No. What do you— Hero?"

Hero lurched toward the arch.

Claire, for once, found herself being the one to have to jog to catch up with him and his long legs. "Hold on a moment! We need to be cau—"

Hero reached the doorway and turned his face to the strange light. The torch fell from his hand, then guttered on the stone. Claire burst forward to face whatever new monster waited.

Springtime.

In their hallway, it was dark and chill in the dead, forgotten realm of the afterlife. But across the threshold in front of them, grass burst from the stones and slowly faded into a thick forest carpet. It swelled with fat moss and large-leafed bushes before giving way to the paving stones of a tidy cottage.

It was a forgettable construction, squat and consisting of conveniently stacked stones and aging wood. The hovel was barely taller than Hero, but one look at the blue-painted door and swept pavers said it was well loved. Flowers of an almost lurid variety burst from boxes by the steps, and smoke rose lazily from the chimney.

"Croak End," Hero breathed. "That's . . . that's impossible."

"What is this?" Claire felt unease and kept her toes away from the patches of false sunlight.

"That's home." Hero's pronouncement left a cold shock in her stomach. Claire returned her attention to the tranquil little scene in front of her. "My . . . my story."

"That can't be. Your book is here. It's likely a trick of the realm," Claire warned. She frowned as she watched a rabbit munch on the grass nearest the threshold. It twitched its ears as if it'd heard her insult. "I had expected a castle for you, the way you talked."

A strange, soft smile broke out on Hero's face. His eyes never left the arch. "Humble beginnings," he murmured. "Castles came later. This is where I grew up. Or next door to it. My place was smaller. Not nearly as nice. My neighbor . . ."

Hero broke off with a gasp as movement stirred at one edge of the arch. He stumbled a step toward the threshold. A lithe young man in dark leathers emerged from the trees, startling the rabbit. He walked with easy, rolling strides, a simple bow slung over one shoulder. His hair was longish and braided, the end of a mahogany plait tickling at his collarbone. He seemed to be whistling to himself, though Claire could hear nothing of the tune.

"Owen." Hero's face warmed beatifically as he watched him. "Owen! We grew up together. He was always there, even when . . ." He paused, looking troubled as he considered it. "How had I forgotten about him?"

Her alarm grew louder with Hero's excitement. Claire clasped his elbow, trying to draw his attention. She could feel the tremor of tension in it. "It's a story, Hero. He's not really there—none of this is. It's got to be a trap. Come away from there."

"He hasn't cut his hair yet. He still has that ratty old bag," Hero muttered fondly, not even hearing Claire. His face softened as he watched the hunter shuck what appeared to be his day's catch onto the porch and kick mud from his boots. "And still poaching. I warned him about that. I always said he would get us both—"

He stopped, all color draining from his face. Claire grew concerned. "What?"

"They killed him." Hero said it levelly, but the words were rimmed in hot rage. His jaw worked as his gaze—never on Claire—turned anguished. Rage set into the curl of his lip and turned his delicate features sharp, cruel. "He stood by me, always protected me, and they *killed* him. Your precious heroes killed him. And I couldn't do anything to stop it."

Claire gripped Hero's wrist. "It's a story, Hero. A *story*. Look at me. Think this through."

"It's not happened yet. I could stop it. I can—" He reached out a hand toward the arch.

Claire knocked his arm down as she stepped in front of him. Only her hands firmly on his chest kept him from brushing past her. "*Listen* to me, Hero. You have to listen. This is just a story, a vision, a trick. Block it out. I know it hurts, but it's *not real*—"

Her shoulder blades slammed into the stone wall behind her and forced the air from her chest. Hero had his arm pressed against her throat. His snarl veered between broken and burning. "You can't see anything past your precious books! We're all just objects to you. This isn't a story. He isn't a *trope*. It *is* real. Owen is real—they are all real. Real to me, real to everyone who loved us. Don't you *dare* . . ."

"Hero—I was . . . I didn't mean you're not—you're—" Claire struggled to get back the breath that had been knocked out of her, but the muscled vise at her throat presented a challenge. "It's a trick. Hero, you need to stop and think. You need to listen to me, and you need to listen to me *right now*. Please."

Claire shifted. Hero looked down and saw Claire's hand clenched on the hilt of the sword at his hip. Truthfully, Claire's fingers were numb, and the scabbard was in the way. She doubted she could do any harm at this angle, but she met Hero's gaze as he looked back up. She swallowed hard and repeated the only word that was making it through his panic. "Please."

Claire's hand began to cramp up. She didn't dare move, didn't dare speak again. The moment felt stretched and fragile. Then something broke. A raw emotion flickered over his eyes, then was gone. Hero sagged and drew back.

Claire wobbled a moment, then sank halfway down the wall to breathe. When she looked up, Hero had his back to her, was silhouetted against the dappled sunlight streaming through the arch. The hunter, Owen, had retreated inside the cabin. Hero stared sightlessly at the front door, the smoke curling in the clear, white-blue sky.

"I could have saved him. I could have saved all of them. I could have fixed it this time. I could have—"

Claire feared for a moment that he'd take that final stride across the threshold and disappear into sunlight despite himself. But in the end, his shoulders crumpled. Hero's gaze fell to the floor, and he jerked away as if it burned. "Sorry, Owen."

He took a stiff, halting step. Paused just long enough to offer Claire a hand. Claire took it, pulling herself up on unsteady feet. They shared no glances this time. They said nothing more.

They walked. Drawing out of the light and continuing into the permanent shadows of the labyrinth.

THEY ENCOUNTERED NO MORE doors, no more possible futures. When they finally stumbled on another set of stairs, they took it and found themselves back in the dust-swirled ruins where they had begun. Twilight cast long shadows over the tops of the stones, cooling the air in the labyrinth quickly. Hero had left his torch behind, and without Claire's supplies, they were soon plodding down paths in the dark.

Once they'd cleared the stairs, words came more easily. The farther they walked into the dark halls, the closer Hero and Claire drifted to each other. Words were harsh, stiff things between them, sparking like stones, but they walked, arms brushing together, in silence. The unnatural quiet of a world halfway to not there.

When they stumbled into the last dead end in a series of wrong left turns, Claire shook her head and slumped against a corner. "Let's just rest here for the night." Even immortal souls could get tired. Humans in the afterlife ate and slept, not because their bodies needed it, but because their sanity did.

"Dead end. How apt."

"Don't be dramatic."

Hero grimaced and glanced around, as if looking for wood to make camp, but when nothing but hard earth and stone appeared, he sighed and slid down the opposite wall. Nervous hands, without a task to busy them, played over his knees.

"You should have seen the castle," Hero finally said.

Claire tensed, uncertain where his thoughts were taking him. Her mind flashed on the cabin in the woods and the handsome boy with the bow, and she opted for a neutral answer. "Is that so?"

"It was the kind of thing I think you would like. Big library, all the creature comforts. None of this hardscrabble adventuring for me. I had a manse, servants. Fluffy bed, a lovely study, and the most charming wine cellar you'll ever find . . ."

"A rags-to-riches aristocrat, then?"

"Not quite. Rebellion is easy. Being clever, striking out where it hurt . . . I was good at that, as you might expect. We were so virtuous, so confident in our rightness. Being right is easy, but then ruling is . . . complicated." Hero looked thoughtful before reverting to the shrug that Claire had begun to recognize as carefully crafted carelessness. "I prefer the term 'philosopher king.'"

"Of course you do." Claire's lips curled into a smile. "What possible motivation could you have to be a villain with a life like that?"

"I never felt like the villain. We were overthrowing a corrupt system, me and Owen. We were going to fix everything. And then he was killed, and I didn't want revolution; I just wanted revenge. And then . . . you turn around one day and realize you have a kingdom that hates you, no matter what you try to do. You begin to hate them a little too." Hero quieted for a long moment. "I thought I could change it for the better, you know. Make her see the truth of it, see what a world she was wasting."

He wasn't speaking of Owen anymore. Claire didn't have to ask what "her" Hero referred to. For an unwritten book, there would only ever be one "her" or "him." The one who'd failed to let him live. Claire half expected him to say more, but the topic of his own book seemed to unsettle him. His gaze went distant and lost at some point over Claire's shoulder.

Watching him withdraw, Claire became aware of a muted, sympathetic twist in her chest. And then, to her surprise, some of her own grief began to thaw. She'd be a hypocrite to dismiss it now. She studied him for a long moment. "Your author must have thought of you often."

Dark green eyes blinked, and Hero returned from his thoughts in a daze. "Why do you say that?"

Lightness felt wrong in a place like this, so she offered a shrug instead. "There's a lot of things that can wake up a book. But one theory is books are pulled awake by their author's dreams—believe me, I know how that can go wrong. But to wake up and take shape like you did, to escape despite the Library's precautions and find her so fast. You're just so"—Claire made a vague twirl of her hand—"alive."

"I much prefer it to the alternative." Hero rubbed the space between his eyes. "Not that it's done me much good."

"Yes, well . . . Women of a tender age don't take to sudden breakups well." Claire suppressed a smile. "If you weren't a villain in her brain before, you certainly are now."

He dropped his head to his knees and a dry chuckle rumbled in his chest before seeming to stutter and trip over itself. He looked up, alarmed. "Is that how it works? Did I— Was I fated to inspire my own author to make me a—"

Claire saw the gears threaten to spin off the tracks in his brain, and she couldn't suppress the laughter that bubbled out. Hero stopped with a startled look, which only made Claire laugh more until she was drained. Too exhausted to be stern.

"Oh, Hero." She shook her head. "Even the Library doesn't know how stories are made. Or not made, in our case. Try to put together who you are, why you are . . . Well, that's the path of madness."

"I'm glad you find my existential crisis so entertaining, warden." Hero's voice was arch, but it was softened by the curve of his lips.

They fell into a tentative truce of quiet. The chill of the stone wall was seeping into her spine, and Claire shifted, trying to find a comfortable spot. It was going to be a long night. There was a glimmer as Hero's eyes tracked her fidgeting.

"Do characters forget themselves, warden?"

"You should know better than anyone."

"Not from damage, I mean. Can characters forget their stories for good?"

"What a curious question . . ." Claire frowned in his direction in the dark. "Why do you ask?"

Hero seemed to chew on his answer a moment. "When I—when we— Oh, bother, it's annoying containing multitudes. I used to be part of the whole, speak for the whole book. I *was* the book. All of us, all our dreams, fears . . . even the bratty, idiotic heroes. But that's begun to fade. I can't feel the others anymore. I'm beginning to feel more and more . . . singular."

Alone. Hero's voice quieted as he said it, his eyes closed, as if he could dismiss the conversation through sleep if it became too uncomfortable.

He was afraid, Claire realized with a start. It must be a disquieting feeling, being alone in your own head for the first time. "You're still a character tied to a book, but you're also becoming an individual. Exposed to things other than your story, you may be changing from how you were written. It's one of the reasons the Library quiets the characters that wake up."

"Except damsels."

"Except the occasional damsel, yes. But only after their author is al-

ready dead and gone, and there's no risk of damaging a potential book,"
Claire allowed. "They change, grow. . . . The damsels become people. I
used to think only damsels did that, but you're proving that wrong.
There's more to every one of us than what our story intends."

Hero's eyes slit open. "Is that why you defended me back there? You
think you've tamed yourself a villain?"

"Not in the slightest." Claire smiled as she made out the unwritten
man's startled expression in the dark. "It just doesn't matter."

"It doesn't matter? What, in the philosophical 'we're all damned anyway' sense?"

Claire shook her head. "Stories are, at the most basic level, how we
make sense of the world. It doesn't do to forget that sometimes heroes fail
you when you need them the most. Sometimes you throw your lot in with
villains. Neither Heaven nor Hell is very happy with us right now." Claire
leaned her head back. The weariness hit her all at once as she looked up
at the strange configuration of stars that peeked through the ruins. They
twinkled red and purple, she realized. Nothing was familiar in this place.
"Whatever you are, your story's still unwritten."

Again, silence. She thought he'd nodded off, but then Hero spoke up
quietly.

"Claire."

"What now?"

"You're not expecting a happy ending here, are you." His words were
a statement rather than a question.

The breath staggered in Claire's throat. She kept her eyes closed. "No.
Not since the ghostlights went out." And not since Leto. There were
things Claire still couldn't say. "Maybe it ends well for the Library, if it's
still standing. Stop Andras, protect the Library. That's what I intend to
guarantee. But for me, no."

"That's a shame."

"Indeed."

Hero seemed to consider. "I don't think I'm going to like mocking a
different librarian. Maybe I'll run away again."

"You'll do no such thing. Sleep."

Whether Hero slept or not, he didn't speak again. Claire listened to the far-off groans, felt the chill stone beneath her cheek, and almost regretted the silence. Almost asked Hero to start chattering again. But she didn't, and eventually she slept and dreamed as she knew she would. Of bronze scales and red stories, and remembered books turned to forgotten graves.

DIM LIGHT PEEKED UNDER her eyelids. Claire woke up tasting dust and ozone on her tongue. The weird nontaste, nonsmell of a dead world. The sun hadn't quite crested the tall labyrinth walls yet, leaving everything in the half-baked purple of dawn. The dead end was empty. That caused a shrill of panic, but when she turned her head, she saw Hero striding back down the passage.

Claire wiped a hand over her cheek. "What time is it?"

"Absolutely no idea," Hero chirped, and shrugged. "You only slept for a couple hours. I figured you needed it."

"You didn't sleep?"

"The accommodations were a little sparse for my tastes. Soon as it started to get light, I took the opportunity to scout out the next intersection. Followed left to another dead end, so I suspect we can be rebels and go right without ruining your glorious left-handed strategy."

Claire took in Hero's appearance. His clothes were filthy. She suspected hers were as well. His aristocratic coat hung open, having lost a couple buttons somewhere between Valhalla and the literally godforsaken maze they found themselves in. He sported scratches on his hands and a welt on his cheek from their headlong tumult through the catacombs. He looked weary but approached none of the exhaustion and hopeless dread that Claire felt. Stories were always resilient in their own ways.

Authors, not so much. Claire still felt half-dead as she dragged a hand over her face. "You shouldn't have wandered off alone. There's something else in here with us. We heard it last night."

Hero stopped in front of her. "Concerned for my safety, warden? I'm touched."

"Merely concerned you'll attract the beast to me. Or take a wild hair to run off again. Not sure I have the energy to chase you, to be honest." But Claire said it with a weak smile. Hero offered his hand, and she allowed him to yank her to her feet.

"Perhaps breakfast will improve your mood. Slice of diabetes?" Hero opened his hand and offered her one of the tiny snack cakes that she'd seen him trying with Leto in the Mdina kitchen. It was perfectly preserved in cellophane, if a bit squished.

"We've been on the run for our souls, and you've been hiding *cakes* on your person?"

"What? It's not as if anyone else thought to pack provisions." Hero took offense. He began to close his hand, but Claire snatched the treat before he could withdraw it. She tore the wrapper and crumpled the cellophane into her pocket.

"I thought you hated sugar," Claire mumbled around a mouthful of frosting, to which Hero shrugged.

"I suppose I'm still figuring out what I hate."

"Where'd you learn a word like 'diabetes,' anyway? I thought your book was more fantasy based. Don't tell me Brev had you read a medical text."

"Leto made a joke, and I made him explain it." Hero's eyes went distant before he swiftly shifted the topic away from that memory. "How do you think they're doing?"

Not Leto. The Library. Brevity. Andras. "I can't know until we get out of here," Claire admitted. The cake felt less sweet, turning to mud on her tongue. "It's been too long, but time between realms can do funny things. Brevity's smart. I'm hoping the reason we've heard nothing is because she called up the wards. The Library's not defenseless. But it's more built to keep books *in* rather than keep anything out—"

"The irony is delicious," Hero interjected.

"And Andras has the pages," Claire finished with a scowl. "Those pages, that codex . . . if Lucifer made it, it's a part of him. Like Hell itself. Even a portion of one could tear down a ward, and Andras has ten whole pages. I might be happy that the angels don't have it, but Andras . . . I'm afraid what he wants to do is even worse."

"You'll just need to take it back, then."

"Yes, of course. I'm sure the Horrors will be happy to listen to a deposed librarian. Without any of her tools of office. Without a library."

"You have a library. A library of one." Hero tapped his chest and flashed her a carefully practiced thousand-watt smile, only slightly dimmed by the smear of sand in his hair. "I'll have you know I'm worth a hundred of those boring old books."

"And an arrogance to match the worth." Claire tried to sound harsh and failed.

"It's all part of my charm. I—" Hero stumbled, as if his foot had tripped on air. He gripped the stone wall with white knuckles as if he suddenly wasn't sure of his feet.

"Hero?"

"Just a moment. I feel . . . peculiar," he muttered through clenched teeth.

Claire studied him, then felt her pulse stop in her throat. The color began bleeding from Hero's bright, brassy bronze hair. It formed cool wisps before evaporating. She looked to the hand pressed against the wall and saw a band of symbols glowing on his wrist. It was bright crimson even as all his other colors were being drained out. Her gut clenched, and the cake fell from her fingers. "The IWL."

"The what?" Hero followed her gaze to the stamp on his wrist. Sweat began to bead on his temple, his face white with distress. "That can't be. *You're* the librarian."

"Not necessarily. Not if Brevity's done her job."

"What? But that's absurd—" He was fighting it, but Claire knew the pull of the Library always won. She saw the panic flare in his eyes as Hero came to the same conclusion. "Not yet, dammit!" He glared up at the air above them as if the Library's interworld loan was something to be bargained with.

Claire felt her heart slowly turning to lead. The little parts of her that had been restored by sleep and food and banter, the illusion of hope—those bits were fading along with the peach of Hero's skin and the blue of his worn coat.

"The Library needs you. It's all right." Her voice was eerily calm even in her own ears. She was a writer; she could lie for him.

"No. Wait. Hold on. Just try—maybe you'll come with?" Hero snatched at her wrist and clamped down hard enough to pinch. His face was beginning to shimmer, just at the edges.

Claire forced her lips up, a halting smile. "Maybe."

She was a better liar with words than with deeds, and she rarely smiled. It was no surprise that the alarm increased in Hero's eyes. His grip on her wrist loosened but he refused to let go. "You can't just—"

"Take care of them, Hero. You promised."

Hero's eyes widened. "Claire—"

The shimmer fell inward and absorbed him. There was a snap, a rush of air. It tingled over her skin, replacing the pressure of Hero's hand with a lick of sharp static.

Silence. She became aware of the sound of harsh breathing. Sharp, staccato gasps of air. She realized it was hers.

The passage suddenly felt too dark, too small, and her vision wobbled. The cake was still splayed on the earth at her feet. She made to pick it up, but instead found the stone scraping harshly at her spine as she slid down the wall. She did not cry. Heat stung her eyes, and she stared sightlessly at the chocolate frosting smudging her fingers.

And Claire was alone.

35

BREVITY

Books change. We change. It's time the system changed.

I will change it. For me. For the books. For our souls. The story can still be rewritten.

Librarian Poppaea Julia, 48 BCE

[Annotated at a much later date, with a heavy, bleak ink:]

We are subjects to our own natures. Books must be true to their stories, and whether we're dead or alive, the role we're given will win out. Accept your duty and find peace. Fighting against your nature is only madness. Learn from Librarian Poppaea's tragedy, apprentice.

Ibukun of Ise, 991 CE

THE IWL WAS NOT a gentle process.

It did not ask, did not offer; it *retrieved*. So Brevity expected an annoyed book when she'd summoned him. She expected a haughty, insulted, snarky book.

Brevity had not expected a train wreck of grief and fury.

Hero had barely materialized from the summons when he gave a half-inhuman snarl, he spun, and Brevity found herself against the opposite shelves with a hand at her collar.

His eyes were narrowed, and his face wore an unfamiliar expression of pain. "You had no right!"

This was not how an IWL request went when Claire did it. Brevity bit down on her frustration and summoned as much authority as she could with books between her shoulder blades. "I am a librarian, and you are under—" But Hero cut her off, with more growl than words.

"You *left her.*"

That trembly feeling threatened in her chest again, alarm laced with panic, but Brevity held on. "The boss will be fine. She always is. We, on the other hand, are in *trouble.*"

Hero finally took note of the thundering beneath his feet. It'd only gotten worse, now accompanied by a distant warning creak. He released his grip and stepped back. Not all of the anger drained from his face, but his shoulders thrummed with new tension. "You may be correct. But Claire's trapped. You need to send me back."

"What? What happened?" Brevity faltered and noted for the first time Hero's state of disarray, the fine layer of dust and sand and regret. Her eyes widened, but the walls shuddered again, and she shook her head. "Explain on the way."

By the time Hero had sketched a quick outline of what had occurred in Malta and beyond, Brevity had led him through the center of the Library. She paused to rescue fallen books and grab scabbards from armor displays, shoving them into Hero's arms as he talked.

The little hope that she'd possessed began to drift as he got further into the story. When Hero recounted Leto's sacrifice, the hope had guttered entirely. When Hero sank into his own concerns about Claire and the labyrinth, Brevity latched onto the one thing she didn't need hope for.

"Boss will find a way. She's a real librarian, not—" Brevity stopped, squeezing her eyes shut against where that thought was going. When she opened them, she could feel the certainty in her own voice. "Boss isn't gonna be stopped by nothing."

"You didn't see that place." Hero's free hand jerked through his hair and betrayed his anxiety. "Just send me back, and I'll relay the situation—"

"I can't."

Hero stopped, nearly dropping the stack of sheathed blades in his arms. "What?"

"I can't send you back. If you were still in Valhalla, sure. But you said it was a forgotten realm—I can't send you back somewhere we don't have a path to."

"But you just—"

"An IWL is kind of a one-way trip. Besides, the Library is sealed and . . ." Brevity paused as another jolt rolled through and rained dust down on them from the stacks. "And I need you here."

A muddle of decisions warred on Hero's face, and for a moment Brevity wondered if she really would have to lock him up with his book. Then a frown tipped the scales, and he settled for a terse nod. "Andras?"

"Only makes sense, given what you said. The wards are hol—" Brevity staggered as the air was snapped from her lungs. Hero put out a hand to steady her as the lights shifted from white to purple and back again. Hero's hand was probably the only thing that kept her from curling up on the floor. "Something just took the first ward down."

"How many wards do we have?"

"Three. But the first ward is the *dream* ward. If that one went . . ." Brevity faltered. "They're supposed to hold up to *demons*. What could . . . Oh no." She turned and Hero had to tilt so she didn't smack on the business end of the swords he held. "You said he's got the codex pages. He's using the pages as weapons."

Hero blinked. "He can do that?"

"It's the *Devil's* Bible. Boss couldn't even touch the pages. Who knows what he inked them with?" Brevity's stomach sank. She said the words so she didn't feel them too hard. "If he's burning up pages to get in, the wards aren't going to hold."

Hero stopped. The floor shivered beneath them as the thundering took up again. His knuckles whitened and curled around the bundle of scabbards. "What do you need me to do?"

It was a question that appeared to cost him something to ask. It helped, just a little. Brevity drew her shoulders up. "Clone yourself, perhaps procure an ancient artifact of great power while you're at it?" She gave him a game smile as she caught a hail of books that fell from the nearest shelf.

Hero stared. "How can you be so blithe in the face of imminent demise?"

All she needed was an audience. Brevity swallowed the lump in her throat. "Practice. Remember who I work for?" There was a particularly loud impact, and she shot an anxious glance down the aisle, where she could see the ward lights still floating above the desk. The second light was stuttering rapidly. "Not good. Let's hurry and . . . I dunno, set up some blockades, maybe?"

"I assume there's a plan?" Hero asked. "Because if it's two against an army of demonic Horrors, I think I'd rather just take my chances on the regime change with the damsels."

"Well, without being able to reach Walter, we're kinda—" Brevity halted midstep, felt like an idiot, and let out a squeal. "Damsels. Oh, you're *brilliant!*"

Hero managed a confused "Of course I am . . ." before following to see what he was brilliant about.

Brevity changed course, mentally scolding herself. She'd been so worried about filling Claire's shoes, about being a librarian, running the Library as Claire would want, preserving the books as Claire would do— failing where Claire would have succeeded. She'd tried so hard to think and act like Claire, when the answer was staring her in the face.

She had been thinking like Claire. She'd been thinking of the damsels as books, things to preserve and curate.

Not people.

The glass-set door cracked as Brevity barged into the damsel suite. The occupants were gathered in uneasy clusters, likely already worried from what Charlotte and Aurora had reported. A dozen sets of pretty eyes narrowed as they took in Hero with his arms full of weapons.

Brevity could positively *feel* the blush that radiated as Hero shifted next to her. "Plan, muse?"

"Plan," Brevity confirmed. She took a deep breath and dropped her face into something apologetic. She turned to the damsels and cleared her throat. "Hey, guys? I need a moment. I'm so sorry, but I'm going to need to restrict all of you to your books for your own safety. The Library is experiencing technical difficulties with our wards—mainly demons bent on destruction, see—and should the wards fall, it'd be best if you're out of the way. So if you please can make your way to your books—"

"*What?*" a blond woman interrupted. She wore a leather catsuit that frankly defied the laws of physics and anatomy. She looked like a spy or, rather, some spy's poorly written sidekick. She must have been new if she was still wearing that thing.

"I know this is very sudden, ladies." Brevity kept her voice slow and calm. "Hero and I will do our very best, but it's likely that you'll experience a change of management in the near future. Andras is determined to possess your books and he has Horrors—"

She was drowned out by a swell of murmurs from the damsels. Charlotte, appearing to have her puritan sensibilities insulted more by the disorder than by the news, let out a sharp whistle to silence the group. She turned to Brevity. "What does a demon want with us?"

Brevity exchanged a mournful look with Hero. "We think he intends to use books as magical power for his coup. Or possibly bribes. For the court."

That brought the protests back in force. "I'm *not* being someone's reward again," a princess with white hair said.

"At least you didn't get fridged in yours." A curvy woman in a pencil skirt slumped into a chair. "Where's Claire?"

"Claire's on her way . . ." Brevity faltered. "But we might be on our own for now. But now . . ." Brevity raised her hands. "No need for distress. We have Hero here and—"

"Heroes don't do *shit*," a firm voice spoke up. The damsel wore what might have started its life as a gauzy peasant gown, but at some point, it had been ripped and tied and stitched and paired with utilitarian fatigues until they resembled more of an androgynous apocalyptic soldier than a damsel. They spit and glared with open hostility at Hero. "Except die first. They do that well."

"I don't—"

"They're kinda right," a curvy alien with lavender tentacles said shyly.

"Your books—"

"Our books suck," Charlotte said, and Brevity really *would* have to find out where that slang had entered her vocabulary. "We're stronger outside of them." She waited until she received some scattered nods from around the room. She squared up to Brevity. "So give us weapons."

"What?" Brevity placed a hand to her chest, widening her eyes. "I couldn't. I'm the acting librarian and you're—"

"We're damsels. Unsuitable ones at that—isn't that why we're here?" Charlotte picked an imaginary fleck from her skirt. At some point, she'd modified it to make it easier to walk in, Brevity realized. Modeled after Claire's, perhaps. Charlotte crossed her arms. "Maybe that just makes us people now."

"And people always have a choice," Hero added softly.

"Look, even a hero gets it," someone else muttered with only a small amount of disdain.

Charlotte nodded. "We're people. And we aren't sitting back and letting some old man tell the story for us again."

A low agreement, hesitant at first, trickled through the room. The damsels seemed divided, but the quiet broke when Aurora, silent as always, padded forward on hooved feet. She inspected Hero's arms and reached hesitantly for the scabbard of a blade nearly as long as she was tall. It wobbled in her hands, and she stepped back. She was followed by a chubby boy in a wizard's robe. The leather-clad spy was next, selecting a thin dagger.

She sniffed. "No guns?"

"Tell me about it," said Hero.

And then the rest of the damsels began to take up arms.

Hero divested himself of all but his own sword, and soon enough they were busy pulling out unwritten combat books and conferring. Hero withdrew to where Brevity stood in the doorway, shoulder bracketed against the frame. She was running through the time left. They would need a plan. Barricades. Units. Tactics.

Hero tilted his head. "That was clever, what you did there."

"What was?" Brevity acted surprised.

"Making them volunteer. Tricky."

"I didn't *make* them do anything. I just had faith they'd come up with the right answer." Brevity sniffed. "Inspiration means having faith. It's . . . it's what muses do. What I did, once."

"You must have been a brilliant muse," Hero said.

A quiet smile grew on Brevity's lips. "I was. Now I'm a brill librarian. Let's get to work."

36

RAMIEL

No story is insignificant. That's what the existence of the Unwritten Wing teaches us. No escapist fantasy, no far-off dream, no remembered suffering. Every story has meaning, has power. Every story has the power to sustain, the power to destroy, the power to create. Stories shape *time*, for Pete's sake. Once upon a time. Long, long ago. Someday. And then what happened?

Living author or dead, written or not, your story shakes the world. That's common sense to a muse, and the idea librarians are supposed to honor. That every story, every human, matters.

The hard part is convincing ourselves first.

Apprentice Librarian Brevity, 2010 CE

LIGHT BLUE CAPSULES SPARKED a dull constellation against a navy blanket. They were that medical blue: the color of latex gloves and bitter chalk, but dulled by the bedroom's yellow-tinged lights. They held the attention of the boy curled over them with a hunger-pang intensity.

When Rami went looking for the remains of Leto's soul, he found a cluttered bedroom floating in darkness. Inside, a haggard teenager hunched over his bed, knees drawn and bony. The pointed ears and the oiled skin were gone, but Rami recognized the tangled curly hair, the soft brown coloring, the gaunt jut of the chin from the demon-boy he'd met.

He was Leto, and yet he wasn't. He was what Leto would be born from. Guilt and regret and self-loathing.

Rami knew exactly what that looked like.

The boy fixed sightlessly on the pills, tugging one end of the blanket to make the little blue ovals twitch back and forth. Back and forth, up and down. As if balancing the scale.

"You already know what happens." Rami made his voice as gentle as possible.

The teenager raised his eyes dully to where Rami stood in the corner of his bedroom. The boy's face didn't change. Didn't register surprise, as if a strange angel popped into his room at midnight every day. He made no move to cover up the dozen pills before him. "I deserved it."

"Do you want to tell me why?" Rami already knew what he would hear, but the question wasn't for him. He had to step carefully, so carefully here. Pulling a soul from its memory was a fragile process, and Rami was aware how desperately out of practice he was. The memory seemed already to be fraying at the edges; an eerie vignette of dark blur muddled the corners of the room.

"I . . . He's dead because of me. I killed him." The boy started toying with the pills again.

Rami gestured. "This doesn't look like where society keeps a murderer."

"I might as well have killed him. Darren, he . . . We were friends. Since we were kids. But lately he was just so . . . annoying. And always complaining. I tried. I tried!" Frustration flickered to life in Leto's voice, giving it an uneven edge. "I invited him to stuff! He shit all over everything." He flicked a begging glance to Rami, but the angel said nothing.

He clenched the blanket in his hands as his eyes diverted again. "It's like he wanted to be miserable. He was always threatening to kill himself. Always talking about it for attention. I just . . . You panic the first few times, because you care, right? But after the twentieth time, it felt like it was just talking. He was on about it again and . . . I snapped. I said, 'Sure,

yeah. Hurry up and do it if you're going to do it already.' God, I was . . .
'Just do it or shut up,' I said." Leto's breath became ragged, his voice thick
as he swallowed. "So he did."

"I'm sorry," Rami said.

"Don't." The boy was suddenly tense. "Just . . . say anything but that.
Don't. That's what they all said. All they ever say. I kept waiting for someone to figure it out. Read the texts he was always sending me. Ask questions. Figure out I'm the reason that . . . But no one did. Everyone just
knew we were friends. Everyone's sympathetic, everyone's sad. I'm not
sad. I'm mad. I'm so—" Leto screwed his eyes shut again, and his voice
broke. "But everyone's so fucking *sorry*."

"You really think they'd blame you?"

"They should. I . . . Darren never cared about normal stuff. The guys
at school called Darren— Well, they called him a lot of things. I dropped
him just to impress guys who couldn't give two fucks about me. I abandoned him." More pills crept between the boy's fingers, and the shadows
stirred across the floor. "Betrayed him."

Rami watched the blue dots leaving dust on clenched hands. "You
think this will help?"

"Nothing helps. Nothing fixes this."

"Nothing stops it either," Rami said. "The hurt doesn't stop just because you turn your back on it."

The boy was silent a moment, knuckles white. "Does it even matter?"

"It always matters to those you leave behind. You broke her heart, you
know."

His shoulders hunched. "Mom won't care. She—"

"Not your mom. Claire."

Confusion replaced some of the tension on the boy's face. Memory
foggy. "Wh-who?"

"The librarian." Rami stepped forward. Not aggressively, but as one
would come around the bedside of a sick person. "It's time to remember,
Leto. You've tortured yourself enough."

"The librarian." Leto repeated the word. His brow furrowed, and the boy seemed about to dismiss it. In this permeable place of time past, grief spent, Rami could almost taste the memories as they cracked through the boy's brain. A headache, gravelly sand, bronze chain, bronze hair. Sun on stones, snack cakes. Ale and ravens. A kiss. Papers and tea. *Uncomfortably squishy.*

Leto shook his head to clear it. "That's not. I haven't. I still have to—"

"You already have. There's no need to relive this," Rami said. "Take my hand, and we can talk."

Leto's gaze drifted from Rami's outstretched hand, was pulled again to the constellation of pills in his palm. "Who are you?"

"You can call me Rami."

A familiar twinge crossed his face. Leto frowned. "You were chasing us."

"I'm not now," Rami said. "I just want to help."

"Did it matter?" Leto rubbed his eyes. Rami could feel him fluttering between two memories, two kinds of now. Past and present warring. That was another feeling Rami knew well. "Did any of it ever mean anything?"

"We make our own meaning, like everything else in life. What matters to you now?"

"The Library." Leto flinched, an apparent realization like ice water. "They were trapped."

Souls usually didn't pivot this fast. Rami grew concerned. "Easy, easy. You're forgiven. You're not in Hell anymore—"

"Who's that?" Leto interrupted, frowning toward the other side of the bedroom. Rami swiveled around, half expecting to see a parent, a teenage friend. But the corner was empty to his eyes.

"What exactly are you seeing?" Rami asked hesitantly. Saving souls didn't mean they necessarily came back intact either.

"Old dude, kinda looks like a hipster? He's got glowing creepy eyes and a suit and . . . striped hair? Like a tiger. Who does that?" Leto froze. "He's . . . familiar. Why do I know him?"

A demon with tiger-striped hair and a cold light in his eyes. No, Andras didn't belong in the mortal world. Not in the memory of a tragic, senseless death. It was wrong, just wrong. Rami felt a chill on his neck. "Did you see him here . . . before? The first time around?"

Leto clenched the pills in his fist before nodding, eyes still locked on the corner.

Rami scrutinized the corner of the room, but whatever Andras had done once upon a time, he was not there now. If the demon had something to do with Leto's human death . . . he'd been planning something longer than anyone expected. Worse, he'd involved the mortal world and unaware souls like Leto to do it. It crossed an unconscionable line, one that signaled larger ambitions than just Hell. Alarm built in his chest, and Rami was eager to be out of the memory. "Let us leave, Leto."

"That's not my name. . . ." The boy frowned. "He said—he said he could make it all go away. Take me someplace better. And then it hurt, so much. He lied. What about you? Are you really helping?"

"I can only try." Rami had to answer honestly. The room felt darker, as if the shadows were folding in on themselves. The memory was unraveling, and they couldn't be caught inside it. "This memory . . . I tried to catch you sooner, but this was all that was left. We need to get you out of here to have a chance."

Leto's eyes reluctantly drifted away from the corner of the room and back toward Rami. He considered. "What about the others?"

"The . . . You mean the librarian?"

"Yes." Leto was already beginning to fade.

"Just . . . take my hand, and we can talk."

Leto considered the blue tablets in front of him. "You know, it didn't hurt as much as I thought it would. Dying." He slid off the bed and turned toward Rami.

Rami let out a breath as Leto took his hand. "It's not meant to. The pain in death isn't the dying. It's the wounds we leave in our wake."

He cast one wary eye back to the empty corner where Andras had once been, then swept them toward Heaven.

❖ ❖ ❖

RAMI DIDN'T LET GO of Leto's hand until they safely set down in Purgatory. He brought him in far from the processing desk and the Gates, wanting to let the boy fully regain himself before overwhelming him with the bureaucracy that was Heaven.

Rami felt a rush of relief as he looked at the teenager. Leto had color in his cheeks, an alert interest in his eyes that said he was centered and aware. It had been close—rescuing a ravaged soul was always a delicate process—but he was whole and stable.

They stood a little apart from the meandering mass of souls that shuffled by them as Rami took stock. Leto's eyes focused on the dazed dead waiting in a tidy, if unwieldy, line. This far away from the desk, the quiet was eerie. The dead didn't have much need for small talk, so the limitless space was filled only with the shuffle of feet.

When Leto's eyes drifted back, Rami felt the question. "You remember now?"

"Yes, I think so." Leto ran a hand through his hair absently before touching his rounded ears with a jerk. "If this isn't Earth, why aren't my ears—"

"You are purified." Rami saw Leto's incredulous look, and he waved a hand. "I know, stilted term. Heaven loves them. You were never wrong to begin with. But it means you're not sentenced to be a demon anymore. An act of sacrifice can do that. You've remembered and forgiven yourself for what you did when you were alive."

"I didn't do it to be forgiven." Leto shook his head. "What I did—"

"Forgiven doesn't mean no regret. We'll always regret the wrongs we've done. It just means you aren't punishing yourself for it."

Leto folded his arms. His morose look was surprising, given the circumstances. Most forgiven souls couldn't race to the Gates fast enough. Rami tried again. "That means you don't have to go back to Hell."

Leto's eyes widened. "Oh no, you have to take me back. We have to go to the Library immediately."

Rami frowned. Perhaps there had been some damage after all, some touch of insanity. He touched Leto's shoulder and willed calm into the boy. Leto's shoulders drooped, and Rami began guiding him through the crowd. He skipped the line of waiting mortals entirely—surely even Heaven would understand some line cutting, given the circumstances. "You really don't mean that."

Despite all reason, Leto persisted. "I do. And I think you're going to take me."

"I think you are misinformed."

"No. You came after me after a crocodile creature . . . god . . . monster-thing tore up my soul. Somehow, I don't think you do that for everyone. Why me?"

Rami furrowed his brow. "It was a brave thing you did, there. Even if you're misguided about what side you're on. You didn't deserve to disappear."

"Maybe, maybe not. I think it's because you wanted something. I'll be honest—I'm not helping you do anything to hurt the Library. But"—Leto looked cagey, and proud of himself for it—"if you get me back to the Library, maybe the librarian will listen to you."

Rami let go of Leto's shoulder. His touch had made him calm and obedient but obviously hadn't dissuaded him from his loyalties. Rami crossed his arms. "You're awfully shrewd for a purified soul."

Leto grinned. "Turns out you can learn a lot of things in a library."

"And willful."

"I think I was always that," Leto said. "I just forgot for a while."

Rami snorted and considered the offer. Uriel had ordered him to find a path into Hell. Even if Uriel's orders mattered little to Ramiel now, it was no major concession to agree to go back. He wanted to see what had become of the librarian. But it would not be safe; he had intended to leave the boy at the Gates. The fact remained that Leto was a purified soul now. Bringing him back to Hell risked condemning him all over again.

It was a risk that didn't sit well with him. "You won't be able to touch anything or anyone there. One touch, you risk your soul being corrupted again, reverting to your original judgment."

Leto's eyes fished toward the distant Gates and back. "I understand."

Rami wasn't confident that he did. "You won't be able to help them."

"But you can," Leto said.

Rami shook his head. "That's not why I would—"

"You help people. That's what you told me. The Library is under attack by a dude who wants to ruin everything. Aren't demons, like, your natural enemy or something?"

"I'm not a part of Hell or the Library."

"Are you part of Heaven, then?"

Guilt settled in Rami's stomach like a stone. "Not precisely."

"And do you think Claire is working for evil?"

"She's Hell's lib—"

"That's her title. Is *she* evil? Is what she's trying to do evil?" Leto insisted.

Rami was not accustomed to moral debate with mortals. He ground his teeth. "No. Not as far as I know."

"Did she try to do anything to harm Heaven? Even when your partner tried to kill her?"

Rami sighed. Uriel really wasn't giving the best impressions of Heaven. "You heard about that."

"For an angel, that didn't seem very nice."

"There were—it wasn't—it's not as if—" Rami fell silent. There was no defending Uriel's lust for revenge. Hadn't Rami already come to that conclusion? Why did he seek to defend Heaven, after all this time?

Leto appeared ready to pounce at the opening. "I hated myself so much I hurt innocent people and it *sucked*. I'm . . . I'm not doing that again. How about you?"

They were approaching the processing desk. Rami slowed as he saw his replacement noticing him. The cherub was an eager sort and tipped his head respectfully. Rami's eyes slid past the desk to the guards at the Gate, then to the high tower, where he knew Uriel's office was.

Leto was bound for Heaven, but Uriel would detain him first for information. And what would Uriel do to a spirited, distinctly uncooperative soul like Leto?

Chances were that Rami wouldn't even be able to get them into Hell. His old access had likely long since been revoked. Even if he did . . . Heaven was invading Hell anyway.

That was all he was doing, Rami reasoned, even as a different decision began to take root. He pushed it aside and tugged Leto around to head back down the hill, away from the eyes of judgmental guards and eager upstarts.

"You're purified, and I'm not rescuing you again. If I agree to this, there are going to be some ground rules."

37

CLAIRE

The trouble with reading is it goes to your head. Read too many books and you get savvy. You begin to think you know which kind of story you're in.

Then some stupid git with a cosmic quill fucks you over.

Librarian Fleur Michel, 1721 CE

CLAIRE WALKED.

After Hero had left she'd stayed there for a time, staring at the walls, not quite seeing anything while the shadows lengthened. She didn't know how much time she'd lost. Even with the ruthless sun progressing in the sky, time had a way of shifting and skittering out of her grasp.

Her body ached from the cold stone. In her chest there was a troublesome hollowness that grew and crowded her heart and lungs, making it hard to breathe. But Claire won the argument with her body, and one foot in front of another, she walked.

She kept taking lefts. It seemed pointless to change their plan now . . . *her* plan now. Claire trailed one hand along the wall to keep her path straight and her mind from drifting.

She had all the time in the world to drift now. It was hard not to follow the thoughts. Brevity would not have resorted to the IWL unless something dire had happened. Andras had the pages, and Andras wanted the Library. There was a faint hope that Hero could assist and they could hold out long enough.

Long enough for what, though? Claire was lost in a dead-end world. Beatrice and Leto were gone. But what bothered her most was that Andras could have gone this far without Hell noticing. It wasn't possible. Lucifer and all his generals were too powerful, too paranoid for that. Either Andras had bested all of them in his scheming or . . . Lucifer had allowed it. The Library had become part of the game.

Claire had always been aware that the Library and its books were pawns. Andras himself had taught her enough about the intrigues and deadly maneuvers the demons made in Hell's court, but she'd never imagined the Library was a pawn Lucifer paid attention to.

Andras had paid attention. Claire knew there was more to the Library than her literary ghosts. Some demons came to read, either out of curiosity or to understand the genuine magic of human imagination. But she also knew there were demons that ate dreams instead, consumed them and extracted pleasure and power from the destruction. Obviously, the Library was kept apart from the rest of Hell for just that reason.

Lucifer had to know. He had to know about Andras's goal. There were too many coincidences. Perhaps he planned to sweep in when they were all dead and start over. She'd read the histories. She knew Lucifer had used purges to quell uprisings in his realm before. She knew she wasn't the first librarian.

She knew hers wasn't the first Library in Hell.

But the books. The books couldn't be purged. They most definitely could *not* be parceled up, doled out, and fed to the vile underbelly of Hell. She had to get back. Get back, get in control, somehow find a way to destroy a demon with the power of the words of Hell's god, the Arcane Wing, and a legion of Horrors at his command. Just getting out of this blighted place would be a feat.

An exit, naturally, presented itself the next time she turned a corner and faced another dead end.

She was just about to let out a groan when she saw the arch. Wedged in the corner where two stone walls met, lost nearly in shadow, stood a darkened doorway. It was roughly the same shape and build as the one they'd encountered up the stairs, only the light was more muted. Lamplight, not sunlight.

"Oh, is it my turn now?" Claire muttered, wary of a trap. She brought her nose as near to the surface as she dared.

Lamplight and leather. Her breath snagged in her throat when she recognized it. Beatrice's office was much as they'd left it, stacked with an aftermath of shuffled books and used teacups. Claire caught herself leaning forward, listening for footsteps. Even on this side of the arch, she could make out the distant sound of the Mdina streets that filtered in through the open window. It was night, the only light spilling from the desk lamp on Beatrice's desk. Claire could just make out several bottles and plastic bags that hadn't been there before. Hope clotted in her throat. If Beatrice had survived, she could be just out of frame. Stepping away to care for her injuries, or her book.

Her book. If the struggle with the Hellhounds had damaged her book, she'd need repairs. If it was damaged and poorly repaired, it could fall apart, stranding Beatrice outside her book or, worse, trapping her inside— Oh, no. Claire's hand clapped at her side, where her bag of tools should have been. Her skin was tingling and somehow the arch had moved a breath away from her nose.

Claire jerked herself back and clamped one hand on top of the other. Heat stung her eyes. Bea. The thought was enough to twist a sharp pain through the numb despair in her chest. Her book could be just on the other side, hurt from ensuring their escape, dying, needing help.

She knew—she knew if she went through, if she found Beatrice, Hellhounds or not, she would not go back. One step and she could rest. One step and she could be *accepted*, loved, cared for. One step and all the rest of it could end.

She'd rejected the idea before, but it washed over her again in a way that she was too tired, too grieving to resist. The idea was strong: to rest, to stop, neither to run nor face her past.

Her eyes burned again from the powerful attraction of it. She'd felt the power of an easy escape before. When she'd said the god words that had banished Gregor.

So she said a different word instead.

"Fuck."

The heels of her hands dug roughly into her eyes as she stumbled back. She ground them in until she saw stars. She screamed. *"Fuck!"*

She'd been looking for an exit, thinking of those left behind, and the labyrinth had presented her with what she desired. Like it had with Hero. But this wasn't a temptation built on happiness; it was one built on despair. "Not again. I won't. Not—"

A wordless rage tore at her throat. She flung one sneaker at the arch. The shoe sailed through the air before passing harmlessly through a shimmer of lamplight and disappearing. Not as satisfying as she needed. Claire let out a growl and flung the other shoe after for good measure.

The rage drained out of her just as quickly as it had come. "Sorry, Bea," she muttered, then frowned down at her feet. "And now I'm barefoot again. Bloody fantastic."

The images of a dead Leto, a wounded Beatrice, paper corpses and ink blood, swept through her. Claire twisted and ran from the dead end, down the path toward the rumbling bellows that echoed from the center of the labyrinth. Ghosts at her back, monsters ahead.

THE HOWLING GREW LOUDER until Claire could feel the vibration jostling the organs in her chest. The air felt like it opened up, walls widening at the next intersection. She slowed as she turned the corner.

The endless dirt paths of the labyrinth fell away to a wide, paved courtyard, each cobblestone dotted with a jade symbol in stone. Half-finished pillars rose every few yards like shattered bones, forming a loose ring around an otherwise barren space. Ragged flags of saffron yellow hung limp from the tops. It was approaching what passed for day here, and the sun throttled down, heating the stones and dwarfing the shadow of the beast that hunkered in the center of the yard.

Claire didn't realize its true size until the creature rose from the stones and began to pace.

Shaggy hair hung off massive shoulders that appeared mostly human until they ran up to meet a monstrous head. Horns thick as oaks arched out from both sides of its skull. They glowed a deep, blackened red. The beast's head was turned away, but even from afar, Claire could tell that its features were gnarled with muscle, and hairs as stiff as needles.

The minotaur skulked past one of the pillars, knocking great blocks aside. It had to be twice the size of the giant Hero had faced in Valhalla.

But what drew her attention, what made Claire take a step away from the wall, was the large iron key that swung from a ratty leather strap around its neck. There was no door in sight, but Claire had read enough fairy tales to know what it unlocked.

The beast halted and sniffed the air, giving a great roar as it turned. A familiar roar. "ABANDON ALL HOPE, ye who enter here! Beyond me lies the city of woe. Before me waits—"

"*Walter?*" Claire stepped forward before considering the wisdom of her actions.

"An' *no mercy* will you . . . ah, oh. Oh."

The minotaur swung its head around. It was a strange, bull-like face, crisscrossed with old scars and tumorous clefts. One eye was milky red in its socket, but the other one lit up with recognition, and there was a familiar set to his bulbous chin. "Hullo there, Miss Claire. You really shouldn't be here."

"A situation I'm trying to correct as quickly as possible, I assure you." Claire felt relief like a kind of giddiness. She approached the Walter minotaur—Waltertaur?—carefully. "It's really you, isn't it? What on earth are you doing here?"

"I'm the gatekeeper. My duty is to guard the gates." Walter puffed up before tapping his knuckles together abashedly. "All gates."

Claire frowned. "The gates of every realm? But I didn't see you in Valhalla."

"Sure you did! Ah, apologies to Hero next time you see 'im, please?"

Claire squinted. She saw no similarity to the giant in the ring when she and Hero had faced the trial to enter Valhalla. He'd been quite thoroughly Viking and wielded . . .

"Widowbane!" Claire remembered the overlarge maul now, glittering with the same shadowy red of the minotaur's horns and Walter's teeth. "You were the bludgeon. You never told me."

The Walter minotaur nodded. "That was me. Well. Part of me. One of me. An aspect. I don't like talkin' about it, precisely. It gets all rather higgledy-piggledy."

"It does indeed." Claire paused as a thought occurred to her. "You're the gatekeeper. You're *every* gatekeeper. Does that make you—"

"Death," Walter said quietly. His gaze gentled and he rubbed his neck, a gesture familiar enough to make Claire's heart ache. "Some call me that, yeah. I always rather liked 'Walter.'"

"Oh." Claire chewed on her cheek. She'd entered the labyrinth expecting to find death and here he was. And he'd been her friend all along. No matter how far she ran, she couldn't escape the feeling of a story. "Regardless . . . I am very glad to see you, Walter. I need transport back to Hell, immediately. There's an emergency."

"I see. Ah, then may I just see your ghostlight, ma'am?"

Claire drew out the cold wax candle from her pocket. It was just as dead as Leto's lighter had been. The tiny stub was crumpled on one side from having been wedged against her hip as she slept.

Walter bent nearly in half to lean his one working eye over it. His face was solemn as he looked back up. "Yer a mortal soul out without a ghostlight, Miss Claire."

"I am." Her fingers curled protectively around the cold piece of wax and stuffed it back into her skirts. At the bottom of the pocket, her fingertips grazed some bits of paper that whispered to her, but she left them there for now.

"That's a mighty shame." Walter took a step back from Claire, and pity was a strange twist on his ageless face. "See, I'm supposed t' eat any regular folk that pass through here. It's kinda why I'm here."

"Now, wait one moment, Walter. You know I'm the librarian—"

"And you shouldn't be here without a proper ghostlight. Makes you a lost soul, ma'am." Walter began rolling his shoulders.

"I'm not anything of the sort! I had a light. There were extenuating circumstances." Claire took a step back. Walter might be Death, but she couldn't quite believe that the Walter she knew would attack her—in any realm. But he appeared to be preparing to do just that. "Can you at least tell me what is supposed to happen here?"

"Well. Screamin' and bleedin' mostly." Walter paused. "I try to eat you, you try to fight, and then you try to run. It don't work out. Your soul gets swallowed and feeds the realm."

"This place has a rather concerning preoccupation with devouring souls," Claire grumbled, rather than feel the flutter of nerves at the way Walter stretched. "Your realm's god dies, and you all turn carrion? No, I suppose it'd be cannibals, since you don't wait until a lady is done with her own soul first."

Walter had the grace to look abashed. "I didnae exactly write the rules, ma'am. I hope ye know this is rather off-putting for me too."

"Yes. Well, eating your colleague is a bit of a faux pas."

"Yeh could just turn around and go back into the labyrinth."

"I'm afraid not. There are pressing matters elsewhere," Claire said. "Besides, it's dull, and I didn't bring a thing to read."

Walter's shoulders dropped. "Then I'm afraid I gotta eat you."

Claire reached for any question to make Walter pause in his warm-up. "What happens if I win?"

"Huh. Well, no one does that."

"But if I did?"

"If you did . . . well, you get to claim a boon, I suppose. In the old days, yeh got to reincarnate on Earth as a kitty cat. But I don't think I got the mojo to do that anymore."

"Good. I rather mistrust cats." Claire considered. "What's your secret?"

"Ma'am?"

"Oh, come, now. I'm an unwritten author, and this whole blighted thing feels like a tale. I know how stories go. Every monster at the center of the labyrinth has a hidden weakness. A trick for the hero to find."

"Oh." Walter was flummoxed. "No one's just come out and asked that before."

"But you do have one?"

"Well. Yes." Walter mulled it over. "I'm not sure I can just tell you like that."

Claire tilted her head. "Is there a rule against it?"

"Well . . . no." Walter's face lit up, pleased, as he gave his full attention to it. "My eye."

Claire inspected both the brown eye fixed on her and the milky white orb opposite it. "Your eye? What? I am supposed to hit you there?"

"Not exactly. I . . . probably can't say any more."

"I see." Claire sighed, skittering back toward a pillar as Walter appeared to square up. "But knowing that, a hero could escape this place?"

"You're no hero, ma'am." Walter was mournful as he said it.

"As this realm keeps on reminding me."

"I'm awfully sorry about this, Miss Claire." His clear eye was watery, even as he stamped his hooved feet and angled his horns down.

Claire reached a pillar and felt for the curve of it behind her. "Apology accepted, Walter. These things do happen."

Walter opened his mouth and the booming howl that came out was much less mournful and much more horrifying than it had been from a distance. He charged.

Claire spun behind the pillar and stumbled back as Walter's impact sent several man-sized stones tumbling from the top. She regained her footing, turned, and ran.

Hurtling headfirst into stone did not slow a minotaur much. Walter shook his head once, then charged after her. Sharp red claws that had not been evident a moment before gouged the wall as he went. Claire ran for the exit, but the junction where she'd entered the courtyard was nowhere to be seen.

The Greeks always loved their tragedies. She shoved the grim thought from her mind as she caught sight of a flash of yellow. One of the pillars' ragged flags hung lower than the other. At Walter's next charge, Claire took the moment of disorientation as he hit the wall to run toward the pillar. She grabbed it and scrambled her feet against the stone. Bare feet worked to her advantage for once. Her toes found the small holds between blocks, and she hauled herself to the top.

Walter circled the wall with a snarl but paused as he looked up. "Don't be a silly wiggins, ma'am. This will go faster if you come down here."

"I prefer not to." Claire ran her hands over the top of the pillar, looking for something, anything, to slow down the minotaur. She shoved a hand in her pocket, and her fingertips hit paper. She took a breath as she drew it out. The ragged end of the Codex Gigas's calling card fluttered in her palm.

The text, as usual, was mostly illegible from the tear, but Claire saw the beginning of a word where the location would be: "Hell, Unwri—" Andras was already at the gates of the Library, if not past the wards.

The calling card was not the codex, merely an artifact of the Library. But it was tied to the book, and the book held ancient destructive power. Books tended to bleed and wander, especially old ones. There was a chance, a remote one, that the card had some residual enchantment of its own.

Claire had hoped to save that chance for later, but later was gravely in question now.

Walter quit pacing and began to back up, stamping the earth with his head down.

Claire fumbled back in her pockets and withdrew the ghostlight candle. She quickly squeezed, warming the wax with her hands, and crumpled the calling card remnant around it, making a projectile that would be easy to throw. It stuck, but just barely.

Walter charged, canceling any other preparation she could make. The entire pillar rocked as he hit, and the minotaur dug ruts in the stone as he continued to press his full weight on the displaced stone. Claire held dearly to the top flagstone; it began to pitch.

She clutched the candle to her chest and kicked away as she fell through the air. But something clamped over her right leg and squeezed like a vise.

It arrested her fall sharply enough that her hip jolted, sending fire up her side. Her knee shrieked and Claire screamed along with it.

Pain watered her eyes when she opened them. Upside down, Walter's knotted face looked like a rotten potato. He held her aloft in one hand, as easily as one would dangle a mouse by the tail. He regarded her with sad, bloodshot eyes and lowered his jaw wide.

Claire got a glimpse of daggerlike incisors and wide, flat teeth made for grinding bone and flesh. Her fingers clenched the candle, and as Walter drew her chest toward his gaping lips, she swung back and let the fistful of paper and wax fly.

She'd meant to aim for the eye. She hadn't forgotten what Walter had said.

But Walter dropped his head back and squeezed his eye shut as he brought her near. The ghostlight arced through the air and pinged dully on a great black tongue before it hit the back of the minotaur's throat.

Walter gagged and snapped shut his mouth out of reflex, latching down on the papered candle. A perplexed look crossed his face. A muted rush of air sucked his cheeks.

Then a sharp burst of blue and green flame lashed out through his nostrils, out shaggy ears, past his lips, even from beneath heavy eyelids. Walter's grip loosened as his good eye went glassy, and Claire had a moment of terrifying free fall before they both hit the dirt.

A limp, meaty arm, covered in thick red-brown fur, broke her fall. Claire scrambled back to get out of reach, but the arm and the clawed hand attached to it remained still.

Her breath was ragged and loud in her ears. It took another moment before she could process that Walter wasn't moving. She slowly shoved to her feet, wincing as her knee shrieked in protest. Likely torn ligaments there. If she could get back to Hell, they could be tended to. First things first.

Walter's barrel chest shivered, barely moving, muscles twitching under heavy scars. The air held a sizzling sound, and the smell of charred meat suggested that the calling card was still working on the poor creature's insides.

Claire leaned over and caught sight of the iron key askew on his neck. As she reached for it, a great clawed hand came down on her wrist and made her heart skip a beat.

But the claws did not tighten, did not tear. Claire looked up and saw Walter's good eye just cracked open. Sluggish blood trailed from every opening on his face. Walter made a weak snarl that was intended to be a smile, and released her to point a trembling claw at his bone-white eye.

The eye was the key.

Claire swallowed a lump in her throat and nodded. "I'm sorry, Walter."

The minotaur didn't speak but closed his eye with a smile that seemed almost proud. A final gout of flame trickled over his lips, and his chest stilled.

Claire extracted herself from his arm and hobbled around to the side of his head. She considered the dead eye lodged in a tumorous skull.

This would not be pleasant work.

SHE'D HAD NO TOOLS, just Walter's own limp claws. By the time it was done, her skirts were tacky with blood, her fingers trembled, and her hands felt as if they'd never be clean again. But a sphere about the size of a grapefruit and the color of bone sat heavy in the palm of her hand. It was completely smooth and was translucent in sections. Not an actual eye, but . . . something else.

That was the problem with defeating the gatekeeper: no one was left to explain how to open the gate.

Claire turned it over in her hands. She hobbled up to this pillar and that, pressing the white surface against random stones. Hoping something would happen. Nothing did, and the urgency to get back merged with injury and exhaustion to eat at what patience she had left for analysis.

"Hell and harpies." She had just pulled away from another pillar in disgust when light hit the orb as she held it up. Claire blinked and squinted as she held the sphere in front of her.

The courtyard transformed. Through the eye, the world became a wash of milky shadows, but it also became a world of doors. Claire turned a slow circle. Everywhere she looked, narrow gates lined the walls. And the pillars—the pillars. Each pillar held a series of tiny, physically impossible doors that hinged off the pillar like wheel spokes off an axle.

The courtyard became a crossroads.

"But no signposts. Which one?" Claire muttered. The orb responded by pulsing brightly and Claire nearly dropped it in surprise. When she brought it back to her eye, she saw that the doors were colored now. Each gate now held a door front decorated with unique lines and painted one of a multitude of colors, more than she would have believed existed.

She considered the one in the wall nearest her. It was ivory with metal inlay, every detail gilded. A flock of chubby-cheeked infants frolicked across it, each bearing wings and a golden horn, while some frankly terrifying figures watched from above, borne up by greater wings. Claire could guess the destination for that one, and she chuckled as she stepped back.

Hell would be easy to find. But she couldn't just drop into the Library in the middle of an invasion and expect a solution to present itself. Claire pivoted as she considered the gallery of pathways around her, a tickle of a plan beginning to form in her head.

38

RAMIEL

The inhabitants of Hell are not the most welcoming neighbors, but a smart librarian will never be adrift for resources. Remember the other libraries, other realms, other paths. Build good fences, make good friends, and keep your laundry indoors. Leave just enough doubt in their minds to make yourself not worth the trouble.

Librarian Gregor Henry, 1982 CE

HELL WAS A SERIES of hallways.

It was monotonous and maddening, and Rami still couldn't believe it. The door had been open. The old paths into Hell, paths Rami hadn't walked since he'd abandoned Lucifer's upstart rebellion so long ago, had still been open. The way between worlds had still risen to appear when Rami willed it. No tricks, no force, no begging needed.

It was as if Hell had been waiting for him. In the eons, ages, millennia since then, Lucifer hadn't shut him out. Uriel's mad plan had turned out to be right. For some reason, even as a Watcher presumably working for Heaven, Rami was welcome in Hell.

The prospect, and the possible reasons why, disturbed him deeply.

Leto, however, experienced no such concerns. The boy brightened up considerably once they'd reached these interminable hallways. He behaved as if he wanted nothing more than to hug each pillar they passed.

Thankfully, he kept his arms at his sides and carefully walked in the center of the hall, per their agreement. Leto was a purified soul, and if he could stay that way, he could still pass the Gates. But souls were grasping things. The slightest encounter with the wrong influence here could corrupt and damn him all over again. Just walking the grounds was dangerous enough, and Rami had insisted that the boy stay two steps behind him when trouble presented itself and touch nothing besides the floor beneath his feet.

He allowed Leto to take the lead once they passed the trials of the anguished in the outer ring and approached the Library. The boy appeared to have blossomed, rather than being drained from his trials; he glowed. His ears stayed rounded and his skin stayed youthful and warm. He toyed with his messy coils of hair absently. How had it been possible that Rami had ever mistaken him for a demon? Leto hummed a tuneless pop song under his breath as he guided Rami past hallways drenched in the sunsets of alien stars, down grand staircases falling into disrepair, through ballrooms that still contained the last strains of music.

They encountered no one, which just set Rami more on edge. It was very quiet for an invasion. Either they were quite late, and the battle was done, or the opposition had been so weak as not to warrant a defense. Neither possibility boded well for the Library. It left Rami considering what he would do should they even reach the doors.

He was so busy chasing these thoughts around his head, he nearly ran into Leto. The teenager was frowning at a large alcove. A low, empty platform grounded the otherwise empty space, and it was this platform that seemed to concern him.

"The gargoyle should be here," Leto said.

"A gargoyle?"

"Well, a headache in the form of a gargoyle. I really should have asked its name. . . ." Leto trailed off as he looked down the hallway. "Oh! There he is!"

The teenager took off toward a large form that stood frozen at the far end of the hall. A chill of alarm shot up Rami's back, and his hand drifted to his sword as he ran. "Leto! Stop!"

He caught up with Leto as he stumbled to a stop near the unmoving form. It was a statue of dull, jagged stone and with a great head and wings that brushed the hallway's tall ceiling. It appeared to be caught in mid-attack, arms and wings extended, muscles bunched. It didn't move but still seemed to shift and twitch, never quite fully in focus. When Rami cautiously circled the statue to inspect its face, a disorienting pulse of pain bloomed in his head.

Rami looked away with a wince. "This is your gargoyle?"

"Yes. But when I knew him, he moved around more. . . ." Leto's brow furrowed in concern. He reached his fingers out toward one frozen wing before catching himself. "Something's wrong with him."

"Perhaps he's best left as he is."

Leto shoved his hands in his pockets and paced around, then back up as if to get a better view. On his third step backward, the air crackled a warning. Rami's shout was too slow.

Violet light filled the hall and shot at Leto's back. The next moment, the teenager flew across the marble floor, and the light briefly coalesced into a wall before fading away.

Leto crumpled against a wall. Rami felt relief when he let out a breathy groan as he reached him. "Are you all right?"

"For the record, I did not touch anything. I swear." Leto accepted help sitting upright, and he rubbed his shoulder with a wince. "What was that?"

"A ward." Rami stood and approached the space where the wall had formed.

"That's good, right? That means Andras and the other bad guys haven't gotten in yet."

"No." Rami inspected the air. He brought out his sword and held it just over the space. Black and violet light arced between his blade and the ward, though it didn't shock again. He sighed and put his blade away. "This is a temporary ward. Strong but hastily formed, not tied to anything. It isn't anchored to the Library."

Leto's face fell as he looked down the hall. Beyond the invisible ward, they could see the great double doors that Rami assumed led to the Library. Muffled shouts and thuds could just barely be heard. But a full-scale resistance, a successful resistance, should have been much louder, producing sounds of fighting that could be heard even at this distance. Rami worried what they would find. They could be merely walking into an enemy encampment.

"So how do we get past it?" Leto asked.

"We can't." Rami stepped back to inspect the lines of power that were just visible now, crisscrossed through the air. "I said it was hasty, not that it was weak. Whoever constructed it has got something powerful feeding it, supplying energy. We would need something even stronger to disrupt it, even for a moment. We would need nothing short of a miracle to bring it down."

"I might be able to manage that." A voice came from down the hall. "But you're not setting foot in my Library."

Rami's sword came to his hand as he pivoted, low in front of Leto to shield the human soul from whatever was coming.

But down the hall was a familiar figure. Claire was in a filthy state, braids wild and skirts torn, brown skin dusted with grit and something redder, but her glare was as fierce as ever.

"Peace, Librarian." Rami lowered his sword.

"Oh, no. *No peace*," Claire spit out the words over what sounded like an increasing mass of birds in the distance. "I told you I would make you pay for—"

"Claire?"

Leto poked his head around Rami's shoulder. Rami watched the fury fall from her face, replaced with shock. Leto stepped out from behind Rami, and the librarian's eyes broke with a kind of hopeful light. The words that fell from her lips were so vulnerable they pulled in his chest.

"Leto . . . that can't— You were— You're here, oh god . . ."

And then she was running toward them. Rami realized she was hobbling, favoring one knee with a twitch of pain on her face every time she stepped. Her skirts were stiff with blood, and she wore multiple amulets slung around her neck and bound around her wrists. She was also barefoot, which struck him as perhaps the most odd.

Rami remembered himself and took two steps to lift a broad arm to bar the librarian's path.

Claire skidded to a stop, and the murderous look was quick to return as she snarled at him. "Get out of my way, or I'll remove your arm for you. I have a bauble for just that."

"Apologies. You can't, Librarian. Do you notice anything different about our young friend?"

Leto held still with a sheepish blush for the inspection. Claire's brow furrowed. "He looks fine. More than fine, he's whole. He's *here*, he's . . ." She stopped. "He's human. Not a demon. Oh, *Leto*. You're human."

"He is. And his soul is bound for Heaven as long as nothing here corrupts him. Nothing touches him."

"Including me." Bitterness and fresh loss flickered across Claire's face and then were gone. "Did you remember, then?"

"I remembered." Leto flushed with embarrassment, voice a little shy. "I was . . . Matthew. Matthew Hadley."

The smile froze, half-formed across Claire's face. Her voice dropped to a strangled whisper. "Hadley?"

"Yeah . . ." Leto rubbed his arm. "Uh, but please, I'm still Leto."

A complicated pain struggled across Claire's face, and it took Rami a moment to put it together. He'd read the brief on the librarian before all this started.

Claire Juniper Hadley.

Born 1944, Surrey, England. Married in London, 1965. Died 1986. Survived by a husband and one daughter.

A daughter who hadn't married but had moved to America to raise a child of her own.

Rami risked a glance between the two. The wiry, coiled hair, the dark eyes, the stubborn jut of the chin. Claire was a darker brown, Leto's eyes more amber, but it was there, yes. If you squinted and allowed for two generations of genetic muddling, which humans were good at. But the way Claire was looking at Leto, like a mirage in the desert, made Rami's heart clench in sympathy. He knew what it meant to see the familiarity of a home you thought you'd lost.

And he knew what it was for that home to be just out of reach. Which made what he said even harder.

"Leto . . . has been through quite a lot of shock today. His soul is fragile," Rami murmured to Claire. With considerable effort, she shook herself, and only Rami noticed the mist trembling at the corners of her eyes.

She dropped her gaze to her feet a moment before drawing a hard breath. "Right. Right. It just explains . . . Never mind." She looked to Rami. "You saved him?"

Rami inclined his chin. Rather than expressing gratitude, Claire nodded, jaw clenching into a hard line. "Nothing is going to lay a hand on him."

"Are you okay?" Leto approached as Rami dropped his arm, but they kept a wide gap between them that spoke much. "You look . . ."

"It's been a . . . rough day since you left." Claire's lips twitched. "Turns out, I'm shit without my assistants."

"The blood . . ."

"Not mine."

"The knee?"

"Mine," Claire said with a wince. "But it's fine now that I'm back in Hell. Phantom pain."

Leto and Claire looked at each other, and it seemed to Rami that Leto had to read the tension welling in the space between. Finally, Leto coughed and pointed. "Something's wrong with the gargoyle, I think."

"Right." Claire embraced the diversion. She approached the gargoyle and ran a motherly hand over one flank as she murmured, "Oh, my friend. What did those bullies do to you . . . ?"

It was the first opportunity that Rami had to watch her work. Claire circled the giant stone statue once. She stopped and ran a hand up and down one shoulder, as if working her fingers along a seam. Then she nodded to herself and began sorting through the beads bound to her wrist. When she found what she was looking for, she hauled herself up one side of the creature, bare feet braced on the gargoyle's haunch, and twisted a large colorless bauble and rapped it along the stone.

On the third rap, the creature shuddered to life.

Rami and Leto had to dodge as the gargoyle's wings swept around. The creature released an infuriated howl that had been caught in its throat, and its dimensional flickering increased. Claire had to hang on to the curve of its shoulder to keep from being displaced. "Easy, old friend."

The gargoyle seemed to calm with a few more murmured words from the librarian, though Rami could not look directly at its face to see what specific effect they had. After a moment, it crouched to gently allow Claire to clamber off. She patted its haunch and straightened her muddled skirts.

Rami eyed the collection of jewels that hung around Claire's neck. When he looked at them just so, the air filled with whispers. "Are those what I think they are?"

Claire turned to him with a sour smile. "I made a supply run before coming here. Picked up a couple things, made a few friends. The Arcane Wing is shockingly unattended right now."

"Are they strong enough to bring down the ward, then?"

She shook her head. "Not nearly powerful enough." Claire reached into one skirt pocket and withdrew her hand, closed over something. A cruel smile twisted at her lips. A smile that suddenly spoke less of heartache and more of dark, vengeful things.

"But this is."

She opened her fingers and a crumpled scrap of paper, pillowed by cloth, drifted on her palm. A familiar scrap of paper. A scrap of paper that glimmered with dark green script and whispered of destruction and had started this whole mess.

Rami's eyes widened, and so did Claire's wicked smile. "I'd hoped to save it for Andras's traitorous face, but this will have to do." The sound of beating wings and dark tidings rushed closer, and a gust of air stirred them from around the corner. Claire canted her head up, a gleam in her eye. "Will you join us, Watcher?"

39

BREVITY

❧

Stories can die. Of course they can. Ask any author who's had an idea wither in their head, fail to thrive and bear fruit. Or a book that spoke to you as a child but upon revisiting it was silent and empty. Stories can die from neglect, from abuse, from rot. Even war, as Shakespeare warned, can turn books to graves.

We seek to preserve the books, of course. But we forget the flip side of that duty: treasure what we have. Honor the stories that speak to you, that give you something you need to keep going. Cherish stories while they are here.

There's a reason the unwritten live on something as fragile as paper.

Librarian Gregor Henry, 1974 CE

A CHARACTER'S COLORS FADE when its book is destroyed.

Brevity stared at Aurora's unmoving face, her heart a fist in her chest. If you were human, and if you closed those eyes, she might just be napping. Sleeping anywhere—balanced on books, on the couch in the suite—as she was prone to do.

If you did not look down and see the jagged holes that had been carved through her thin cotton jumpsuit and the tiny chest beneath. If you did not see the flurry of shredded, ink-stained paper that littered the character's body. If you were not a muse who could see the absence of light where color should have bloomed.

Brevity knelt and picked up a scrap of paper that eddied by, rubbing her thumb over it. She tried to catch her breath, to hold on to the idea of how they'd gotten here; the fall had been so fast.

Not all the damsels had chosen to fight. Some had retreated into their books, but enough had decided to stay that Brevity and Hero felt they could mount a proper defense. Hero had a mind for fighting dirty, and Brevity had been surprised at his fierce, determined plan. He'd moved swiftly between damsels, helping one locate books on swordsmanship and combat before moving on to the next one.

"Why in damnation aren't there any unwritten *guns* in this place? Or unwritten grenades, flamethrowers?" Hero had complained early on.

"First of all: fire. *Library. No.* Second . . ." Brevity shrugged. "Weapons stopped being art. Fickle human progress."

Hero had grunted and bent to help with another barricade.

They moved the damsels into position, loose groups of three that at least gave them a fighting chance. They readied a stockpile of weapons and projectiles—pilfered, again, from anything in the collection that was not nailed down—around the reinforcements.

And they had waited. Tension strung through the Library in different ways. A princess with cropped raven hair cried quietly, even while holding her sword up with a determined grip. The moll in the flapper dress had cracked jokes and produced a pack of smokes from nowhere. (Not allowed, but Brevity hadn't had the heart to confiscate them.) A severe nonbinary mechanic with overalls and greased hair had surprised Brevity by moving quietly from group to group, shushing the teary and comforting nerves.

Instead of feeling anxious, Brevity felt moved to help. Hero found her at the front barricade when he came to kick her out.

"He needs you." Hero emptied his hands of the last of the weapon supply. Brevity's eyes wordlessly drifted to the door as it shuddered again, and Hero fiercely shook her shoulder. "If Andras wants to take the Library, he'll need to confront and defeat the acting librarian, yes? That means you."

"But—"

She should have protested harder.

"The best way you can defend the Library is to not let Andras's men get a hand on you." Hero was firm. "They don't have the Library if they don't have the librarian. I don't care how this fight goes. No matter what happens, don't let them see you."

"That's not—"

She liked to imagine she'd fought more than she had.

"It's what Claire wanted." Hero's jaw was hard. He winced, closed his eyes, and took a sharp breath to correct himself. "It's what Claire *wants*. You have to stay free long enough for her to get here, right? Or this is all lost."

And she'd agreed; of course she had. She told herself the flighty, trembling feeling in her heart was nerves, not relief, as she retreated to the stacks, behind the barricades. By the time the second ward fell, they'd thrown together what Brevity felt was a reasonable stand. Perhaps they wouldn't even need her.

And then the final ward began to shudder. Hero had cast Brevity a grim glance full of warning before moving to his position at the front of the barricades. Brevity positioned herself adjacent to the damsels guarding the rear, at the entrance to the stacks. This group was composed of the youngest damsels, including Aurora. Unsteady, they looked to her. She sought for something encouraging to say, one last performative act of bravery. But the moment passed.

The final ward fell.

There was no fanfare, no horns. The final blood black light above the desk merely died. The doors fell open, and a moving shadow swept into the Library. A legion of teeth and ambition. Brevity caught a glimpse of Andras at the back, flanked by the largest of the eldritch Horrors he called apprentices.

There was no chance to surrender. Whatever had transpired above, Andras evidently had no illusions about the Library's agreeableness. He would accept nothing less than total submission.

The damsels rushed to meet them. They came out swinging. Trained by unwritten war books, they spun and struck in precise, disciplined units. Brevity felt her heart swell as they engaged with Andras's demons and Horrors. It was a chance. They would take it.

Brevity offered a coward's assistance. She had an advantage as a muse. She could fade-step in the Library, flickering from one shadow to another whenever a demon or terror drew too close. She retreated to the top of the Library's great stacks and stood on top of the long rows of shelves, flinging whatever detritus she could at demonic heads.

But it hurt every time she stepped back while damsels rushed forward, and watched them fall on dark creatures their authors couldn't have dreamed of. Even in the dust-clogged corners of a Library at war, Brevity could make out the shadow play of books as they died. It was the flare that got to her: the last, furious struggle of purple, red, green, blue, white, before they finally dispersed like smoke. And each time she left another person—another unwritten person, her books, irreplaceable and in her charge—to fight in her place, she dug another grave in the back of her mind and put herself in it. Her only comfort was that she couldn't argue with Hero's tactics. They were pushing them back. They would win this.

And then the wyrm appeared.

Andras's voice was a charged command in the air, and a wave of granite scale flowed in from the hall. It was not the largest of Hell's serpent servants, but it was large enough to create a solid wall as it slunk, lightning fast, around the back of the damsels' line, shattering barricades in its wake. Its body glinted with armored charcoal scales, and it opened a darting mouth to loose a spray of acid that destroyed an unwritten rug on contact.

Brevity was frozen, hidden and too far away. She could only watch with her heart in her throat. The damsels, already engaged with Andras's forces, had no way to retreat. The wyrm threaded through the Library's defenders. It didn't even need to strike; it simply constricted, breaking the lines and driving the damsels on to waiting claws, teeth, and blades. It didn't take long for Andras's monsters to find their weakness.

Their books.

The damsels who stayed to fight had chosen to carry their books. The damsel suite might have been safer, but with so much at stake, damsels were stronger staying closer to their books. It freed their movement, allowing them to strike and maneuver like dervishes, but it also left them vulnerable.

Carrying the means of their existence like hearts in their hands.

Aurora had given Brevity a shy smile as she'd patted the breast pocket of her jacket earlier. Her pocket had shimmered a happy, vibrant teal. It made a perfect target for the claws of the Horror that tore through her with less than a thought.

Brevity saw her fall. Saw the shock and terror and the fade from teal to gray to hollow air. She flickered, just once, as if trying to return to her book. But her body flinched back into the ink-soaked carpet, corporeal and agonized. Brevity waited, like a coward in the shadows, until the Horror turned away to seek a new target.

Brevity fade-stepped, flickering from one shadow to the next, until she reached the girl's side. She was already fading, violet skin seeping to gray. Her body was drifting to paper and ash before her eyes. A book turned into a grave. Brevity instinctively reached out and tried to press a hand to the wound, but more of her disintegrated under her fingers. Brevity's hand came away black with ink and ash.

She stared at her palm, long after the small body had dusted away, long after it was safe, as the dying raged in her ears.

And then it quieted, which was worse.

She fled back through shadow, twisting through the stacks. Some of the great shelves had been brought down by the wyrm's thick body. Others lost their books and rocked worrisomely, but the Library was vast, and there were many places for a coward, a failed muse, a failed librarian, to hide. Brevity was about to move again when she heard a strangled cry. Deeper than the damsels', and angry.

Hero.

Brevity flew across the stacks, stepping out from the shadows as much as she dared. She peered over the edge just in time to see Andras withdraw a short dagger from Hero's arm. Hero was flat on the ground near the wide double doors, a hand crushed under the clawed foot of one of Andras's largest Horrors.

The wyrm had stopped seeking the remaining damsels and coiled in a circle around its master and his victim. More Horrors drew closer, appearing from deeper in the stacks. Sensing blood in the air, a decisive end.

What that implied about the fates of the remaining damsels made Brevity's chest ache.

Andras twirled the dagger in an idle grip before flipping it in his palm and plunging the blade into the meaty part of Hero's thigh, pulling another scream from the unwritten man. Ink pooled from a handful of other similar wounds, and the whole right side of Hero's face was swollen underneath the black ink and ash.

Hero tried to twist to his feet, kicking out hard with the injured leg, but the wyrm's coiled body left no room to maneuver. The Horror standing over him shoved him down and redoubled his weight on his wrist. Andras, evidently tiring of the show, waved him off and dragged Hero to his knees. He waited while the Horrors bound him, tapping his fingers impatiently.

"I've been fighting books, books, nothing but books, since I got here. But not a librarian in sight. Someone's shirking their duties." Andras's voice echoed, silky and dangerous. The flat of the dagger tapped on Andras's chin as he studied Hero's wounds like a painter would a canvas. His features, which Brevity had previously considered stern but fatherly, were now sharp, hungry. "Why don't you be a good book and tell me where your masters are? Where's Claire?"

Hero's eyes were glazed with pain. He said nothing.

"Come, now, Hero. We drank together in Valhalla! I know the way you strain at your leash. I sympathize, even." He petted Hero's bloodied cheek, dragging claw marks through the soot. Hero flinched. "So I know you wouldn't come back to this place on your own—if you're here, then she is too. Why suffer for those who keep you prisoner?"

Andras's second-in-command held up a square, ragged book. Brevity squinted until she recognized the too-white pages. Hero's book. The Horror shook it open and raked its claws over the front page, shredding it delicately.

Hero's shoulders shuddered, but then an odd sound came. It was like a wet squelch—a broken cough—until it resolved into a laugh. Claws hesitated on the page.

"You'd be doing me a favor," Hero croaked. His head lolled on his shoulders, eyes sliding around the ceiling until Brevity realized he was searching. They lit on the shadow where she hid, and a ragged smile forced its way onto his blackened lips. "The librarians are weak, perfidious beasts. If you need them, then I wish you good hunting. They abandoned us."

"I think not. Claire is my creation. I groomed her for many things, but I could always rely on her stubbornness." Andras tilted the point of the blade under Hero's chin. "Ah. Or should I be looking for the muse? She'll be easier to break."

Hero closed his eyes. His head drooped. "Go to hell."

Andras made a disappointed cluck of his tongue. "That's not much of a profanity here, you know. If you're not going to make yourself useful, I have no need for a broken book in a place full of them." Andras flicked the blade carelessly, opening another bloom of black ink on Hero's chest.

Brevity was in shadow before she realized it; then she was at the base of the stacks. The wyrm blocked her view. Damsels were dead and it was in her *way*. She opened her mouth. "Stop!"

Slowly, the wyrm's body shuddered into motion and pulled away to reveal Andras. Brevity stepped forward. Her skin crawled as the monster shifted behind her, closing her path. Books lay torn everywhere, crushed under the wyrm's weight. Pages slipped beneath her heels. Wet clung to her cheeks. She crouched down to inspect Hero when she reached him.

Up close, the ash-gouged wounds and pooling ink were even worse. Hero's lip was split and black with ink as he managed to open his good eye. His words stumbled through a broken mouth. "We had a plan."

"I improvised." Brevity had to whisper to keep her voice from cracking. "I'm not strong enough to be a hero."

Hero's laugh was small, brittle. "Me neither."

"I am prepared to accept the Library's surrender," Andras's cool voice intruded.

Brevity drew her eyes from Hero. Andras was smiling. "I'll surrender, but the books stay. You have to promise no more books are destroyed."

Andras's smile grew. Not pleased, amused. "Is that all? The Library is no good to me burned. I'll spare your pets, for now."

A little of the sour tension leaked out of Brevity's shoulders. But then Andras glanced again toward Hero.

"It would be unwise to leave insurrectionists at my back, however." Andras made a motion. The Horror holding Hero's book moved before Brevity could react. Claws grasped a handful of pages and tore.

Hero's whole body stiffened, and his eyes rolled back. He didn't scream, which worried Brevity even more. As if someone had cut his strings, he fell forward.

Hero's colors had always been subdued, held close to his book. Simmering navy, the occasional gilded shadow of pewter and green. Hero, the character, had been colorful and bright enough for both. But Brevity felt it, like a shriveling under her hand, when his colors began to fade. Brevity gripped him by the shoulders and could only watch as Andras's Horror grasped for another handful of pages as the scraps floated to the floor.

The blizzard of pages drifted through the air. The last scrap of paper landed on the carpet. As if marking finality, it was accompanied by a deep, earth-shuddering *boom*.

Then another, more out of place: *boom*.

The entrance to the wing flew open. The heavy oak doors rocked back on their hinges. As Andras's temporary ward dropped, electrified air swept through the space, carrying in with it the smoky residue of powerful magic and a crackle of lightning. A monstrous figure blocked the doorway, wings splayed, and the gargoyle let out a howl that came from every direction and multiple dimensions at once.

The echo died a moment later, and smoke settled in tiny eddies around the feet of three figures.

A gawky and thin teenage boy.

A soldier holding a sword kissed with lightning.

And a woman.

Claire flicked a gaze of cold fury around the room before landing on Andras and his men.

"Get your hands off *my book*."

40

CLAIRE

It's not just for the sake of the authors and the books that we keep the unwritten sleeping. Yes, we have to preserve the stories, and yes, the trauma an escaped book could do to an author is significant. But the whole situation is rotten for them, isn't it? Coddled away to sleep in some dusty realm?

Might be, the unwritten have an idea or two of their own on how their story should go. Might be, they'd have reason to be angry. Pray they never wake up.

Librarian Fleur Michel, 1798 CE

THE STENCH OF CRACKLING leather and burned ink stole the breath from her lungs. Claire tried to breathe through her mouth, until her tongue clotted with paper ash. The Library's tall stacks slumped like defeated giants, ripped from their moorings and spilling their contents in a trail of paper and leather around the front lobby. Black blood and fading sheaves were the evidence of those crushed underfoot or eaten by the wyrm's acid. So many books damaged, so many stories lost.

Claire's eyes were reserved for one book in particular.

Soot and ink nearly completely covered Hero's skin, painting his bronze hair gray. He was barely conscious, but swollen and split lips twitched up as he tried to open his injured eye. The Horror held a claw over Hero's pages, uncertain what to do now.

Andras forgot his game entirely as his yellow eyes lingered over

Claire, taking in her patches of blood, stopping at the amulets looped around her neck. For the time being, surprise and the dangerous sizzle of Rami's sword kept the Horrors at bay. The gargoyle creaked at her back, wings flexing to create a protective shadow over their heads. It let out a low, warning rumble. Claire raised her hand, and it stilled.

Andras's eyes narrowed. "It appears the Hellhounds have not lived up to their reputation."

"Can't blame them too much for their failings," Claire said. "Demons are so unpredictable."

"We share that with humans." He opened his mouth as if to say something more. *It would be just like him to have a dramatic speech,* Claire thought. But he seemed to think better of it. His hand twitched, and the time to talk was over. "Kill them."

The Horrors surged like the tide.

Rami strode forward and met one group, gray feathered coat billowing as he buried his blade in the chest of the first demon that approached, then pulled it cleanly out to strike at another. The smell of ozone and storms and fury filled the air, and he moved like a powerful dervish. A building storm of lightning and force. Ramiel, the Thunder of God.

The gargoyle had swept aside the nearest Horrors with one hand, and the wyrm surged and attacked. The serpent twisted and coiled around the bellowing creature. The wyrm was bigger, but the gargoyle's stone skin was slick, difficult to gain purchase on. They clashed in a titanic roil of scale and stone that knocked another shelf to the ground.

Out of the corner of her eye, Claire saw Leto hunker behind a shelf near the door as he'd promised.

Leto. Matthew Hadley.

He might have been, what, a nephew? Grandchild? Had it really been that long? The impossible thought had a stranglehold on her heart. In a whisper, while they prepared in the hallway, Rami had told her what he knew and how he'd found Leto. It was too much for a coincidence.

And too much to think of now. Claire ducked as a wing swept over her head, and she focused her attention on the demon at the eye of the storm. Andras took one look at the titans clashing over their heads, cast a sour look at Brevity, then turned and ran.

Claire cursed and rushed forward to where Brevity supported Hero. The Horrors were beginning to move again. "Arlid! Anytime now!"

A grackling cry built from the doorway. A conspiracy of ravens, all those freed from the Arcane Wing and more, shrieked in and swept wide passes through the air, out of the reach of the demons. They dove in groups to rake sensitive tentacles and scalps of the Horrors, claws coming away bloody. The flock swept around and hurtled themselves at the ground. Birds disappeared in a flurry of feathers and came up leather-clad fighters, wielding thick swords and cruel sickles.

Andras's Horrors, suddenly flanked, whirled and lost formation. Arlid cast the nearest one a manic grin and lopped its spiny head off.

A shattering sound drew Claire's attention. Two ravens had cut off Andras at the entrance to the stacks. The demon held them at bay with his strange black dagger. Then he ripped a red-gemmed bauble from his coat and flung it against the nearest shelves. An unnatural fire bloomed where it shattered. Claire's heart stopped as the first books began to crackle. She staggered to her feet.

Then another row of unwritten books smoldered and leather began to boil and pucker.

"Brevity!" Panic made Claire's voice shrill and sour.

"On it!"

Brevity didn't bother with running: one moment she was behind her; the next, she emerged from a shadow near the flames. She ripped a light globe from the wall as she passed and bolted toward the fire, dodging Horrors and ravens locked in combat. She twisted the globe sharply until it turned blue and began spraying a fine jet of delicate, glimmering foam at precise places on the shelves. The foam evaporated the moment it touched the books, taking the fire with it. "I've got this!"

Claire turned back. Andras stepped over the burned bodies of the ravens. He tilted his head, as if acknowledging her, before disappearing into the stacks. She cursed and moved after him.

"Claire."

The hoarse voice arrested her steps. Hero had propped himself up on the ground and made attempts to bunch his coat over the worst wounds. Black ink spread too fast between his fingers. His face was swollen and blackened on one side, but the undamaged part of his mouth curved into a familiar, bitter-edged smile. He shifted, grimacing as he did, and pushed his sword. It skittered across the floor to stop at Claire's feet.

Claire took the weapon and found her heart in her throat, wondering how much pain he could survive without a book to repair back to. The question must have bled onto her face. Hero waved her on. "Go. End this."

Claire clutched the sword to her chest, turned, and ran into the stacks.

THE STACKS HAD BECOME narrow ravines of shadow. Between the fighting and the fire, the globes that had so reliably lit dark corners were gone. The deeper Claire went, the less the damage, these shelves being more removed from the initial battle. Only a few jostled books scattered the aisles. She could just see the retreating flutter of Andras's coat as it threatened to disappear at the far end of the aisle.

He wanted her to follow him. Would have some trap in mind. But Claire just wanted this over.

Her knee protested as she ran, slowing her down. A wheeled ladder leaned against the shelves to the right, and she leapt, landing on it with her full weight to send the ladder flying. A few kicks picked up speed, and Claire could see the back of Andras's head clearly now. She was gaining on him.

Then he disappeared around the corner at the end of the row. The ladder hit the end of the track, and a black blade swept out at chest level. Claire flung off the ladder, barely avoiding the wicked edge as it bit into the wood.

She landed hard on her hip and slid across the polished floor. When she came up, Andras had his dagger free but was still.

"Whatever happened to 'I could never hurt you, pup'?" Claire hissed. She slid Hero's sword from its sheath and held it out unsteadily. Her hands were trembling something awful. She was a *librarian*. She knew next to nothing about swordplay or fighting. She hadn't had the heart to tell Hero that.

The corner of Andras's lips twitched. "I said I could never *kill* you. I would never lie to you, pup. This?" The dagger swayed in his hand. "A single piece of soul stone. Didn't do much to Hero earlier, but the soul of the book isn't in the paper, is it? It's high time yours took a rest, Claire. You've earned it, though it needn't have been this way."

They were deep in the bowels of the stacks, and the sounds of fighting were muted. The smoke had disappeared. Hopefully that meant Brevity had the fire damage under control. Claire edged around the demon. "Rubbish. You planned all this. *I know* what you did to Leto."

Matthew. Claire cradled his real name in her chest, pressed under her heart. She wouldn't forget it. She'd forgotten many things, but she would not forget Leto.

Andras tilted his head. He backed up a step and Claire followed, not willing to let him run again. "Finally put that together, did you? Frankly, I'd hoped you two would have that reunion sooner. You always were adopting strays, pup. I gave you a real one."

"You killed him, and you think I should be *grateful?*" Incredulity gave way to fury. Andras raised his blade in warning.

"The boy killed himself. I just greased the rails as a gift to you. I hoped having him around would make you happy. Soften you, make you more open to new opportunities. I needed you. I knew the codex was out there, but that *damned* city was warded. I needed a tracker, and a stubborn one. We could have worked together."

Claire's lip curled, though the disgust felt reserved for herself. So many deaths at her feet. Leto, the damsels and demons. Beatrice? No. Claire shook her head. "How in the world did I ever consider you a friend?"

Andras sounded sad. "You used me just as much. It's what friends do."

Andras hadn't moved. He wasn't retreating, but he wasn't pressing his obvious advantage either. Claire frowned, risking a glance from him to the shelves and back. He traced her suspicion and his smile grew. He rested a possessive hand on a shelf. "Since we're in the business of reunions today . . ."

Claire narrowed her eyes; then ice raced down her spine. The name was stamped in small gilded letters on the spines of the books under his fingers: CLAIRE JUNIPER HADLEY.

Her books.

She hadn't realized they were so deep in the Library.

Her books were not part of the main collection. After what had happened with Beatrice, she'd gathered up all the unwritten books bearing her name and archived them in the most obscure corner of the Library, tucked them between books whose authors had died thousands of years ago. She'd told herself it wasn't for herself but for the books. Beyond her temptation, surrounded by ancient and satisfactorily sleeping books. She allowed herself to pretend it was merely a side benefit that she never had to be reminded of her past failures.

Even now the temptation was still there. Her hands itched, ached to reach out to touch, to thumb over the pages. She might have forgotten so much of her past life, but her stories—the stories never faded. Unspent words stayed, like ink in the blood. She felt cold and hot at once, hollow with the ghosts she carried.

Andras watched her reaction with growing pity. "I always do my research. It took some time for my men to find where you'd tucked them. I thought I taught you better, Claire. The first rule of the game is a simple one: never keep a secret that can be used against you."

Claire's mouth felt dry. She dragged her eyes away from the shelves. "Funny words for a creature that does nothing but lie."

"Two different beasts: deception and secrets. Deceptions are when you lie to others; secrets are when you lie to yourself." Andras made an impatient motion, waving his blade over the shelves. "We could debate virtues all day, but I know you, pup. Shame to let such an impressive collection of books go to waste."

The blade spun in his hand, and the black tip brushed against a green-bound book. It left a smear of ink: Hero's blood. It gleamed wet for a moment before the ink ignited. Claire flinched and bit back a cry as black flames flared and the book fell to ash.

"Step down, Librarian," Andras said.

There was a nib of leather in the ashes, a fleck of gold. Claire tried to turn away, but her gaze locked on a scrap of shadow drifting from the shelf. It was a portion of paper, entirely turned to ash but held together, for a breath of a moment, as if it hadn't forgotten how to be a page. Darker striations of ash marched across the middle—the *ink*. She could almost make out a snippet of a paragraph, and the laconic, cold voice of the historian told her, from the back of her mind, that she would be the last soul to read these words. A sob hiccuped in her throat, and the puff of air was enough: the ash page dissolved between her outstretched fingers.

The destruction of a book was a shame, but the grief that suffocated her all at once wasn't for a book. It was for people: like Hero, like Beatrice. God, she'd been every kind of fool. Her voice felt ash-choked. "I buried them because I wanted to forget them. Why would I care what you do?"

"I don't think that's true." Andras turned a prospective gaze over Claire's collection. "Which book do you think that was, now? A random adventure, a romance? Your one moment of genius? I've already met your idea of a hero—quite crude, by the way. So terse, so unlikable. Better that woman never got written. But I'm sure in one of these you dreamed up your ideal love too. Do you think you memorialized your beloved family somewhere, since you couldn't be bothered to remember yourself? Is there a story there for your daughter? Perhaps this one."

At a word, another book folded into char and soot.

"Just as well." Andras tutted. "They obviously didn't try to remember you."

It wasn't her forgotten daughter he was destroying, and Andras knew it. Her daughter was a human who had lived and grown old. Andras was killing the lives trapped between pages here, innocent lives. Lives that relied on the Library for protection.

"You can't win, Andras." Claire's voice trembled. She breathed through her nose and it felt like screaming.

"Oh?" The blade paused in Andras's hand. He tapped his bottom lip. "Do you think you'll just wish me away, like you did Gregor? I'm a demon. Hell is my very nature. Your 'words' won't work on me."

"I won't need them to stop you." Claire swallowed. The fear stuck beneath her collarbone. "Your Horrors will be eliminated by Arlid's ravens. I've turned your own wing's collection against you. Lucifer is never going to grant you your title again after such a defeat. What can you hope to gain with this? You're never a sadist without reason."

"Call it a morbid curiosity to see just how much of your past you'll ascribe to the fire. That's what I liked best about you, Claire. You were so *selfish*, so human." Andras's gold gaze was bright as a coin and twice as greedy, but it wasn't cold. It simmered with regret, which was worse. Claire caught the moment when he steeled himself for an act. "Did you ever wonder why I call you pup?"

"I assumed fatherly affection, but that's obviously wrong."

"When I found you, you were a whining puppy. Broken, grieving your silly books. Like a kicked dog. Would have rolled over and played dead for anyone. *I* took you in. *I* kept you safe." His words curled, ripping over into a snarl. "You owe your station to me. You owe me this. I know you kept the scrap. Smart girl, but you burned that up getting in here, didn't you? I admit I had to do a bit of the same. Tragedy, but I . . ." He patted one pocket. "I had just enough to spare. With the Uwritten Wing in hand, I can trade the rest of these for enough power to challenge Lucifer himself, if I so desire."

"You can burn the Library, but you won't possess it," Claire said, and she blinked, realizing the truth of it. It gave her the strength to raise her chin. "Brevity and I will resist you with everything."

"And that's why I have this." Andras flipped the blade over in his hands. Claire realized the black surface gleamed not like metal but like polished crystal. "Good-bye, pup."

The blade moved at her, fast and glinting like a minnow in water.

Claire threw the sword in front of her as she stumbled back, using it more as a shield than a riposte. Andras flicked his wrist and turned the movement against her. The sword wrenched out of her hands and flew down the aisle.

Andras stopped, sighing as she clutched her bruised wrist. "This just isn't fair. I knew I should have taught you swordplay." He moved again, taking advantage of her reaction to kick her solidly in the gut. Claire crumpled to the floor, breath seizing in her lungs. She felt Andras stop behind her, a cold shadow. He was toying with her. Andras would win any fight, fair or otherwise.

Claire understood it then. She stayed on her knees.

"Hear me," Claire whispered, words lost to the floorboards. "Hear me, please. I have done my best, but we need you now. If you ever had power, if you ever cared about this place and those in it, *please*, I need you now."

Andras heaved a long sigh. A toe nudged her spine. "Praying? I'm disappointed in you. Even if Lucifer was the worshipping type, he's abandoned you. I thought you were better than cheap begging."

"Please," Claire breathed. She leaned against a shelf of books. The leather was cool against her cheek. Nothing stirred beneath it. She squeezed her eyes shut with effort. "This isn't how the story ends. Not yours." Hers, perhaps. But hers wasn't the only story inked in the bones of Hell.

The whispers, when they came, were nothing more than a soft hush of wind. Claire opened her eyes and turned.

Andras still held a disappointed frown, dagger out as if he was waiting for his fancy to take him. His gaze stumbled, catching on something just over Claire's shoulder. She held very still. She felt the figures at her back, dozens of them. No, not dozens.

Hundreds.

And she knew the books were awake.

Books woken up after a long, very long, sleep. Heroes and villains and damsels and knights. Monsters and rogues and saints and madmen. Books and stories and characters and conflicts from ages long past, furies and passions honed over an eon to a killing edge. Aliens and monsters and queens and mercenaries and children. They crowded the hall behind her and clung to shelves; those with wings and tails crowded overhead. Dozens, hundreds, more. The weight of the wakened Library balanced, heavy and infinite, in the air.

They didn't bother with the niceties of dimensional physics. Out of the corner of her eye, feet flickered against the floorboards. Boots turned to hooves turned to heels turned to soft shadow. The only thing constant was the weight, the weight of a million gazes on her back. The pressure was like a great wave, obliterating and terrible. And when it turned its gaze on Andras, a tremor shook through the demon's shoulders. His hand fell to his side, and Andras began to back up. Claire felt the pull of the tide of old stories, hungry ghosts, and dug her knuckles into the floor. It was all she could do not to lose herself with it.

Andras's voice was haughty but unsteady. "I'm the Arcanist, Grand Duke of Hell. You can't—"

"We can." The words came to Claire's lips, like grave dust. "We are the dreams that did not die with the dreamer. We care nothing for the dark."

"Nonsense. I'm a demon! I can offer you freedom, escape, *power* beyond imagination."

"We are *imagination.*"

Air rushed out of the aisle, sucking Claire's breath with it. When she felt the first figure pass her, like a trace of frost over her skin, the prudent thing would have been to close her eyes. There were things human minds weren't meant to comprehend, and Claire felt her own mind pressed, spread too thin. But she'd called this. She'd asked, and the Library had answered. She'd woken them up. All of them. She ground her hands against the wood until her nails splintered, and she looked up.

Andras backed into a wall, shoulders hunched, with his dagger out. Not in a proficient pose like before, but sweeping, searching for a target. Figures coalesced in the air between them, like a mist swirling on a current. His blade passed through the chest of the nearest figure. It parted like water and then, instead of disintegrating, the figure solidified and power spread like a ripple. Andras's eyes were gold-and-black cat eyes, all human traces gone, when they found hers and caught.

"You're not a murderer, pup. Have mercy. You know me. We could have—"

A dark-skinned woman, ageless and terrifying as the dawn, appeared out of the shadows at Andras's back. A rush of power and a spike of light forced Claire to squeeze her eyes shut. When she opened them, empty air hung where Andras had stood.

The dagger clattered to the hardwood, loud as Claire's pulse. It was no longer black, but as silver as Andras's hair, with a tiger stripe of faintly glowing amber.

Claire took an unsteady breath, realizing too late that the ghost woman's attention was now on her. Her starless black eyes gained weight, as if feeding from the judgment. Claire tried, with the parts of her mind that weren't screaming, to identify her. The woman didn't seem like one of Claire's own characters, or any damsel that had appeared in the past. This wasn't a character that had ever woken up under Claire's care, perhaps had *never* woken up. This was a character from an old book, breathtakingly old, a book conceived when characters such as this were not women, but *forces*, faces of the gods.

That gaze held Claire immobile, and pressed down like stone. It saw every fleck of ash on her cheeks, the smoke heavy in her hair, every callous disregard she'd ever had. It saw the ink that stained her fingers, time and time again, and measured her life in cruelties. Somewhere distant, she could hear Brevity's high voice calling her name. They were looking for her now.

But the Library had already found her. The Library would not bring the others here until it was done with her.

Andras had been asking the wrong person for mercy. The mercies of the Library were dust and silence. She was caught in a sea of ghosts, a trap with jaws of ink and bone. The pulse of dreams beat at her skin, pressing in, and hundreds of hungering eyes palmed at her soul. Tasting, testing, finding it wanting. The accusation was there. The accusation and weight of every book that'd burned today. Claire distantly wondered which faces in the crowd were of her creation.

All seemed equally judging, but that was familiar.

The woman in front drew toward her. Claire felt locked in place, but dragged a word from her throat. "Wait."

It was only a shred of a whisper, but the specter paused. Claire swallowed and tasted iron. "You have a right to be angry. Give me a chance to fix it. I—" She distantly heard Brevity's voice again. "We can fix this. I might have failed you, each of you, but the Library wasn't abandoned today. You had no shortage of champions. You are the Library; we are the librarians. *Let us serve.*"

Stories end. The words nearly split Claire's skull. She winced. The woman at the fore drifted toward her, hair suddenly white, fire instead of shadow.

"Yes. And that's my fault. Only mine." Claire struggled to breathe. "Please. I'll accept what I must do to make amends."

The woman was as still as a statue, and she considered.

41

RAMIEL

There is no apology for my acts. We have a choice, all of us, in seeing the world and system we participate in. At some point, we are confronted with the cost. What suffers for happiness. What dies for life. Even Caesar couldn't keep such a thing hidden, the blood that waters an empire's soil. You have a choice. You can choose to close your eyes and enjoy your lucky position on the good earth. You can choose to walk away.

Or you can choose to rebel.

Librarian Poppaea Julia, 48 BCE

RAMI WAS LEARNING MANY things today.

Hell had a pet gargoyle. Ravens fought like warriors. Books bled ink. And dead bodies stank, even in Hell.

The last lesson was the most pressing on his mind as he covered his nose with his sleeve, clearing a spot on the floor of debris before the gargoyle deposited the final body on the pile. The Library had become a graveyard.

The Horrors, when slain, decomposed at an accelerated rate and had turned putrid before the fighting was even over. The young ladies—Leto had referred to them as damsels before Brevity staunchly corrected that they were their own goddamn heroes now—were fading and so fragile, their forms were like spiderweb and ash where they'd fallen. Rami had made one attempt, just one, to right a dying damsel, but the body had folded into dust. Brevity had made a wounded sound, and Rami couldn't even bring himself to wipe the ash from his face.

Arlid and her raven folk made little effort to help, of course. The warriors were more inclined to scour the stacks, finishing off with judicial glee any Horror they found, but Arlid delegated a young leather-clad boy to tend to the injured book they called Hero.

The boy had bandaged the unwritten man's wounds as best as possible. Brevity directed him to prop Hero on the couch near the front desk. She gathered his mangled book where it lay, but that was as much as could be done until a librarian could repair the damage. Hero lay on the couch unmoving, fading in and out of awareness, though every time he woke, his face turned toward the entrance to the stacks.

Finally, against Rami's advice, Brevity took a few of Arlid's folk and plunged into the stacks after Claire. Fool girl. It wasn't safe, but the muse was frantic to find the librarian. She'd only grown more so after a discomfiting breeze had whipped through the stacks before dying down again.

The minutes had ticked by, but neither raven nor librarians emerged. "How much more?" Leto asked, hovering by the desk. The boy had kept out of the fighting, but helplessness drained his features. The boy looked tired, scanning the death and destruction at the front of the Library. Several of the Library's tall shelves had been damaged in the fighting, upended as much by the gargoyle's own maneuvering as by Andras's forces. The stacks cracked and groaned, leaning against one another like broken old men. Books, paintings, and other unwritten artifacts were scattered on the floor. Rami hadn't allowed Leto even to help with pickup.

"That's the last of them," Rami said. He stepped back as Arlid approached with a blue-flamed torch. The smell drew a wince as she placed it to the bodies, but the magical fire sputtered and burned cleanly, smoke neatly drifting out the hallway to mingle with Hell's usual ash- and anise-heavy air. Damsel and demon alike were ascribed to the elements. Rami said a silent prayer. To whom, he found he wasn't quite sure.

"Was it worth it?" Rami muttered.

Arlid heard and arched one thick brow. "Beats me, Watcher. My kind slaughter each other, everyone gets up for sunrise again the next morning. Ask your librarians."

"If they return." Rami cast a look toward the still shadows of the stacks.

"They better. The little one took some of the flock in with her." Arlid made it sound as if she would take it as a personal offense if the search party failed.

The fire did quick work, burning blue and clean, never straying toward the shelves of tempting paper nearby. They were just watching the embers when there was a pop and a familiar teenage yelp of surprise behind him. Rami sighed and turned to remind Leto not to touch anything.

The air left his chest in a rush.

A shattered star stood just beneath the arch of the Library doors. Uriel, archangel of the Heavenly Host, Face of God, proud, holy, eternal, stood straight as a blade in the chaos of the Library. Her fractal wings were fully unfurled, and razor blades of light scissored and lashed gouges into the door molding. By her side, Leto stood stock-still.

Perhaps due to the angelic fist clenched around his throat.

"Uriel!" Rami's legs decided to work again and he jolted forward. "What are you doing?"

"What you should have done, the moment you entered this unholy place." Her voice was silk over frozen stone. Uriel didn't have a weapon, didn't need one. Her pale fingers curled around Leto's neck like a collar. It was threat enough. The whites of Leto's eyes were wide, and his cheek twitched from the effort to breathe around Uriel's grip.

Her hand tightened as Rami advanced. He frowned in confusion at the archangel. "How did you—"

"I followed you. Your fallen path was not so hard to find once you made me aware of it."

"That's— The threat is over now." Rami raised his hand. It was difficult to keep the tremble out of his voice. "Leto is an innocent human soul. He's not even damned—he's Heaven's now. We saved him. That means—"

"That means *nothing*," Uriel snarled. Her arm shook for good measure, drawing a stuttering yelp from Leto. The light at her back splintered and doubled, growing from wings into a lashing scorpion tail. She was losing control. "Not when a Watcher, one of Heaven's first creations, dear to the Creator's heart, would turn traitor and help these *things*."

"No one here is a *thing*. They're human, or harmless spirits, or ..." He trailed off, not quite sure how to describe Arlid's ravens or the gargoyle. He caught leather-clad movement at the edge of his vision. Arlid stepped up behind him, hand dancing over her weapon, calculating the space between them and the angel.

His heart ached, already drowned in too much bloodshed today. He had to stop this before it turned foolish. "I haven't betrayed anyone, Uriel. And I can't condone harm to a human soul by our hands."

"You have no standing to judge me. A failed Watcher, the sad, pathetic beggar at Heaven's Gates." Uriel's grip tightened, sending a flush of strangled blue frost to Leto's cheeks. The teenager's hands flew up and clawed weakly at her wrist. Rami didn't realize he'd moved until the lightning crackled up and down the blade in his hands.

Uriel's eyes ignited and leaked flame. "*You* would dare draw a blade against *me?*"

Rami opened his mouth before he realized he couldn't deny it. But Uriel began to bleed pale wildfire, and panic leapt into his mouth instead. "Leto! Close your eyes!"

The room flared as Uriel shed her skin. Behind him, he heard a strangled cry and a flutter of raven wings. Only Rami could stand his ground as shards of light spit from the angel's back like needles, and her face became a mask of fire. Leto was a dark, cringing blot against Uriel's wrath, and Rami could only hope he'd followed orders. A human mind was not equipped to see the face of god.

When Uriel's transformation completed, her voice was splintered crystal in his ears. "*You dare?*"

Rami swallowed, calling lightning to his blade, which he kept pointed low. "It seems I do. Let the boy go, Uriel." Leto whimpered, and Rami was ashamed that he was uncertain whether he could really strike the Face of God.

He didn't have to find out.

"Rule number twenty-three. No fighting in the Library."

A voice, infinitely weary, rang out from the front of the stacks. Rami turned. Claire's arm was looped over Brevity's shoulder. The muse had her eyes screwed shut against the light, but Claire leaned heavily on her assistant. It took Rami an unbelieving moment to realize she stared directly into the blinding face of god with a dull, distant stare.

"The *abomination*." Uriel's mouth hissed flames. "You will suffer for your crimes."

"Always threats with you people," Claire said, unblinking and cold. "You need to leave, angel. The Library is closed and Hell will not claim you."

"I am of the High Host of Heaven and you are *all* in judgment." Uriel was unhinged, burning from within. One glowing hand squeezed on Leto's throat, pulling a wounded noise from the teenager. "I will crush your sinner beneath—"

"*Kheladgis*," Claire said. Then words started to pour from her mouth. Dark, guttural things. They must have been words, but they took on a life of their own as they left her lips. They became black holes, sucking the air from Rami's lungs. They became embers, searing ash into his eyes. They became silk, caressing his skin before slithering by like snakes on a hunt.

A shudder flinched through the room. Uriel had time only to curl her lips in a snarl. Her light fluttered from blinding to translucent, insubstantial. Like a flame suddenly deprived of air. Her scything wings melted into mist, and her hand dissolved from around Leto's neck like dust cleared by the wind, leaving the boy staggering.

She was gone.

It took three ragged breaths of staring at the empty space before Rami's mind could do something other than scream. He spun toward Claire, though he had the sense to lower his weapon as he did so. "You . . . Uriel. Did you just . . ."

"She was hurting Leto. There are certain words . . ." Claire trailed off. She leaned more heavily on Brevity and let her guide her to her desk. "She was not of Hell. I did warn her the Library was closed."

"But she's . . ."

"She'll likely find her way back to Heaven again in a while. Give or take a decade."

Unmade. Uriel, highest of the Host, the avatar Face of God, had been unmade by a librarian. Rami could feel the absence of her, a well in the universe that all of Heaven tilted toward. There would be aftershocks of this for decades, centuries even. For lack of any ability to process that, Rami focused on sheathing his sword. Claire leaned heavily on the desk, rubbing the space between her brows.

"You were able to look at her, yet you're . . . ," Rami said with wonder.

"Not mad? I wouldn't go that far." Claire's smile was paper-thin. "It's been a day for nonsense. I'm full up on madness and horror." She took a breath and turned. "Are you all right, Leto?"

"Yes, ma'am. Thank you." Leto sagged against the wall near the door and rubbed his neck. He was technically leaning on a shelf full of books, but Rami didn't have the heart to force him to stand. His neck was still frostbitten, but slowly it warmed under his fingers. Claire's eyes swept over the boy, a hundred unspoken words in her worried eyes. She said nothing.

Rami found himself glancing about the room, alone in Hell and uncertain of the weight of his conscience. An unmaking of an archangel shouldn't even have been possible. Claire had just murdered one of the highest of the Host, his commander, in front of him. That would be a declaration of war for any angel, fallen or no.

He could draw his sword, right now, and smite all of them. He'd be in the right. They'd all be dead in the coming war between the realms, but he'd be right.

But somewhere in Ramiel's long and winding existence, right had stopped feeling like the best place to be.

His gaze wandered until it came to Leto. The teenager smiled, tentative, encouraging, at Rami. The boy would never know why he'd ended up in Hell's Library. A muscle in his jaw worked, and Rami took a slow, shuddering breath. He lowered his eyes to the scorch mark where Uriel had stood. His hand fell from his sword hilt.

"Do you need to go file a report or something?" Claire kept her question neutral, though the cant of her shoulders telegraphed that she was expecting a poor response.

Rami nodded stiffly. "Eventually. Heaven will need to know the archangel is . . . delayed."

Claire blinked, and of all the impossibility of her acts, *this* was what surprised her. "Delayed."

"It's accurate," Rami insisted.

"Delayed." Claire nodded to herself and turned, as if surveying the damage for the first time. She sucked a sharp breath of air in through her teeth.

"We won." Brevity had found her voice, though it sounded thin as spun sugar. She had a kind of hollow-eyed look when Rami considered her. Claire shrugged her arm free of her assistant.

"This," the librarian said, with a particularly ruthless kind of self-loathing that Rami knew well, "this is not winning."

Brevity didn't appear to have a single denial for that, but she straightened. There was in her sharp features a resolve that Rami hadn't noticed before. The kind left after a fire. "We're here, aren't we?"

Claire met that gaze for a long moment. Rami couldn't claim he knew either woman well enough to know what was being transmitted without words, but he knew the look of survivors when survival was not expected.

"Right. To business." Claire nodded, and Brevity began organizing the few remaining damsels into groups to gather the books that were yet salvageable from the battlefield around them.

Rami saw Claire's eyes stray toward the couch where Hero lay, but she resolutely turned to face the raven captain instead. Arlid and her flock had finished greeting the ravens from the search party and held themselves near the door, obviously preparing to leave.

"Arlid," Claire said levelly. "I see you were helpful as ever."

"Glowy things, burning things, not our fight." Arlid grasped Claire's forearm in a grudging shake. "You freed our kin and asked for help fighting demons, not angels."

"Just so. You did hold up your end there."

"A good fight." Arlid's kohled eyes glittered with amusement. She nodded at the chaos. "Your place looks almost as bad as the storyteller's now."

A ghost of a smile hit Claire's lips. "Just missing a few drunken Norsemen."

"We could spare them."

Claire glanced to the gathered raven folk. "Any losses?"

"Two. A hurt for the flock. But your saga women fared worse."

"The damsels, yes." Claire's eyes slid to Brevity, and the muse looked down, eyes carefully turned away from the pyre. "They were characters, not warriors, but they defended their home."

"They fought bravely. It was a good death."

"Good deaths exist only in stories." Claire's voice was grim with loss, a sound Rami knew well. "In any case, thank you again. This wasn't Valhalla's fight."

"It wasn't. Consider yourself indebted, feather and bone," Arlid said before her smile grew sharp. "But the chance to strike against the demon who had imprisoned and experimented on my flock for so long and abused the raven roads? Anytime, Librarian."

They shook once again, and the ravens departed, maintaining their human forms until the sound of wings filled the hallway.

Claire sank down on a chair with a deflated sound. She stared at nothing for a moment before turning her look to Rami.

"You'll be taking him again."

The hurt in her words made it obvious she was speaking of Leto. Whatever had happened in the stacks—not to mention all that had led up to it—had drained her. The weight of it was recognizable to Rami, the discovery and immediate loss of family she hadn't even known she'd had.

Claire looked drawn, but she was waiting for an answer. Rami nodded. "I have to. He needs to enter Heaven before he risks corruption."

Leto hovered near the couch, not seeming to know where to put himself without touching anything. He furrowed his brow at Rami. "I feel fine. Surely I can stay and help—"

"No." Rami was firm on that point. "However, after Leto's processed . . . I would like permission to return."

Surprise startled the grief from Claire's face momentarily. "Return?"

"To the Library. I should . . . I would like . . ." Rami was confounded by his own words. To *like*, to want anything. To seek anything beyond forgiveness was something he hadn't been faced with in many, many years. It felt weightless, and terrifying. There had been a time when he'd still had the right to wings; he hadn't always been earthbound. The memory came to him unbidden, that breath in flight, when you've stepped off solid ground and your mind hasn't quite made up whether you want to fly or follow your shadow to the ground. He abruptly wanted to cry, but he grunted instead. "I would like to return to . . . discuss. How I can help."

Claire's brows remained a few inches too high, but some humor gleamed in her dark eyes as she considered. "Return, and we'll see what happens.

"Brevity," she called over her shoulder as she drew herself up from the couch. "Come say your good-byes to Leto."

"Don't I get a say in this?" Leto sulked, his eyes on his feet as Brevity approached him. His cheeks were pink as he glanced at her teary face. "Ah, c'mon. It's not like I'm dying . . . again."

"That place better treat you good." Brevity sniffed, and it was obvious it took great effort not to swing her arms around his neck in a hug. "If not, you just go ahead and damn yourself all over again."

"That's . . . that's not how it works," Rami muttered, mostly to remove the pained grimace from Claire's face.

Leto just flushed. "You're going to be a great librarian someday, Brev. The best."

"You bet." Brevity rubbed a tear off her cheek. "The Library will always have a place for you."

"Only if he remembers how to brew a proper pot of tea." Claire made a face as she hobbled over. Injury or not, her limp was more pronounced as her energy flagged.

"I'll practice in Heaven," Leto said. "You'll tell Hero I said . . . bye?"

"I'll improvise on that with a little more eloquence, but sure."

Leto drifted for a hug, but caught himself when Rami shook his head. Leto let out a long sigh and rubbed his neck. "Thank you, ma'am."

"Still calling me ma'am." Claire drew herself up, voice aloof and eyes wet. "I give up. Rami, get the kid out of here before I decide to keep him."

"You heard the lady." Rami squeezed Leto's shoulder.

"I mean it. Thank you. I was . . . The Library saved—"

"You saved yourself. You write your own story here." Something crumbled, just enough for Claire to wrap her arms around herself, as if making sure they didn't do anything they weren't supposed to do. She smiled. "I'm . . . I'm glad I got to meet you, Leto. Go. Be good. No—be better than good: be happy."

42

CLAIRE

Here is how you make a sheet of parchment: Soak a pelt in a scouring bath until it softens. Scrape the hair off. Treat the skin with astringent tannic acids. Rack and torture until tight.

And here's how you make a story: Soak a life in mortality. Scrape the soul.

Librarian Gregor Henry, 1899 CE

FOR THE SECOND TIME in as many days, Claire sat down and began to repair the binding of Hero's book.

His was not the only book to be repaired. Claire kept her eyes pinned on the tattered binding in front of her, but she could nearly hear the hurts of the hundreds of torn, crushed, burned unwritten works around her. The books trodden underfoot by Horrors, the carpets with holes eaten by acid, the paintings torn by raven blades.

Claire didn't see books; she saw graves.

She saw a thousand lives on each cindered page. Here, a band of adventurers, suffocating in a forest. There, a pair of lovers, entombed in the moment before a kiss. There, torn beneath the edge of a fallen chair, the teenage outcast that never learns they are something more.

A thousand stories, caught middream, eviscerated from the possibility of being real. Some, granted, were never to be written—their authors were long dead—but others had authors just beginning to dream them. Each book was magic, a potential never to be duplicated. With a book destroyed, they faded all the same. Worlds trapped, suffocating on the page.

One thought suffocated more than most. Not long ago, it wouldn't have bothered her at all. She'd called them things. Pressed a scalpel against their hurts and called them unreal. When books were merely as enchanted objects, annoying simulacra. But now . . . now their deaths smelled of ash and acid and ink turned sour.

And as little as she cared to admit it, overriding it all was the concern for the still body on the couch next to her.

Hero had drifted in and out of consciousness during the confrontation, but once the ravens left and the danger passed, he'd succumbed to a deep sleep. Most of the fresh pages she'd stitched into his book just days ago had been clawed and torn. The front cover was blackened with char, and the edges were sodden with ink and soot. If possible, he'd done even worse injury to himself than before. She hadn't been able to get a proper conversation to assess the origin of his injuries, but Brevity had told her an absolutely ridiculous tale of Hero's . . . heroics.

She would have to be careful not to use that phrase in front of the vain creature. There would be no living with him.

Claire found herself hoping there would be *some* living with him.

She glanced to the couch and gave another grunt, pushing it all out of her head. She focused on rebinding Hero's pages. Again. Slice the strands of old thread, divide the signatures. Trim the papers. Mark the new spine. Cut the groove. Fit the cord. Reconnect the signatures. Adjust the press. Thread and stitch. Thread and stitch. So much threading and stitching.

She worked the finishing chain stitch up the spine, tied it off, and leaned back to rub the numbness out of her fingers. She let her gaze wander to give her eyes a moment of rest. The Library sank into a sepulchre of quiet.

Rami had departed with Leto, promising to return when he was able. She worried he would encounter questions that were best left unanswered, but the Watcher seemed confident in his ability to maneuver

Heavenly bureaucracy. She hoped he was right to be so confident; she'd had enough of war.

Brevity, after orchestrating a cleanup of the worst of the mess, expressed a preference for hovering over Claire like a rather concerned sparrow. After Brevity checked her tea needs for the third time, Claire had sent her off to the depths of the stacks to inspect the ashes of her burned books.

The memory of flames igniting under a black blade unsettled her focus again. Claire took a long sip of tea. Her books. Her arrogance. Beatrice. Her longing for Earth. Andras had only played on the foolish secrets and tender fears that Claire had kept. He'd set the fire, but she'd provided the tinder to burn it all down.

Andras had always said the game was just children playing in the dirt, exposing wiggling things to the light of day.

And she was exposed now. Brevity had gasped when Claire instructed her to assess and repair her books.

"Yours, boss? Are you sure you don't want me to bring them up for you, and—"

"No." Claire shook her head. "Things got . . . stirred up when I confronted the Arcanist. It's best if you repair them. I trust you."

The surprise that sparked across her assistant's face, blooming into starry joy, made Claire deeply sorry for the diet of harsh words she'd fallen into over the years. A habit she'd never given thought to before. She sent Brevity off with supplies, drowning that introspection under a swig of tea as she focused on Hero's repairs.

Whatever else would happen due to her rash invocation of the Library, she could fix one book.

Feeling returned to her fingertips and she rubbed out the tingles as she dug through the drawer for the binding paste. Claire startled when Rami cleared his throat. The fallen angel slouched against a bookcase, deep in the collar of his feathered coat. His broad olive features, usually grim and sure, held an uncertain, shy question as he looked at her.

"Leto passed the pearly gates?" Claire asked.

"With flying colors," Rami said. "He seemed a little put off at the idea of paradise. It won't surprise me if he's running Purgatory within the month."

The thought made the hollow in Claire's chest warm, mending a little. "That's . . . good."

A whisper of a smile was there, then gone. "I'm sorry you didn't have longer with him. If you like, I could try to find the records, see if he was—"

"No. Andras as much as confirmed it, and . . ." Claire hesitated. "He's where he's supposed to be now. As am I."

A stymied emotion settled in Rami's frown. Claire was new to the company of angels, but she had begun to suspect his innate sense of *justice* was frequently going to run smack against her desire to be left alone. She sighed. "What?"

"In Mdina—Brevity mentioned you left behind someone dear. If you like, I could—"

Beatrice. Claire's fingers seized up painfully. She cursed and rubbed her knuckles, forcing herself to breathe slowly through her nose. Beatrice had sacrificed herself. Yet, if the labyrinth's blasted portals could be believed, she escaped. Might have escaped. No one knew whether Beatrice still existed, book or woman. Bea always did like the allure of a mystery. Claire sighed.

"It's a kind offer, but . . . no. Our stories are . . . separate now."

Rami made a frustrated noise. "Still. It's obvious you cared—"

"No trouble finding your way back, then?"

Rami accepted the diversion for what it was: a closed door. He shrugged. "No trouble. It appears . . . Hell accepts me."

"How curious. His Pissypants doesn't usually take to drifters. But then I hear you two have a history." Claire softened the words with a nod to the pot on the caddy beside the desk. "Tea?"

"I prefer coffee, if you have it."

Claire made a face. "Well, now you definitely can't stay."

Humor fell flat, as it often did for her. Rami's gaze trailed to the materials on Claire's desk. She saw it skim over the small ridge of books and land on the amber and gray dagger perched on the corner. The gleam of the blade seemed to wink at them.

"You're really certain you caught all of him in that thing?"

Claire refused to divert her attention to the blade. Andras didn't deserve it. "The parts that were trying to subjugate all of us, at least. If he can stage a coup from a scabbard, he deserves the whole realm."

"But how did you do it?" Claire gave him an offended look, and Rami backtracked. "No offense intended, Claire, but you were limping and holding that sword like a dead fish when you ran after him."

"Yes. I suppose if I keep my position, I should probably fix that training gap." Claire ignored Rami's alarm. "I can't actually take all the credit. Andras made a fatal error. He angered the Library."

"Even *I* know not to do that. Human dreams. Prickly." A voice dusty as the grave made both Claire and Rami jump. The demon at the door padded toward them without invitation.

Rather than the archaic clothes that Andras wore, she was clad mostly in supple, flowing rose leathers, tooled with flowers and polished to a sheen. Wild hair the color of cold steel, unkempt and proud, bushed around a sharp face of worn tan skin. She looked like precisely everyone's grandmother, if one's grandmother kept the blood of her enemies under her nails.

"Malphas." Claire said the name of the general of Hell's armies on a sigh. Lucifer's second-in-command; all of Hell knew her name better as a whisper.

Malphas gave a regal smile.

Claire crossed her arms with obvious resignation. "I stave off political intrigue, put down a coup for Hell, and he couldn't even be bothered to come himself?"

"You don't seem happy to see me, kiddo." Malphas's eyes were gold like Andras's, but they lacked even the artificial warmth of his. She was cold and ancient as burial iron. Other demons called her the War Crone, and it suited. Mother of war, grandmother of death. As she approached, her leathers became less rose colored and more a shade of blood-soaked hide. Loss flowed like a river around her. She flicked a glance around the ravaged Library lobby. "If this is what 'staved off' looks like, I advise you not to enter politics."

"Saints preserve me from such a fate," Claire said just to watch Malphas frown.

Malphas's eyes slid over Rami. A hook of a smile appeared. "Ramiel. I thought Heaven's warhorse had been tamed into a mule. What are you doing here?"

"I keep my own business." Ramiel's words were stilted.

Claire risked a glance. She'd always considered the fallen angel a stiff soldier type, but this was new. He stood ramrod straight, his large, calloused hands clenched at his thighs, with the prey's instinct that complete stillness was the only way to avoid drawing unwanted attention. Malphas had that effect on longtime acquaintances.

"I see you two know each other," Claire murmured. She waited until Malphas stopped at the edge of her desk. "If you came for a debrief, we don't have a final tally on the damages yet."

Malphas waved that off, as if the domain of numbers and loss was for weaker minds. "I came to see for myself this codex. Something that made Andras finally show his hand must be powerful."

"I'm afraid that's not possible."

Malphas caught the flat note in Claire's voice, and the crow's-feet at the corners of her eyes tightened speculatively. "You're too intelligent to defy me. Do you mean the pages are already destroyed?"

"Is that what a good librarian would do?" Claire met Malphas's level gaze. "The Library is secure and Lucifer's secrets are safe. You can tell the court that."

"Yes . . ." Malphas's lips thinned before transforming into a positively terrifying gentle smile as her eyes landed on the dagger, concern forgotten. "Such a compact little prison. Precious."

Claire stifled a groan at the affectation. The gentler Malphas became, the bigger the ball of dread grew in her stomach. Rami twitched and drew closer behind her. "In a way. I'm not certain on the specifics of how Andras created it, but it captures a being. Just not the one he intended," Claire said.

"Andras always had a better mind for deception than strategy. I was the one to toss him out the first time, you know." Malphas plucked up the blade, holding it this way and that. "A useless weapon, but the court will have a trophy."

"You mean the Arcane Wing," Claire corrected her, earning a flash of warning displeasure. Malphas was a long-standing, revered general. The War Crone had no enemies, because her enemies were all dead. Claire kept her thoughts from her face. "It is an artifact of the Library's Arcane Wing and belongs there. That doesn't change just because there's a demon in it now."

Malphas considered. Bony fingers, hard as granite and with blackened nails, tapped along the edge of the blade. "Our lord has ways of dealing with failed rebellions."

"Failed," of course, was the key word. Claire knew Lucifer encouraged the plotting and backstabbing in the court as a way to keep his most powerful demons distracted. With a general like Malphas safeguarding his throne, he could afford the chaos. "And if His Vilest would like to come and extract Andras's soul for punishment, he's welcome. But until there's a new Arcanist in place, I'm sure Lucifer would agree that my charge is to guarantee no artifacts wander off the inventory."

Malphas set the dagger down by the nearest stack of books, losing interest. Instead she focused her full attention on Claire, which felt a queer mix of predatory and maternal. "About that. You have stolen from my army."

It was a flicker of a moment, a trick of the light, when a shadow melted across Malphas's features and turned them from wizened to skull-like, then back. Claire held the fear in her mouth rather than swallow and draw attention to her exposed throat. "As you said, I am too intelligent to cross you, Malphas."

"Yet I smelled the burning from the hallway. Those Horrors and that wyrm were mine. Andras was mine, despite his reassignment. So it falls to me to name a new successor." The train of thought behind Malphas's granite eyes was impossible to guess. "There are several well-established demons campaigning for the honor—"

"No demons," Claire said, more harshly than was wise. "I won't share the Library with another grasping, plotting viper. There's too much power in the Arcane Wing. The Arcanist needs to be someone who has no interest or *ability* to profit from it. Andras was proof enough of that."

"As you said, you are intelligent," Malphas mused. She leaned forward, patting Claire's cheek with sharp fingertips that left cold grit there. Then the crone demon tapped her fingers at her wrinkled throat, making an obvious show of considering. "But if not a demon, then who? That knocks out a sizable portion of qualified candidates."

Claire felt like she'd volunteered herself out onto a crumbling ledge and was now being asked to tap-dance. She traded a wary expression with Rami. The fallen angel gave a little nod, and she turned back to Malphas. "Rami would make an excellent curator."

Malphas's smile tilted over the edge from amused to disgusted. "A fallen angel is no better than a demon—worse, in fact, if he's proven to have such *pliable* loyalties. What's to keep him from making a play?"

"I have no interest in any game of yours, War Crone." Rami still looked as if he was waiting for an ambush, the mouse under a cat's paw, but he squared his shoulders. "In fact, I will only stay with the stipulation that I swear no oath to you or your throne. I believe that disqualifies me for any titles or honors in the court, does it not?"

"You are just as weak willed as ever," Malphas hummed. "But an interesting pawn. You should lend him to me, Claire."

The tremor that ran through Ramiel was palpable at Claire's back. She smiled. "I'm short staffed as it is. I couldn't possibly spare him."

"Just as well. He needs a strong hand." Malphas's face fell into carefully crafted disappointment, maternal and knowing. "Either way, I'm not sure an angel has the credentials. What do you know about Lirene's Eighth Circle Artifice Bond?"

Claire's eyes flew to the untidy pile of artifacts she'd pilfered from the Arcane Wing, and her stomach dropped. She immediately knew where this was going even as Rami faltered. "I . . . I know danger when it must be contained."

Malphas made a clicking noise with her tongue. "Oh, sweet, sweet Ramiel." She studied her nails before turning her attention back to Claire. "He's an angel with not an ounce of guile. The artifacts would eat him up on day one. We need someone with the acumen to deal with trickster artifacts. The strength to bring them to heel. Someone who has experienced the finer betrayals in life."

Claire pursed her lips. "I said no demons, Malphas."

"No demons. I had a different, reasonably *intelligent* mortal in mind."

Malphas's meaning was impossible to dodge, but Claire tried anyway. "I already have a position and responsibilities. I am Hell's librarian."

Then Malphas gave her a coin-flip smile, half-pitying and half-pleased, as she made Claire's veins run cold with two words.

"Are you?"

The air stole out of her lungs and they ached. Claire refused to flinch from Malphas's predatory stillness, but she ran her fingers idly over the paste brush still in her hands, tracing the wood against her calluses. When had she developed calluses? Bodies weren't supposed to change in Hell. "Any soul sentenced to the Library remains until they've processed their sins."

"Or failed in their duties."

Claire clenched her jaw so hard it hurt. "I just repelled a hostile invasion of the Library."

"By leaving a path of destruction through three realms and dead dreams in your wake. Even I was impressed, but death is my purview, not yours." Malphas's mood flipped. The jaws of the trap fell shut. "The librarian is supposed to protect the Library, not the other way around, child. How many books were lost because you went on this wild-goose chase? Leaving without permission on a stolen ghostlight alone would sentence any normal soul—"

"Oh, do save me the posturing." Claire found herself on her feet, and Malphas raised a warning brow. "Lucifer knew what was happening. He had to. There were too many coincidences that had his tacit tolerance, if not approval. The codex pages. B—the collector and wards at Mdina. Deny it all you want—" She held up a hand, which only increased the murder in the old demon's eyes. "But he kept you from the Library and sent no aid when we closed the wards. That alone says he knew and condoned what was going on. Hell broke faith with the Library first."

Malphas waited until Claire reluctantly sat again before speaking, fond and soft, which was when she was most dangerous. "If—*if*—our lord had an inkling of Andras's ambition, and *if* he decided to test Andras's loyalty by dangling a morsel in front of him—"

"That sacrificial morsel being the pages of the codex, my Library, and my people."

"*If* he did as you say," Malphas continued, "then he may have taken precautions to limit damage. And he must have had the faith—misplaced, in my opinion—that you would produce the necessary outcome. That doesn't mean there aren't consequences for your actions, child of man. We have no control over that."

The way she said it, with the calm of the ageless, made a final, awful piece snap into place in Claire's brain. Her anger fell. "This isn't coming from Lucifer at all."

"No." Malphas leaned back, crossing scarred, muscled arms. "When Hell comes for you, little mortal, you'll know it."

Claire tried to ignore that. "The books . . . have a grievance?"

Malphas cast a look around the ash-strewn hall. "Wouldn't you?"

The Library had always been not quite quiet. Silence was always built on the susurrus of rustling pages, the creak of leather spines, the rumbles of stories sleeping fitfully. There was none of that now. The books slept, but dreamlessly. It turned the Library into a tomb, and again the dust of a thousand books turned to graves clogged Claire's chest. "And the Library chooses its librarian," Claire said dully. "But in the stacks, they—it, the Library—withdrew. It gave me a chance to make things right."

"And that's what you'll do, as Arcanist," Malphas said. "The Arcane Wing will no longer be a threat."

Claire knew it wasn't wise to look away from Malphas, but she found her gaze had drifted to the cluttered desk in front of her. The new stitches on Hero's book had tightened. Claire picked up scissors and began mechanically snipping off the loose ends. She had cleaned up only two knots when Malphas broke out with a terrifying sound: laughter.

"Despair is such a dull look on you. Don't start boring me now." Malphas leaned over the desk, looking every inch the dotty, harmless old woman she pretended to be. "You'll still work in the Library, of course. There's plenty of work to do to clean up your mess. As you said, the Arcane Wing and the Unwritten Wing are the allies that make the Library. I never had much patience for reading, but it gives Hell an air of erudite respectability."

"As Arcanist, I get to choose my assistants." Rather than let it sink in, Claire latched onto a demand at random. She glanced briefly at Rami. "I won't work with those vile creatures Andras had in here."

"Easy enough. You destroyed most of them anyway," Malphas reminded her. She slid off the desk, rolling her shoulders like she'd won something. "I'll leave you to give your pawns the good news."

The demon disappeared in a swirl of iron and cinnamon. Claire stared at her desk. She found herself preoccupied with the knots twisted on Hero's book, noting the irregularities for trimming. Her hands clenched when Rami cleared his throat.

"I can go find Brevity. If you . . ." He trailed off when Claire nodded, and he turned and disappeared into the stacks.

Claire tilted her head back and closed her eyes. She drew in a slow breath and exhaled firmly, driving out any thought of the changes to come. She shuddered, eyes squeezed tighter.

When she could be sure of herself, she twisted in her chair and squinted at the unmoving body on the couch. The body whose face hadn't moved but whose breathing had shifted just slightly when Malphas appeared.

"I suppose you heard all that."

A whisper of movement tugged up the corner of Hero's lips. He kept his eyes closed, but his color was better. When his lips parted, Hero's voice was hoarse. "Didn't want to interrupt."

"Rami was concerned about you. You could have said something."

"I like playing hard to get."

Claire snorted. "You do love a chase."

Hero couldn't quite manage a laugh, and when he tried, it turned into a pathetic, stumbling cough. He licked his lips with some effort. "*Did* you destroy all the pages of the codex?"

Claire's smile was bitter. "Maybe. Maybe not. Better to let the courts wonder. The Library will be vulnerable for a while. If I did destroy them, we're fair game. Open to being swept up by the next demon with a hunger for power. If I *didn't*, then I'm a threat only Lucifer has the authority to address. Until they know, even Malphas will stay out of the Library."

Hero huffed weakly. "Clever."

"I learned from the best." Claire's eyes dodged to Andras's dagger. She turned back to the book in front of her and picked up the paste brush again. "For now I'll need to finish fixing your binding. *Again.*"

"Maybe you'll get it right this time."

"Everybody's a critic," Claire muttered as she began to apply the paste where the binding would adhere to leather. She worked in quiet for a few moments until Hero spoke again.

"I heard you, you know."

Claire turned and saw Hero had cracked one eye open with great effort. His gaze glittered, beneath the bruises and black filth. Claire turned back to her work. "Heard what?"

"When you confronted Andras. You said '*my* book.'"

"Is that what you heard?" Claire felt a small smile grow on her lips before she remembered herself. Loss welled in her stomach as she shook her head. "No books are mine now."

For once, Hero didn't have a response.

◆ ◆ ◆

THE DOORS TO THE Arcane Wing protested as she pushed them open. Claire stood at the entrance a moment, squinting as she indulged her gloomy mood with the darkened interior.

It had taken much talking and two pots of tea to get Brevity to accept her sudden promotion. The muse had ranted and railed, and at one point Rami had had to restrain her from fade-stepping right to Lucifer's court herself to set things right. But in the end, she'd slumped down beside Claire on the couch, sulking dully.

"This sucks, boss."

Claire silently agreed, but she rolled her eyes at Brevity. "Only because it's new. You will be an adequate librarian if you—"

"But after all we did. That I— It's not *fair*."

"What *ever* gave you the idea that Hell's Library would be fair? You should know better by now. Stories are capricious at the best of times, and . . ." She bit off the lecture that might make her feel better but would only increase Brevity's hurt. Tears had just finished drying tracks down her face, but the muse looked close to waterworks again. She slipped her hand into Brevity's. "You've already proven yourself to be a champion of the Library. You're *strong*, Brev. You'll be an admirable librarian. Better than I was. Look at it this way. You can finally brew all the atrocious strawberry-whatsit tea you want."

Brevity pulled together the broken bits of her smile. "And you'll be there?"

"I'll be around," Claire said evasively. "Just not when you're stinking up the place with that rubbish."

There might have been kinder ways to pass the mantle, but Brevity had experience reading between Claire's words. She rallied to help Claire finish restoring Hero's book. Claire had chosen to rebind him in a vivid green leather cover—primarily because it matched his eyes, but also because it was bright enough to annoy his aesthetic. The book was repaired, but the front pages remained stubbornly blank. No matter what techniques she attempted, Hero was still exiled from his own book.

He'd taken it in stride and seemed to at least get more color back in his cheeks as time went on. His eyes were back to their usual calculating mischief.

Brevity began the long work of putting the stacks back in order (the gargoyle had done the kindness of righting the fallen shelves before returning to its post in the hallway). Hero helped where he could, primarily by grumbling loudly from his recovery couch. After a few days, Claire felt confident enough to leave them to their work.

The Library would go on without Claire. The stories already had.

Rather than indulge in the morose thought, Claire decided to return to the Arcane Wing the artifacts she'd stolen and see what her new posting would bring. It was just as gloomy as she remembered. The shelves and cupboard stood ransacked where she'd raced through, scooping up anything Andras had left behind.

The raven cages, naturally, stood open and empty at the back. Arlid had taken back her people, leaving the place oddly silent. Claire ran her fingers over dust-coated shelves as she worked her way back, trying to place amulets and rings back where she remembered them.

"One shelf up. It was next to that atrocious violet crown."

Claire placed the piece and turned to see Hero lounging against the open doors. "Lounging," perhaps, was not the right word, as the doors contributed a great deal to keeping Hero's battered body upright. His arm was in a sling, but his wounds were beginning to heal. Scar material, pale as parchment against his tan, was beginning to form in spiderwebs along his jaw. Skin puckered and curled over his temple, marring his much-lauded cheekbones. Time would never fade the scars entirely.

Hero was marked, changed from how he was written, but it didn't appear to affect the mocking smile at her questioning look. "I have an excellent memory and humans think of the ugliest things."

"Yes, well, someone dreamed you up."

"You wound me, warden." Hero placed the fingers of his uninjured hand to his chest, bitterness keeping his voice from being as light as it should have been. He gestured to his face. "I suppose there's no being mistaken for a hero now."

Claire turned back to the shelves. "Don't be silly. You could be a grimdark darling. Heartless and rugged."

"Rugged. Now, there's something I've never been called." Hero chuckled, the act of which made him grimace. "But this place is dark enough for both of us."

"Andras was not a bright person. Spaces match their owners." Claire gave the warren of bleak cages a baleful look.

"So why isn't it changing?"

The way Claire blinked at him elicited another chuckle that looked like it hurt. Hero rubbed his ribs ruefully. "It never occurred to you. You're still thinking of this place as Andras's. It's yours now, isn't it?"

It stung a little, but Claire had to nod. Hero made an imperious gesture. "Then Claire-ify it. Oh—*clarify*! God, I'm clever."

"Please stop," Claire groaned, and surveyed the lab, if only to shut him up. It was too dark, too sterile, too much a cross between Frankenstein's laboratory and a Gothic parlor. She concentrated, remembering the golden glow of the Library, shabbily appointed chairs, and hot tea. She couldn't re-create that, but perhaps she could create something adjacent.

The shift was slow, like that of a photo developing in a dark room. Color slowly seeped into the walls, warming the wood. Pools of light sprang up with lamps where there were none a moment before. The orientation of the lab seemed to pivot around her until all had changed. Claire twisted around slowly to take it in.

Tidy cubbies built of dark wood made neat rows along the sides of the large room. Each row was spotted intermittently with a globe lamp. An ordinary lamp, not like those in the Library she knew, made of frosted glass and brass, but tidy and functional. Generous worktables dotted the front, gleaming with polished wood and more brass tools lit by overhead lights. It was warm, orderly, if too mechanical. Not quite the Unwritten Wing, but approximate. Some tension slowly began to leak from Claire's chest.

Hero made an approving sound in his throat, soft and a little surprised. "Nicely done."

"It . . . it will do." Claire dusted her hands, though she hadn't used them, and focused on Hero. "I suppose you're here to blackmail me. You were going to run off and tell the courts what a horrible librarian I am, weren't you?"

Hero pursed his lips and looked away. Claire thought she almost detected red in his cheeks. He reached a hand up to rub his cheek but stopped when his fingertips touched the scars. "I . . . was angry when I said that. Besides, I suppose that's lost any bargaining power now. Now that you're not . . ."

Claire shrugged. "They could always demote me to janitor."

Hero chuckled and winced. Up close, Claire could see there were still feathers of bruised ink clinging to the skin around the scars. "Shouldn't you be resting?"

"Shouldn't you?"

Claire snorted, turning her head to survey the room again. She was aware of Hero's watching her for a reaction. "I suppose I wanted to see the place. And give Brevity some room to settle in."

"You haven't been exiled, you know. The Unwritten Wing needs plenty of help. One big, happy Library, after all."

"One big, happy," Claire repeated.

Hero rolled his eyes. "What are you going to call the place?"

"Call it? It's the Arcane Wing."

"That's incredibly boring. Besides, I can't see calling you the Arcanist. How about . . . the Vaults?"

Claire wrinkled her nose. "Too steampunk. Arcane lab?"

"Too nerdy. You do lock things up. How about the Cells?"

"What, so you can keep calling me warden? No, thanks." Claire's smile stilled as her eyes landed on the empty cages at the back. Her chest felt hollow. "Maybe a place like this shouldn't have a name."

"Oh, come, now." Hero made a sharp noise. "I won't have you sulking down here by yourself. You're no fun when you brood."

"I'm no longer here for your amusement. Not your librarian now, remember?"

"True. You're not the warden anymore." Hero considered. "I suppose I'll just have to run away again. Brevity won't have time to miss me for a while."

That was bait that Claire was in no mood to ignore. She whipped her head back around and stabbed a finger at Hero's chest. "You absolutely will not. Brevity will have a hard enough ti—"

"Peace," Hero interrupted, and slid his gaze lazily around her face before coming to a conclusion. "How about a truce? You stick around, I'll stick around."

"That's blackmail."

"Is it?" Hero mused. "I thought that's what friends did."

Claire pressed her lips together, silenced by that. Artifacts gleamed underneath their new, cozy lights. Gems winked with dark eyes, all turned toward their new keeper. The force of the gaze felt heavy on Claire's shoulders, harsh but not hostile. The wing listened. The wing watched.

Hero broke the spell after a moment, clicking his tongue. He squeezed her arm.

"Come on, Claire. New story. There's work to do."

ACKNOWLEDGMENTS

This book started its life as a nonsense short story about a nervous demon courier and a grumpy librarian. It was a long, winding road from an idea in my own Unwritten Wing to here, a finished book in your hands. It was not the first book I ever drafted (there are many, many trunked novels), but it was the first book I truly wanted to believe in. I don't know how I'll ever be able to properly thank and acknowledge every kind person who helped this strange book on its way, but I'll try.

Thank you, first and foremost, to my agent, Caitlin McDonald, who believed so much in this book that she forgave the fact that it came attached to an author with the personality of a magpie. And to Rebecca Brewer at Ace Books, who championed it onward. Without Caitlin's and Rebecca's considerable skill and energy, Claire and the gang would not have made it the last mile out of the Unwritten Wing. I also want to extend my sincere gratitude to the entire Ace and Penguin Random House team, including Jessica Plummer, Alexis Nixon, and Dan Walsh.

Special thanks to writer friends and mentors who read early drafts and yelled at me until I explained how living books actually worked: Teresa Nielsen Hayden, Scott Lynch, Steve Gould, Sherwood Smith, Chris Wolfgang, Jennie Goloboy, Tyler Hayes, Jo Miles, and Elizabeth Kalmbach (and Cru). Thank you to Rebecca Littlefield, a dear friend who was the one who heard me go, "Ha-ha, but what if a library in Hell . . ." and ordered me to write it. Special thanks to Jennifer Mace, who helped me check a few Britishisms, and John Appel, my consultant on all matters pointy-things related. All errors are my own.

Thanks to Jilly Dreadful's Brainery class, and the amazing Viable Paradise workshop community, who helped me put the book through the fire and melt out the (many) flaws. All my love, gratitude, cheesy weasels, and space whales to the writers of the Isle, VP20, and the Pub. I would not still be doing this without you.

Love and gratitude to my family, who have always encouraged my writing even when they did not entirely (or even partially) share the interest. To my sister, for understanding what it takes to get here, and my mom and dad, who didn't, but were proud of me anyway. Look, Mom. All those book fairs and bedtime stories paid off. Dad—it's not a cowboy story but I hope it'll do.

And to my husband, Levi, to whom this book is dedicated: thank you. You were my first reader, the one who gave the crucial initial shove out of my personal Unwritten Wing, and have been there for every word, weasel, and win. You are and always will be my favorite story.

A. J. Hackwith is (almost) certainly not an ink witch in a hoodie. She's a queer writer of fantasy and science fiction living in Seattle and writes sci-fi romance as Ada Harper. She is a graduate of the Viable Paradise writers' workshop and her work appears in *Uncanny* magazine and assorted anthologies. Summon A.J. at your own peril with an arcane circle of fountain pens and classic RPGs, or you can find her on Twitter and other dark corners of the internet.